Grace in all Her Steps

Laura Longthorne

Published in 2014 by FeedARead.com Publishing

Copyright © The author as named on the book cover.

First Edition

The author has asserted their moral right under the Copyright, Designs and Patents Act, 1988, to be identified as the author of this work.

All Rights reserved. No part of this publication may be reproduced, copied, stored in a retrieval system, or transmitted, in any form or by any means, without the prior written consent of the copyright holder, nor be otherwise circulated in any form of binding or cover other than that in which it is published and without a similar condition being imposed on the subsequent purchaser.

A CIP catalogue record for this title is available from the British Library.

Cover design by Emma Masters ©

For Martin and Moira

*Grace was in all her steps,
heaven in her eye,
in every gesture dignity and love.*

John Milton, Paradise Lost

Prologue
7th May 1915, RMS Lusitania, North Atlantic Ocean

Lord and Lady Goldhurst hurried along the deck towards the lifeboats. Lady Goldhurst was irritated with herself for not objecting more forcefully to this journey. It had been her husband's idea to sail from New York back to England in water teeming with U-boats, aboard a passenger liner without proper naval protection. The German embassy had issued a warning but her husband insisted that they were 'using scaremonger tactics' and would not dare attack a passenger vessel carrying so many Americans. This was not the first time he had been wrong, but it was certainly the first time that it had really mattered.

Nearly ten minutes ago a torpedo from the German U-20 hit RMS Lusitania, throwing its passengers and crew into turmoil.

As they neared a lifeboat, Lord Goldhurst guided his wife and his mother-in-law, Lady Malholm, into a line of shivering women being helped in with much haste and little decorum. Fear had softened Lady Malholm's normally severe face. Her thin lips quivered and the wrinkles gathered in folds across her forehead and chin - a look that Lady Goldhurst was unused to seeing. It frightened her.

"I can't swim, Catherine! You know I've never been able to! And I'm so terribly afraid of the sea." Lady Malholm said.

"Don't fret, Roberta, you'll be safe inside the lifeboat and you'll be with Catherine. I won't be far behind you and we can't be far from Ireland; the navy's bound to be on its way. No need to panic."

Lord Goldhurst spoke with gravity, as always, but Catherine knew from the tremor in his voice that he was not entirely convinced by his own words. He turned away from Lady Malholm to face her and spoke in a quieter, uneasy tone. "Stay calm and be brave, my dear. I will see you in a few moments." He kissed her on the cheek with dry lips and nodded towards the crewman waiting to help them into the boat.

"Make sure you get on a lifeboat as soon as possible, George." Despite her initial vexation with her husband, Lady Goldhurst hated the idea of leaving him on the deck of the doomed vessel.

A grim smile darkened his face, "Don't worry about me."

The officer overseeing the lowering of the lifeboat shouted orders to begin just as the last woman had sat down. Jerking to life, the boat bucked its way down the side of the ship, thrusting the women to and fro, forcing them to stagger into one another. Lady Malholm was nearing hysteria, crying into her daughter's ear about water and waves and drowning. Catherine closed her eyes.

George Goldhurst watched in horror as his wife's lifeboat swung pendulously, narrowly missing the heads of those leaning over the side of the lower decks. Outraged he shouted to the officers charged with the task of lowering the boat at an acute angle on the fast sinking ship.

"What the devil are you doing, men? You're knocking those ladies about like dominoes! For God's sake, hold your ropes steady!"

The two officers ignored him and exchanged grim looks. The lifeboat continued lurching towards the sea.

Lord Goldhurst pushed his way over to them. "Did you fools not hear me? My wife and my mother-in-law are on that boat and I don't care for your slack handedness. They're going to fall into the water if you don't get a grip and God forbid they do, for I shall have your necks!"

He felt his face flush and that sharp, tight feeling in his chest he often experienced when he was excessively vexed. The last time must have been when Grace knocked his father's Velázquez from the wall of the upstairs gallery. What a foul mood she had been in that day.

One of the men addressed him in a placatory tone, "Sir, we're low'ring the boat the best we can, given the circumstances. The ship's goin' down fast so let us do our job without interference and things will go along much smoover, right?"

Ignoring the man, Lord Goldhurst moved closer to him and attempted to yank the rope from his hands. "I will lower this damn boat myself since this ship's crew have proven themselves incompetent!"

So shocked was the officer by this man's audacity that, for a moment, Lord Goldhurst was successful in capturing the rope. However, he quickly recovered himself and tried to hustle it from the older man's grasp.

"Oi, what the 'ell do you think you're doin', you madman? You're gonna empty that boat; you don't know wot you're doin'. Gimme that rope, now!"

As the two men struggled the second officer called out "Bloody Hell! The boat's capsized, they're all out!" The two men gaped over the side. Sure enough, twenty or more women were gasping and splashing in the water around the upturned boat. Lord Goldhurst's heart constricted tighter in his chest as he tried to spot his wife.

"See what you did, you stupid bastard! I told you to leave off, now we've lost anuver lifeboat - and there's still U-boats in those waters!" Lord Goldhurst heard the man's voice, jeering and accusatory and turned on him.

"How dare you! My mother-in-law can't swim and my wife is stuck down there in that freezing cold seawater because you can't hold a rope properly! We need to go down and help those ladies. Go and get another boat - I'll come with you."

The man stared at him in disbelief and let out a hollow laugh, "You must be jokin' mate. I don't take orders from you." He began to turn away when Lord Goldhurst powered towards him, preparing to deliver a punch to the face. The officer, however, was faster and thumped the older man on the bridge of his nose. Lord Goldhurst fell back onto the sodden deck, gasping, his head spinning. Seconds later the hot, metallic taste of his own blood began to seep into his mouth.

The officer paused for a moment; a brief pang of guilt overcame him; he was easily half Lord Goldhurst's age and much stronger. He considered helping him up and checking if he was all right, but his fellow officer was calling and he hurried off.

Lord Goldhurst slowly collected himself and got to his feet, spitting bloody saliva onto the deck. What would Catherine say when she saw him? Catherine. He forgot she was still in the water. He had to get to her, and to poor Roberta.

Suddenly, a second, violent explosion below deck knocked him backwards and pulled at the ship from underneath, dragging it down rapidly. Once upright he noticed a shadow slowing stalking the deck. Looking up he saw one of the ship's funnels heaving towards him in slow motion: black and solid. 'Is this really how it ends?' he thought, 'or am I imagining the whole thing?' He had just suffered a punch to the face after all. "I really ought to have afforded more sympathy to those poor devils on the Titanic," he murmured just before the funnel smashed onto the deck, crushing him instantly.

The lifeboat lowered unsteadily, rocking from side to side, throwing the passengers into one another in undignified embraces. Lady Malholm gripped her daughter's hand, her face paler and paler with every swing.

Catherine glanced up, scanning the length of the sinking ship and to her horror saw men, women and even children flung about the ship's decks; two men were even propelled over the side into the water whilst countless others clamoured to get on board the remaining lifeboats. 'This is how it must have been aboard the Titanic', she thought, with an overwhelming urge to urinate; most unlike her, but from what she could smell, a few other ladies on board shared her feelings, if not her restraint. She shivered and wrapped her arms around her lifejacket. She had almost forgotten about the cold, such was her panic, but the sea wind was picking up now and she prayed that the boat stayed dry inside as it hit the water. There could be nothing worse than getting wet on a cold day like this with no shelter.

They were approaching the waves in what Catherine considered to be an alarmingly fast rate, too fast to bear a steady landing. She braced herself and concentrated on controlling her bladder. She was still, after all, Lady Goldhurst of Goldhurst Estate in Rutland; her husband was Lord George Goldhurst, who owned one of the largest shipping franchises in Europe. He would know what to do; he would rescue her and she must not let him down by giving into petty primal urges, even if she was surrounded by predatory U-boats with a sinking thirty-two thousand tonne ship beside her.

Her thoughts were soon interrupted with piercing screams. Their boat had hit the water too fast and at a clumsy angle, hurling them into the bitter grip of the North Atlantic.

The icy sting of the water found its way to Catherine's body instantly, working its way into the folds of her skirts, her bodice, her undergarments, making them heavy and unbearable. She tried to scream for help but shock held her voice in and instead she found herself choking as wave after wave hit her in the face. She groped blindly in the freezing water for something to hold onto. All around her companions were screaming and splashing more water into her eyes, making it almost impossible to see, although she could smell something - was it smoke? At last she managed to force an eye open and squinted to see if she could spot her husband on the top deck. He would have witnessed the boat capsizing; he would help them.

All at once, someone grabbed her and clung onto her back, shrieking horribly and splashing more than the others. It was Lady Malholm, but in the confusion Lady Goldhurst thought that someone was deliberately trying to drown her by dragging her under. She screamed and tried to push the assailant off before she recognised her mother's contorted face.

As she tried fruitlessly to calm the elderly woman, who had never thought it necessary to learn to swim, Catherine heard a bang that seemed to shatter her hearing completely. A flash of light was follow by a huge plume of smoke, which engulfed the ship, but Catherine Goldhurst had little time to panic as she and Lady Malholm were sucked under water with the force of the explosion. Catherine pushed against a ceiling of water above her, cursing her lack of enthusiasm for swimming lessons as a young girl. Her paltry strokes were no match for her opponent and her lifejacket could do nothing to help: a dead weight around her torso. She laboured to reach air and light but the strength of the Atlantic and the sinking ship conspired to drag her further and further into the depths. She felt herself tiring and knew she was seconds away from opening her mouth to liquid suffocation. In one final moment of lucidity she thought of her children and her home in Rutland. What would become of them? Was Edward capable of taking care of them all? And what about Grace?

Catherine's questions would never be answered. She closed her eyes and opened her mouth. The Atlantic and the Great War had claimed their next victim.

Chapter One
11th May 1915, Kinwell, Rutland
Alice

Reverend Samson's monotonous voice reverberated across the graveyard and hung in the still May air. I caught only parts of his speech: 'tragedy beyond comprehension...merciless slaughter...Germans...in God's hands...sadly missed in the parish...grieving children.'

My parents, Lord George and Lady Catherine Goldhurst, had travelled to New York two months ago to visit my sister Louisa, despite constant warnings from the Home Office about U-boat attacks on British ships. How very like my father to ignore all reasonable advice; how very like mother to avoid refuting him.

Next to me, my sister Charlotte spluttered out wails and sighs as she dabbed at her eyes. Less than three civil words had been uttered between her and my parents since the war began and yet here was the picture of inconsolable grief.

I looked across to my older brother, Edward, in his captain's uniform - dry-eyed and solemn - but the concertinaed brow betrayed the fear I knew he felt at the prospect of managing Goldhurst Estate alone, especially with a sickly wife and child.

Then there was Grace. Poor Grace - Thirteen years old and orphaned. I watched her drift around the graveyard, a gangly isolato, walking up to each headstone, her nose almost pressed against the granite, tracing her finger along the lettering, mouthing the names of the deceased. Martha, her nanny, followed closely behind, smiling and nodding when Grace looked round at her for approval. My little sister had barely aged over the past five years. Her round, solemn face was framed with lank, mousy waves tied into a haphazard bun with tendrils straggling around her forehead like mice tails escaping from underneath her bonnet. Her brown eyes were alert and inquiring but devoid of any other expression. They were angelic eyes but you would be lucky to receive more than a glimpse of their beauty; Grace avoided eye contact the way Charlotte avoided modesty. Unlike my older sister and I, fashion had no place in Grace's world. Her dress was functional and familiar; certain frocks for each day of the week and woe betide anyone who disrupted the pattern. When Louisa married, my mother tried to coerce Grace into wearing an ivory bridesmaid's dress for the wedding (which was on a Friday - green dress day). The offending dress was deposited into a hole (hand-dug) next to the rose garden and Martha spent half an hour excavating the dirt from underneath Grace's fingernails. Needless to say, she triumphed in wearing her usual green and beige dress to the wedding, one that I had made for her when I was sixteen and had had to alter about five times as she grew taller.

Reverend Samson was coming to a close just as Grace lolloped along the mossy path towards me, clearly excited despite the serious look on her face. "Alice, there are four headstones with Martha on them: Martha Deane, Martha Fife, Martha Norbury and Martha Grant; two headstones with Alice on it: Alice Reynolds and Alice Morris; three headstones with Charlotte on: Charlotte Hodges, Charlotte Nash and Charlotte Billson; ten headstones with Edward on them: Edward Allen, Edward Vince, Edward Jones, Edward Glover, Edward McDonald, Edward Tate, Edward Deane (I think he may be related to Martha Deane), Edward Morris, Edward Charles and Edward Price." Grace breathed and stared at me intently.

"Interesting. What about Louisa?" She blinked, expressionless, spun around and jogged back up the path. "No, Grace, I didn't mean look for them now! Come back, Grace, come back!" I shouted but she had a job to do, which no one was going to prevent.

"Don't worry, I'll go and bring her back, Miss." Martha smiled and set off up the path to retrieve the wayward girl.

I trod the familiar path to Robert's and Gregory's graves: two identical granite oblongs, four feet tall, protected by the shade of a yew tree and worshipped by geraniums and hyacinths at their bases. My parents' memorial stone would join theirs next week, so they could be with them in spirit, if not in body. More than a week had passed since we found out about the tragedy and still I had not been able to cry. I hoped that looking at my poor dead baby brothers' graves would induce tears as it usually did. But there was nothing - not one sob.

I had helped Edward arrange the service, calmed and comforted Charlotte, written endless letters to various relatives and family acquaintances and now, on the one occasion I could allow myself to grieve normally, I was disappointed to feel no lump rise in my throat, no tears stinging my eyes, just emptiness. Perhaps it was shock or stress, or perhaps I was afraid that if I began to cry there was a real danger that I would never be able to stop.

I saw the remainder of my family trudge out of the church with the reverend. The melancholy mood, the overwhelming shadow of grief, reminded me of a summer afternoon five years before, during the dark days after my baby brother, Robert, had died. Mother's family had come to visit and offer their support. The subject eventually turned to persuading Mother to do something about Grace, as it often did when my grandmother came to stay. Grace herself was unusually perky and bright. This particular afternoon she spent wandering around the rose garden with Martha, counting the petals on the flowers. The rest of my family were drinking and idling on the lawn. Mother's mother, Lady Malholm, was a stiff, unapproachable woman, committed to Victorian principles of obedience (particularly in children), propriety and upholding reputation. The day was balmy and the air was so thick that it seemed to swaddle us all in its uncomfortable blanket.

Nevertheless, my grandmother wore her usual restrictive crinoline garb, buttoned up to the throat, sucked in at the waist with a hard, bone corset. She only ever wore drab colours (black, grey or dark hyacinthine) after her husband died in 1905, so that, with her long grey hair and deep voice, she reminded me of a witch. In truth I only recall seeing my grandmother wearing clothes that were not dark on one occasion: my Aunt Cynthia's wedding twelve years ago, in 1903.

On this afternoon she waved a huge fan in front of her face with such languor that I was sure it scarcely produced the slightest draught to relieve her glistening face. Her expression was perpetually austere: the narrowed eyes and the thin, colourless lips; so pursed one would be forgiven for believing she had no lips at all. My mother sat next to her wearing lighter, more fluid cream skirts, her pale skin matching the hue of her gown. I remember her heartbreak that week. I pitied her. Robert's death had aged her.

Aunt Cynthia and her husband, Sir John Radcliffe, were also there that weekend. Uncle John was jolly and drunk in a whey-coloured linen suit and straw boater hat. Aunt Cynthia and my father's sister, Aunt Edith, spent the whole day trying to better one another with tales of their children's recent accolades.

Charlotte and I were not quite old enough to be accepted into their fold, so we remained on a woollen tartan picnic rug, her pretending to read and me sketching the house, both of us trying and failing not to eavesdrop on the elders' conversations. In truth I begged to stay in my room as I did every day following Robert's death, but Mother insisted that I join them. I was so miserable and tired from lack of sleep (for at least a full year after the incident I was plagued with sleepless nights or harrowing nightmares so that I struggled to stay awake during the daytime, let alone converse with anyone) and all I wanted was to seek refuge indoors, upstairs with my sewing machine. It was the only thing that kept me going.

After a while, Grace emerged from the rose garden and plodded over to where the adults were sitting. "Mother, I counted every petal on the rose bushes. How many do you think there are?"

"I don't know, my dear." My mother smiled weakly at her and put down her drink.

"Guess." She pressed. Mother sighed.

"I really don't know, Grace. Can you go and play with Martha, I'm talking to Grandmama." My grandmother regarded Grace like a curious stray cat that had found its way into our gardens and outstayed its welcome.

"Well, there are one hundred and thirteen thousand, four hundred and fifty seven. Eighty thousand, three hundred and twenty nine red petals, twenty thousand, five hundred and twelve yellow petals..."

"Please, Grace, not now." Mother said.

"...And twelve thousand, five hundred and fifty nine white petals."

"Young lady, can you not see that your mother is tired and grieving the loss of your poor little brother, God rest his soul. You are not helping her by standing there impudently spouting this nonsense." My grandmother interjected.

Grace interrupted her, "I asked Mr. Healy how many petals were in the rose garden and he said he had no idea and would go to his grave not knowing the answer. So I told him this morning that I would count every single petal and tell him the answer tomorrow and he said he would bet me a penny that I would not be able to count them all, so..." My grandmother's face was close to imploding with rage. Mother sat back and covered her forehead with her hands.

"What on earth is wrong with this child? Nearly nine years old and babbling the most tedious nonsense with no consideration for her poor mother and no respect for her elders! Selfish insolence is what I call it." She clicked her fingers and gestured to Martha, who was loitering nearby and, with a sweep of her crinoline skirts, she turned her back on Grace and spoke to Mother in what she considered to be a hushed tone.

"This child needs to be sent away...some place where her behaviour can be corrected once and for all. Catherine, I have heard of a place near York; I wish you would let me help you deal with this child for you. She has been a strain and a disgrace all her life and you are doing her no favours by letting her run amok with just a maid for supervision."

Mother sighed, "Thank you Mama, but this is not the time to discuss it." She glanced over at Grace who was rooted to the spot. "Martha, please take Grace inside and give her a bath and a change of clothes."

"Of course, m'lady. Come along, Grace." Martha placed her hands delicately on Grace's shoulders and began to steer her towards the house.

"Do they have rose gardens in York?" Although directed at Martha, my grandmother thought the question was aimed at her.

"I beg your pardon?" Her tone was acidic and I cowered from my place of relative safety, silently willing Grace to stop talking.

"Do they have rose gardens in York? Because if they do I won't mind going there, I can count all the petals on their rose bushes. Maybe they'll have more than Mr. Healy and it might take me a whole month to count them. Maybe even a whole year. They might bet me more than a penny...two pennies! And maybe they'll have a hedgehog for me to look after, like the one that lives near the back door that I gave milk to. Maybe we should leave some food for him tonight, Martha?"

"Enough! Be quiet! I do not want to hear another word from you. Take her inside and put her to bed." My grandmother gestured wildly towards the house and Martha hurried Grace away from her. I heard her questioning Martha about rose bushes, hedgehogs and York as they weaved their way across the lawn, up the stone steps and into the house.

My grandmother breathed heavily, rousing herself into another speech about Grace's deviant behaviour. "That girl is trouble." The fan beat back and forth wildly with each word. "Catherine, this house is no place for a child like that. She is insane and she grows worse every time I see her."

"Catherine," Uncle John chipped in, "the child just needs some professional help. There are all kinds of new fangled treatments for," he hesitated, "you know, lunatics."

Mother sat up. "Grace is not a lunatic, John. She *is* different from normal children and I admit we need some help with her, but I will never hand her over to one of those awful asylums. Nor will I send her away unless I am satisfied they have her best interests at heart."

"If you ask my opinion, children like that need the madness beaten out of them." Grandmother added, ignoring Mother.

"Don't be so medieval." My mother snapped. "That awful Mr. Irvine wanted to wire her up to some machine and shock her. We need to try a different approach - a more humane approach."

"Well, you know where I stand on the matter. You should send that child away from Goldhurst Estate, out of the way." She leaned across to my mother, "especially as Edward, and soon Charlotte, are at ages where they need to be married and settled."

"Mother's right, Catherine," Aunt Cynthia added, "you don't want to hinder their opportunities. Both Edward and Charlotte are very eligible; a mad sister attached to the family may be too much of a compromise. You don't want them tainted by association."

Mother sighed again, "Of course I want to see all of them happy and settled without having to worry about Grace. You seem to forget, though, that she is my daughter too and she needs my protection more than the others."

"At least say you'll allow me to look into alternative arrangements?" Grandmother implored.

Although I sat a distance away from the group, my grandmother's voice travelled across the lawn in a shrill wave. My sketch was awful. I had sketched the house before and much better than this. The conversation was distracting me. My mind was not engaged in art today. I ripped up the paper and slipped back into the house with no more notice than a sideways glance from Charlotte.

Goldhurst Estate was the result of my great-grandfather's profligacy; his success made him a fortune and plucked his family from their lower-middle class life, planting them into one of splendour. The man wanted to showcase his success, so he changed his family name from the modest 'Hurst' to 'Goldhurst', creating Goldhurst Estate. Every gold-leaf door knob, every ivory napkin ring, every polished teak chair that he acquired was an elaborate gesture; a reminder to the world that he created this dream from virtually nothing and that he was equal to any of those who inherited their ancestral estates. The central staircase rose majestically opposite the heavy front doors. As a child, Grace refused to enter through the front of the house; it reminded her of a monster's mouth. It wasn't until last year when she accidentally ran through it thinking that a wolf was chasing her (it was an Irish Wolf Hound, escaped from a neighbouring farm), that she overcame her fear.

As I climbed the stairs to the second floor (Grace's was the only bedroom up there, except for some of the servants') I glimpsed pallid young maids in plain, dove-coloured dresses and aprons scurrying in and out of the rooms downstairs, like industrious mice, no doubt trying to accommodate my grandmother's exacting standards.

Approaching the second floor I heard Martha's soft voice floating through the gap. It was a soothing voice, each note rising and falling effortlessly, her slight Derbyshire accent, adding warmth and openness; the antithesis of my grandmother's shrillness.

As I pushed open the door she looked up and finished the page she was reading. Grace was kneeling next to the bookcase, lining up her books in regimented lines and perfect alphabetical order. Martha smiled at me. "Hello Miss Alice. Would you like to finish the story?"

"Yes, all right. But afterwards can I talk to you about something?"

"Of course you can." She said.

I settled on to the bed next to Martha and finished reading 'Little Red Riding Hood', Grace's favourite. "'Little Red Riding Hood' again, Grace? You always read that, why don't you read the one I bought you last week - 'Jack and the Beanstalk'?"

"We read 'Jack and the Beanstalk', but, I didn't like it." Grace spoke without looking up. "You can't get magic beans and there's no giant up in the sky because his castle would be too heavy for the clouds to hold it up and if he was too high up he would freeze."

I wondered why she objected to such fantasy when she had not once questioned the plausibility of an anthropomorphic wolf. "You have a point, but it must be rather boring for Martha to read the same book over and over again."

"Martha likes reading it, don't you?"

"Quite right!" Martha said. "Now, what was it you wanted to ask me, Miss Alice?"

"Do you mind if we talk outside?" I lowered my voice and nodded towards Grace, knowing full well she would have heard me anyway.

"Of course," Martha replied and we left Grace to order her trunk of toys - smallest to largest.

We stood outside in the corridor; muffled voices could be heard, but not understood, from downstairs. A door opened and closed. The house was broiling that summer; its bricks enclosed the heat and emanated a feverish warmth well into the evening. Martha faced me.

"What's the matter, Miss? Is there something wrong with your sewing machine again?"

"No, it's nothing to do with that." I paused, choosing my words with care. "I'm worried about..." I stopped and lowered my voice. "Do you really think they mean it? About sending Grace away?" Her sweet smile was replaced with pursed lips and a furrowed brow. "Only, I don't think she would cope. Those places, they're. Well, you know yourself when we visited St. Giles'. They're ghastly, absolutely ghastly and I can't believe Mother is even allowing Grandmama to discuss sending her away to one of those horrid places."

Martha placed her hand over mine "Don't fret about it, Miss Alice. I know Lady Goldhurst would never send Grace away. She would have already done it if she really wanted to. She's just going through a hard time with your poor little brother's passing." I shuddered despite the warmth. Was this the moment to tell her?

"Martha, do you think they'd send her away if..." I hesitated.

"If what?"

I swallowed, "If Grace did something naughty that would upset people?"

Martha's hand dropped back to her side; her expression was serious now and her eyes were fixed on me. "I don't quite understand what you mean, Miss Alice. Has Grace done something naughty?" The question hung between us and I shifted uncomfortably. I knew I couldn't go back now.

"There is something you don't know, something no one knows except Grace and I." As I tried to explain, tears began to form in the corners of my eyes and my heart drummed in my ears. "Please, Martha, promise you won't tell anyone, Grace will be in more trouble than we can ever imagine and we'll never see her again, I know it."

Martha's voice grew urgent, "What is it? Miss Alice, you're starting to scare me now."

I swallowed down the lump rising in my throat and looked around the cheerless landing. I could hear Grace's monotonous hum from behind the oak door. Another door opened and slammed downstairs. I swallowed again and told Martha our secret, drawing her into our conspiracy that she swore she would take to her grave.

Edward came striding across the graveyard, Charlotte close behind him still sniffling and sighing melodramatically. My brother's expression was weary. The burden that had been placed on him so suddenly seemed to be bearing down on his shoulders. The house; the estate and the business; an ailing wife and a young child; the war; the servants and the money; Charlotte and I and, of course, Grace. These were Edward's responsibilities now and responsibility was not something that he embraced. Our father had always been so controlling he'd never really needed to worry about anyone but himself. He had assumed he would have at least twenty more years of freedom after he married before responsibility of this scale was required of him.

He married Sarah four years ago. Our parents and hers had arranged most of it and, from what I could tell, Edward liked her a lot. She was beautiful and amenable, but her parents neglected to mention her sickly constitution. We found out later that she had suffered from pneumonia as a child and had never fully returned to health. Soon after they married Sarah became ill more and more frequently, spending most of her time fighting off infections or convalescing. Her maid and the doctor saw far more of her than her husband, or even her child.

Children was the other issue. Sarah had suffered two miscarriages that I knew of and Sophie, my niece, was born two months premature, meaning her underdeveloped heart would plague her for life. Understandably, my brother was devastated and found it difficult to cope with this new life of malady and uncertainty. Edward had always liked things done the easy way, with minimal disruption to him. However, this very philosophy of leaving important decisions to others had backfired when it came to marriage. As a result, Edward began to spend less and less time at home with his wife and child, preferring to stay in London or Liverpool to deal with the family business. When Father established the motor car factory, Edward, who had always been so reluctant to involve himself in that side of the business, practically jumped for joy when he asked him to manage it for him.

The outbreak of war last year had been an unlikely liberation for him. He whole-heartedly joined up as a captain in the Lincolnshire regiment and was sent to France soon afterwards. Edward saw this as a chance to escape for a while and as a way to imbue some excitement and heroism into his life.

His expectations, however, were soon suppressed. He was injured during the battle of Ypres and brought back to England. Shrapnel had implanted in his shoulder during an explosion, permanently damaging the muscles and the joint. Edward was not able to lift his right arm more than a few inches and would not be capable of carrying anything heavy (including his child) for the foreseeable future. His early retirement from the army hit him hard and he became even more distant than before. He flew into rages or hid himself away completely for the first few months. Some local men tried to persuade him to join the Lincolnshire Territorial Force but this did little to lift his spirits. The news of my parents' deaths was the pinnacle of a hellish few months for my poor brother.

As he strode forwards, Edward looked straight through us to the car waiting in the lane to drive us back to the house. "I need to get back before noon," he addressed this comment to no one in particular as he walked towards the iron gate and the waiting driver. I looked across the graveyard; Martha was trying her hardest to coerce Grace into meeting us at the car, to no avail.

"You and Charlotte go ahead, we'll walk back. It's a lovely day after all." I foresaw the quarrel if I suggested waiting for Grace. Edward grunted and climbed into the car without uttering another word. Charlotte stepped in after him dabbing her eyes that were surely dry by now. The engine started and they chugged away.

I turned and walked along the winding path into the graveyard towards Martha. By now Grace was flitting around the headstones looking for 'Louisas'.

"I told Edward we would walk back to the house." Martha smiled and nodded. She was no fool; she knew Edward's temperament as well as me.

Eventually Grace came running back to where we stood, her face flushed and her clothes askew. "Two Louisas: Louisa Pearson and Louisa McCrorie." She said in triumph.

"Goodness, well done Grace, you found them all!" I congratulated her on her small, personal victory and wondered whether I wished my thoughts to be as simple and carefree as hers. On a day like today I certainly saw the appeal of thinking like Grace, but I had to admit I did sometimes pray thanks to God that none of us were like her.

"Let's head home, Grace. I don't know about you but I'm quite peckish." Martha took Grace's hand as we walked out of the graveyard and across the road, but she extricated it immediately and galloped a few feet ahead of us.

"Can we walk back through the woods? I want to see if I can spot the hedgehog today."

"Yes, why not? Who knows, you might be lucky today." I said.

We set off through the village and took the path leading through the woodland stretching from Kinwell to the edge of Goldhurst Estate. Grace soon became bored by our pace of walking and gambolled ahead, stopping occasionally to peer into the trees or patches of bluebells.

When we were half way home we stopped at a little stone bridge, crossing a small river. Grace leaned heavily on the flat stone and rocked back and forth on her heels, staring into the water.

"No ducks today." She said and wandered over to a nearby colony of nettles, scuffing her boots across the path.

"Be careful around those nettles and don't drag your feet, duck." Martha called.

"No ducks." Came a muttered reply.

"She's desperate to find that hedgehog." Martha chuckled but was interrupted by a shriek.

"Martha, look!" Grace was jumping up and down pointing at the ground.

"What is it?" We both rushed to the spot she was indicating and saw a tiny baby bird discarded under a patch of nettles; it had only just begun to sprout some downy feathers and could not have been more than a few days old.

"Oh, poor little mite! It must have fallen out of the nest, or a predator may have dropped it..." Martha said.

I stared at the wretched little creature, so weak and pitiable, left to rot under a clump of weeds so soon after breathing its first gasps and feeling the warmth of its mother's wings. A tiny stolen life.

"Let's bury it under one of these trees." Martha scooped the bird up in her handkerchief.

"Under the monkey tail tree - that's my favourite." Grace said hurriedly.

"That's all the way back in the village, Gracie, how about over there, amongst those beautiful bluebells." She walked ahead a few paces, scooped up some earth with the edge of her boot and place the little dead bird in the hole, covering it again. Grace had lost interest and wandered on again, but I couldn't move. The sadness felt like a heavy weight inside me, anchoring me to the bridge, unable to move. I was suddenly aware of a large lump growing and growing, constricting the flow of air in my throat. I gasped and sank down on the top of the bridge, grief pouring out of me.

"Miss Alice! Oh, don't get upset." Martha ran to me and put her arm around my shoulders. "Don't worry about the bird, Miss, he's all right now."

She fell silent, holding me while I cried and shook for at least ten minutes until we were interrupted by a husky voice, "Martha! Alice! I think I've found the hedgehog!"

Chapter Two
20th July 1901, Goldhurst Estate, Rutland
Martha

Even a farmer's daughter has difficulty getting out of bed at five o'clock in the morning every day, for there are very few things in life that are worth getting up for at that cheerless hour. However, the sun dawning over Goldhurst Estate in summertime, I have to say, is a treat that can rouse the weariest soul. Watching the light crawl across the horizon towards me, together with the chorus of larks nesting in the rafters above my window never fails to set me up for the morning's labour. And there is always plenty of it.

The Goldhurst family, as I was told by Mrs. Brickett, the housekeeper, on my first day of employment, are not an old aristocratic family like the Templetons (her previous employers), who inhabited the next closest estate. Instead they had inherited their wealth from Lord Goldhurst's great-grandfather, who made a fortune in shipping.

"They may not have the titles and heraldry of the Templetons or other landed families," she told me that first day, "but at least they can hold their heads up high and say that their ancestors achieved their fortune from good, honest hard work." I nodded inanely, trying to take it all in. "You won't find anyone as hard-working as Lord Goldhurst, which is more than some of those lazy so-and-sos can say." Being a farm girl, I couldn't argue with that.

She went on to tell me that the house had been designed by some celebrated architect, who had also been one of Queen Victoria's favourites at one time or another, although I forgot the chap's name almost straight away.

The house was almost a perfect square and its bricks were a reddish colour that made it appear rather jolly on the outside. The windows were large (except, of course, for the attics, where the servants slept) and were framed with white sills that, I was reliably informed, were a pain in the neck to maintain. Scattered around the back of the house were stables, housing some of the finest thoroughbreds in the county. Cottages, potting sheds, a large greenhouse and an even larger garage were also outside. The jewel in Goldhurst's crown, however, had to be the gardens. I'd never seen such big and attractive gardens before. Whenever I had a spare moment I liked to just gaze at the lawns and the rose garden from one of the second floor windows, imagining that they were mine. Some of the servants said that Lord Goldhurst had hinted at bringing some fallow deer to the park from Burghley, although I couldn't picture it. They'd mess up the beautiful greenery, the roses, the delphiniums, the tulips...animals are more trouble than they're worth, in my opinion.

The family had recently installed a new fountain and a boathouse, for their young son Master Edward - a keen sailor. Although I believe this pastime was encouraged by the boy's parents to stop him from sporting around in the woods, a stone's throw away from the far side of the lake. Even after eleven months I couldn't fathom how one family could have so much land to themselves. It seemed to stretch for miles and they owned a number of tenanted farms in the county. I felt the ache of homesickness whenever my mind wandered to the farms or the countryside; I hadn't seen my mother or brother for almost six months and I seldom had time to write a decent letter.

So, rising at five o'clock was not too much of a chore on days like this; I was used to it. I had been working at Goldhurst Estate for almost a year and before that no one in our household could justify sleeping past six o'clock when there were chores to be done.

This particular day followed the same routine as always: after waking at five, I, along with the six other housemaids, crowded into the draughty servants' bathroom for a quick wash, taking it in turns to splash and gasp. The water always varied in temperature from cold to freezing, even in the balmy heat of summer.

On with the uniform next, including the loathed corset, as if our job wasn't difficult enough. Still, I have the pleasure of making Ms. Vermaut's coffee afterwards.

Ms. Mathilde Vermaut, Lady Goldhurst's maid, only ever drinks coffee in the morning instead of tea, like all the other servants. Looking at the two of us, you wouldn't think that a thin, glamorous woman from Paris would have anything in common with a housemaid from Derbyshire, but like me Ms. Vermaut came to Rutland in search of work after her father died and the family found themselves in debt. I used to find Ms. Vermaut haughty and unapproachable until one morning I found her weeping uncontrollably in her bedroom and discovered that she was even more homesick than I was. Since that day we got along fine enough.

"Ms. Vermaut?" I tapped on her door and it opened with a flourish. "Bonjour Mademoiselle Vermaut. Voici ton café." I enjoyed using the little French that my mother had taught me. She had once hoped that I would follow her and become a teacher or a governess.

"Ah, merci mademoiselle." Ms. Vermaut replied throatily and whisked the tray into her room.

Then the real chores started: lighting the fires and cleaning the rooms allocated to me (the nursery, the library and the morning room). This I had to do before my own breakfast at half past seven, just before the family ate theirs, since I could only start making the beds after the family went down to breakfast to avoid them catching sight of me or the other maids. Heaven forbid if they ever saw me! I think that was the hardest part of my job - knowing that I worked for people who could barely tell me apart from six other girls. Our job was to clean and beautify the house like a troupe of sprites, descending on every room as soon as it had been emptied then disappearing as promptly as we had arrived.

On this particular day there seemed to be rather more of a commotion about the house. Dorothy, one of the other housemaids with whom I shared a room, soon informed me that Lady Goldhurst had gone into early labour and the doctor had been called as a matter of urgency. I knew the lady of the house was pregnant and had been feeling rather under the weather recently, but I also knew that her child was not due for at least another six weeks. Indeed, Dorothy confirmed that she had gone into labour prematurely and we were all to pray for her safety and, of course, for the safe arrival of her child.

"His lordship is beside himself, you know his first wife died in childbirth, don't you?" Dorothy said in hushed tones as she fumbled with the keys to the spare linen cupboard.

"No, I didn't even know his lordship was married before."

"Oh yes, Miss Louisa is only Lady Goldhurst's step-daughter and a half-sister to the others."

"The one who was married last month?"

"To the American gentleman, yes." She said.

"Dorothy, for God's sake hurry up, girl!" Mrs. Brickett screeched down the corridor, causing us both to start. Dorothy emitted a yelp, grabbed a pile of towels and shoved them in my direction.

"Go on!" She hissed, "and don't tell anyone what I just told you."

At eleven o'clock, shortly before Doctor Scott and a nurse arrived, the wailing began. Bloodcurdling cries which, I imagined, were the sounds a person makes when being tortured to death or murdered very slowly and as painfully as possible. From that moment onwards we abandoned our usual jobs and worked together to help the doctor. We maids were expected to rush up and downstairs all day, bringing fresh towels, water, remedies, refreshment for the doctor and nurse and all manner of things in between. I vaguely remembered my mother giving birth to my younger brother years ago and had heard stories of other women in our village going through the ordeal, but nothing prepared me for Lady Goldhurst's appalling screams of pain; the panic and the sheer length of the labour. It was enough to make me vow never to have children.

At half past ten, after eighteen hours of work, tiredness ran through every muscle and bone I possessed and a quiet moment was gratefully received. Sitting down at the table in the servant's I rested my head, quite past caring what Mrs. Brickett would say if she found me. Lady Goldhurst's howls echoed in my ears as I drowsed. I imagined her pain and pictured a wolfish child howling as it came into the world, unapologetic of the pain it had caused.

"What on earth?" Mrs. Brickett's squawk roused me so that I almost fell off the chair. "You lazy girl, lying there snoring whilst the whole household works their fingers to the bone trying to save two innocent lives! You should be ashamed of yourself!"

"I...I'm sorry, Mrs. Brickett, I...I was just having a quick sit down, I've been on my feet since five..." Mrs. Brickett was grumbling to herself, ignoring my weak attempt at an explanation.

"You're lucky I caught you and not Mr. Brooks or you'd be out on y'ear. Here," she thrust a pile of towels and a pail of warm water into my hands so forcefully I nearly dropped it all. "Make yerself useful; get this lot upstairs to the girls in Lady Goldhurst's bedroom. Off you go, don't stand there gawping at me!" I made as swift an exit as I could, given the heavy load and she stood glaring at me, arms folded as I struggled up the steps.

Outside Lady Goldhurst's chamber the din was unbearable. I was so frightened I almost turned and ran away, the impulse to do so was so great, but neither did I fancy another tongue lashing or worse from Mrs. Brickett.

I knocked and entered the chamber of doom where I feared the wailing would make my eardrums erupt. The air was hot and clammy with sweat and panic, and the smell was equally unbearable. The stench of human waste, lavender, stale air, antiseptic and perspiration was a stronger, more nauseating concoction than I had ever smelled on the farm. Ms. Vermaut was leaning over a sweating and screaming Lady Goldhurst, wiping her forehead delicately and moving her lips as if in prayer. She may well have been praying, singing or reciting poetry for all I could tell; the noise was so loud I couldn't hear a word of it, despite only being a couple of feet away. In spite of these horrors, I couldn't help staring at Lady Goldhurst; it was the first time I had been in a room with her and seen her this close.

I was suddenly aware of Ms. Vermaut glaring at me. I recovered myself and placed the towels and water gently next to the doctor and turned, relieved to leave the hellish chamber.

"Where do you think you are going?" Ms. Vermaut's shrill French accent stopped me in my tracks. I stared at her, puzzled. "You have been sent here to help the doctor, non? So help him then!" She gestured in irritation at Doctor Scott who was washing his hands and frowning in the direction of his patient.

"Oh, I, no I wasn't sent up to help." I said, skulking by the door, longing to be on the other side of it.

"Well, you have no choice, this child is in the middle of being born and I need some help. Come here, girl." Doctor Scott said. I gulped and walked over to the bed as if in a dream. I was so empty and scared I thought I might faint.

Doctor Scott was possibly the calmest, most composed man I had met, but even he appeared flustered. He barked orders at me and I did what he told me mechanically and as quickly as I could manage. Lady Goldhurst breathed in and out rapidly, like a steam train chugging out of the station. I was vaguely aware that Doctor Scott was ordering her to push and keep pushing as hard as she could; he had sent me over to the basin to create a makeshift bath so he could clean the child and wrap it in warm towels when it appeared.

As I tried to ignore Lady Goldhurst's cries, which had reached a climax, a new sound cut through the din - the squawking, gargling, yelping noise of the newborn infant. Doctor Scott held him up: a tiny boy with dark matted hair and oddly coloured skin – purplish blue. The doctor bustled over to the basin with him after congratulating Lady Goldhurst for her tremendous efforts. I slunk away and made myself useful by mopping at Lady Goldhurst's legs and feet, which were saturated in blood and other unnatural looking sludge. The poor woman was still screaming and crying; she had obviously been at it for so long that she was hysterical and didn't realise that it was all over.

"Help, Doctor! I think there is another one coming!" Ms. Vermaut yelled across the room.

"What?" I looked up and saw another tiny, round head budding before my eyes. I gasped in disbelief and shouted, "Doctor Scott, come quick!" terrified of the cub pushing its way towards freedom. The doctor looked from the newborn in his arms to where I stood at the end of the bed.

"I have to tend to the boy; you will have to deliver the child yourself. Take a deep breath, my lady, keep pushing as hard as you can, and you, my girl, need to gently, but firmly pull the child out from underneath the shoulders when it comes." I had no time to think, the creature was moving rapidly into being, covered with blood and slime as lambs are born on a farm. I reminded myself of how many times I had seen animals born at home in Derbyshire; it was no worse than that. At the time I didn't think of the magnitude of the job in front of me; I would be the first person to touch this new life.

Gritting my teeth, I seized the writhing infant with both hands and pulled her out (for I saw soon afterwards that it was a girl). I wrapped her in a large, clean blanket and held her up howling to Lady Goldhurst and Ms. Vermaut.

"It's a girl, my lady!" I cried, but the poor woman was so exhausted she barely smiled, instead letting out a whimper of exhaustion. Doctor Scott instructed me to cut the umbilical cord, thus severing the last attachment between mother and daughter. The little girl was now a human being in her own right. She looked different to her twin brother. Although not large, she was certainly much bigger than him; her skin was rosy pink; her hair was darker and thicker and her cries echoed around the room as she filled her little lungs with air. It was then that it dawned on me - Lady Goldhurst's new son was not crying. Nor had he been crying for some minutes. Busy as I was in the task I had been given I had blocked out everything else, for now I also noticed a pair of maids had entered the chamber and were scurrying around, attending to Lady Goldhurst like ants rebuilding a nest. Doctor Scott finally faced us with the tiny bundle nestled into the crook of his arm. No one dared to speak.

Lord Goldhurst burst into the room; a look of joy mixed with worry on his face. He saw the baby wailing in my arms and bounded over to take a look at his new child. I shivered; it was the closest I had been to either of my employers. He was a middle-aged man with dark hair tinged with silver around the sides of his head. I lowered the blanket slightly and propped his daughter up so he could have a clearer view. As soon as he saw real flesh and blood his face relaxed into a smile.

"A girl, monsieur." Ms. Vermaut clarified from the bedside. Lord Goldhurst nodded without taking his eyes away from the baby.

"Ah, another girl, Catherine? Well she seems healthy and has a fine set of lungs on her so thank heavens for that. Not too many complications were there doctor?" Lord Goldhurst had not yet spotted the grim reaper in the corner of the room. His eyes soon wandered over to him and once again I watched his expression change from happy relief to puzzlement to apprehension. Doctor Scott's grave expression and knotted brow were no comfort. He spoke slowly, addressing Lord Goldhurst.

"My lord, your wife gave birth to twins. I'm afraid, I'm dreadfully sorry to tell you that the boy didn't pull through." He looked down at the small, lifeless bundle in his arms. "His heart was very weak; it simply couldn't beat on its own. Sometimes, with twins, there is a more dominant one..." He began to tail off before collecting himself, "and there's nothing we can do in such circumstances. I am truly sorry my lord and lady."

Time seemed to stand still for a moment in that awful room. I was suddenly aware that I shouldn't be there. I felt like an intruder. I was just a seventeen year-old housemaid and I had already done more than my duty. Then Mrs. Brickett was at my shoulder, lifting the bundle away from me and subtly indicating the door for me to leave.

"Well done, Martha," she whispered, "get yourself to bed." I mustered a feeble smile and walked stiffly out of the room, leaving them all to grieve.

Once out of that stifling den I heard an unearthly wail. The sort of sound you would expect to hear when a mother loses her child.

I barely had time to digest the night's events, for sleep came quickly and swallowed me into its warm fold. I dreamed of a pair of wolf cubs, downy and bright-eyed, playing in a dense forest. They began fighting - snarling and snipping at one another amidst ghostly howls. One cub clearly had the advantage in terms of size and aggression. It suddenly doubled in size as the howls grew louder and mist began to appear, creating a boxing ring around them. The larger cub grabbed its brother by the jugular and snapped his neck with several forceful shakes. The wretched body of the brother cub drooped from its jaws like a wilted lily. The triumphant cub released the lifeless sack of fur and bone and gave a long, low howl to the moon before heading into the hills alone.

Lord and Lady Goldhurst decided upon the name Grace for Gregory's twin sister a couple of days after his death. They thought it was fitting, as she was their saving grace: a healthy baby to take their minds off the tragedy.

Little Gregory's funeral was held a week later. It was, of course, a grim affair made all the more upsetting when the tiny coffin was lowered into the ground in Kinwell churchyard. It seemed so unnatural, the earth swallowing up this little baby, his life not even begun.

Almost all of the servants were in attendance as well as Lord Goldhurst, Master Edward, Miss Louisa and her new husband and some other family members. Lady Goldhurst was too ill and too bereaved to attend and Lord Goldhurst thought it would be too upsetting for his younger daughters.

Life carried on as normally as possible at the estate. Oddly, I felt more content working there after that awful night. Being present at the birth of the twins ingratiated me somewhat to Lady Goldhurst and she acknowledged my presence more and more. One day, about four weeks after Gregory's funeral, she summoned me to her room to thank me for my help that night. I must have looked ridiculous for I was blushing beetroot the entire time. However, she didn't seem to notice and even asked if I wanted to hold the baby.

In spite of her charming name, Grace didn't prove to be quite the blessing that her parents had hoped for. From the moment she was born she filled every corner of the house with wails and screeches. Her nursemaid desperately tried to settle her, but nothing could stop the crying. It was a terrible howling, throaty cry that seemed almost animal. For that reason, Grace's nursery was moved to the second floor of the house and remained there permanently.

Lady Goldhurst sent me upstairs, with Mrs. Brickett as chaperone, to see the baby. I admit, at the time I had no particular urge to see or hold the child banshee, but I was young and eager to please my employer, so I went, not wanting to seem ungrateful for the honour.

The noise was unbearable as we approached the dreaded room; it was far worse than hearing Lady Goldhurst's wails that night because they never stopped.

The nursemaid's soothing words were more like frantic pleas, barely audible over the din. With trepidation, we entered (knocking seemed a waste of time; she would never have heard). Mrs. Dylan, the nursemaid, turned around, startled and red-faced. "Can I help you?" She shouted.

"Lady Goldhurst has sent us. She wants young Martha here to hold the baby for a minute." Mrs. Brickett shouted back.

Mrs. Dylan grunted and held the howling child out to me. "Gladly, I need a sit down; I haven't eaten a crumb nor drunk a drop since five o'clock this morning." The baby was thrust into my arms and she bustled out grumbling to herself. I looked helplessly from the screaming bundle to Mrs. Brickett.

"Well, I have a million and one things to do, Martha, so stay with the child until Mrs. Dylan comes back." Before I could protest she hurried out after Mrs. Dylan, almost slamming the door behind her.

I tried coaxing and cooing and rocking the little red-faced girl but nothing seemed to work. If anything she howled louder than before and I was sure Mrs. Dylan would blame me for it when she returned. I looked around the white-walled room, it didn't look much like a nursery yet, except for the cradle and several toys scattered in one corner. However, I did notice a bookcase with a handful of books on it. I decided that a story might help as it had always helped to soothe my younger brother when he was a baby.

There were only four titles on the shelf: 'The Children's Book of Nursery Rhymes', a couple of Beatrix Potters and 'Little Red Riding Hood'. I chose the latter as it had been one of my favourites as a child. Retrieving the book, I sat in Mrs. Dylan's rocking chair, propping the baby up against my arm so she could see the pictures as I read.

"Once upon a time there was a dear little girl who was loved by everyone who looked at her, but most of all by her grandmother, and there was nothing that she would not have given to the child." Grace's howling appeared to lessen, so I read on, pointing at the pictures in the book as I read.

Half an hour later I didn't even notice Mrs. Dylan enter the room as I was finishing the story. Grace had been quiet for at least fifteen minutes and her small, dark eyes were darting inquisitively over the pages of the book. Mrs. Dylan looked astonished.

"Heaven's above! How in God's name did you get that child quiet?"

I shrugged. "She seems to like this story."

"Well, maybe you can come here for half an hour a couple of times a day to let me take my lunch and dinner? That Dorothy is next to useless. I'll talk to Mrs. Brickett about it."

So for the next six months I visited Grace and read her the same story over and over, each time she stopped howling and listened, fascinated. The visits became more frequent and longer as Mrs. Dylan was often at the end of her tether with the screeching baby. I can't say that I was pleased at first; I had never been that fond of children, but I felt sorry for the little wailer. She was avoided by everybody, nobody spoke kindly to her and she seemed unhappy with the world, even at her young age.

It soon became apparent that I was not the only one who felt uncomfortable with my new duties. Dorothy, who had taken great delight in reminding me that she was senior to me in the house, resented the way that I had somehow overtaken her in terms of status and responsibilities. She ceased speaking to me unless it was to bark orders or complain that I had not swept the floors properly or not dusted the sills thoroughly or that I breathed too loudly when

I was asleep. All chance of friendship broke down when Mrs. Brickett informed Dorothy that she was to take over from me in making Ms. Vermaut's coffee every morning.

One morning I entered the servant's hall to see Dorothy and three other housemaids whispering and giggling in the corner.

"Sssshhh, she's behind you!" one of the maids whispered to Dorothy, who craned her neck to see me staring at her, red-faced.

Instead of appearing embarrassed she laughed and said, "I don't care if she hears, she's not my friend. Friends don't betray you and..."

Mrs. Brickett bustled into the servant's hall and looked from me to Dorothy wide-eyed, "What's this? What are you all doing congregating down here when there's work to be done? Get along now, all of you!"

We hurried into the corridor and I heard Dorothy snigger and say, "Mrs. Brickett had better watch out, Saint Martha will be looking to take on her job next."

Chapter Three
19th July 1907, Goldhurst Estate, Rutland
Martha

When Lady Goldhurst asked me to become their young daughter's nanny and carer two years ago, shortly after her fourth birthday in 1905, I was pleased, although not surprised considering I was practically doing the job already. It was a relief to get away from Dorothy, for by then I was bold enough to ask to be moved to another room closer to the nursery.

Mrs. Dylan remained Grace's nursemaid for the first year before declaring she had had enough of the 'demon child' and walked out. She was the longest serving nurse or nanny to date; others came and went in quick succession; one or two didn't even last a day. They all said the same - Grace was trouble - she was too much for them to cope with and she needed professional help. At first, doctors blamed her premature birth for her slow development and erratic behaviour. But as time went on without improvement, her parents became more and more concerned.

At the age of three Grace had not begun to speak or walk properly. She used to slither or crawl around and grunt, screech or howl like a pup. Even at the age of five her speech was limited to 'yes' and 'no' and little else. Her lack of communication, her frequent tantrums and her habit of making strange noises during the night drove people away, even servants, who had little to do with her. There was also her aggressive streak: Grace often became frustrated when she didn't get her own way and expressed this frustration through violence.

I remember one incident vividly, about a year ago. Lord and Lady Goldhurst had paid a speech doctor from London to come and work with Grace to see if he could get to the root of her problem. The gentleman was pleasant enough and very patient with her, but it was clear that Grace was not going to make his job easy. Although I was not present when the incident took place, I did witness the gentleman leave the house cursing loudly with blood streaming down his face and I imagine some rather unsightly teeth marks imprinted on his nose.

Once every three months, Grace had to be sedated to allow Ms. Vermaut to cut her unruly hair and, on one occasion, she became so maniacal that we feared that she may try and stab Ms. Vermaut with her own scissors.

The most memorable episode by far, however, happened a few weeks after her fifth birthday last year. It was a gorgeous summer's day and I promised Grace a walk to the village to feed the ducks, for it was last summer that she first developed a keen interest in them. I found it rather sweet and harmless until she began imitating the sounds of the ducks as we tossed dry lumps of bread at them and it drew some rather puzzled stares from the villagers.

Before we intended to set off, I left Grace watching Miss Alice and Miss Charlotte singing and dancing in the morning room while I went to change her bedclothes, for she was prone to night time accidents back then. When I returned, Miss Alice and Miss Charlotte were bickering about something silly and Grace was nowhere to be seen.

"Miss Charlotte, Miss Alice, where has your sister gone?" I asked, trying not to panic too soon. They stopped and looked at me in confusion. A quick scan of the room and Miss Alice's eyes widened as she realised that she had gone.

Miss Charlotte, however, just sighed and shrugged, saying, "Where you last left her," turning her back on me.

"I left her with you two for no longer than ten minutes. You were supposed to be keeping an eye on her." I scolded. Unlike some I had no tolerance for Miss Charlotte's uppity manner. She was far too young to be so arrogant.

"Mama and Papa pay *you* to look after her, not us!" She smirked, seating herself at the piano.

I was about to make some retort, but Miss Alice got there first, "Do shut up, Charlotte. Honestly you're so rude and she's right, *we* should have been looking after Grace; she's our sister, after all." Miss Charlotte rolled her eyes and continued to leaf through her sheet music. "We need to help Martha look for her, Charlotte." She added as she began walking towards the door, throwing a backwards glance at her sister, expecting her to follow.

"She can't have gone far in a few minutes. We don't need three people looking for her and besides, I need to practise this song for when Mama and Papa return from Paris." With that she began playing, her face was pure indifference.

"What if something's happened to her? Don't you care?" Miss Charlotte ignored her younger sister and continued to play. Miss Alice huffed and scowled at her as she hurried out to help me find my lost charge.

"I'll look upstairs, you start down here, Miss." I said. "If I see any other servants I'll ask them to help."

I dashed up the polished staircase and flung open each door, shouting Grace's name. Every room I found was empty and my calls went unanswered. She had never really taken a liking to the game hide-and-seek, so I saw no need to look under beds or inside wardrobes, except as a last resort.

After about ten minutes I decided to search the gardens, wondering why I hadn't thought to look there first. As I hurried outside I heard a loud commotion: screams, howls, loud voices and ducks' quacks coming from the direction of the lake. I ran, shouting Grace's name again and again.

As I reached the lakeside I was met with pandemonium. Grace was rocking wildly on the bank, dripping wet, flapping her arms like a wild thing whilst howling and shrieking with her eyes closed. Miss Alice was desperately trying to quieten her and lead her away from the water's edge, almost in tears with the effort. Next to her, also drenched, was one of the under-gardeners - a young lad from the village - half-heartedly trying to help Miss Alice get the screaming child up the cant towards the house, but he hung back with a look of terror in his eyes. Whilst this was going on, a raft of ducks were quacking away angrily, annoyed at being disturbed so abruptly.

The whole scene looked so utterly absurd that I forgot everything for a moment and started laughing. Miss Alice and the boy stared at me in amazement, but they too soon cracked grins and joined in. After about a minute Grace's screams subsided and even she sat down and began chuckling to herself; a strange, snuffling little laugh, but a breakthrough all the same. We laughed on the bank like a group of madmen for a few minutes before continuing to coerce Grace back inside and into a bath. It was then that Miss Alice told me what she had seen.

"One of the servants said they had spotted her in the garden heading for the lake, so I ran down there and called to the gardener's boy to help me. We got there just in time to see her flap her arms and run towards the water as if she was trying to take off! She must have watched the ducks do it and convinced herself that she could do the same. Luckily the boy could swim so he dived in after her."

"Thank heavens for that!" I said, getting some fresh clothes out for Grace.

"Yes, but, oh the poor boy!" Miss Alice began giggling, "Grace started thrashing and screaming and splashing him as he was trying to pull her out. He must have dropped her about six times, poor thing!" I chuckled at her story but couldn't help feeling nervous.

"Oh dear, Miss Alice. I really don't know what is going to become of your sister. I shall have to watch her like a hawk after this. It's just fortunate your parents weren't around to see it." I sighed and watched the girl splash and quack in the tub.

"Don't worry; Mama says she'll grow out of it." Miss Alice said cheerfully. "Besides, Papa said he's bringing one of the best doctors back with him from Paris to see Grace. I'm sure he'll be able to help." She smiled encouragingly at me and left the room.

Indeed, the Goldhursts had consulted all manner of specialists, from doctors, psychiatrists, speech experts, priests, apothecaries and even mystics. I had heard all sorts of explanations over the years, from mutism, hysteria and imbecility to partial deafness or short-sightedness. Their recommended treatments ranged from home-made herbal concoctions, electric shock therapy, institutionalisation, brain surgery, cold baths, singing to her, ignoring her, castor oil, exorcism, laudanum or good old fashioned prayer. Throughout her childhood we tried them all but none seemed to work. Each time another of these experts left I found myself called upon to pick up the pieces and carry on with Grace as best I could. Since a baby, she had always reacted better to me than the others. She was calmer; she cried and shouted less; she listened to me; she was rarely violent towards me. She seemed to trust me. I never found out why this was. Perhaps it was because I had been there from the beginning, perhaps because I was younger than the others, or spoke to her differently. I could only guess. Although looking after her had been challenging, it had not been without its pleasures. I was the first person to hear her utter her first words (aged five) three months ago. It was simply the word 'red' (she was asking me to read 'Little Red Riding Hood'). Excitement and relief swept through me as I knew her parents were desperate to hear her talk.

It was moments like this that cheered me and encouraged me to keep going. Besides, I far preferred looking after little Grace to the daily grind I endured as a housemaid and I was allowed my own room like the other nannies or governesses. The family were not keen for me to become Grace's full-time nanny due to my age, my lack of experience and my lack of schooling. I tried to tell them that my mother had educated me and my brother at home when we reached the age of eight and I was more than capable of teaching a child, but they were still reluctant. It wasn't until the nineteenth nanny left that they gave in. I still had to do a bit of cleaning, tidying and cooking from time to time, but that was more than bearable.

Excepting Mrs. Brickett, Mr. Brooks and occasionally Ms. Vermaut, I had little to do with the other servants. It didn't bother me, I had never grown close to anyone, except Dorothy at the beginning, and they couldn't deny the fact that they could never care for Grace without being driven insane.

Tenacious was the word that Grace's grandmother used to describe her. It was a word I hadn't heard before and after some investigation I decided it was a good way to describe her. She was certainly stubborn and impossible to persuade when she didn't want to do something.

This day, the eve of Grace's sixth birthday, Miss Louisa, or Mrs. Avery, as I kept having to remind myself to call her aloud, was visiting along with Lady Malholm, her ladyship's terrifying mother. Miss Louisa was heavily pregnant and full of excitement for she and her husband were going to live in America after the baby was born. Lady Malholm, however, was full of disapproval; her shrill voice floated up the stairs carrying questions such as: is it sensible to raise a family there? Where will you buy your clothes? Are the servants all former slaves? Will you be able to receive letters? before expressing her concerns about the American accent.

"It's taxing enough having to get used to your husband's accent, without you and your children talking like yanks too." She huffed. I closed the door to the nursery in an attempt to shut out her voice.

Miss Louisa's young daughter, Moira, was asleep upstairs meaning we had been banished to the second floor nursery. Grace was counting using her abacus, an unlikely favourite toy she had received last Christmas. A few minutes later, there was a knock at the door and Miss Louisa walked in.

"Hello my little Grace! My, how you've grown!" Miss Louisa had the patience of a nun and always made a particular fuss of Grace, despite getting little more than a grunt or a scowl in response. She spoiled Miss Charlotte and Miss Alice too, and they adored her so much that they often cried when she left again. They would be devastated when she moved away.

"I would love a stroll around the garden with all my sisters before dinner, and Martha too, of course."

"Very well, Miss...Mrs. Avery. I'll just fetch her boots."

During summer afternoons the gardens of Goldhurst were at their most beautiful. The light touched the treetops and the surface of the distant lake, highlighting the gentle ripples caused by the breeze. We were accompanied by Miss Alice but not Miss Charlotte, who had been invited to a friend's house for tea. Miss Alice, who at thirteen was almost as tall as her twenty-five year old sister, linked arms with Miss Louisa and chatted happily about her dressmaking lessons that she was receiving from Mrs. Birch, a local woman in Stamford.

"Mrs. Birch is simply the most wonderful teacher. She's taught me how to use a Singer sewing machine, how to measure and cut patterns and now we're learning how to crochet. I just wish I had my own machine here, in the house, I hate asking that beastly Mademoiselle Vermaut. She's so odious and rude!"

"Now, Alice, remember she's very busy; it's jolly nice of her to let you borrow it at all."

I gathered from their conversation that Lord and Lady Goldhurst were uncomfortable with the arrangement with Mrs. Birch, but Miss Louisa was full of encouragement and promised to speak to her parents about getting a Singer for Alice to practise on at home.

Soon the conversation turned to Grace's birthday and although she was unable to answer all her sisters' questions, she did seem to enjoy the attention. Her movements were more vigorous and her eyes were brighter, her face more inquisitive. Grace had started to echo sounds she heard more and more frequently and would occasionally repeat individual words I said to her aloud, depending on her mood. This afternoon she was in fairly good spirits and was happily chirping away, imitating a thrush.

"Look Grace, a rose. Isn't it beautiful? Rose...Rose....Rose." Miss Alice repeated the word slowly and deliberately, looking at Grace who was lolloping along in her own fantasy. "There are red roses, pink roses, yellow roses, such gorgeous roses this year." Miss Alice persevered, with one ear cocked in anticipation. Like her older sister, Miss Alice was a sweet girl and very patient with her sister. I was pleased to see that since Grace had started talking, she had begun to take more of an interest in her. Miss Charlotte wasn't in the least interested. She was embarrassed and irritated by her, although she told her parents she avoided her because she was afraid, which I doubted very much. Master Edward, being the son and heir, was treated quite differently, and kept quite separate from the girls when they were growing up, being sent away to boarding school, and now university, for most of the year. When he was at home he rarely bothered with any of his sisters and would usually ignore Grace completely if he happened to hear or see her. I always felt quite intimidated by Master Edward; it was hard to imagine him being a year younger than me.

"Rose." A weak, husky voice interrupted my thoughts. Miss Alice spun around and clapped her hands in delight.

"Oh Grace, well done! Yes that's right, these are roses!"

"Rose." Grace repeated without changing her expression or looking at us. Miss Alice didn't mind though, she beamed like a sun ray as we carried on across the garden.

After a few more failed attempts to get Grace to speak, we headed back towards the house. The sun was beginning to set and cast an amber glow across the gardens. Clumsily, Grace pranced on ahead and Miss Louisa turned to us, a serious look on her face.

"Poor dear. It's a shame I won't get to see her progress; you must write to me in New York and tell me how she's getting on." Miss Alice insisted that she would write every week, to which Miss Louisa smiled and said once a month was more than sufficient. "You must both promise me that you'll look after her. There are people in this family who would prefer that she were not here. I don't believe Mother would ever send her away but others will certainly try to persuade her nonetheless. Please try and protect her as much as you can for she desperately needs friends and supporters." Miss Alice, wide-eyed and open-mouthed nodded earnestly. Miss Louisa smiled and said, "I know a thing or two about being an outsider in this family. Now, I'd better go up to the nursery to see to Moira. Bye bye Gracie." She called blowing a kiss in Grace's direction. "See you in the dining room, Alice." She said kissing her sister on the cheek. "Bye Martha." She smiled at me and walked up the stone steps and into the house.

"Time for supper, Gracie." I said as we headed towards the staircase.

"Do you know what day it is tomorrow, Grace?" Miss Alice paused and, realising she wasn't going to get an answer, continued. "It's your sixth birthday! You're growing up very fast." She turned to me. "Do you know if we're doing anything special for it?"

"I've got her a little present and a card. I'm not sure what your mother and father have got in mind. I suppose it's a surprise." The comment was more for Grace's benefit; for I knew Lord and Lady Goldhurst would not be planning anything to mark the occasion. They had realised quite early on than any kind of excitement or change from their daughter's usual routine could lead to an outburst, a fit of screaming, or worse. The whole family knew that scolding or any normal punishment issued to a naughty child had no effect on Grace; therefore the best thing was to do nothing to provoke her.

Once back inside, Miss Alice said goodnight and kissed Grace gently on the cheek. She squirmed and rubbed the spot.

"Before you go upstairs I have a little early birthday present for you." She reached into her dress pocket and retrieved a beautiful, large pink rose. "Mr. Healy cut it for you, especially". Grace took it from her and stared at it, her expression unchanged as Miss Alice walked away.

"Come on Gracie, duck, time for a story and then bed." I steered her towards the staircase and heard a small, wispy voice reply, "Rose".

Chapter Four
28th October 1909, Goldhurst Estate, Rutland
Martha

Three months after Grace's eighth birthday her parents decided to employ yet another psychiatrist specialising in child behaviour named Mr. Irvine. Lord Goldhurst had heard about him from an acquaintance in London; apparently he was well known for his effective, if radical, treatment of children with 'cognitive behavioural problems', as he put it.

That morning, late in October, Mr. Irvine arrived at half past eight and was ushered into Lord Goldhurst's study; no doubt he was offered a sizeable fee for his services.

Grace had finished her breakfast and I was wiping the breadcrumbs from her mouth when Lady Goldhurst bustled in to summon her downstairs to meet the latest stranger.

"Come along, Grace, dear." She said waving her outstretched hand at her daughter. Grace ignored her and went to sit on the window seat with a copy of 'Snow White and the Seven Dwarves'.

"Grace, you heard me, come on, we can't be rude and keep our visitor waiting." Her mother continued brightly.

"I don't want to go downstairs. Martha needs to read to me like we do every morning." She mumbled without looking up. Lady Goldhurst shot me a look of desperation. I knew what I had to do.

"Just go with your mother now, Miss Grace, and we'll read Snow White in a few minutes." Lady Goldhurst looked hopefully at her daughter, who was unmoved. "I can't read you the book until you go down with your mother. Just like Red Riding Hood was not allowed to play until she had visited her grandma." I continued with a tone of regret.

"What?" She said without looking at me. "How do you know that?"

"It's true, I know more about that story than you think." I said, winking at her. I hated lying to her, but sometimes it was the only way. Slowly, she plonked the book down and dragged herself towards the door, hugging herself, refusing to make eye contact or to hold her mother's hand.

Once downstairs the three of us entered the library where Mr. Irvine was waiting. Lady Goldhurst had asked me to accompany them to meet the gentleman, as much for her own sake as his.

When we first walked into the room, Mr. Irvine had his back to us, and steadily turned to face us as we made our entrance. He was a red-haired man of about forty with waxy skin, the colour of wet pastry. His hands were planted deep inside his pockets. To me, he looked more like a police constable than a doctor. On closer inspection, I saw the red spikes of hair protruding from his thin head, which pointed towards the ceiling, making it look like a large arrow, and his quick, watery grey eyes reminded me of a whippet we once kept on the farm. His dress and appearance was nothing out of the ordinary; he wore a dark grey suit, much the same as all the other doctors or professors I had seen. But his manners seemed rather odd; almost brusque. Firstly, I found it rude that the man stood in front of Lady Goldhurst with his hands wedged into his pockets, making no attempt to extract them to acknowledge her greeting. Secondly, he had a queer way of looking at Grace that instantly made me uncomfortable. Finally (and I couldn't explain it), I had a general feeling of unease around him. I suppose it was what most folk would call intuition, for I hadn't seen or heard of the man until today, yet the feeling was so overwhelming I wanted to grab Grace's hand and run out of that room, away from him.

"This is Miss Grace Goldhurst, my daughter, Mr. Irvine. Say how do you do, Grace." Lady Goldhurst smiled and coaxed. Grace lowered her chin to her chest and fixed her eyes on the carpet.

"Martha needs to read to me now. We always read at nine o'clock, after breakfast." Grace muttered to her feet. She was still refusing to hold anyone's hand or stand next to one of us. Lady Goldhurst rolled her eyes and sighed, casting our visitor an apologetic look.

"Your nanny won't be reading to you today, Miss Goldhurst. I will be working with you this morning. Your mother and father are very worried about you. I understand that you haven't even learned to write properly yet! You're growing up and you need a proper education so you can become an intelligent, amiable young lady. I'm sure you don't want to grow up to become a *burden* on your parents now, do you?" He said, stretching his mouth into a grin. I winced when I saw the rows of little, pointed teeth.

Lady Goldhurst stared at him as if wanting to say something but unable to find the correct words, so she spoke to Grace instead. "My dear, you know your father and I are very worried about the way you are..." she paused to consider the most appropriate word, "conducting yourself, and misbehaving for the tutors that we bring here for you - some of the best in Europe, I might add. It grieves us deeply, as we want the best for you. I want you to grow up to live a normal happy life like your older brother and sisters." Her voice wavered slightly. "So, please, darling, just try your very hardest to get along with Mr. Irvine and do as he tells you, for me? He's an expert and can help you if you let him." She smiled encouragingly at the tenacious girl, whose brow was furrowing deeper and deeper until I thought her entire face might cave in. Her folded arms were creeping higher and higher up her chest and her eyes were locked on the burgundy carpet.

Then the humming started. Quietly at first, but steadily louder and louder into a sound resembling a car engine.

Lord Goldhurst suddenly appeared in the room, red-faced and eyes blazing. For a moment I couldn't believe how much he looked like Grace. "For God's sake, child! Stop that dreadful noise at once!" His wife relayed their conversation and Lord Goldhurst apologised to Mr. Irvine and stood directly in front of his daughter. "It makes no difference what sound you make, you are not getting your own way this time, my girl. Your mother and I have had enough of your insubordination." Grace continued her humming, shriller still, and stared at the ground as if her father were invisible, which angered him further.

Mr. Irvine simply smiled, unfazed by the din and placed a long, bony hand on Lord Goldhurst's back. "Why don't I spend some time alone with Miss Goldhurst? Believe me, I'm used to such behaviour and the noise won't stop until her audience leaves."

He began to usher us out of the library, with the confidence of one who had been there for years. I didn't want to leave her; the dreadful uneasy feeling remained. "Perhaps I should stay with her too, ma'am. For the first few minutes at least." I whispered to Lady Goldhurst.

Mr. Irvine fixed his cold, watery eyes on me for the first time and responded, before Lady Goldhurst could, "No, that won't help matters at all. In fact, it will make it significantly worse. This child is clearly too attached to over-indulgent nannies and she cannot hope to progress unless we remedy that." I felt my face flush, partly from the anger I felt towards this rude stranger but also because of shame. Was I doing her more harm than good? I hadn't thought of it before.

I was forced to follow Lord and Lady Goldhurst out of the room, leaving Grace at his mercy. I saw her with her hands covering each ear, humming furiously as the door closed behind us.

Muttering to himself, Lord Goldhurst strode back to his study without another word; Lady Goldhurst took my arm and steered me away from the library door.

"We have great faith in Mr. Irvine. He's a miracle worker, by all accounts in London. He has worked with all kinds of people and even cured one girl of madness completely." Lady Goldhurst gibbered away, more for her own benefit than for mine so I nodded my head every few words to reassure her I was listening. "He started his career at Broadmoor Lunatic Asylum, doing some marvellous work with the patients, then went on to study psychiatry with some well-known doctor, I can't recall his name, but he is quite famous in Europe." She waved her hand absently. "Anyway, I think he will be the one to finally get somewhere with Grace. I have a good feeling, Martha." I was unconvinced. If he was so wonderful, why wasn't he Doctor Irvine instead of Mister? But it was none of my business.

"At first I was put off by some of the stories of the...methods he has used, but now he has explained them to Lord Goldhurst, I'm not worried in the slightest. If we want results we have to try different therapies."

"What methods does he use, if you don't mind me asking m'lady?" I was already dreading the answer. We had reached the morning room and Lady Goldhurst closed the door before facing me.

"Well, he has been known to use this newfangled electroconvulsive therapy, which sounds quite beastly, but it's quite safe, he assures us. They're using it in America and on the continent too. Apparently it's working wonders with patients at his hospital in Scotland. He told Lord Goldhurst that a young man came to him three months ago, completely wild, unable to form a coherent sentence and terribly aggressive. His family had given up on him and sent him to Irvine as a last resort. Well, to cut a long story short, after just two months of this electro therapy he was cured! He was calm, talking normally, eating normally - a complete transformation. He's a naval officer now, can you believe?" She smiled and sighed. "Can you imagine the possibilities for Grace if he can do the same for her?"

I shuddered at the thought of that red-haired fiend torturing my Grace. I wanted to shake her mother, for I was sure she had lost her senses. "Lady Goldhurst, I know you are Miss Grace's mother and you have her best interests at heart, but this electric therapy sounds...terrifying. It's all very well inflicting it on a madman but remember, Miss Grace is only eight years old. It could do some real damage, m'lady, she could be shocked out of her senses completely."

To my great surprise, a grin spread across Lady Goldhurst's face. "Martha, I believe its aim is to frighten people *in* to their senses!" She chuckled. I felt my face flush again, not from embarrassment, which would probably have been my reaction a couple of years ago, but from outrage at this woman's stupidity.

"Sorry, that was a poor joke." She said, touching my arm. "In all seriousness, Mr. Irvine is *not* going to electrocute my child. He has made it quite clear that it is a last resort. He's simply going to assess Grace today to calculate the best course of action. Really, Martha, of course we wouldn't let him do anything as radical as that!" She laughed at me and turned to leave the room, leaving me to gawp like an idiot.

"Now, I have a few things that need collecting from Stamford. Could you take Charlotte and Alice with you in an hour? They could do with a bit of air."

"Yes m'lady. I'll go and tell them." I replied stiffly.

Five hours later Mr. Irvine had left, but not before giving his verdict to the Lord and Lady of the house. Grace needed expert help in a proper psychiatric institution (just like the one he ran in Scotland, coincidentally). On closer inspection, Mr. Irvine concluded that the child must have suffered a blow to the head at some point during birth or early childhood since the cause didn't appear to be moral or genetic, considering none of her family suffered from mental disorders or moral depravity. As I had been present at Grace's birth and had been around her almost every day, I found this unlikely, but her parents lapped up this neat explanation that in no way incriminated them. Mrs. Dylan's name was raised as the guilty party who must have dropped the poor child and hid the truth from her parents.

Mr. Irvine persuaded Lord and Lady Goldhurst that Grace would never improve if she remained untreated and in the care of amateurs. So a trip to Scotland was arranged for the following month to visit St. Giles' Psychiatric Hospital.

Immediately after Mr. Irvine left, Grace would not talk to me, would not listen to me, would not cooperate with me. I knew I had lost her trust and I wasn't sure how long it would take for me to regain it.

The same afternoon I discovered marks on the poor child's wrists and ankles; Mr. Irvine had obviously restrained her in the library as he 'assessed' her. I reported it to her mother straight away, who seemed unmoved. She said she already knew about it; he had told them that she attacked him and he needed to restrain her. No wonder she distrusted us all, we had left her alone with this devilish stranger who wasn't even a proper doctor.

Over the next month, as the marks faded, I managed to regain some of her trust. However, the date of our Scotland trip was looming and I felt powerless to help her, especially as her parents seemed to be pinning all their hopes on Mr. Irvine as a kind of saviour.

On the morning of our journey north, I tried to stay enthusiastic. Despite what people thought, Grace was not stupid and she certainly knew when something was wrong. She wasn't keen on travelling and she hated surprises, so Lady Goldhurst suggested that the whole family go, in order to settle her nerves. In the end Miss Alice was the only sibling who came with us. Lord Goldhurst wanted Master Edward to stay in order to take care of some business and Miss Charlotte said she wouldn't be joining us as she was coming down with a fever and couldn't possibly survive the long, cold journey all the way up to Edinburgh.

We set off just after half past seven and had a fairly uneventful journey to Peterborough station. Lady Goldhurst, however, had been sick all the way and had to lie down in a separate compartment on the train for the majority of the journey. Grace and I also sat separately due to her excitement and the noises she always made when travelling by train.

She sat on the floor and chugged along with the train, emitting a shrill whistle, mimicking the train's own whistle every time it sounded, slowing or accelerating depending on the train's movement. Her body remained rigid, only her head and arms bobbed up and down like a puppet's. To watch, it was quite fascinating. She got the sounds just right and seemed to be in her own little world. Her father stressed that the door remained closed all the way to Scotland, in case someone looked in and saw what was happening. After about two hours, she exhausted herself and fell asleep in my lap.

We arrived at our hotel in Edinburgh just after two o'clock. Lord Goldhurst was forced to ring the hospital to postpone our visit until the next morning due to Lady Goldhurst's ill health, which had worsened in the last two hours. So, with Miss Alice and Ms. Vermaut attending Lady Goldhurst and Lord Goldhurst occupied with some business, Grace and I were left to explore the hotel and the sights of Edinburgh by ourselves.

The hotel, aptly named The Regency, was a grand affair of plaid curtains; thickly woven carpets and dark wood staircases. A selective littering of ornaments and vases filled with fresh flowers and thistles added some character to it. The other guests looked similar to Lord and Lady Goldhurst: wealthy, busy and important, with an entourage of servants trailing obediently, a step or two behind.

"Martha, Grace!" a familiar voice cut through the jabbering in the lobby. Miss Alice hurried towards us.

"Oh good! I was worried you had set off already and I had missed you. Mama is asleep and Ms. Vermaut is looking after her so I can join you on your walk." She beamed. "I brought my easel and water colours. Let's walk to Arthur's Seat, via the castle, the views are rather spectacular."

The three of us walked out onto the cobbled streets and headed towards the castle. Miss Alice had visited Edinburgh three years ago with her aunt and was happy to be our guide.

An hour later we were at the top of Arthur's Seat. She set up her easel and began to paint the view of Edinburgh, insisting that Grace and I sat in the foreground. I had always liked Miss Alice, she was a sweet, polite girl; a little dreamy and absent-minded at times, perhaps, but certainly a great deal more kind and sensitive than Miss Charlotte or Master Edward. I had always thought that she shared some similarities with her younger sister. She was content in her own company and often became engrossed in tasks, labouring at them for hours on end, namely painting and sewing. She was extremely skilled at both, but sewing and dressmaking in particular.

After a while, Grace became bored with sitting and trotted off around the summit collecting stones, bringing them back to a pile a few feet away. It was a cool, cloudy day and the breeze brought calm to us all.

Miss Alice was engrossed in her painting and bit her lip in concentration, now and again muttering to herself, words which were carried away by the wind. She might as well have been alone on that hilltop.

Only when she had finished did she speak, asking for my opinion on the masterpiece. "My word, it's super, Miss Alice!" I was full of admiration for her talents, but she wrinkled her nose and tilted her head to one side, squinting at the painting.

"Thank you, but it's certainly not my best. It's so difficult to capture these clouds well." She gestured towards the sky and shook her head as she spoke. "Ah, I just don't have the skill for it!" and with this self-criticism she rubbed her hands together with an air of finality. "We should head back - it's getting late. Do you want this?" She held the painting out to me.

"What, to keep?" I said. She nodded. "Oh, Miss, I couldn't take it, it's so beautiful, don't you want to keep it?" She wrinkled her nose and shook her head forcing it into my hand.

Grace had constructed two tracks around the summit with the stones she had collected. She was now busy chugging up and down them making the same noises as she had on the train. It took many attempts at cajoling, coaxing and coercing before we managed to get her to leave and she only gave in when we allowed her to bring the pile of stones with her in Miss Alice's easel bag; it seemed a fair deal.

I showed Grace the painting on the way down, pointing out the two figures in the foreground as her and me. She stared at it for a moment, unmoved, then concluded, "That's not me. I'm me," before racing to the bottom.

As we neared the hotel, Miss Alice spoke about the next day's visit in a low voice. "I really don't know much about these sorts of places. Mama and Papa would never send Grace away to a lunatic asylum, but if they find a nice, private place for children of respectable families then I think it's sensible to keep an open mind. Mama worries about her constantly. She can't read or write and I don't know how she's going to cope with adult life if she doesn't improve soon. It is an awful situation, don't you think?"

"It is a worry. But Miss, don't you think your sister has improved over the last few years? Considering she never even used to speak I think she's come on in leaps and bounds. Who's to say all that good work won't come undone if she's sent away to live with strangers?"

She considered this. "I see your point, she has made progress, but is it enough?" I remained silent and avoided her eyes as I could feel a lump rising in my throat. Miss Alice had always seemed more understanding of Grace. Out of all the Goldhurst children she had been the most affectionate and accepting of her. Perhaps that was changing.

"I don't want to upset you, I know how much you mean to her and vice versa, but if she has a better chance of leading a normal life with the help of these people at the hospital we need to consider it. Grace may not be happy there at first but she will no doubt grow fond of it by and by. Like I said, we need to keep an open mind and think of what is best for her future."

Fortunately, as we had reached the hotel, Lord Goldhurst's valet was heading towards us to tell us dinner would be served in an hour. I led Grace away upstairs without saying another word to her sister. I felt useless, I didn't want her to go to this hospital, or any other for that matter and I was certain that Grace didn't want to either, but what could I do? I was just her nanny. She was slipping through my fingers and I had to accept it.

After breakfast the next morning the family and I drove to St. Giles' Hospital, about ten miles outside Edinburgh, near a small town called Kirklear. The building was nestled between rolling hills and heaths. It was an attractive white building and the grounds were more attractive still, but the uneasy feeling I experienced when first meeting Mr. Irvine extended to this place he managed. It reminded me of the setting in a gothic novel: beautiful, wild, secluded, supernatural, yet with the potential for danger.

The wind, which had picked up during the night, whipped the sides of our car and jostled us together so that it was strangely relieving to see Mr. Irvine opening the door to offer refuge.

He welcomed Lord and Lady Goldhurst with exaggerated warmth once inside. Miss Alice smiled politely and even Grace seemed indifferent to the place. She had shown no signs of dislike or alarm and fiddled quite contentedly with the wooden duck figurine Miss Alice had bought her on the way back to the hotel the previous evening. All night I had thought about Miss Alice's comments to 'keep an open mind' and do what was best for Grace. I had no choice but to accept her view and look on St. Giles' in an optimistic light or a neutral one at least. However, my intuition would not allow me to trust this Irvine chap. I felt sick at the prospect of leaving Grace here with him.

Our tour of St. Giles' was uneventful and eerily quiet. Mr. Irvine informed us that all the residents, except the very sick, had gone out for the day to visit Hadrian's Wall and had left shortly before our arrival.

"You will note, Lord Goldhurst, that we refer to the patients as 'residents' here. I feel that the term is more conducive to familiarity, you know, personable care which is sadly lacking in the state-managed or larger private institutions." Mr. Irvine simpered, pleased with the way that Lord Goldhurst nodded in approval.

I turned away to hide my disgust. The view I was faced with out of the window was one of wild beauty: the wind lashed the trees, forcing them to bow towards the ground. The sky had turned to a grizzled, dark grey and rain piddled to the ground in fat drops.

"Oh dear, it's a wretched day to be out hill-walking at the border. The poor devils will be soaked, if not blown away first!" Lord Goldhurst's comment drew my attention back to the conversation and I saw Mr. Irvine's eyes dart to the window before settling on his visitor with a smile.

"Aye, my lord, I daresay they will find shelter in a local inn or head back if it becomes too rough. Now, if you follow me, I'll show you some of the patients' private rooms and the treatment rooms."

After a glimpse of the empty private rooms, the kitchen and the lounge, our host led us down a deserted corridor towards the building's annexe. The wind had reached a fierce climax and hurled rain against the window panes. The glass rattled and the whistling hit an unbearable, shrill note. Grace, who had been walking beside me, was now several feet behind, covering her ears and dragging her feet in protest. I tried to soothe her but I knew it was useless; the humming had already started.

On first impressions the treatment rooms were not too different to the other private rooms we had seen, if a little colder and blander. However, the equipment in the corner of the one we saw chased away all the images of the cosy private rooms. There were several angry-looking machines in wooden boxes, covered with knobs and wheels and wires dangling to the floor. I noticed afterwards that the bed was on wheels and by the sink were all the usual paraphernalia of a doctor's surgery: gloves, scissors, bottles of solution and cotton balls. A diagram of a human brain framed the wall behind the bed and the whole room smelled of disinfectant and rubber.

Mr. Irvine had barely begun to explain the room's function before Grace interrupted him. She ran circles around the bed and hummed along with the sound of the wind; louder and louder until it echoed off the walls. Miss Alice and I tried to calm her with words and foolishly tried to stand in her way as she was running, which only made her hum louder.

When Lord Goldhurst and Mr. Irvine joined in the effort she retreated into a small space between the machines and a bed-side table, humming frantically but still clutching her duck.

"Allow me, Lord Goldhurst, I know what to do." Mr. Irvine said. Lord Goldhurst, flushed red from embarrassment and exertion and began to protest, but Mr. Irvine held up a hand in an assured manner and moved forward.

Miss Alice and her mother stood by the opposite wall clinging to one another; Miss Alice whispered something and Lady Goldhurst closed her eyes. Her husband gawked at Mr. Irvine, clenching and unclenching his fists and I, unsure of whether to intervene or not, stood dumbly looking on as Mr. Irvine crouched to Grace's level and inched closer. The humming grew louder.

"Now Grace, this behaviour has to stop. Remember what we spoke about a few weeks ago?" He shouted to make himself heard over the din and clasped Grace's wrists as if to prise them from her ears. I didn't hear the rest of his speech as an almighty scream bounced from all four walls, followed by a deeper, desperate shout and the wooden duck sailed across the room, clattering as it landed at Miss Alice's feet.

Suddenly, Grace was racing past me, out of the room and round the corner out of sight. I ran to the door. The girl could move like a greyhound when she wanted to. A nurse vaulted out of the way as she flew past, her skirts kicked up behind and her hair had loosened and hung like a frayed rope down her back. Then she vanished around the next corner. For a moment I heard nothing but the rustle of material and the heavy clopping of boot soles against tile. In spite of the commotion, a warm feeling of satisfaction bubbled in my ears. Hopefully this meant she wasn't to be admitted here after all.

This feeling was not to last as the next image I saw was several male attendants sprinting after her; Lord Goldhurst pushed past me and ambled along in pursuit of the younger men.

I became aware of sobbing behind me. Lady Goldhurst had collapsed on the bed with wheels, her hands covering her face. Miss Alice gaped at the door the same way I had before collecting her senses and going to soothe her mother.

Mr. Irvine was the only person not fixated on the door. He paced and cursed and dabbed at his wound like and angry bear, made all the more furious by his being ignored. I took a proper look at the damage Grace had caused: a red mass of blood stained his pale cheek; two trails of it ran down and settled in the ginger brush of beard.

"Beast! The feral little beast bit me!" I heard him curse and I scowled in his direction, leaving Miss Alice to offer apologies.

Grace was eventually found an hour and a half later, curled up under a thick gorse bush a few yards outside the grounds of the hospital - soaked through and frightened. It took some time to persuade her to come out (in the end only the wooden duck secured the victory) and I returned with her to Edinburgh immediately.

I wasted no time in bathing Grace and putting her straight to bed with a dose of tonic. An hour in the cold, wet Scottish wilderness with only a day dress, I feared, would result in a chill or, at worst, a fever. Luckily, Grace gave in without much resistance. The day's events had clearly drained the poor child of all her usual tenacity.

I still desperately wanted to find out what had passed between Grace's parents and the awful Mr. Irvine after we had driven back to the hotel.

After dinner I approached Miss Alice, who was alone in her room, to find out.

"It was all very queer. Despite what happened, Mr. Irvine insisted that Grace should be assigned to his care at the hospital, to everyone's amazement, as you can imagine. He said that she was 'a most challenging and urgent case' and he strongly advised, no, *insisted*, that she be removed from the family home and consigned to a proper psychiatric hospital with immediate effect."

I was shocked, "Why on earth would he insist upon it after what she did to him? He clearly hated her for it."

"He claimed that her outburst and attack on him proved what he already knew: that she is a deeply troubled and dangerous child and no one could tell what she was capable of in the future if she didn't receive adequate professional care right away."

I was livid. How dare this man - a stranger - dictate what was best for Grace, for whom he had no interest or love?

"Miss Alice, please tell me they're not sending her there. I couldn't bear it. I don't trust him and she would be miserable, I know it." It was a bold move to express my feelings to my employer's daughter, but I had to try and save her.

She looked at me, unblinking, "I agree with you. There is something underhand and rather sinister about that man. I wouldn't trust him with my pet cat, let alone my sister. The way he cursed and swore about Grace...and those awful machines, and those noises..." She shuddered and broke off.

I looked at her quizzically. "What noises, the wind, do you mean?"

She hugged herself as she continued. "After everybody went to look for Grace, Mama and I were walking back to the main building with Mr. Irvine and I heard some bizarre noises coming from a section of the place we hadn't seen. As soon as Mama was settled in his office I went to see where they were coming from but Mr. Irvine stopped me. His manner was so completely changed; I thought he must be delirious from the injury."

"What do you mean?" I said, wanting to know it all.

"He was so very rude, raising his voice and practically frogmarching me back to his office. After that any doubts I had were confirmed."

"What sort of noises did you hear?"

She frowned, "I can't be certain, but it was a wailing and a shouting, and then some screaming - women's screams. Lord knows what or who it was, I know it's not unusual to hear strange screams in a hospital, but he was adamant that all the residents were out hill-walking. It wasn't coming from the hospital wing, where the sick patients were."

My heart was beating fast, I put my hands to my head and thanked the lord that they hadn't left Grace there.

"Anyway, I told my parents that I didn't trust him."

"What did they say?"

"Papa was harder to convince but Mama was more sympathetic. She's been crying for most of the afternoon. In the end she told Papa that she would never speak to him again if he sent Grace there. It worked in persuading him against the idea. For now, at least."

"For now?"

"Papa was adamant that he will continue to look for a suitable care home for Grace. But it won't be St. Giles', thank goodness."

I was relieved by Miss Alice's news and impressed with the way she had defended her sister. "Thank you for doing that, Miss. It was brave of you to face Mr. Irvine like that."

She sighed and sank onto the edge of the bed. "I do love Grace terribly: she's my sister. And I just feel so frustrated that I can't do more for her. I wish Louisa was here; she was always so good at talking to people and saying the right thing to make one feel better."

"I know how you feel, Miss. But Grace is getting there; small steps and she'll get there."

She sighed again and fiddled with the fabric of her skirt. "I think we've all been rather naïve about the severity of her problem. Look what she did to that man today. He may have deserved it, but what if she attacks someone again?"

"She's still only young; she'll grow out of it. Besides, she only does it when she's scared. I'll keep a closer eye on her."

"But Martha, what if you decide to leave? Grace is already dependent on you and she wouldn't be able to cope if you left. We have a responsibility to ensure she's looked after, or better still, can look after herself, for the rest of her life. At the moment it looks like she will never be able to do that."

I saw Miss Alice in a new light. I had always viewed her as a sweet young dreamer. She was clearly wiser than her fourteen years; however, she underestimated my attachment to her sister.

"Miss Alice, I'm not a doctor, or a psychiatrist. I can't promise that I'm going to 'cure' her of her problems." Ashamed, I felt a lump rise in my throat and swallowed hard to get rid of it. "However, I can promise you that I will always be there for her as long as she needs and wants me. I won't be going anywhere. And I don't think many doctors can say the same."

Miss Alice smiled. "Thank you, Martha, that's awfully sweet. Grace is lucky to have you." She kissed me on the cheek and said goodnight.

There was a small sitting room at the back of the hotel, removed from the bustle and grandeur of the lobby at the front. The room glowed warm orange. A large fireplace dominated the majority of one wall and armchairs of various sizes and styles crowded around the hearth as if waiting for some old storyteller to settle down for the evening.

Ms. Vermaut and I were the only people in the room at first. She led the way to the biggest couple of tartan chairs by the fire and relaxed before the fire, whisking out a cigarette, attaching it to an amber holder and lighting it with the effortless movement of a professional.

She offered one to me; I declined. I had never liked the smell or taste of tobacco.

This was the longest conversation I had ever had with Ms. Vermaut and, after a few minutes of polite talk, I asked her more about her family and life in France.

"My father was a maitre d'hôtel, first in Paris, then in London where he met my mother. He worked at The Ritz for a short while, but mostly at The Savoy. He was there for six years before we moved back to Paris." She paused and inhaled deeply on her cigarette. "My mother was a dancer when they first met. She could have been very successful if my father had not got in the way!"

"She must have been very good."

"She was exquisite to watch – graceful, fluid, rhythmic. But she had to give it all up to support us. She tried to get back onto the stage in Paris when we were older, but by then she was too old and no one wanted her. I watched her a few times when she did amateur performances. She danced beautifully. Such a waste of talent." She shrugged and stared into the fire.

"You had a very glamorous upbringing compared to mine. Rural Derbyshire doesn't really compare to Paris and London."

She stubbed out her cigarette in the silver ash tray placed in the middle of a small table between us, a smile playing on her lips. "Yes, I can imagine nothing worse than living on a farm in England. It does not exactly suggest sophistication or excitement." She chuckled at my expense. I had brought it on myself by mentioning it.

"Well, my parents may not have been sophisticated but they are honest and intelligent. Or should I say was in the case of my father." I paused, mentioning my father was always upsetting. "He owned one of the most successful farms in the county before he became too ill to manage it. And my mother was a governess for a number of years before she married. She taught me everything I know." I must have sounded defensive judging by the way Ms. Vermaut held her hands up in surrender.

"My apologies, I meant no offence."

A silence fell between us before she addressed me again, "I suppose we are all of us very similar; we want to make our parents proud and feel miserable if we let them down." As I was rolling this comment around in my mind, I couldn't prevent my thoughts from wandering back to Grace. It seemed the same subject was on Ms. Vermaut's mind. "Lady Goldhurst told me about what happened today." Another cigarette was lit. "It is a sad business. There are *some* things I really don't envy her."

A middle aged man and woman entered the sitting room deep in conversation and headed for the opposite side without acknowledging us. Ms. Vermaut lowered her voice and moved her head closer. "If I tell you something, you must promise not to tell another soul until it becomes public knowledge." Her look was serious.

"Of course." I replied.

"Her ladyship is with child, again." Ms. Vermaut sat back in her chair and sucked on her cigarette, watching my face expectantly.

"Really? That would certainly explain her ill health. I am happy for her and Lord Goldhurst." My voice sounded neutral and unaffected by her information. In reality a hundred thoughts were taking flight. Was this the reason for bringing Grace here? How would she react to the news? What if the child was like her?

Disappointed that her news had not induced more of a reaction, Ms. Vermaut started a new line of enquiry. "Alors, I am sure you are relieved that they decided not to leave the girl at this hospital?"

"Of course I'm pleased. She's far better off with her family and with people who care about her than with some strange doctors who are only concerned with money and using their patients as experiments."

She nodded her head as she exhaled a cloudy stream. "Oui, I agree this was not the right place for her, from what her ladyship said. As to being with the family, I don't know. They, and you, are not equipped to look after her properly I think and she is becoming very aggressive from what Lady

Goldhurst has told me. Surely she is better being with people who understand her and can help her? Her family would be too..."

"Forgive me, but you can't possibly comment on the subject for you only understand the situation from Lady Goldhurst's hearsay. You don't spend any time with Miss Grace. You don't know her, so I would appreciate it if you kept your opinions to yourself."

Ms. Vermaut looked taken aback. "Excuse me, I may not know the child well but I live under the same roof as her and I can see what she is like. I also see the effect she has on her mother. I know you have your own reasons for keeping her at Goldhurst Estate which perhaps clouds *your* judgement on this subject."

I narrowed my eyes at her. "What do you mean by that?"

She shrugged, "You have a very comfortable, well-paid job at Goldhurst. That would all disappear if she was sent away and you would end up back on a farm or in service, would you not?"

Her words rang in my ears, goading me. Unable to control my outrage I stood up so quickly it made Ms. Vermaut start. "How dare you! Who are you to judge me? You're a servant the same as me and your intimacy with Lady Goldhurst doesn't make you superior to me in any way." I made to leave the room but hesitated and turned back. "You're quite right. You don't know the child well and if you cared about her half as much as I do you may begin to understand the fear that I feel every day knowing that she relies on me to protect her from people like you and them, and I dread the day that I cannot offer her any more protection."

I was aware that the couple in the corner were staring at me and the last thing I wanted was a response from Ms. Vermaut. I practically ran from the room whose comforting orange glow had become unbearable. I had said too much and longed for the day to end.

Chapter Five
16th March 1910, Goldhurst Estate, Rutland
Grace

Today Mother shouted and shouted and shouted and shouted for ninety eight seconds which is four seconds longer than the time I picked all the petals off the roses to prove to Mr. Healy that there were two hundred and twenty six thousand, nine hundred and twelve petals on the roses in the rose garden.

When I woke up, Martha brought me some tea and read 'Little Red Riding Hood' to me while I drank it. After that I had a wash, cleaned my teeth and got dressed. Because it is a Saturday and it is the summer, I wore my blue dress with the white lace and white shoes. I went downstairs to eat my breakfast in the big nursery: two slices of brown toast and one egg. On Tuesdays, Wednesdays, Thursdays, Fridays, Saturdays and Sundays I eat my breakfast with Martha in the big nursery but I have to eat it in my bedroom on Mondays because Martha has to clean the big nursery then.

After breakfast I cleaned my teeth again, anticlockwise this time, that's very important. Then we went for a walk. Alice used to come with us on Saturdays but Martha says she is too busy now sewing dresses. She has made lots of dresses for me. I don't like sewing. I don't like the needle. Once, Martha made me help her sew a cross stitch picture of foxes in the woods but I ran out of green thread halfway through and then pricked my finger and it bled for more than five minutes so I shouted and said I was never sewing again. I have never sewn again.

We walked to the village to feed the ducks. I like feeding the ducks. The best place to go is near the stone bridge because the small ducks that can't normally eat the bread because of the big ducks live there and they can have a chance to get the bread first (Martha taught me that trick). Then you have to go to the part of the river near the mill because the swans are there and they get the bread second. Then you can go to the main pond near the church so the rest of the ducks (the big ducks) can get the rest of the bread because they should get some bread even though Martha says they are mean and tough. Sometimes there are ducklings and they quack when you get too close.

Each duck is not allowed more than three bits of bread. One time a big mean duck was stealing all the bread (he had eaten five bits and wanted more!) so I had to go in the water and tell him to stop being greedy. I fell in and the ducks quacked and quacked and quacked and quacked and my watch was in the water so I don't know how long they quacked for but they were very loud and some of the mean ones pecked and tapped me with their beaks (Martha said their ducklings were scared of me). I pretended to be a big, giant duck (but with no feathers) and I quacked twice as loud a pecked them back.

Then Martha pulled me out and took me home. She said I smelled like fish and duck poo. That time Mother screamed and screamed and screamed and screamed for forty second and made Martha throw my clothes away.

After feeding the ducks (they all had just three bits today) we went to the post office to post Martha's letter to her mother. She told me she is old and live miles away. She said she likes ducks like me and Martha do.

We walked back home through the woods. I like to look for hedgehogs but I've only seen one in there when I was six. I like the woods.

When we got home, Mother had guests so she said I had to stay in the big nursery. Martha said we should read a storybook. We looked on the shelf. There was: Alice's Adventures in Wonderland, Cinderella, Beatrix Potter: The Tale of Peter Rabbit, Treasure Island, Hansel and Gretel, Journey to the Centre of the Earth, Beatrix Potter: The Tale of Jeremy Fisher, Sleeping Beauty, Beatrix Potter: The Tale of Squirrel Nutkin, Beatrix Potter: The Tale of Jeremy Fisher, Beatrix Potter: The Story of Miss Moppet, The Elephant's Child, Beatrix Potter: The Tale of Tom Kitten, The Children's Book of Nursery Rhymes, Rapunzel, Rumpelstiltskin, Beatrix Potter: The Tale of Jemima Puddleduck, Beatrix Potter: The Tale of Mrs Tittlemouse, Beatrix Potter: The Tale of Two Bad Mice, Black Beauty, Little Red Riding Hood, The Wonderful Wizard of Oz, Beatrix Potter: The Tale of Mrs Tiggywinkle and Beatrix Potter: The Tale of Benjamin Bunny. I had to line my books up again, as all the Beatrix Potter books should be together.

I chose 'Little Red Riding Hood'. We've read it eight hundred and ninety-two times since I was four. I like the bit when the wolf dies. Martha told me there is always a huntsman in the woods protecting us from wolf attacks. I hope I see him in the woods one day to say thank you. Wolves are my worst animal.

After we ate lunch (I had a jam sandwich with white bread, two biscuits and an apple) in the nursery. Mother came in and said that Martha had to help Charlotte and Alice get dressed and do their hair because their servant is on holiday, so she told me to go out and help Mr. Healy in the garden. Mr. Healy digs and makes roses grow really big.

I walked out of the servants' door and I saw Charlotte's cat, Rosie. I don't like Rosie, she meows and hisses at me. She is the same colour as the wolf in 'Little Red Riding Hood' - grey and horrible (but not as big). I walked past the cat but she followed me and kept following me into the garden. I tried to push her away with my foot but she hissed like a snake and scratched my ankle and made it bleed. I hissed back at her and meowed twice as loud, but she wouldn't go away, like the big mean ducks. I wanted to get rid of Rosie.

I asked Mr. Healy where the huntsman lived so I could go and ask him to get rid of Rosie but he told me there was no huntsman in the woods, he lives in the village (I will have to tell Martha because she still thinks he lives in the woods).

I went into Mr. Healy's shed where he keeps his gardening tools. He has a pile of brown sacks in there for bulbs and soil to go in. I took three of them, and some string. I like Mr. Healy's shed.

Then I went to find Rosie. She was quite hard to find but I found her licking her paws outside the kitchen. I crept up on her the way the huntsman creeps up on the wolf in 'Little Red Riding Hood' and put her in one of the brown sacks. Then I put that sack inside the other brown sack and that one in a bigger brown sack.

Walking to find the huntsman in the village was hard because Rosie was hissing and meowing and scratching, even through the three sacks. She was getting even nastier because she knew that we were going to the huntsman and she was worried that he would get rid of her.

When I got to the stone bridge something Rosie had nearly scratched through the sacks and was going to escape! So I threw her in the river (there were no ducks on this bit of the river today). She was meowing really loudly so I meowed twice as loudly back until she sank underneath the water and disappeared. I thought she might turn into an otter and swim up and down the river (I like otters) but she didn't.

Martha was looking for me when I got back and she made me go upstairs to have a bath and change my dress because it was all muddy and had twigs and burrs stuck to it. I would like to live in the woods, like a huntsman or a hedgehog, then I wouldn't have to change my clothes all the time and I would probably see other hedgehogs or otters or ducks.

Martha asked me to wear my white dress with yellow flowers on it and my yellow shoes, which I usually wear on a Saturday if it is warm. It wasn't very warm today but Martha said I had to wear that or my Sunday dress. I didn't want do that so I had to wear the white dress with the yellow flowers on and the yellow shoes.

I ate my dinner at six o'clock in the big nursery with Martha (white bits of chicken, three potatoes and five carrots) and she read Beatrix Potter: The Tale of Mrs Tiggywinkle to me.

I had forgotten about Rosie until I heard Charlotte screaming and crying in the hallway and Mother shouting and shouting and shouting. She came in and her face was all funny and pink. She was saying that I did a bad thing for throwing Rosie in the river and Charlotte came rushing in screaming and screaming and screaming and screaming really loud (I couldn't time it because they were both screaming at the same time). It was so loud that I had to cover my ears and scream and scream and scream and scream twice as loud to make them stop and Father came in shouting loud as well and hit me very hard on the bottom eight times with his cane which made me scream even more and I tried to get them away by throwing all the books on the shelves at them to make them go away. I don't like it when they shout.

Finally they all went away and left me but they locked me in my room. They said I had to stay in my room all day tomorrow.

Martha said a neighbour saw me throwing Rosie in the river and came round and told Mother and Father. She said Charlotte was so upset she was still crying two hours later.

I don't like cats. Or dogs. Or wolves.

Chapter Six
25th March 1910, Goldhurst Estate, Rutland
Martha

The atmosphere in the house following the cat drowning was worse than I had ever known it. Lady Goldhurst was tired and unusually bad-tempered whilst her husband stormed off to London all week with Mister Edward, claiming to have urgent business. Despite not saying it aloud, I knew that they blamed me for not keeping a closer eye on Grace. However, sweet little Miss Alice argued on my behalf and reminded her ladyship that she had instructed me to help her and Miss Charlotte to dress that morning so I couldn't possibly be in two places at once.

In part, I did blame myself for not foreseeing the incident. I had spent every day with Grace for eight years, yet still I could not predict her behaviour. That morning she had been so calm and well-behaved; there were no signs of mischief or violence in her. Likewise, I knew she had a particular dislike for the cat, but she'd never harmed an animal before. I had to admit, I still didn't know what was running through her mind.

Grace's actions did little to improve the relationship between her and Miss Charlotte. She had begged her parents for a cat for years and it was unlikely that she would be getting another one now.

Once more, there was talk of sending Grace away to all manner of places. Even Mr. Irvine's hospital, St. Giles', was mentioned by Lord Goldhurst, who had clearly forgotten the dreadful morning spent there five months before.

The family had been aloof with me for the first few days, during which time I had an idea that would ease the tension of the household. I approached Lady Goldhurst with my suggestion one morning after breakfast.

"Pardon me, Lady Goldhurst, but could I have a word with you about Grace?"

Her ladyship had been drinking tea with her mother, Lady Malholm, a terrifying woman who glared at me like a wild fox that had wandered into the house. Lady Goldhurst gestured for me to come in and continue.

"I was wondering if, given the..." I searched for an appropriate word, "events that have happened recently, whether it would be possible for me to take Grace with me to visit my family in Derbyshire?"

Lady Malholm narrowed her eyes; but Lady Goldhurst's expression remained stolid.

"I hope you don't think it impertinent my asking. It's just, I think she'll like the peaks and the countryside, plus the fresh air will do her good and it will give you a chance to rest..." I felt myself babbling and my face flushing as the two formidable women stared at me in silence. Lady Goldhurst set down her teacup and spoke in a weary voice.

"I think it's a good idea. You have my permission, as long as you promise not to let her out of your sight. You can take her for a week and Brooks will arrange a car to drive you there tomorrow morning. You had better go and see to Grace's things."

I stood gaping for a moment as I was not expecting such swift consent. I thanked her and turned to go but Lady Malholm spoke in her shrill, scolding way that was all her own, "And do make sure that you observe Lady Goldhurst's instruction this time - do not let the child out of your sight for a moment, do you understand, girl?"

I swallowed with difficulty as my throat was dry and nodded several times too many, "Yes, your ladyship, of course." Lady Malholm clicked her tongue impatiently, signalling that I had outstayed my welcome and, making a hasty curtsey, I left the room to break the news to Grace.

We set off at eight o'clock the next morning, under a cloudy sky, threatening rain. Miss Alice was the only Goldhurst to bid us farewell; Lady Goldhurst and Lady Malholm were still asleep and Miss Charlotte had refused to acknowledge her younger sister since last week.

For most of the journey Grace remained quiet, managing no more than two words per response to my questions, which mostly consisted of 'Are you all right?' or 'It's not much further, would you like a drink of water?' She seemed to enjoy watching the countryside rushing past out of the car's window and I certainly liked the novelty of being in a Rolls Royce. As with every one of these episodes, it would take some time to build up her confidence and get her to talk to me at length again; she had scarcely spoken since she was punished, even refusing the offer of a 'Little Red Riding Hood' reading.

As we neared Bradcote, the familiar landscape made me grin like a child coming home from a long holiday. There was something comforting about the distant peaks and woodland that remained the same regardless of the season. Every time we turned a corner or peeked over the brow of a hill a new scene was revealed, even more delightful than the previous. Green farmland dotted with sheep, hillocks striped with crumbling stone walls and the unmistakable scents of the countryside brought me back to my childhood. I was home.

Grace seemed indifferent to the views but pricked up her ears when I described the various animals to be found in the area. As we neared my old home, Pick Farm, I felt a stab of nostalgia. This had been my home for the first fifteen years of my life and in my heart it would always be my home. Except now it was 'Pilgrim's Farm' and belonged to a wealthy Yorkshireman. Although little about the place had changed, it was unrecognisable to me. I knew my family weren't inside to greet us and I thought of my poor father, who had broken his heart when he was forced to sell up - a lifetime's work taken away in a matter of weeks. It was too painful to think about, so I turned my mind and my eye away from it.

"Now then, Gracie, we're almost there! It's the next village along this road." She barely nodded, her eyes were still locked on the window. "There's so much I want to show you: the peaks, the river, the woods, the caves, the horses..."

"Can we feed the ducks?" The husky voice interrupted.

"Of course! Maybe we can do that this evening."

"Not too late or they'll be in bed."

I nodded, "Where do you think they sleep?"

"In the reeds, of course!" Of course, I thought.

Fifteen minutes later we arrived at Clematis Cottage in Bradcote village. I had only lived there a few months before I left home to take up my post at Goldhurst Estate. Since then my mother had transformed the place. The walls had been washed and painted white and the roof re-thatched. Likewise, each room inside had been lovingly painted, cleaned and decorated with paintings and the odd photograph. New furniture and rugs also brightened up the once shabby house. It would never have a patch on Pick Farm, but it was a comfortable and cheery little place nonetheless.

"Oh, you haven't seen the garden yet." My mother ushered us towards the back door once we had eaten and settled in.

"I've brought the old pond back to life since you were last here, and I've got a chicken coop too so there's fresh eggs every morning."

"Fresh eggs, Gracie, doesn't that sound lovely?" She had pottered ahead and was staring in wonder at the chickens. A row of brown and white plump, feathered bodies shifted on the other side of the wire, clucking contentedly.

My mother took my arm and led me in the opposite direction. "Are you going to tell me the full story now? I'm more than happy to have the poor girl here but I'm astonished that her parents let you bring her with you."

My face grew warm. "You don't think I'm to be trusted, then?".

"Now then, Martha, don't get upset, I wasn't implying that you weren't fit to look after her on your own. I know how capable you are. You think the world of that child, it's just, with her father being a lord and her mother from a noble family, it's a bit odd her being here, from an outsider's point of view."

I sighed, "Yes I know. There is a reason for it, but, I don't think now is the right time to discuss it. She's sharper than most people realise; I don't want her to overhear anything and get upset again."

Grace was crouched, softly clucking along with the hens when a great quacking stole her attention. A portly duck waddled across the garden towards her from the far side of the pond, flapping its white wings in annoyance at having been disturbed.

Grace's normally inexpressive face changed from shocked, to hypnotised, to delighted and in as much time the hens were abandoned.

"Quack, quack, quack, quack!" She echoed the duck's sound and flapped her spread arms, a ghost of a smile on her lips.

"Oh, stop that racket, Jimmy!" My mother shouted, fetching some bread to appease the animal.

"Does this duck live in your garden? For God's sake, Mam, are you trying to set up your own farm in this cottage?" I said teasingly.

"No, duck," she laughed, "I found him by the river about six months ago with a damaged wing. He was much smaller then, practically a duckling, and with no mammy duck, so I brought him home to look after him until his wing healed and, well, he never left!"

"Why did you call him 'Jimmy'?"

"Ah, well, it was Jemima first, after Miss Puddleduck, but then I found out she was actually a he, so Jimmy replaced Jemima. I see Miss Goldhurst approves of him." She nodded towards the pair who were staring at each other with mutual interest.

"She loves ducks so she'll enjoy her stay here."

Sure enough, for the rest of our stay Grace spent almost every day in the garden with the good-natured duck and I had to fairly drag her out of the cottage for walks and days out to explore the peaks.

During the morning on our second day, there was a knock at the door. My mother was busy feeding the chickens so I answered it, expecting it to be my brother Bill.

Standing in the alcove inspecting the hydrangea in the flower bed was a tall man with auburn hair who I didn't recognise. His clothes indicated he was a working man: a grey cotton shirt with sleeves rolled up to the elbow; dark brown trousers held up by braces and slightly muddied boots. He wore a cap, but immediately removed it when he saw the person at the door wasn't my mother.

"Ah, um, sorry to bother you, Miss." He mumbled, looking down at his boots. He had a young face but the rest of him seemed older.

"I'm, err, after Mrs. Pick." He looked at me briefly and I noticed the unusual eyes: green, dabbled with specks of brown.

"She's in the garden." I replied, willing myself not to blush for once.

"Oh, is that Eric?" My mother's voice sawed through the awkwardness.

"Shall I get started round the back, Mrs. Pick?" He called.

"Yes, please. This is my daughter, Martha, by the way. I'm sure you remember her, she was good friends with your sister years ago."

"Nice to see you again, Miss Pick." He inclined his head and sloped away around the back of the cottage.

"Eric Patterson, Emily's brother. Do you remember him? You used to play with them when you were little." My mother said.

My face burned when I recalled the memory. When I was seven years old and Eric had been six, his sister and I had teased the poor boy mercilessly. Once we had tricked him into removing all his clothes and thrown them into the duck pond in the village. Poor Eric cried and was taunted by the other boys for a good number of years afterwards. Emily found it hilarious, until her mother wiped the smile off her face with a slipper and banned me from coming to their house. I was suitably ashamed of my actions and had only really gone along with it under the mischievous Emily's instructions.

"I don't really remember him."

"He's been a godsend with the gardening. He took care of the pond and built the chicken coop, a wonderful help. He just has the flower beds to finish and I'll have the perfect country garden."

My mother bustled around singing Eric's praises then turned to me suddenly. "Go and ask him if he would like a cup of tea, Martha."

"Oh, yes, all right." Reluctantly, I headed through the kitchen and out the back door. Grace was sitting on the step silently staring at Jimmy, the copy of 'The Jungle Book' my mother had given to her lay forgotten in her lap. I patted the top of her head, but she didn't react.

Eric was busy digging near the pond and didn't look up as I approached. He hadn't forgotten what I did; he hated me for it, I thought. "Would you like a cup of tea, Eric?" I focused on his spade, watching it rise and fall, anything to avoid eye contact.

"You don't have to bother on my account." He said without stopping.

"It's no trouble, Mam was making a brew anyway."

"Please, then." He said, before hurriedly adding "Martha", lifting his eyes to look at me quickly; one green flash before turning them towards the earth again. I hurried back into the kitchen before he could notice me blushing.

Much to my horror, Mother invited Eric to tea that evening, along with my brother, Bill, and his wife, Jane. I took Grace to visit some of the local farms to take my mind off the evening ahead. I couldn't help but feel betrayed by my mother. She knew that I longed to see my brother and Jane, and with Eric being there as well I knew I wouldn't be able to relax and be myself. I felt uneasy around Eric. I had behaved so cruelly when we were children and it was mine and Emily's fault that he was picked on at school for so long. He must have hated me for all these years. I flinched when I thought of it.

My thoughts were interrupted by a sudden, loud whinnying. "Listen, there must be horses on this farm."

"I can't see them." Grace's said in a raspy voice.

"Let's ask if we can have a look. I'm sure the farmer won't mind, I think I know him."

The farm was owned by an old friend of my father who was more than happy to let us see the animals. Grace stood for some time staring at the horses, fascinated.

"Martha, who decided what noises the animals make?"

Grace's questions kept me on my toes. "I suppose God decided, when he created each of the animals. It probably has something to do with their size, it would look rather silly if a huge elephant squeaked like a little mouse."

Grace continued to stare at the horses and slowly nodded, apparently satisfied with my answer.

"God is the man in the sky." She said.

"Yes, well he isn't just in the sky, he's everywhere, all around. Do you remember we talked about him?"

"I've never seen him, though. I think you got that bit wrong, I think he's just in the sky, above the clouds."

I smiled, "You don't have to see God to know he's there. Sometimes you can feel that he's there."

Grace turned to me with a startled look in her eyes. "How can you feel him if you can't see him? Is he a ghost? I don't like ghosts, they're scary."

"No, he's not scary, I meant you can sense that he is looking after you and that he loves you, like a father."

"I already have a father. I don't want a ghost father that I can't see."

I had tried numerous times to explain the idea of God and religion to Grace, but each time she seemed more confused.

"God created the world, human beings and all the creatures you see around you, so he is everyone's father, not just yours and that's why we respect him and give thanks to him in church every week."

Grace considered this. "I don't like church."

I sighed, "I know you don't. Now come on, we'd better get back home for tea. Say goodbye to the horses." I made sure we walked the long way back, avoiding the church.

Eric accepted my mother's invitation to tea and to make matters worse she insisted I sit next to him so I couldn't avoid talking to him. Grace had already eaten and was happily playing in the garden with the duck, so I didn't even have her as a distraction. It was obvious by now that my mother had planned it all. She had sent me several letters after Bill married nearly a year ago, hinting at her desire to see me married and settled as well. However, I had tactically ignored these parts of her narratives. If she had hopes of romance between me and Eric she had no hope. I felt awkward around him, partly due to my shame at having treated him badly and not apologising all those years ago; partly because I was not used to male company. Almost every day for the past eight years had been spent with Grace; I didn't even talk to the male servants much and I had certainly never had any followers before. I cringed at the thought.

My sister-in-law was four months pregnant and Bill spent much of the dinner discussing how he was going to decorate the spare bedroom and Jane was currently half way through knitting her second blanket. After a while they questioned me on the goings on at Goldhurst Estate before we all lapsed into a lazy silence, interrupted with the odd comment about the weather.

Soon after, my mother, Bill and Jane began discussing events in the village amongst themselves, excluding Eric and I, no doubt to my mother's delight. She gave me a sly wink and I looked away, praying that Eric had not noticed.

I decided to be polite, more for his sake than for my mother's. "I wanted to thank you, Eric, for helping my mother with her garden. It looks beautiful and the chickens are a wonderful idea. I'm sure she feels more at home here now."

"You don't need to thank me. Mrs. Pick made all the decisions; I just put it together, really. It's been no trouble."

Again, awkward silence filled the space between us as I scrabbled around in my head for something suitable to talk about. I stared resentfully at my mother who was now excusing herself to fetch the pudding.

"How is Emily? I heard she's married to a soldier and has a family of her own. Do you see much of her?"

"She lives up near the border so we don't see them very often. I've only seen the youngest once, at his christening. She writes every so often, though."

"Oh, I see. Does she like living up north?"

"As far as I know, yes."

Thankfully my mother returned with a dish of apple pie which provided a distraction from talking.

"Eric, duck," my mother said after everyone had finished, "are you still going into Derby tomorrow afternoon?"

"Aye, Mrs. Pick, about one o'clock."

"Oh good. You wouldn't mind if Martha came with you, would you? She needs a few things and I don't think she'll have another chance to go before she leaves."

I turned to my mother, wide-eyed and furious at her interference. "I thought you and I were going into Derby on Thursday, with Grace." I felt my face grow red.

"I thought I told you, Martha, I can't make Thursday now as I told Mrs. Kimbell I'd look after her boys that afternoon. It'll be too much of a rush. I'll watch Grace as well so you can get your shopping done in peace. Eric can show you around. I'm sure he won't mind, will you, duckie?"

Poor Eric blushed and I narrowed my eyes at her. "No, I have to take Grace with me. I can't leave her with you for a whole afternoon, she wouldn't like that."

"Oh, nonsense. She'll be fine and she might even make some new friends."

"No, Mam, I insist. I know you're trying to be helpful, but I'd rather she was with me."

"Well, we can discuss that later, but either way, Eric, will you take Martha with you?"

Eric looked at me and mother like a frightened rabbit, backed into a corner.

"Yes, Mrs. Pick. Of course."

Furious with my mother's pushy interference I took Grace to bed as soon as our guests left and then went to sleep myself in order to avoid speaking to her. In one of her letters, which she had sent around the time of my twenty-sixth birthday, she had mentioned that she had been twenty-six when she met and married my father and expressed her hope for similar good luck for me. Perhaps she had been planning this since then, especially as Bill, who was four years younger, was now happily married.

The next morning I broached the subject with her, determined to put an end to her embarrassing meddling. "Mother, why do you keep trying to force Eric Patterson and me together? I know he's as embarrassed about it as I am and it's not fair. I didn't come here to be humiliated, nor does he deserve it after the kindness he's shown you."

She looked at me in mock surprise. "I don't know what you mean! I haven't been forcing you, duck. I just thought it would be a nice change for you to spend some time in the company of someone your own age, and it will be for Eric, too. You know he's the last one at home with his parents and I think he gets a bit bored. It will do you both the world of good. I don't know why you're getting so mardy about it."

"Is it just that? Are you sure there're no other schemes running through your mind, perhaps involving me in a white dress standing at the altar?"

She laughed, "No, of course not! What makes you think that?" I raised my eyebrows and she sighed, sitting down at the table, beckoning me to do the same.

"You can't blame me for trying, or for caring. I just want you to be happy, like I was with your father. We've got a lot in common, you know, Martha."

"I know you mean well, but I'm not like you, Mam. I'm happy with my work and I'm in no rush to abandon it all to get married."

She patted me on the hand. "I know you may feel like that now but what about in a few years' time, when you're thirty? It may be too late to find someone and I'm afraid you're going to be alone, with no children and no love in your life. I'll worry about you. Listen, I felt the same as you once, but looking back I'm so relieved I took a chance and left my job to marry your father when I did. If I'd refused him I doubt I would ever have married, nor had a family."

"Listen, I'm perfectly happy. Besides, if I did want to get married, believe me, this is not the way I'd go about it - forcing two strangers together and expecting them to fall in love - it's ridiculous! And it's very out of character for you, because you're not a ridiculous person."

She smiled, but there were tears in her eyes. "I am sorry, my love. I've been silly! I just worry about you at that house."

"Whatever for? Have I given you reason to worry?" I asked in puzzlement.

"Please don't take this the wrong way, my duck," she pleaded.

"Well until I hear it I don't know how I'm going to respond."

She ignored me and carried on. "From what I've seen, Grace is a lovely child. Her behaviour may be...strange, and it's clear she will never live a normal life. But, I can't help worrying about the stories you've told me. Her parents obviously want her to get professional help, so sooner or later you're going to be out of a job and then what? You'll find it hard to get another that pays as well in the area and the chance of marriage may have passed you by."

I stood up and turned away from her, looking out the window at the March drizzle being scattered in all directions by the wind.

"I don't want to upset you, Martha. But remember, I know what it's like to work for a rich family. They may treat you like one of them and flatter you now, but believe me, they won't think twice about getting rid of you as soon as you're no longer needed. I've seen it happen to many good servants in my time. And Grace, I'm afraid, has grown so attached to you, of course, given your kind nature and commitment to her."

"You speak as if it's a bad thing." I spat.

"It will be for her when the day comes when you'll be taken away from her. The more attached you both become, the harder it will be. I don't want to sound harsh but...she's not your child and she never will be."

I was taken aback. I opened my mouth to speak but tears pricked in the corners of my eyes and I turned away to hide them.

"Sorry, my duck, but I had to say it. She may seem like your child but you must always remember she is the daughter of your employer."

"Mother," I said very quietly. "I can't believe you think I'm daft enough to regard Grace as my daughter! I take back what I said, you have turned into a ridiculous old woman since my father died."

"Martha!" She stood up, her face a picture of shock, as if I had slapped her on the cheek.

"I have to get Grace up." I interrupted. "Oh, and Lady Goldhurst is pregnant again, so who knows? I may have two children to look after. They won't want to get rid of me then." I swept past her without waiting for a response. My last remark was petulant and defensive and it left a sour taste. This visit was supposed to be a chance to get away from Goldhurst Estate and its problems; for me, it was creating even more. Deep down I knew my mother meant well. However, at the time I was so furious with her I avoided her all morning.

At lunchtime Grace and I returned from a long walk which had taken us into the heart of the surrounding countryside. Grace had been content until the last half mile and had plonked herself in the middle of a muddy road in protest as her feet hurt. What should have been a two hour walk took well over three hours and Grace was smothered from head to toe in wet mud that was now caking dry, making her look like a clay statue. The sight and sound of her quacking had drawn more than a few puzzled stares as I hurried her back to the cottage. Despite all I had said earlier, I couldn't help but pray that Eric was not around to see my wild hair and dirty old walking clothes. And Lord knows what he would make of Grace.

My mother had lunch waiting for us when we finally arrived and, to her credit, was extremely patient with Grace as she whined and howled at my insistence of her taking a bath during the daytime. An hour later all my previous anger and resentment towards her had disappeared and I felt rather guilty for offending her.

"I'll pop round and tell Eric that you won't be going with him to Derby." She said softly, taking her overcoat from its peg.

"No, Mam, you don't have to do that. I'll go with him to Derby. That is, if you don't mind keeping an eye on Grace. I hardly think she'll react well to another spot of walking anyway."

"Oh!" her eyes brightened as she replaced the overcoat.

"Don't get any more ridiculous ideas into your head, I'll go with him today but after that I don't want any more interfering. I'm not going to ask him to be my sweetheart."

She smiled, "All right, duckie, if that's what you want that is fine with me. You'd better nip upstairs and get ready before he arrives."

To my surprise, Eric proved to be a fairly agreeable travelling companion and talked a great deal more than he had done at tea; he seemed to open up considerably when we left the village. He told me that he had received a letter from Emily that morning informing him that he was going to be an uncle again. I asked him to pass on my congratulations. I told him a little about my life at Goldhurst Estate, but no more than I had to.

Upon arrival in Derby, Eric showed me around the town, including his brother's butcher's shop where I was generously treated to half price sausages and pork chops. Just as the conversation was drying up he left me alone to carry on with my shopping. Perhaps in some ways my mother had been right; I was enjoying the attention of someone my own age, for I scarcely received any at Goldhurst. The way that Eric had changed overnight did seem rather strange to me, but I assumed he must be shy and now he knew me better, and people like my mother were not interfering, he felt able to relax.

When Eric dropped me back at the cottage at five o'clock I expected it to be the last time I saw him. But, incredibly, he asked me if I would like to take a walk in the peaks the next day. His reason being that he wanted to show me 'the most beautiful area in the county', as he called it.

"It's rarely visited as folks tend to stick to the usual trails marked out for them. You can't leave here without seeing it."

I wasn't keen to spend another afternoon with Eric. Not because I hadn't enjoyed his company, but my mother would surely get the wrong impression and I was not prepared to leave Grace alone with her again.

"It sounds lovely, Eric. However, I will have to say no as I need to look after Grace."

"That's not a problem; we can bring her along too. She's a good little walker, so I've heard. She'll enjoy it."

I smiled weakly, unable to think of another excuse. "Well then, if you don't mind we would be happy to come with you."

Eric beamed, "Wonderful! I'll pick you up at one o'clock again tomorrow." He tipped his hat and walked back down the garden path.

As I suspected, my mother was overjoyed to hear I was seeing Eric again and even tried to persuade me to leave Grace with her. There was no way I was going to agree, even though she had been remarkably well-behaved. I wasn't prepared to take a chance.

At one o'clock sharp Eric arrived with his horse and buggy and we set off into the spring sunshine. Grace had been stubborn as she wanted to bring Jimmy the duck with her and was now treating me to silent disdain for refusing her. However, Eric's enthusiasm more than made up for it; he chattered about the landscape and the wildlife to the point that I wanted to tell him to just be quiet and let us enjoy the views in peace. We were in the heart of the Peak District now, and as Eric had promised, the area was wonderfully secluded. Craggy green hills rose on every side, creating a private haven of peace and fresh beauty. The road we followed was barely a road at all, more a wide, stony path that caused the buggy to bump and rattle as we progressed at a slower rate.

We continued into another valley and stopped to take in the view. The sun was hidden by clumps of grey and white cloud with two rays piercing through to light up a small area of grass. Sheep moved about leisurely - little white dots on the horizon - emitting high-pitched bleats.

"I want to get out." Grace said suddenly.

"I don't think we can stop just yet, duck." I said to her, looking nervously at Eric.

"There's an inn about two miles from here, I'll head in that direction so we can leave the horse and have a bit of a walk, if you can hold on." He said.

"I want to get out now." Grace repeated and scrambled down without waiting for an answer.

"Grace, wait, it's not safe, the horse may move suddenly." I warned, but she had already jumped down from her seat and began heading away from the road. "I'm so sorry, Eric. When she gets an idea in her head, there's no stopping her."

"It's all right, don't apologise. I'll stay with the horse if you want to have a quick walk."

Embarrassed, I followed Grace who was now ambling along the side of the path. I called to Eric to follow along behind.

She stopped in a field a few feet from the road and stared at the sheep, repeated their 'baa-baas' until the sound became hoarse.

Eventually, I persuaded her to sit back in the buggy as we drove the last mile to the inn. She bleated the entire way, making any conversation impossible.

Eric kindly ordered us drinks as we sat at a wooden picnic table outside. When he came out, Grace refused to sit with us and took up a seat at an empty table where she read 'Little Red Riding Hood' by herself. I was so relieved that the bleating had stopped that I left her to it.

"What do you think then?" Eric said after a short silence.

"I think you were right, it's breath taking. Thank you for inviting us." I replied before lapsing into a more comfortable silence than before. I decided now was a good opportunity to make amends for my past behaviour.

"Eric, I've been meaning to apologise to you properly for the way I treated you when we were younger."

He looked at me, puzzled. I stared into my glass and felt my face grow hot.

"You know, the times when Emily and I teased you about being small and we threw all your clothes in the village pond. It was an awful thing to do and I've regretted it ever since. I'm sorry." I was afraid to look up so I glanced over at Grace then gulped down my shandy.

To my amazement Eric laughed. It was the first time I had heard it: a loud, low, hearty chuckle that seemed to belong to an older man. It was so comical I allowed myself a little giggle as well.

"That was you? I don't believe it!" He exclaimed after recovering himself. "I thought it was another of her friends...and I threw her schoolbag in the river one summer when I was about ten to get my own back! No wonder she was so upset! I got an awful clout from my parents *and* a caning from the headmaster! And it was you all along!"

"Oh, I feel even worse now, if some other poor girl got the blame!" I cried. "Didn't you realise after I stopped coming round to play with Emily?"

"Not at all. I assumed your mam and dad said you couldn't play with her anymore because she was always up to mischief. That's what most of the mams in the village did. Emily was a bad penny as a child. In fact, she's probably still a bad penny!"

"Oh no, what must you think of me!"

Eric waved his hand. "It was years ago, we were children. At least you felt some shame for what you did, which is more than I can say for my sister! You know, I was actually upset when you stopped coming round. I liked you best out of all her friends."

I blushed and smiled, turning around to check on Grace so Eric couldn't see it. But Grace wasn't there. Her untouched lemonade and the book were abandoned on the table, the pages fluttering in the breeze.

"Oh my God! Grace! Grace!" I shouted, ducking to look under every table. "She's not here! Oh God help me! Grace, where are you!" I ran around to the front of the pub to check in the buggy, but she was nowhere to be found.

Eric ran to meet me but I ignored him and ran down the road shouting her name.

"Martha! Wait, come back."

"I have to find her!" I shouted.

"I'll help you, but someone needs to stay at the inn in case she comes back. I know the area better, let me go and look."

"She doesn't know you. She won't come back with you if you find her." I said.

"Martha, she's not down here, you can see for miles, we'd be able to spot her. It's more likely that she's someone near the inn."

"How would you know?" I snapped, causing him to halt for a moment. I stopped as well. "I'm sorry. It's my fault. I should've been watching her. I wasn't doing my job properly; I know better than to take my eyes off her." Hysterical with worry, I began to cry.

"Please, don't get upset. We'll find her, come on, we haven't even asked at the inn yet."

"She's my responsibility; I should never have come out here." I continued blaming myself between sobs as we entered the front door of the inn.

"Have you seen a young lass wearing a grey coat?" Eric asked the barman.

The man continued to rub the inside of a pint glass with a white tea towel, "She's over there playing with the stuffed birds." he nodded to a table near the window where Grace was lining up a collection of stuffed owls, ducks and guinea fowl on the windowsill.

"Thank heavens! Grace, you're all right." I ran over and embraced her; she shook me off, annoyed at being disturbed from her task. "I was worried sick; I thought I'd lost you. Why did you walk off without telling me? Remember you promised me that you wouldn't do that again?"

"You were talking to that man." She said crossly. "I wanted you to read to me."

"You wouldn't sit with us Grace; I thought you were happy on your own."

"I didn't want to sit with that man. I wanted you to sit with me."

"Well I can't always sit with you..." My heart was still pounding and I sat down to gather myself, breathing hard. I looked at the rumpled little face, her eyes dark and moody, hair escaping from her bonnet. Tears spiked the corners of my eyes again. It was my fault. I'd promised Lady Goldhurst that I wouldn't let her out of my sight, not even for a minute. I'd been selfish and I felt utterly ashamed. "I'll sit with you on the way home and I'll read to you then. How's that?" She shrugged and carried on rearranging the stuffed birds. "'Little Red Riding Hood'?"

She glanced at me sideways, "Yes, 'Little Red Riding Hood'."

After I read the story to her twice on the way home we continued the rest of the journey in silence. When we got back to the cottage, Grace ran up the garden path and round the back of the cottage without thanking Eric. As for me, I just wanted to put the experience behind me as quickly as possible.

"Thank you for taking us; it was very kind." I said to Eric.

"It was my pleasure," he replied. "I hope you've recovered from your shock."

"I have, thank you. I suppose I'm a little over-protective of her because of how she is."

He smiled and took a step closer. "You're a caring person, Martha. I know I couldn't do your job."

"Most people don't believe me, but I really enjoy it most of the time." I probably sounded a little annoyed as Eric looked at his boots sheepishly, as if he had been told off before taking a step back.

"Good evening, Martha." He tipped his hat and walked away, then called back. "Can you tell your mother I'll be round at ten o'clock tomorrow morning to finish the flower beds?" I nodded and watched him drive away down the street.

"Martha, you're being ridiculous. Come down and have lunch." As soon as Eric had arrived I took Grace out to feed the ducks and retreated upstairs to avoid speaking to him. I felt a little foolish, but I hadn't been able to sleep the previous night for fretting. I didn't like the way he made me feel yesterday. He had distracted me from my job and I resented him for it, even though I welcomed it at the time. I had enjoyed his company over the last couple of days; he was considerate and pleasant to talk to, as well as handsome. But I didn't want a follower, I didn't want a husband and what was the point in having a friend I knew I would never see? The point of this visit was to spend some time with my family and with Grace. My mother's meddling had prevented that from happening and it was hard to tell whether I was more annoyed with her or with myself for falling for it. It didn't help that Eric always seemed to be at the cottage. At that moment I felt trapped.

"I think Grace wants to eat her lunch upstairs today."

"No I don't." Grace said unhelpfully.

"Come down then, it's ready."

Reluctantly, I went downstairs and sat in the place set for me next to Eric. We exchanged pleasantries then ate in almost complete silence, my mother trying desperately to keep some kind of talk going.

Eventually she announced that she had to go into the village to run some errands and asked me to wash the dishes for her.

I obeyed, relieved to have a distraction, and began to tidy up. Grace had lolloped out into the garden and was counting the petals on my mother's daffodils. I assumed Eric would follow her to carry on with his work; instead he lingered in the kitchen.

"Can I get you anything?" I asked at last.

"No, sorry, I just hope you're not upset with me after what happened yesterday."

"It wasn't your fault, not at all. I shouldn't have snapped at you then, I'm sorry." I smiled reassuringly and he beamed back, pleased with this response.

"I was talking to your mother earlier," he said.

I groaned inwardly. "What about?"

"About you, really."

"What was she saying?" I said, suddenly annoyed with them both.

"I told her how fond I am of you, Martha. I never knew you that well when you lived here, but I always thought you were a nice lass, different from the usual lasses round here. I'm sure you didn't realise, or even notice me, but I'm so glad I've got to know you better now."

I stood still, unsure what to say to him. His face was flushed and he gripped his hat to steady his hands. He looked at me, finally, his eyes green and speckled, like a frog's skin. Such an unusual colour.

"I know how much your job means to you and I wouldn't have said anything if your mother hadn't assured me that you were thinking of coming back here eventually, and that your situation may be changing at Goldhurst Estate in the near future."

My mouth hung open in surprise at his comment, but he hurried on, unaware, "Anyway, what I suppose I'm asking you, Martha, is, do you think you could ever...are you...do you have any feelings for me? And could you ever come back to Derbyshire to live with me? I mean marry me? Could we have a future together? We don't have to live around here if you don't want to. We could move closer to Derby, near my brother, or anywhere, really. What do you think?"

After his rambling he looked at me with such hope and adoration in his green speckled eyes that all feelings of irritation and horror melted and were replaced with the most devastating pity for him. He had convinced himself that he was in love with me, that I was the one for him, the same way I had convinced myself that he wasn't the one for me. I didn't want to say anything,

I just wanted to disappear into the Derbyshire hills and live forever amongst the peaks.

"Oh, Eric, I don't know how to say this..." he looked at me, breath held, "Thank you so much for your kind words, but I don't deserve them at all. I don't deserve your affection."

"Of course you deserve it!" He exclaimed, suddenly taking my hand, "you deserve happiness, just like anyone else, more, in fact."

"Believe me if my situation were different, if I had not left Bradcote, perhaps, I would seriously consider what you're suggesting. But I left Derbyshire a long time ago and whatever my mother has told you is, I'm afraid, not true in the slightest."

His face slowly began to droop and even though he remained still, he seemed to move further and further away from me.

"I have no intention of leaving my job. In fact, I'm needed at Goldhurst now more than ever and my priority will always be Grace. I'm sure you've seen yourself how much I care for her and how much she relies on me. I would never forgive myself if I ever deserted her. I'm very sorry if I have hurt you, but I have to be honest with you and with myself. I'd never be happy; I'd always be worrying about her."

Eric listened quietly and stood perfectly still. Then he dropped my hand and nodded his head slowly, the colour draining from his face. "I understand. Your mother said, well, no it doesn't matter now, I clearly got it all wrong. Forgive me, I've been a fool."

"Of course you haven't, Eric, it's not your fault. I'm so very flattered, no man has ever admired me before and it can't have been easy to wear your heart on your sleeve like that."

"Yes, well, I just feel like a clown at the moment." He cleared his throat and placed his hat on his head, pulling it down over his eyes. "Please tell your mother I'll finish her garden next week, after you've left."

"I really am sorry, Eric, I didn't mean to lead you on, I wouldn't hurt you feelings like that."

He smiled grimly and grabbed his coat from the peg on the back of the kitchen door. "Have a safe journey back and best of luck to you in the future, Martha." He turned with the brisk formality of a soldier and walked out.

"Good bye, Eric." I called after him, but he was already out of the door.

"Come on, Grace, we can't possibly take Jimmy back with us, what would your mother say?" It was the morning of our departure and the Goldhurst's car had been waiting for us for over half an hour. Grace refused to leave unless she could take her beloved Jimmy the duck with her and I knew too well that she could be as stubborn as a bull.

"Jimmy lives here, you can't take him away from all his friends and from me; he wouldn't like that one bit." My mother said.

"Yes, Grace, I know you would hate it if you were taken away from your home to a new, strange place all on your own."

We had tried every line of argument but Grace was beyond reason. I had threatened to leave without her; I had warned her that Mr. Griffin, the chauffeur, wouldn't allow an animal in his nice car; I had tried to convince her that I had spoken to her parents who were very disappointed with her behaviour. None had the desired effect.

My mother took me to one side, "Maybe you should just let her take the duck." This was the first time we had spoken more than two words at a time to one another since the Eric argument two days before. I was absolutely livid with the way she had lied to the poor man and interfered when I had warned her not to.

"How can I let her bring a duck back with us? Lady Goldhurst will be furious with me and I'm sure his lordship would love the leather seats covered in duck mess."

"Well what do you suggest?"

I sighed and looked over at Grace's hunched back and clenched fists. "I've got no choice, I'll have to try and carry her into the car. I'll go and get my chloroform, just in case. Would you get me a clean cotton cloth?" My mother looked alarmed at this suggestion but obeyed. I retrieved the small decanter of clear liquid and some white gloves from my trunk. I hated using the stuff on her and had hoped to avoid using it this week, but the alternative was allowing her to hurt herself or others and I didn't want her lashing out around my mother, despite my annoyance towards her.

"Grace, if you don't come to the car in the next ten seconds I will have to carry you. It's not fair to keep Mr. Griffin waiting and your parents are expecting us."

Her stormy face remained fixed on the pond, and she jerked back and forth as if I wasn't there. My mother place a handkerchief gently next to the chloroform and stood behind me, kneading her hands together.

"One, two, three, four..." I counted slowly.

"Five, six, seven..."

Before I could reach eight Grace shot up, howling, and ran around the garden pulling my mother's flowers up in great handfuls, throwing them on to the lawn, creating a carpet of mangled green corpses.

Behind me my mother shrieked, "Oh Christ, my garden! My flowers! Oh God, Martha! Stop her!"

I grabbed the chloroform bottle and tipped a small amount onto the handkerchief, keeping it at arm's length.

Grace had pulled up almost every flower in a matter of seconds and was stuffing some of the stalks into her mouth in animal rage, growling like a dog, then quacking like a duck. I ran over to her but she howled louder and jumped into the pond. The hens were clucking in a cacophony behind me and

Jimmy was quacking angrily at Grace so that the entire garden sounded like an awful, fractious farm yard chorus.

Grace was momentarily blinded by some water in her eyes; I didn't waste any time and jumped in after her, covering her nose and mouth with the handkerchief whilst trying to gather and hold her arms behind her back. She lashed and howled terribly behind the cotton muzzle; her nails clawed at my hands and wrists; luckily I had trimmed them just three days before, so the damage was minimal.

After a few seconds her howling subsided and her body grew slack. Once I was sure she was unconscious I gently lifted her out onto the grass and climbed out myself. My mother was staring at me, wide-eyed, her jaw slack.

"I'll need to change her clothes quickly." I said, removing the gloves. "I'll change mine first so I'm not trailing pond water around the house." I saw the panic in my mother's face, then, looking at the lifeless body added, "Don't worry, she'll be asleep for a while."

Twenty minutes later I sat in the back of Lord Goldhurst's Rolls Royce with Grace, dry and clean, in my arms. My mother leaned across and kissed me one last time. I still loved her dearly, of course, but our relationship would not be the same after this visit.

"Will the little one be all right?"

"She'll live. Unfortunately this isn't the first time it's happened. I'm so sorry about your garden..."

She waved her hand, "Don't fret about that. It's such a shame for Eric, he planted most of them, but I think he was going to dig them up anyway, and I'll pay him handsomely for it!" She laughed unconvincingly.

"Hopefully now you see why I'm needed so much at Goldhurst." I said.

"It's certainly been an eye-opener." She paused, as if deciding whether to continue.

"The family need me to help them look after her and despite what you think I am happy to do it; it's not a prison sentence."

"I know you do, Lord knows you'd have to! I just worry about you, about your future. I am your mother after all."

"Are we ready?" Mr Griffin called from the other side of the car.

"Yes, thank you. Good bye, Mam, thank you so much for your help with Grace, and again, sorry about the garden."

"Take care of yourself dear. I'll write to you soon."

"Don't forget to apologise to Eric about the flowers." I added, thinking it was little consolation.

The engine started and we pulled away. My mother stood at the edge of the path waving until she disappeared from view.

I watched the village fly past and ebb away, it looked different compared to when we first arrived. I had waited for so long to come back and spend time in my childhood home, with my family, now I was desperate to leave. The houses, the streets, the pond, the people, all seemed overbearing. Of course, they had not changed much - I had. My mother had let me down this week with her interfering and I knew I had let her down too. I felt as if I had betrayed her by swearing allegiance to the opposing side in order to follow my own beliefs.

I looked down at Grace's peaceful face and stroked a tendril of hair back behind her ear. What would I say to her when we got home? For now I would just have to enjoy the calm before the storm.

As we reached the brow of the hill outside the village, I remembered that I had always turned around to have one last look back at the place at the bottom, before leaving it behind. This time I couldn't bring myself to do it. Twisting around would upset Grace's position and besides, I had had more than my fill of Bradcote for the time being.

Chapter Seven
2nd August 1914 Goldhurst Estate, Rutland
Martha

"Grace! Hurry up, will you? I want to get this dress finished before tomorrow." Miss Alice called to her sister. It was a hot summer's day - not the sort of atmosphere that had you begging to stand statue-still in a stuffy drawing room. Grace slouched on the edge of the window sill, pouting, her arms wrapped around her chest as if in a straight jacket. Together we managed to bribe her with the promise of a new toy if she would stand still for five minutes.

At twenty years old Miss Alice had become a fine young woman: pretty, intelligent and talented. Over the past two years she had established her own small dressmaking business, taking requests from many wealthy families in the area, and a few in London as news of her talent travelled.

I felt proud of Miss Alice; although I had always thought highly of her, being the third daughter and fourth child she had often been overlooked in her youth. Miss Charlotte was always the centre of attention and considered to be the prettiest child; Miss Louisa, being eldest and first to marry and have children was often talked of with high regard; however, Mr. Edward, as the son and heir, had always been the favourite within the family. As a child, Miss Alice had never enjoyed attention and, being a sensible child, she was often trusted to amuse herself, which led her to perfect her dressmaking skills. Thus, although Miss Louisa had married a successful American financier and Miss Charlotte had many admirers, in my eyes, Miss Alice was the one who had the most promising future. She had achieved what the other two had not: the possibility of independence.

"How was your time in London, Miss? Did you find a nice shop?"

"No, unfortunately I had a change of plan." Grace grumbled as she spread her arms scarecrow-wide. At thirteen she was a lanky child - almost as tall as me and whippet-thin.

"Mother and Father insisted that I keep things the way they are – small favours for acquaintances and family." She rolled her eyes and sighed. I smiled in sympathy. Unlike me, Lord and Lady Goldhurst did not approve of her ambitions, even discouraging them. With the support of her rich and influential parents, there was no doubt that Miss Alice could establish a very successful business in London or maybe even Paris and New York, as she dreamed, but they refused to assist her with money or contacts. Lord and Lady Goldhurst seemed to think that her dressmaking was a passing fancy of which she would grow tired after a few months. However, their unhelpful attitude only served to encourage Miss Alice to make a success of her venture, whilst creating a rift between them. It was a shame in more ways than one as it meant that she was spending less and less time at Goldhurst and more time in London with her older sister and her family, who had returned from America three years before.

"Of course I've got the machine and the work space in Louisa's house, but it's not the same as keeping my very own shop. I did think about asking Miles for help to start up, but they've already been so generous and with the move back to New York, they have enough to think about."

"I bet you'll miss them."

"Terribly, I thought they'd be back for good, but alas, Miles' work, you know?" I nodded, although in truth I didn't understand exactly what Mr. Avery did for work. "Part of me wishes I could go with them, but I don't think I'd care much for America. Come on, Grace, darling, stand up straight, only a couple more minutes." Grace gnashed her teeth and groaned as Miss Alice smoothed and pinned the seams of her yellow taffeta dress with expert hands, before whipping it over her head.

"Now, hold your arm out for me, dear, so I can measure it again. Gosh, you've grown so much!" Grace huffed but held her arm out mechanically.

"What a beautiful dress you've got, Grace. You will look as pretty as a peony at the christening tomorrow."

"Isn't the saying 'as pretty as a picture'?" Miss Alice laughed.

"Not all pictures are pretty." Grace mumbled matter-of-factly, "some of those pictures we saw in London were ugly. I didn't like them."

"No, you weren't an admirer of the expressionist art, were you? It's not to everyone's taste, but you will be a very pretty picture, not ugly or drab at all!" Miss Alice exclaimed, patting her gently on the shoulder.

"Peony." She muttered. "Can I go now?"

"Yes, all done!"

"Good." She sloped back to the window ledge, looping a discarded length of cream ribbon around her index fingers.

"You've done such a tremendous job on these clothes, as always, Miss Alice. I'm full of admiration."

"Thank you, Martha. You are kind. Would you like to see the christening gown? I finished it this morning."

"We'd love to, if you have time, wouldn't we, Grace?"

"No. Boring." She fiddled with the ribbon, without looking up.

"Don't be rude," I warned.

"Don't worry Martha, we'll go and see it and leave Lady Grace here on her own!" She said loudly, winking at me.

"All right, I will come." Grace shuffled towards us, expressionless.

"Come on, just a quick glimpse as I have to get on with your dress."

She led us down the hallway to the library. The house was fairly quiet since Lord and Lady Goldhurst were visiting Mister Edward and his wife, Sarah, to make some preparations for the christening banquet on the Sunday. Sarah had given birth to Baby Sophie prematurely seven months previous, and she and the baby had been very ill for months afterwards, meaning that a christening was not possible until recently. Thinking of it brought back memories of the night Grace was born. I still shuddered at the memory of Lady Goldhurst howling in agony and the image of Doctor Scott, pale and sweating, holding the tiny dead body of Gregory. After all these years the memory remained as clear as it had the morning after. I pushed it from my thoughts.

"You two are the first to see the gown since it's been finished, not even Edward or Sarah have seen it, so don't tell them!" I grinned and promised on both our behalves; Grace swung her arms at her side, looking uninterested.

Miss Alice whisked a tiny white dress out of a cupboard, "Ta-dah! What do you think?"

The dress was beautiful: white cotton, layered with lace and pale yellow ribbons; the sleeves were shorter than the usual length and made from a sheer fabric with white butterflies embroidered on. "Oh, Miss Alice, it's absolutely gorgeous! What a lucky little girl! It's certainly very different to my lumpy old christening gown. What do you think, Grace?"

She wrinkled her nose and whined that she was hungry. I sighed, "Go and wash up ready for lunch, then. Wait for me in the big nursery." She bolted out of the library and clopped up the stairs.

"I'm sure it'll be a lovely day." I said.

Miss Alice hid the dress away once more and smiled, "I'm looking forward to it. Did I tell you about my special role? Edward and Sarah have asked me to be Sophie's godmother."

I gasped and congratulated her. I was pleased that they had chosen her and not Miss Charlotte. She would make a much better godmother.

"Do you think Grace will be all right during the ceremony?" she said. "It will be a shame if she misses it."

"We'll have to try it. I'll sit at the back of the church with her and take her out if it becomes too difficult."

She nodded and glanced down at a copy of The Times on one of the side tables, her expression became troubled. "I do worry about all this business in Europe, the mood in London is awfully restive; it's all anyone can talk about anywhere. The waiting, not knowing..."

"Not knowing what?" Miss Charlotte bustled into the library, causing me to start.

"We were discussing the situation in Europe. When did you get back?" Miss Alice said, picking up the newspaper.

Miss Charlotte groaned and threw her hands up dismissively, "Oh, bosh! I've heard enough dull war talk to last me a lifetime! Every conversation is the same in London, I wish they'd hurry up and declare it and put every wretched Tom, Dick or Cousin Lyle out of his misery."

"Charlotte! What an outrageous thing to say! And what's Cousin Lyle got to do with it?"

"Eurgh, he's the worst for it. He's become even more of a dreadful bore for it." She plucked two grapes from the fruit bowl and giggled to herself, "He's a war bore!"

"You disgust me sometimes." Miss Alice shook her head.

"Oh come on, everyone we know is thinking exactly the same, even you - admit it!" She giggled again. I looked down at my feet.

"I can speak for myself, thank you very much, and I certainly don't share your opinion. I'd much rather we were not at war; I'd much rather they were announcing peace talks and that scores of innocent men were not going to be sent to die in Europe..."

Miss Charlotte rolled her eyes and held up her hands in mock surrender, "Please, it's too early for one of your impassioned speeches. I only came down to ask you to take in my dress for the christening - I've lost a little weight, what luck!"

At that moment I feared that Miss Alice would hit her sister over the head with the newspaper clenched in her hand and that I would have to break it up somehow. I muttered my excuses and sidled out of the library without them noticing, leaving them to their bickering.

The day of the christening soon arrived and the house was bustling with activity from the first rays of dawn. Mister Edward had chosen to hold the party at Goldhurst Estate on account of his wife's ill health leaving her too tired and weak to organise anything at their house in Stamford. Outwardly, Lady Goldhurst grumbled about the inconvenience of hosting the event with so little notice, but I knew she enjoyed it all secretly. She was happiest when she and Mrs. Brickett were planning dinner and beautifying the house and ordering the staff around. Grace slept through it all, thank heavens, as she loathed any sort of disruption and detested large groups of people. This also meant I could enjoy the glorious Goldhurst morning uninterrupted. There was a window on the east side of the building, on the second floor, and despite being small it received the finest view of the gardens and the lake beyond at sunrise. Although the sun had already risen and was beating a trail of light on everything it saw, no clouds had formed so the sky was a perfect pale blue canvas. If Miss Alice were not so busy I would have told her about it; it would make a delightful painting. She would have captured the colours so splendidly: the many shades of green, the reds, pinks, yellows and whites of the flowers, the metallic shine of the lake, partly hidden by the willows. To me, it was paradise.

"Martha! Martha!" A loud, hoarse voice brought me back to the second floor - Grace was calling for her breakfast no doubt.

With much huffing and griping, Grace was dressed and ready an hour later. Already the plaits that I had so carefully created from her knotty tendrils were being worried and chewed. Suddenly, and without a knock the door swung open. I expected to see Lady Goldhurst flustered and pink with a vase in her hand (she often stored the valuables upstairs when a large party of guests was expected). But it was Miss Alice, smiling and brandishing a black garment bag.

"Oh, Grace! You look absolutely divine in that dress! It fits you perfectly, if I do say so myself." She grinned happily, which made her pretty face look soft and angelic. She wore a lovely lilac gown with a delicate lace neckline and sleeves. She had styled her hair differently, with more of it curled around her face. I always thought she looked much better without a hat as she had such a little head and yards of lovely long dark hair to cover it.

"Now, I've got a little present for you, Martha," She swept over to the wardrobe and hooked a coat hanger on the back of the door. She glanced back at me, smiling coyly and slipped the garment bag off the hanger to reveal another dress - a blue one. I frowned, "It's for you to wear to the christening. I didn't want you to feel left out. What do you think? Try it on, quick; I may need to alter it as I didn't measure you."

I stood dumb, gawping at the dress. It was heavenly - blue silk! I didn't own anything made from silk, except an ancient pair of black gloves that my mother had bought for me for my father's funeral. This shade was far lovelier - pale blue, the colour of the sky I had been admiring just a few moments before.

"I'll watch Grace while you slip into the bathroom." Alice cut through the silence. She must have thought I was too shy to try the dress in front of her.

"Miss Alice, this is too generous a gift, it must have taken you hours to make, and I couldn't possibly..." She waved a gloved hand to silence me.

"Nonsense! You deserve it and I'm not taking it back so I suppose you can either wear it or it can rot here!" She handed me the dress, nodding encouragement. Gingerly I laid it over my arm, as if it was made of glass and I scurried next door.

The silk felt better than I could have imagined - cool and soft, like liquid; it seemed to glide over my limbs and slot into place just perfectly. The arms were short, finishing just above my elbows, and at the waist was a cream satin sash to match the cream lace trim of the neckline. I stood on the balls of my feet to try and get a full view in the mirror, which was fitted high up on the wall above the washbasin. The only drawback I could see was the neckline, which was more revealing than I was used to, but I could easily fix it with a scarf from my own collection. I beamed at myself and hugged the dress to me, never wanting to take it off. I breezed back into the nursery with the air of a girl on the night of her first ball and Miss Alice descended on me, cooing and rearranging the dress.

"You look exquisite in this! Look, Grace, doesn't Martha look beautiful in this frock!" There was no response from Grace, who knelt in the corner with her back to us, chewing her hair ribbon, engrossed in her collection of wooden animals. "Here, this hat will look wonderful with it too." She perched a cream ribboned hat on my head at a jaunty angle and stood back to admire her work. "Perfect! I'll watch Grace while you go and do your hair if you like."

"Oh no, Miss, you've done plenty already, I usually do my hair in here. Are you sure you don't mind me borrowing this hat? I'm sure I have a white one upstairs..."

"No, no, no, that's an old one, you can keep it." She smiled sweetly.

"Well, I'm lost for words, Miss. This is the most generous gift anyone's given me, are you sure...?"

"Martha, please, I wouldn't have made it for you if I didn't want you to have it." She fussed with the sash and dropped her voice, "Besides, given the current circumstances who knows when I'll be able to get my hands on this sort of material in the future. We might as well make the most of it."

"Have you heard any more from London?" I whispered.

She glanced at Grace and leaned in closer, "Papa thinks they're going to declare war today, however, Mother refuses to believe that they would announce it on a Sunday." She rolled her eyes, "I don't know what to think. War...European war, it just sounds so medieval. You would think that, in the twentieth century, our leaders could avoid this sort of thing by talking about it rationally. Or is that naïve of me?" I looked at her suddenly, unsure of whether she wanted me to answer her, but she went on, "I keep hoping that it can be avoided still. I can't think of anyone who actually wants this damned war, excuse my language."

Grace suddenly started coughing, although it sounded more like a barrage of barks. "Stop chewing that ribbon, duck, that's what's making you cough, here." I passed her a cup of water that was placed on the night stand.

"No it's not." She said, emptying the cup in three gulps and smacking her lips afterwards.

"Are you looking forward to the christening, Grace?" Miss Alice said brightly.

"No." She replied, kneeling back to attend to her toys.

"Oh, why not?" She pressed.

"I don't like churches." She mumbled without turning around.

"But you're going to make a special effort today since it's your little niece's big day and you don't want to spoil it." I said, trying to reassure Miss Alice.

"Ah, well done, darling! Do try to be on your best behaviour, so many people are looking forward to it." Grace's face remained inscrutable as she lined her animals up in pairs, with exactly the same distance between them.

"Are many people coming to the service?" I said.

"Quite a few, actually. The Duke of Rutland and his family have accepted the invitation and the Templetons, of course. Oh, Lord, is that the time?" She leapt away from me to the door. "I need to go. You know you're to assemble in the hall in half an hour?"

I nodded, "Thank you, again, Miss Alice."

"You're very welcome; see you both at the church." She rushed out of the room and I listened to her steps fade down the stairs and muffled voices float up from the hall.

"I'm bored, let's play tiddlywinks." Grace's voice was garbled from the length of ribbon that she was still chewing on."

"We can't -" I was interrupted when the door swung open and Lady Goldhurst stood, head-to-toe in cream satin, tulle and pearls, breathing heavily, clutching a Chinese vase normally housed in the drawing room.

"Martha, be a dear and keep this in your room, I don't want it getting knocked over."

"Of course, m'lady," I said, taking the vase and cradling it with care.

"My word, don't you both look delightful!" She exclaimed. "That's a beautiful gown, Martha, very becoming." I blushed and thanked her.

"Now, Grace, dearest, remember what we spoke about last week? You promised me that you would try and stay in the church for the christening service. I haven't forgotten, you know." Grace continued to chew on her ribbon and play with her toys as if her mother had not entered the room. "Please try, darling, for my sake, and your brother's. It's a very special day and you're such a big girl now."

"Grace has promised me again this morning, m'lady."

"Good, splendid. Thank you, dear." She called over, then lowered her voice for my ears only, "Please do something with her hair, before you come downstairs, Martha."

"I want to play draughts." Grace repeated. Lady Goldhurst frowned.

"Not today, Gracie, we're very busy." I said.

Lady Goldhurst stared at her daughter, crouched in a corner, clanging two wooden elephants together, chomping furiously on her green ribbon and sighed, her eyes full of despair. "I sometimes wonder whether her twin brother would have turned out like her. What do you think?" She said, without looking at me.

"Umm, I haven't really thought about it much, Lady Goldhurst." Where was this conversation heading? I wondered.

"Of course, never mind." She shook her head and smiled. "Please be good for Martha, my dear." She turned to me, "Just take her outside if she starts making a fuss. It is Edward and Sarah's day after all. Now, I must go and see if Louisa and the children are ready." She hurried out of the room leaving a scent of magnolia lingering in her wake.

Kinwell church was a pretty building: small, but not poky, ornate, but not too elaborate. The interior did not appear as cavernous as some churches; the ceiling was not too high, the wooden pews were polished to a warm silky finish and a maroon velvet carpet covered the cold stone flags, leading up to the altar. The stained glass windows, depicting the Nativity, the Resurrection and various saints (who I couldn't tell apart, although I think one was Saint Francis), brought some cheer to the grey walls, casting a rainbow of dusty colour with every sunbeam that sliced through the glass. The only unpleasant feature inside the church was the font, which the family now flanked. It was a monstrous grey goblet that looked ready to swallow the baby whole. I couldn't blame the child for wailing when Reverend Samson held her over its wide lip.

Grace despised the church. Despite numerous bribes and pleas she refused to join the family for Sunday service each week. She made such a fuss that Lady Goldhurst gave up the battle years ago. Thus, I had not been inside a church for longer than five minutes since I was sixteen. I didn't miss it particularly, except the hymns, but the vicar in our own parish in Derbyshire was about as ancient as the church and the entire congregation had nodded off during one of his homilies at one time or another. Besides, Grace did enjoy romping around the graveyard and the woods beyond, so I was at least close to the Holy Spirit fairly often.

I had tried to encourage Grace to pray and sing hymns with me on a Sunday morning, to appease her grandmother, Lady Malholm, who called her a 'little heathen', but she wasn't interested in anything to do with religion.

I studied her face as we sat down. She kept glaring at the stained glass windows, particularly the one depicting the resurrection. Lord and Lady Goldhurst and Miss Charlotte were sitting in the front pew, on the same side of the church that we were sitting, joined also by the new Mrs. Goldhurst, who was still unwell and too weak to stand. Mrs. Goldhurst's family occupied the pews opposite. Standing around the dreadful font with Reverend Samson was Mister Edward, holding the baby; Miss Alice and Mr. Avery, Miss Louisa's husband, who was to be the baby's godfather; along with two other ladies and a gentleman I didn't recognise, although one of the ladies looked like Lady Manners, a family friend. Miss Louisa and her children sat in the second pew with Lady Malholm perched on the end of the row; a great black-feathered matriarch. The rest of the church was filling up with family and acquaintances and, when everyone was seated, the reverend spoke briefly before launching into 'All Things Bright and Beautiful'.

I joined in with the hearty chorus (there were some talented singers in the room), but Grace remained seated with her mouth locked tight. It wasn't until the hymn ended that I noticed she was swinging her legs and kicking the back of the pew in front. Each knock echoed around the church, making a hollow sound like a slow rap on a wooden door. One member of the congregation nearly got out of his seat to see who was knocking on the door outside until his wife rolled her eyes in Grace's direction as a way of explanation. My face grew hot and I quietly pleaded for Grace to stop.

"I don't like it in here. I don't like seeing Lord Jesus bleeding." I could see why the crucifix above the pulpit was off-putting. Even from the rear of the aisle I could see the drops of ruby red blood staining the creamy skin of

Christ, his face the picture of despair as his eyes roved upwards towards the crown of thorns pressing into his scalp. The face reminded me of an expression Lady Goldhurst sometimes wore.

"I don't like those windows either."

"Then don't look at them. Look at the baby, or Miss Alice, or your mother." I whispered.

"I want to go outside. I don't like it in here." She shouted, causing a few of the congregation to turn and stare and shake their heads in disapproval. Lady Malholm was the first to turn around in her seat and scowl at us, complaining loudly to Miss Louisa, who smiled sympathetically in my direction. To his credit, Reverend Samson soldiered on as if nothing had happened.

"Grace, remember you promised your mother and me that you would make an effort. The service is only short, I'm sure you can manage to sit through at least half of it. We've only been here for ten minutes." Her face remained stoic, glaring at the stained glass windows from the tail of her eye.

"No!" She pushed past me with surprising nimbleness and force, thrusting the doors open and running around the side of the building. Everyone was staring at me now and angry murmurs began to drown out Reverend Samson's words.

"Carry on, for pity's sake!" I heard Lord Goldhurst call over the din and I ran out in pursuit of my charge, closing the doors behind me.

"Grace! Come here right now!" She had disappeared from sight already. "Grace, where are you?" I trudged around to the back of the church and scanned the tops of the gravestones. I had been a fool for playing along with this. I should have known she wouldn't sit in the church throughout an entire service, even if it was her niece's christening. She had never done so up until today. Were we expecting some sort of miracle?

"Look what I found – roses!" Suddenly she was by my side, waving a bunch of peach coloured blooms at me. "I've never seen orange ones."

"Where did you get those from?"

"Over there." She pointed vaguely behind her.

"Did you take them from someone's grave?" She ignored me and began fingering the thin, curling petals. I put my hands on my hips and lowered my voice to as stern a tone as I could. "Grace Goldhurst, put those flowers back where you found them. You can't steal things from people's graves! It's very disrespectful."

She continued to stroke the petals, rocking back and forth gently on her heels. I heard the collective voice of the congregation rise up into song again inside the church. Hopefully Grace's outburst had not ruined the ceremony.

"Grace, I'm being serious. If you don't put them back I shall have to tell your father."

"But they're orange ones. I need to show Mr. Healy." She whined.

"Mr. Healy's already seen them. You can ask him to grow some for you next season, if you like."

"How do you know he's seen them?"

"Because Mr. Healy is a professional gardener and he knows everything there is to know about roses."

"Why doesn't he grow them, then?"

"He doesn't like the colour. But I'm sure he'll make an exception for you." She stood still, staring at the roses a little longer before turning and jogging back to a large grey cross and placing the bouquet gently onto the earth.

"Well done, that's a good lass."

"Can we walk through the woods to see the hedgehogs?"

"The hedgehogs will be sleeping now. Besides, we have to stay around the church to meet your family when the christening finishes." I paused. "I wish you had tried harder to sit through the service like you promised..."

"Can we go to the little bridge to feed the ducks?" Her pale face stared at me, blank, expressionless, but her eyes sparkled with hope. I sighed.

"We don't have any bread, but we can walk over and see them." She loped down the stone path, through the gate and across the green.

The sun was rising higher in the sky, beating down on a group of boys, who had set up a game of cricket on the green. A cluster of men were gathered near the bridge, their faces serious and their voices urgent. Although I only heard a few gobbets of their conversation as I passed, I could tell they were talking about the war that had not yet been declared. Several of them turned to stare at Grace and me. Their Sunday service had finished over an hour ago and they had already changed out of their best. I nodded courteously at them and one of them tipped his hat and smiled in return.

"Can't we buy some bread for the ducks?" Grace said, leaning over the edge of the bridge, chewing her hair ribbon. Between the churchyard and the bridge her hair had loosened and hung untidily about her shoulders.

"All the shops are closed today." I said.

"Why?"

"It's Sunday, remember? The Sabbath day, the day of rest. No shops are open today."

"Why?" She rocked back and forth on her heels with impatience.

"I've told you about this before. God made the world in six days and rested on the seventh - Sunday. So we do the same out of respect for God."

"Why on Sunday?"

"That's just how it is, duck." She fell to silence, gazing at the ducks in the little river with her chin resting in her hands. The crowd of men slowly dispersed, with just two remaining.

After a while the husky voice spoke again. "What's war?"

"Hmm?"

"What's war?"

"Why do you ask that?" It was a silly question; half of the conversations at Goldhurst Estate involved the word.

"Everyone keeps talking about war. What is it?"

A round of whoops erupted from the cricketers, upsetting a flock of birds, which flew across the green, squawking. I sucked in my breath, wondering how best to explain it to her.

"Well, a war happens when two countries fall out with each other and they can't find a way to make peace."

She frowned a little, "So, what do they do?"

"They have lots of battles; they fight until one side gives up or surrenders, that's the word they usually use. Then the war is over."

She had worried a ribbon free from one of her plaits and was winding it around her fingers. "Fighting is bad. You shouldn't fight."

"Yes I know, but sometimes, if another country is throwing their weight around or doing something they shouldn't be doing, one of the other countries needs to stop them."

"What?"

"For instance, if a big country is picking on a little country, another big country might tell them to stop and they fall out over it." It sounded ridiculously petty when I explained it and I was glad that no one was within earshot of the conversation.

"Who are we going to fight?"

"Oh, Gracie, you don't have to worry about that. We're not actually at war with anyone yet."

"Will I have to fight? I don't want to, I don't like fighting."

"No, no, no, of course not! It's only men that are expected to fight in a war."

"So will Father and Mr. Healy and Edward have to fight?"

"Your father and Mr. Healy wouldn't. They're too old, it's only young men."

"So Edward would need to fight? He might die."

"It won't come to that, duckie, I'm sure. Let's not talk about the war; it's not very nice, is it?"

"No, I think it's silly!" After uttering the final word the ribbon slipped from her fingers into the river, narrowly missing a mallard.

"Oh no, Grace, your ribbon."

"I'm going to get it!" She yelled and shot down the bank.

"Don't you dare, Grace, come back right now!" The thought of her ruining Miss Alice's beautiful dress sent a wave of panic through me. I ran after her but her feet were already in the water; the ducks quacked in alarm at this odd intruder. I reached out and grabbed her arm. "Get out of there now! Your dress..."

She grunted and pulled away from me with an almighty lunge. Both of us fell headfirst into the river. A fishy, brackish taste filled my mouth and the ducks noisily took flight downstream, appalled at being ousted from their home. I stood up, gasping; my clothes weighed me down so that I could barely move. I waded to the bank and collapsed on the soggy grass, tears filling my eyes.

"I've got it!" Grace came splashing towards me, holding the limp green ribbon in the air like a trophy.

I narrowed my eyes; it was boiling up. I couldn't control it any longer. "I told you to stop! Why didn't you listen to me? Why don't you ever listen to me? Now look what you've done! Look at the state of us! Our dresses are ruined! Silk dresses! What is Miss Alice going to say? What are your parents going to say? It's me they'll blame. How could you do this, Grace?" Hot, furious tears streamed down my cheeks, mingling with the weed-scented water drenching the rest of me. "You've gone too far. We can't face your family like this; they'll be coming out of the church soon."

I wiped my eyes and realised that Grace had started bawling. The ribbon that she had held up with such triumph a moment ago was hanging unceremoniously at her side; her eyes were scrunched up in distress.

"What on earth 'appened 'ere?" Two of the men from the little group were standing over me looking completely bewildered.

"I...I was trying to stop her from...falling in and we both slipped." I looked away in shame, rubbing the tears so they blended with the other trails of water running from my hat down to my chin. Grace was still standing in the water, wailing.

"Don't get upset there, lass, it's only a bit o'water." The man who had smiled at us earlier had a soft Yorkshire accent. "Where do you live?"

"They live up at the big house," his companion answered quickly. "Y'know the one?"

"Oh, right, yes I know. Would you like to come and clean up? I live just across the green. Me wife can help you with clean clothes."

I pushed wet tendrils of hair away from my eyes and scrambled up, straightening my sopping gown. "Thank you for the kind offer, but I need to get her home. She doesn't always respond well to strangers." We all looked at Grace.

"Right, er, well, I can take you home in me van, it's parked just up the back of the bakers."

I glanced across the green; thankfully the congregation were still inside the church. "That would be very helpful, but the family will be waiting for us when they come out of the church."

"I'll stop here and pass on the message that you had to go." The second man said.

"Thank you very much." I smiled.

"You're very welcome, Miss..."

"Martha Pick. This is Miss Grace Goldhurst." Grace was still snivelling in the river and it took a few minutes and much grovelling to convince her to follow me to the baker's van. The ribbon remained clenched inside her fist the entire time.

Our Good Samaritan's name was Peter Patrick, he was originally from Bradford but had married a girl from Stamford and they had recently moved down to Kinwell to take over her uncle's bakery. I persuaded him to drop us at the gates at the end of the long gravel drive so we could slip through the servants' hall relatively unnoticed.

Grace, still pouting and sullen, dragged her feet as we squelched up the drive. I felt wretched at having lost my temper with her.

"I'm sorry I shouted at you, Gracie. I didn't mean it; I was just upset that our lovely new dresses were ruined. Miss Alice worked so hard on them."

We trudged along side by side in silence. Grace looked so forlorn I couldn't help but weep again. "Do you forgive me?"

We squelched a little farther and as we neared the servants' door Grace stopped, breathing noisily, her chest rising with each sob. "I'm sorry I made you cry," she croaked, staring at the ground as she said it. I embraced her.

"Thank you, duckie! That means a lot to me." She grunted and squirmed and I released her laughing. "Come on, you, let's wash and get changed."

Much to Lady Goldhurst's triumph, war was not declared on the day of little Sophie's christening, nor was it declared the following day, but on the Tuesday, although we didn't hear about it until the next morning on account of the decision being made at eleven o'clock the previous night. I wondered how on earth the Prime Minister and his cabinet went to sleep after such a momentous decision. If it were me, I would be sure not to sleep for days.

A few of the young male servants enlisted straight away, along with the other young men in the area. Peter Patrick and his comrades marched proudly through Kinwell, the villagers cheering them on their way to France. Edward Goldhurst too, was among the first to join up, as a captain in the First Battalion of the Royal Lincolnshire Regiment. His mother, his wife and his sister begged him not to go; Lord Goldhurst remained silent on the subject but eventually concluded that his son was a grown man and could make his own mind up, wishing him good luck as he went. So that was that.

My ever-reliable mother wrote to me as soon as the war was declared, informing me that a number of men from Bradcote had enlisted and Bill was seriously thinking of joining them. Despite the many posters and cartoons in the newspapers showing women persuading their menfolk to sign up, proudly waving them on their way to the Front, I hated the idea of my brother, my only sibling, going to fight in a war. It was very unpatriotic, but I couldn't forget Miss Alice's words, 'Scores of innocent men are going to be sent to die in Europe.' I hoped she was wrong and that it would all be over by Christmas, like the newspapers said.

Two days after the war was declared, Miss Louisa and her family left their London home and moved to New York, meaning that Miss Charlotte and Miss Alice were forced to remain at home more often. Miss Alice, although disappointed, bore it with patience. She would have to wait until the war was over to continue with her dressmaking enterprise, although she insisted on making her brother's uniform before he left. Miss Charlotte, however, behaved as if war had been declared just to spoil her fun. She whined and wept and argued with any family member who dared to tick her off. Eventually, Lady Goldhurst allowed her to go to London for one weekend a month, to stay with her aunt and uncle, as long as she promised to telephone every day. Miss Alice, meanwhile, entered into the spirit of the Home Front by knitting socks and scarves for the soldiers.

Edward Goldhurst's war was short-lived. He was sent back to Portsmouth in November, having fractured his elbow and dislocated his shoulder during one of the first battles in Belgium. When he arrived back in Rutland he refused to speak to anyone for over a month. It was a dark Christmas, but darker ones were still to come.

    Bill enlisted at the start of November and was sent to the Front a month later. I dreaded seeing an ivory envelope decorated with my mother's sloping handwriting in case it should contain bad news. It had been at least three months since my mother's last letter - most unlike her - since I had received at least one letter every four weeks for the past fourteen years. This letter came with a parcel. She had knitted a white duck for Grace which looked as similar to Jimmy as a woollen duck could. She still asked about him every time she saw me with a letter from my mother.

    I looked out across the garden from beneath the old horse chestnut. A sheet of sunlight had turned the snow a brilliant shade of white and somewhere above me a solitary bird sang a maudlin tune that I thought would never end. I hated everything about this time of year, except the snow, which covered every bare branch it could find, burying the lawn in a deep overcoat of cottony white. I couldn't stand those puny half-hearted flakes that barely covered the ground and disappeared the next day.

    Grace was meandering in and out of the bare rose garden, clutching her new Jimmy and occasionally shoving her face into the sparse bushes so she could lick the snow.

    Pushing my finger under the envelope's flap, I tore the seal and unfolded the stiff pages. There were four - more than usual - and it was dated two weeks previous. It smelled of my mother's cottage - pastry and soap with a hint of lavender. Her letters always carried the same scent, perhaps it was a conscious attempt to persuade me to return to Bradcote more often.

    Her letter began normally enough:

Dear Martha,

    I hope this letter finds you well and that you have not been affected by the snow as much as we have... She went on to apologise for her lack of communication and put it down to her daily involvement with my brother's shop. Since Bill had left, Jane had been struggling to keep the butcher's going on her own. *I've taken on a boy from the village (Simon Brewer - John's son) but he's got to learn as he goes along and, having not worked in a shop before, it's taking him a while to get the hang of it. I've been helping out every day to give Jane a bit of respite. Of course she has Harry and Tom to look after as well but her mother arrived last week so some of the strain has been relieved. The poor girl is run ragged every day but she's adamant she wants to keep the butcher's going for Bill. She wants him to come home to a thriving business; she's convinced it won't be long now, but I must admit I'm starting to have my doubts. Didn't they say this war would be over by Christmas? It's nearly February and if anything it's getting worse...*

    A gust of wind rustled the pages suddenly. I looked up; Grace was following Mr. Healy, trudging behind his wheelbarrow.

    "Grace, don't bother Mr. Healy while he's working." I called over the wind. They both turned around.

    "Don't fret, Martha, she's no trouble." He shouted back. I smiled at his unfaltering kindness and patience. The Goldhursts would never find another gardener like him when he eventually retired.

    I smoothed out the pages, reading from the beginning again. I had considered asking Lady Goldhurst for some time off to visit Bradcote and help out, but I was worried about Grace. Lord and Lady Goldhurst were planning a month's trip to New York to see Miss Louisa fairly soon and I didn't feel it was appropriate to ask. I read on.

    We haven't heard any more from Bill since he landed in France in December. Jane is beside herself, poor thing, but I'm trying to remain optimistic. No news is good news as they always say.

    I had hoped, considering the length of my mother's letter, that it might contain some more news from Bill. It had been nearly three months since he left and we had only heard from him once, and very briefly, in that time.

    The same cannot be said of the Pattersons, I'm afraid. Poor Eric joined up just before Bill and his parents received news of his death a few days ago. I was terribly upset when I heard and his mother is inconsolable. I haven't seen him since he moved to Derby a few years back but I remember what a lovely young man he was; so kind and thoughtful, he did a lot for me and I won't forget him. It seems ever so cruel, so sad and it makes we want to see our Bill desperately, to make sure he's all right. I can't really talk to Jane about these things; it would make her worry even more. Reverend Williams is going to hold a memorial service for Eric next week. I think it's a nice idea, although I'm not sure if his parents will be quite ready for it; their hearts are broken, as mine would be. It's unnatural and cruel for a mother to have to bury her child...

I read through the rest of the letter in a daze. She updated me with village news, Harry's progress and ended, as she always did, by sending her love to Grace.

Have you told her about Jimmy yet? I suppose what she doesn't know won't hurt her. Heaven knows we've got enough death and sadness to deal with at the moment. Let the poor girl think he's immortal. I hope she likes the duck.

Jimmy the duck had died almost a year ago but I hadn't the heart to tell Grace.

She came running towards me, in wonky strides, ungainly as always, and I smiled. She looked happy and carefree, just what I needed to stop the lump in my throat from growing even larger.

"I've found forty six worms in Mr. Healy's wheelbarrow." She croaked. I looked down at her filthy hands and dress.

"Oh Grace, you didn't touch them, did you?"

She blinked, looking confused, "No. I counted them in the soil. Mr. Healy let me use his trowel."

I clicked my tongue softly, "You'll need a bath before dinner, and a change of clothes. Come on, it's getting dark." We headed back into the house when she stopped abruptly and ran back to where she had come from.

"Where are you going?" I shouted.

"I left Jimmy." She called.

The paltry winter sun was wrapped in a sea of grey cloud, casting a gloaming shadow across the gardens. I stood on the steps waiting, rubbing the letter between my fingers. Despite my best efforts my mind wandered back to Eric. I saw his auburn hair and green eyes flecked with brown specks, his shy and serious face breaking into a smile the way it did when we spent the day in Derby and the peaks nearly five years ago. He had written to me once after I returned to Goldhurst, no doubt encouraged by my mother, but I didn't reply. The last thing I wanted to do was to give him false hope and besides, I couldn't think of the right words to say. According to my mother he had never married, but had obviously left Bradcote some time ago. Had he been happy? Was there a sweetheart in Derby who had lovingly sent him on his way? I hoped so. I closed my eyes and tried to stop my lips from trembling. He had felt something for me once. He had made me feel beautiful and loved, if only for a short time. What if I had reciprocated? Would I be a widow now; heartbroken and raising children on my own?

"Got him," Grace was breathless and shot past me into the house. Taking a deep breath I followed quickly behind, calling for her to slow down.

A thump and a man's cry made me halt and turn back. "Mr. Healy? What's wrong?" I couldn't see anything outside and I called for one of the servants, not wanting to leave Grace alone for too long. There was no response. Where was everybody? I walked outside and shivered. The wind had picked up and brushed layers of snow from the bushes' haggard branches. I could see Mr. Healy's wheelbarrow at the far side of the sleeping rose garden.

"Mr. Healy? If you're there can you call to me?" When I received no response I jogged over to the barrow and froze, trying to take in the sight before me. Mr. Healy lay spread-eagled in the snow, his right hand over his chest; his mouth open and his eyes closed. I screamed for help. I didn't want to be the one to find him like this; I couldn't cope. I knelt beside his still-warm body and clutched his gloved hand. Tears dribbled down my cheeks and plopped onto the cold earth. "How am I going to tell her?"

Chapter Eight
16th December 1915, Goldhurst Estate, Rutland
Alice

"What do you think of these decorations, Grace?" Martha and I were helping the servants bring a bit of festive cheer to our morose house. I had spent the previous day creating stars, trees, angels, snowflakes and bells with scraps of cloth and buttons, all of which were now hanging from the branches of a tall fir brought in by Mr. Gribble, the gardener.

"Nice." Grace replied without looking up from her drawing. I was pleased to see that Grace had shown more interest in drawing and painting as she grew older. She usually produced childish sketches of animals and landscapes, but now she was working on a nativity scene with a barn, sheep, donkeys and stars, but no people.

"Where is the baby in the manger, Grace? And Mary and Joseph?"

She shrugged and carried on colouring the sky black.

I knew that Grace had an aversion to young children, particularly to ones that cried; she could not tolerate the sound. I had my apprehensions when Edward and Sarah moved into the house two months ago with Sophie, for I knew the change would upset Grace. Her life had already been upended with the death of our parents and she had regressed considerably because of it. She was intractable to the point of becoming aggressive and refused to speak to anyone except Martha and myself. Even now, seven months later, she would only speak to close family members. In a way it was Grace that pulled me through those dark early months of grief when one found it hard to find a reason to leave one's bedroom and converse with people about anything other than death and sorrow. Grace and my sewing machine, odd as it sounds; they gave me a purpose. I had to appear strong and capable in front of Grace to avoid exacerbating her unpredictable moods. The sewing just gave me pleasure. It always had.

Edward had delayed moving his family to Goldhurst Estate due to his Sarah's continuing poor health, but he was now fully in charge of the estate as well as the family business and, thus, was rarely seen around the house, not even at dinner times. Sarah's sickliness was further aggravated by the move and she spent the majority of her time confined to her bedroom resting, rendering her equally evasive.

So, with its owners indisposed I assumed the unofficial role of Lady of the House and helped with the running of the estate. Charlotte was spending most of her time in London as her beau, Captain Henry De Lisle, was back from France and her not so subtle plan was to try to procure him as a husband sooner, rather than later. He wanted to wait until the war was over; she didn't.

Although they only met him twice, Mother and Father had never approved of Henry De Lisle as a potential son-in-law; I never discovered the reason for this, though I suspected they had heard rumours of his reputation as a philanderer.

"What about garlands, Miss?" Martha's voice roused me from my musings. "I found these ones we used last year. Shall I just give them a clean and put them up?"

"Yes, that would be fine, Martha. We can't justify buying new garlands at the moment and the old ones are just as good." Like Edward, Martha was looking older. Lines I hadn't noticed before appeared when she smiled.

"Grace and I are going into Stamford after lunch. Would you like to join us, Miss Alice?"

"Thank you Martha, but I don't think I will today. I need to finish making those blankets and socks for The Red Cross."

She raised her eyebrows. "You've been sewing all week, Miss. Make sure you don't overdo it. You look exhausted."

"Well it's nothing compared to what those poor men are feeling over the Channel. The very least I can do to repay them is donate a few blankets and some warm clothing. I wish I could do more; one feels so helpless over here when others are risking their lives every day."

"Yes, it's awful thinking about those poor souls, my brother Bill included. He said in his last letter that some of the latest recruits are barely out of short trousers, God bless them. I admire what you're doing, I just worry that you're going to wear yourself out and fall ill, like Mrs. Goldhurst. I don't think we'd all cope without you." Her brow was furrowed in concern, creating a cluster of lines across her forehead.

"Oh, don't worry about me. I'm made of stronger stuff than that. Please do let me know the news from Stamford, won't you?"

"Of course, I'll see you later on, Miss."

I ate luncheon in the morning room, which I had transformed into a makeshift factory with three sewing machines atop wooden benches: two electric powered and my old hand-powered machine in the corner. The older electric machine had belonged to Ms. Vermaut, who had been killed on the Lusitania with my parents. I hadn't been able to bring myself to use it; I thought I might donate it to a charity since I had not been able to trace any of her family.

As I began threading the needle of the newer machine I stared at the old Singer, my first sewing machine, and thought about the day I got it. The memory remained etched as vividly as the outbreak of the war and I often daydreamed about it to dispel the boredom of stitching length after length of khaki wool and thread.

I had been begging my parents for a machine for at least two years, but they had resisted; both seemed to think I would grow out of sewing and I had no need to make my own clothes when we had servants and dressmakers at our disposal to do the work for us. My mother was the most truculent; she didn't want her daughter getting any ideas below her station. "I just don't see the attraction." She would often say and Charlotte would find great enjoyment in teasing me about it. Whenever I tried to explain to them that I wanted to design and create new fashions rather than mending clothes they seldom listened; they weren't interested.

Louisa was the only person in the family who encouraged me to pursue my interest. She asked Ms. Vermaut, to teach me how to use a machine (for I was terrified of her and would never have asked myself) and even introduced me to Mrs. Birch's dressmaker's shop in Stamford, arranging lessons for two hours on a Saturday so I could learn more from her.

Despite her kind efforts, Louisa knew that I really wanted my very own machine. Ms. Vermaut was not the most willing or patient teacher and never attempted to disguise her annoyance whenever I asked her permission to practise on her Singer. I remember how she used to tut and say "it's not a toy" over again, as if I didn't know.

To my delight, on my fourteenth birthday in 1908, my wish was granted. I remember the day well - a mild but grey Wednesday in late November - I woke at half past seven as usual and wore the pretty hyacinth gown I had picked out for the occasion the previous month.

As I went down to breakfast, Louisa, who was staying for two months over the festive period, beckoned me into the morning room and there it was - my very own Singer sewing machine. For a moment time stood still as I ran my index finger along the polished black plate and then traced the ornate gold lettering which spelled out 'The Singer Manufacturing Co.' in a style that made it seem so distinguished. One could tell it was a few years old: the wooden base was slightly worn as was the handle on the hand wheel, but I didn't care. It radiated possibilities and I couldn't wait to start using it.

I kissed Louisa about twenty times, telling her over and over again how much I loved her; how I would never forget the kindness she had shown me. She did warn me, however, not to talk about it too much in front of the rest of our family. Mother and Father still disapproved and were not happy with her for getting the machine, even though it was a gift from her and Miles, bought with her own money. It took a great deal of persuasion for them to allow her to give me the gift; my mother had been adamant that Louisa take the machine back.

From that day onwards I spent part of every day on my sewing machine and soon became an expert in creating simple garments; I made lots for Grace and for Louisa's children. I also made lots of adorable smocks and blankets for little Robert when he was first born, but alas, my poor mother barely had a chance to use them. I shuddered at the memory and prayed that I had been forgiven and that Robert was safe in Heaven.

Mother would only allow me to keep the Singer in my own room and I was never allowed to use it for longer than one hour each day. Of course, this decree was not always adhered to. My parents were so absorbed in the family business (in the case of my father) or preoccupied with Grace and finding eligible spouses for Edward (my mother), that they neglected to check what I was doing. I was quiet, out of the way and caused them no trouble, so I was left to occupy myself a lot of the time, which suited me very well indeed.

Glancing over at the pewter wall clock I was surprised to see it was almost five o'clock; I had been working for four hours without rest and was running low on khaki thread. Making a mental note to buy some more, I turned off the machine and headed upstairs to prepare for dinner. Charlotte was due home at half past five after her week in London and, with Sarah's illness and Edward's absence from home, I had been rather lonely at dinnertimes during the past few days. I was actually looking forward to seeing Charlotte for once.

I stopped when I heard Martha's voice drifting towards me from the back of the house.

"Now we've got to make another appointment and get yet another pair made! You need to stop doing this; you're acting like a small child!"

"What's wrong?" I asked as they approached me.

"Oh, Miss, please have a word with your sister. She's ruined another pair of spectacles - the third pair this month! She just will not wear them and when I make her, she throws them in the river, or out the window, stamps on them, or throws them underneath a horse and cart, like today!" It was unusual to see Martha so worked up into a temper.

"Martha, why don't you go and have a bath? Or do some reading; write some letters and have some time to yourself this evening. Charlotte and I will look after Grace and I will talk to her about the spectacles."

She seemed stunned for a moment. "I wasn't moaning, I, I just wanted Grace to understand that her behaviour wasn't acceptable." Her face reddened and she looked down.

"I completely agree. I will be having a stern word with her, as will Edward when he returns. Now, off you go. It's about time you had a night off." I smiled encouragingly at her.

"No, Miss, I couldn't do that, I don't mind..."

"Please, Martha, do as you're told!" I said laughing at her. She looked up, wide-eyed, then, when she saw I was joking, her face relaxed.

"Are you sure?"

"Yes! How many times do I have to tell you?" I turned her around to face the staircase.

"Thank you very much, Miss Alice, I was going to write to my mam. I won't be far if you need me, though and I'll come down to put her to bed."

"No you won't, I can do it. Go on!"

"Right, well, be good for your sister, Grace." She said and she went upstairs, turning around once to see Grace's reaction. She had not moved, but continued to stare at the carpet swinging her arms by her sides.

I turned to her when Martha had disappeared. "Now, young lady, let's go and sit in the drawing room." I led the way and she trudged after me, head down.

"Why did you throw your glasses under a horse today?"

She fiddled with the buttons on her dress and shrugged.

"Grace, if you don't talk to me I will have to give your Christmas presents away."

"I hate them," she said quickly, "I hate the way they feel on my nose."

"They're bound to feel strange at first, but you'll get used to them if you keep wearing them. Soon you won't even notice you're wearing them."

"I will." She moaned.

"You know you need them for a reason. They help you see things better and if you don't wear them your eyesight will only get worse until everything will become blurry. You wouldn't want that, would you? You'd hate not being able to see the birds or the animals or the roses..." I stopped and drew my hand to my mouth. Hopefully she wouldn't react to the last word.

"I don't like them."

"Regardless of that, you must stop breaking them. Do you realise that every time you smash them or throw them away we have to buy you a new pair? And Martha has to go all the way to Stamford to collect them? They are quite expensive and with the war we need to be so careful that we are not wasteful. Think about those poor children whose fathers are away fighting in France and can't afford new spectacles. They would love to have a new pair and here you are throwing them away! It's very selfish, don't you think?"

"Are Mother and Father coming back after the war?"

"What do you mean? No, Mother and Father are no longer with us. You know that."

"Why don't they come back?"

"Grace, we've had this conversation. You know Mother and Father died seven months ago. We went to their funeral, remember? We've been to visit their memorials in the churchyard."

"They drowned like Rosie."

"Who's Rosie?"

"Charlotte's cat."

"Oh, yes, of course." I said.

"Drowning is different from dying. I saw Rosie again after she drowned."

"I think you probably just saw another cat that looked like Rosie. When someone drowns they cannot breathe anymore and they die."

"How did Mother and Father drown? Were they in a sack?"

"What?"

"That's how Rosie drowned."

I shook my head. "They weren't in a sack. Come on, you need to eat your dinner. You can either sit with Charlotte and me or eat it on your own in the nursery."

"I want to eat on my own."

"Right, we'll talk about the spectacles after you've finished and you will be staying in your bedroom for the rest of the evening for breaking them and upsetting poor Martha."

"Is Martha angry with me?"

"You know she is."

"Is she coming back?"

"Yes, but not tonight. She's having a rest."

She seemed satisfied with this answer and I ushered her towards the staircase.

Ten minutes later Charlotte arrived home. I went into the hallway to greet her and as soon as she saw me she burst into a crescendo of gasps and tears. I moved forward to comfort her.

"What's the matter? Has something happened to Henry?"

"He's fighting a war, that's what's happened! Oh he's so brave! I can hardly bear to be away from him again. He has no idea when he's next back in London and it sounds so beastly over there - all alone for Christmas!" A white, embroidered handkerchief was conveniently retrieved from her purse and she covered her face with it.

"He won't be alone; there will be hundreds of other men in the same situation."

She ignored me, "It breaks my heart; I don't know how I'm going to survive without him!"

I wanted to be sympathetic to my sister; I wanted to be the caring listener, the shoulder she could cry on, but I was tired. I had no energy for Charlotte's histrionics today so I said, "Charlotte, dear, why don't you go and get changed and we'll have dinner together in half an hour? I need to go and see to Grace."

"Why do you have to see to her? Where's her minder?"

"I gave Martha the night off as she was at the end of her tether."

Charlotte grunted. "Aren't we all? That was a stupid thing to do, Alice."

"Be fair, the poor woman hasn't had a day off for months, possibly years. You know these spectacles Grace has been told to wear?"

"What about them?" She snapped, sniffing and blotting her nose.

"She keeps breaking them on purpose so she doesn't have to wear them. She threw them under a horse and cart today in Stamford. I'm just going to talk to her about it and send her to bed early."

"Good! Tell her no one has time for her attention-seeking tricks whilst there are thousands of brave soldiers risking their lives for God and country. Mother was always too soft on her."

"She doesn't always understand that she's done something wrong, poor thing. Don't be unkind, Charlotte, the war has completely confused her, she's lost both of her parents."

"I've lost my parents too, but you don't see me behaving like a spoiled brat!"

I had to stop myself from scoffing at Charlotte's self-appraisal. "Besides," she sniffed, "she hasn't shed one tear over their death. She doesn't even seem to care."

"Like I said, she's not like the rest of us. She doesn't express her feelings in the same way as everyone else; she can't. Just because she doesn't grieve in the same manner as you and I do doesn't mean she isn't grieving. We need to look after one another."

"All right, all right, Alice I think you've made your point, you can get off your soapbox and we'll have dinner in half an hour. Then I can tell you my news properly."

I left Grace twenty minutes later having procured an apology and a promise to give the spectacles a chance when she got her new pair. This was a small triumph for me; Grace had always been stubborn and unwilling to compromise under any of my conditions.

I met Charlotte in the dining room wearing a black chiffon velvet dress trimmed with jet beading and a diamond bracelet that Henry had given her. Although the gown was enhanced with frills in the skirt and a gardenia corsage at the neckline, it reminded me of something my grandmother used to wear.

"Why on earth are you wearing that drab thing?"

She smiled a little and tilted her chin upwards, "I'm wearing nothing but black until my darling Henry arrives home."

I rolled my eyes. "I'll give it a week before you're back in colours. Besides, Henry isn't dead."

She sighed and whimpered. "He might be, for all I know!"

"He hasn't even left England yet, has he?"

"Please!" She gasped, "Don't remind me of his leaving. Let's just eat. I'm famished."

One of the maids began to serve the food.

"Where's Sarah tonight?"

"I thought you went up to see her? She's ill; she hasn't eaten dinner downstairs for a while."

"Still ill? Heavens, what's wrong with her?"

"She's very weak. Sophie is doing well, though." I added.

"Hmm?" She looked up, sipping her soup.

"Our niece, Sophie."

"Oh good. And how did you get on with the devil child?"

"Don't talk about her like that. She's been very good, in fact." I paused. "Excepting the spectacles."

"Wonders will never cease!"

"She was asking about Mother and Father earlier. She seemed to think they were coming back."

"Gosh, really? She's mad as a hatter if she thinks that!"

"Sad, isn't it?" She nodded and the maids took away our soup bowls.

"Do you miss them?" Charlotte asked after they had left.

"Of course, don't you?"

"Of course." We stared at each other for a moment, Charlotte opened her mouth to speak again but soon closed it when the maids returned with the main course.

"Hmmm. Anyway, do you want to hear my news or not?" Charlotte had always had the ability to flit from serious to trivial within a matter of seconds.

"Yes, let me hear it." I said.

"First of all, the most exciting news is: Henry is going to propose next time he's back!"

"Propose what?"

She clicked her tongue, "You know what, don't be ridiculous, it doesn't suit you."

"What makes you think he's going to propose to you?" I said coolly.

"I don't think, Alice, I know. I overheard him talking to his sister about a ring."

"Oh, well that explains everything then!" I rolled my eyes.

She dropped her cutlery onto her plate, "Why can't you just be happy for me, instead of being jealous all the time? It makes you sound like a bitter old hag."

"Believe me, Charlotte, I'm not jealous of you in the slightest. In fact, I pity you. You hardly know this man and you're a fool to want to get married during a war."

"What do you mean I hardly know him? We've been courting since before the war."

"Exactly, you met him a week before he left for France and since then he's only been home twice so you've spent twenty days with him at the most. How do you know you love him or that he loves you? What if he just wants your fortune?"

"He's not like that; you don't know him at all. We've been writing to each other almost every week. That's how I know he loves me. And his family is *very* wealthy, he has plenty of money, he doesn't need mine."

"Two or three weeks together, a handful of billet-doux and a cartload of money does not equal a successful marriage. What if he comes back from France crippled? Or blind? Are you prepared to care for him for the rest of your life?" Charlotte's face froze. She seemed stunned by this question. Clearly she had not thought of every eventuality of war.

I pressed on, "I've heard of husbands and fiancés returning with awful injuries. If you're willing to become a widow or a permanent nursemaid at the age of twenty four you're a braver person than I am."

Charlotte looked at me with an agonised expression, her lower lip fluttering. "Why are you saying all of this? It won't happen! It won't happen to my Henry!"

"How do you know? It could happen to anyone and didn't you just say that you don't know whether he's alive or dead a few moments ago?"

"Stop!" She cried. She was silent for a moment then continued to slice a piece of lamb. "All right, maybe I'll wait until the war is over before marrying him. It won't be much longer anyway, he says." She narrowed her eyes at me. "Although I don't know why I'm listening to you, you've never been in love, except perhaps with your sewing machine." She snorted; I ignored her.

We ate the rest of the meal in silence, Charlotte clearly disturbed by the thought of marrying someone with a disability.

After the servants took away our plates she seemed to perk up, however.

"Prepare yourself for my next piece of news, it's quite shocking."

"Go on." I said.

She leaned closer. "Sarah's not likely to come down tonight, is she?"

"I doubt it, she's ill, why?"

"The news concerns Edward." She said smugly.

"Our brother Edward?"

"Well I don't mean Prince Edward."

"What about him?"

She looked over both shoulders and, satisfied that there were no eavesdroppers, continued in a hushed voice. "Henry, and I were at the theatre yesterday evening, with Florence and Gerald, and we saw Edward there too - with a woman - looking very intimate."

I frowned, "Are you sure it was Edward?"

"Certain. He was about eight rows in front of us, but I didn't notice him until the show was over. Henry and I followed them out and I got a good look at his face, and hers, it was definitely Edward."

"That's queer. He told Sarah that he was at the Liverpool factory until Friday. Why would he lie?"

Charlotte laughed abrasively. "Don't be naïve, Alice, he's obviously having an affair with this woman."

"That's absurd. I hope you haven't been saying things like that in front of our Aunt and Uncle; Edward will be livid and quite right."

She snorted. "What right has he got to be livid when he's the one who's been unfaithful?"

"For God's sake, Charlotte, keep your voice down! I'm sure there is a perfectly reasonable explanation. The woman was probably an acquaintance, a friend whose husband is away and needed a chaperone, perhaps."

She raised her eyebrows, "Friend or not they looked rather familiar when they got into a cab together outside the theatre. And if it was all so innocent why didn't he mention it to his wife? Why did he tell her that he was in Liverpool?"

"I don't know, maybe he did tell her. Maybe you're just jumping to conclusions the way you tend to do sometimes. What did Cousin Miranda say about it?"

"I didn't tell her. Only Henry, Gerald and Florence know, and now you. I must say it's abominable behaviour, he's gone down in my estimation. The woman wasn't even pretty."

"What did she look like?" I had to admit my curiosity.

"I didn't see her that well as it was dark, but she looked about my age and height, she had dark hair and wore far too much make up. She wasn't nearly as pretty as Sarah and her dress was cheap and garish." She winced. "You wouldn't approve anyway."

I shook my head trying to take it all in. "I just can't imagine Edward doing something like that. He's not the sort of man to betray his wife, especially when she's so unwell."

"I think we should have a good look in his study tomorrow to see if we can find out anything else about this woman."

"Not on your life, Charlotte! I'm not poking around in my brother's private belongings."

She shrugged, "Suit yourself."

I grinned. "There I was thinking that you were going to update me of events on the Western Front."

"Oh, yes. Henry did tell me all about it, but I must confess I've forgotten everything he said."

An icy grey and drizzly morning greeted us, doing little to lift the spirits of the household. Charlotte and I had planned to spend the morning in Stamford, but she refused to leave the house in such weather. So I spent some time with Sarah, who was feeling well enough to face some company.

Her bedchamber smelled of Vapo-Resolene and stagnant air; I was desperate to fling open a window or two, if not to let in new air, then to permit some light, for the heavy purple curtains trapped us in near darkness. Sarah was propped up into an almost sitting position and in the gloom she reminded me of an elegant vampire from a Victorian gothic novel.

"Sophie is getting so big and clever too; she is starting to say a few words already, isn't that incredible?" She said in a weak, watery voice. I nodded and gushed along with her. In truth I wasn't sure whether this was a remarkable achievement or not as I had not spent much time around infants, except Grace, and she was hardly a model of conformity. Then there were the few short weeks when Robert came along. I shivered at the memory.

"Have you heard any news from Edward?" I knew she was going to ask me about him at some point and I desperately wanted to avoid it. Luckily (or perhaps unluckily) I had become rather skilful at hiding the truth over the years.

"No, I expect he's awfully busy." She looked disappointed. "You know how he feels about contributing to the war effort. I doubt we'll hear from him before Friday."

Sarah lay back on her pillow, lines etched across her face, like Martha's. She was so pale her skin was almost transparent; her lips were a light shade of violet. All colour and life had been sucked out of her by illness and lethargy; but she was still beautiful. Her long golden hair and orb-like face had captivated Edward not so long ago, how sad it would be if she wasn't enough for him now. Things had changed. How could they have foreseen what life would be like three years after their engagement? It wasn't anybody's fault that Sarah was so sickly; it wasn't anybody's fault that Edward had been shattered by the war. Could I blame him for what he was doing? I suddenly felt uneasy sitting with Sarah. I felt guilty, like a spy.

"You look tired, Sarah. I think I should let you sleep."

"You will tell me if you hear from Edward?"

"Yes, of course. Don't worry about him, concentrate on getting yourself better."

The weather had upset my plans to get more supplies from Stamford. I desperately wanted to make another load of blankets, socks and vests for the soldiers before Christmas. Frustrated, I tried to persuade Charlotte to come with me, despite the weather; however, when I found her she was furiously writing an intense epistle of love to Henry and didn't want to be disturbed. Besides, the weather had got considerably worse: ragged drops of sleet hit the windows creating a mushy film on the sills. I had to resign myself to the fact that I would have to stay inside in idleness for the time being.

Grace had been very quiet all morning. I had gone to see her before breakfast, but she was still asleep. As it was ten o'clock I presumed she was now up and about.

Martha was in a better mood when I entered the nursery, but Grace sat in a corner, hunched up with all her stuffed animals around her.

"She's been rather sombre this morning. She woke up late and has hardly spoken to me. I think it's her way of saying sorry, or at least acknowledging she was wrong." Martha informed me. We managed to coax her into sitting at the little table and she began to draw what appeared to be a gnome.

The room darkened so much that we had to switch on two lamps. "It's a shame about this dismal weather; we won't be able to collect the new glasses until tomorrow if it continues." I said.

"I telephoned to let Mr. Smyth know we needed another pair as soon as possible." Martha whispered.

"What did he say?" I said.

"He was very good-natured, actually; I'm sure he had a chuckle about it."

"He's probably rubbing his hands together; the amount of money he's earned from our family is probably enough to pay his bills for a year."

Martha smiled and looked over at Grace, who was silently scrubbing the paper with a black crayon.

"Thank you for letting me have a break yesterday, Miss. I shouldn't have made such a fuss, I'm sorry."

"You more than deserved a night off; you have more patience than the rest of us put together." Martha blushed and mumbled thanks. Her modesty annoyed me sometimes, whenever I paid her a compliment she turned scarlet and squirmed as if it were unbearable. She had dedicated the best part of her life to Grace, to our family, and never expected any praise or reward. She would have made a splendid nun, I thought.

"I forgot to ask yesterday, was there any news from Stamford?"

"There was some news, although I'm afraid a lot of it isn't very pleasant."

"Go on." I said, swallowing hard.

"Mr. and Mrs. Kennery, the couple that run the butcher's, their son was killed in action a number of weeks ago. Mrs. Kennery was fretting as she hadn't heard from him for a long time. Likewise, Mrs. Clough's son was killed and one of the Carter boys."

"How awful, does that mean Mrs. Clough's alone now?"

Martha nodded, "Although her sister and niece have asked her to go and live with them in Peterborough. I think she will."

"What about Captain Knowles, any news of him?"

"As far as I know he's still at the front. The twins, the Teanby twins from the smith's, are both dead. Well, one is certainly dead the other is missing presumed dead."

I closed my eyes for a minute and saw the grinning red-haired Teanby boys, who had once sung in the church choir. "They were the same age as me. I can't believe all these young men have gone. It's too awful for words. I can't imagine what their parents are feeling. We must rally around them at Christmas, do what we can."

"There was some other news I think you'd be interested in, again, it's not particularly jolly."

I sighed and looked out at the watery, grey December day. "Is there ever jolly news these days?"

Grace suddenly stood up and took her completed drawing to her pinboard.

"Let me do that, duck." Martha said, reaching out to take the drawing from her.

"No." Grace held it against her breast and pinned it up herself. It was of an old man with a grey beard and hair; a pink, round face; and matching brown boots, gloves and hat, surrounded by brightly coloured presents against a sooty black sky.

"What a lovely picture of Father Christmas." I exclaimed.

"It's not Father Christmas." She snapped back.

"Oh, who is it then?" I said.

"It's Mr. Healy with his flowers in heaven."

"Thank you ever so much, Mrs. Birch, this will keep me going until mid-January at least."

I had been forced to wait three days before I was able to venture into Stamford. The weather had worsened considerably overnight; the roads and paths had transformed into lethal slides of ice and snowfall.

"You're welcome, m'lady. I admire what you're doing for the men over there."

Mrs. Birch's dressmaking business had been so successful during the twenty years since her shop opened that she was able to take on several girls as apprentices before the war. As her shop grew in popularity she opened a small factory and took on more girls to meet the demand for her dresses, coats, hats and gloves. She was on the brink of expanding her shops to Lincoln and Peterborough but, alas, it was not meant to be. Her husband, who helped her run the business, mostly by using the profits to keep up his gambling interests, died a few months before the outbreak of war, leaving her with enough debt to make life difficult. I had always felt a tremendous sense of loyalty to Mrs. Birch; it was her shop that Louisa took me to in order to learn how to cut patterns, sew appliqué, embroider, crochet and design my own fashions. She had also been very helpful over the years in providing me with various fabrics, cloth, buttons and sundry materials that took my fancy. Without her advice I would not have had the confidence to start my own business.

"It's the absolute least I can do for them. It's all I can think about. I want to help them in every way I can."

"We all feel the same." She said, nodding enthusiastically. I saw my opportunity.

"Martha told me that your business has suffered in recent months."

A look of shock passed her face, which she quickly absorbed. "It's to be expected, Miss Goldhurst. People have got to watch what they're spending; folk have got more important things on their minds than nice clothes. I don't blame them; the men are away, so who's going to admire their frocks?" She chuckled mirthlessly. "Two of my girls have left to be munitionettes - two very experienced girls who I thought were loyal to me. They said they wanted to be more involved in the war effort, but the truth is they're being paid almost double what I can give them, and they're working two and a half extra hours each day. Emma has had to leave to help her sister out with her nephews and nieces and I had to let poor little Kathy go - I couldn't afford another 'prentice with things as they are."

The poor woman looked close to tears. In all the years I had known her I had never seen Mrs. Birch cry, not even when her husband passed away. I had always admired her unyielding pragmatism.

"I was expecting the war to be over by now and things back to normal. Now I have no idea what I'm going to do. I owe two months' rent on the factory, I can't afford to pay the girls that are still here and I haven't even been able to buy gifts for Christmas." She suddenly let out a wail and sobbed into her hands. It was an unnatural sight - like watching one's father or older brother weep. I offered her my handkerchief.

"Mrs. Birch, I want to help you, I have a plan." I pulled up a chair beside her; she looked at me in puzzlement, tears still dripping down her face at a slug's pace.

"You know The War Office is granting contracts to private businesses to produce munitions, guns, heavy machinery and the like for them in their factories?"

She frowned, her face clammy and pink like a baby's, "Yes, Miss, what about it?"

"Well I've been making a few enquiries about doing the same, except for army uniforms and clothing instead of weapons. I wanted to make them at the house but you need a proper factory in order for the government to consider you for the contract. Mr. Goldhurst's not likely to let me convert the house into a factory, so I thought we could use yours and I could come and help you manage it."

Mrs. Birch blinked and stared at me, her mouth slack. "Miss Goldhurst, that's a very clever idea, but to be perfectly honest with you, I don't even think I'll last until Christmas, the bailiffs are coming to collect the rent this week and I don't have it, it's too late."

"No, it most certainly is not! I will pay the rent from now on. I thought I could be your business partner, just until the war is over and everything returns to how it was, and then I will bow out gracefully and let you carry on as you were."

"Oh, m'lady, I couldn't possibly let you do all that for me. It's not your problem to solve. I'm very grateful to you for even thinking about me, but it's my ship, I need to go down with her."

"Mrs. Birch, if you refuse my offer I will take it as a personal insult. You have done so much for me over the years - it's thanks to you that I know how to make clothes at all - and I would give away everything that I have before I saw your dress shop disappear." Emotion was rising in my voice and the poor woman was watching me with wonder. "As a child I used to look forward to coming to your shop so much. Even though my mother didn't approve of me spending so much time there, I didn't care, I just wanted to be around the clothes and the machines and the patterns," I smiled, "I owe you more than you know. Please let me do this one thing for you, please?"

Her lower lip began to quiver again and she stood, holding out her right hand for me to shake. "Thank you, Miss Goldhurst, or should I say partner?"

Elated after my meeting with Mrs. Birch, I forgot to collect Grace's new spectacles and had to turn back. I must have been an odd sight, grinning to myself as I strolled across Red Lion Square towards Mr. Smyth's shop. As well as helping a dear friend I couldn't wait to learn more about running a larger business. Like Charlotte, I had my own plans for the future, and they didn't involve marriage just yet. The previous evening, I had wanted to tell Charlotte how, after the initial hopelessness, losing our parents had made me feel stronger, more in control and more determined to rely on myself rather than Edward. I missed my parents; every day I wished that they were still here, but another part of me felt like I had been set free; although I would never admit it aloud.

Goldhurst Estate looked like an illustration in a children's book as the car trundled up the gravel driveway. Snow coated its every extremity, as well as the surrounding trees and lawns. The fountain was completely buried in a white cottony layer and Mr. Griffin had to slow down to a snail's crawl to avoid ploughing into it. I cleared my throat; it was dry and sore, which meant a cold was on its way. But I couldn't help but feel festive and began to hum some carols.

As we drew near to the front door I admired the wreath that Aunt Edith had given to us three Christmases ago; it was still as good as new. Our approach had been so slow and lengthy, Brooks had clearly seen the car coming and opened the main doors automatically. I thanked him and we stood admiring the decorations when Charlotte poked her head out of the library door. She was back to wearing one of her usual colourful gowns, but her expression was dark enough to make up for her betrayal.

"I told you you'd be back in colours." I smirked.

"Where have you been?" She yelled over my voice, "Grace is in a beastly mood and I don't have the time to deal with her."

"Do you ever have the time to deal with her?" I retorted, but she was already stomping away from me, into the drawing room. I sighed and asked Brooks to bring me some lemon and honey after I had spoken to Grace.

After checking the nurseries and finding them empty, I approached Grace's bedroom. It was eerily quiet. I held my ear to the door and knocked twice.

"Come in," came Martha's reply. I pushed open the door and gasped. The room was in such a state my first thought was that a wild animal had got into the house somehow. Milk, bread, cheese and fruit had been thrown across the room; the entire contents of Grace's wardrobe had been emptied onto the carpet, along with all her books and toys from shelves and boxes. Grace herself was crouched in a corner, a curtain of mousy hair concealing her face. She was rocking gently back and forth clutching something to her chest.

Martha held a finger to her lips and gestured towards the open door. We retreated into the corridor and she pulled the door until Grace could just be seen through a small gap. She spoke in a low voice, "She was in a complete frenzy about an hour ago, Miss; I've only just got her still and quiet, so keep your voice low, if you don't mind."

"What happened? What caused it?" I hissed.

"I thought there was something wrong with the food at first, that lot is her third helping," she indicated the food strewn across her room, "but it wasn't. It was because she couldn't read 'Little Red Riding Hood' on her own; she couldn't see the words properly. I tried telling her that she needs to wear her glasses, but she was so wound up she just went mad, I'm afraid."

"This could be a great opportunity to persuade her to wear them; it could work in our favour." I held up the brown leather glasses case, "I've got her new pair here, let me explain to her again why she needs to look after them."

Martha looked worried but nodded.

"Grace?" I pushed open the door and approached her slowly. She was in the same position, rocking gently, still holding what I now saw was 'Little Red Riding Hood' to her chest.

"Darling, the reason you can't read your book is because you need to wear your glasses. You see, this is why you can't keep breaking them, because you need them to see things properly. Here, I have your brand new pair, why don't you try them on and see if you can read 'Little Red Riding Hood'?" She stopped rocking, which I took as sufficient encouragement. I held the spectacles out for her to take. Slowly she reached out and took them, clasping them tightly in her hand. I looked round and smiled at Martha, who appeared to be holding her breath.

"Why don't you try them on?" I said to her, smiling. At that moment I don't know what I expected to happen. I knew that Grace hated wearing the spectacles and I knew from experience that when she was in a frenzy it was wise to leave her alone. But nothing prepared me for what happened next.

In the space of a few seconds she smashed the spectacles against the wall, causing several pieces of glass to become embedded in her hand. She then started howling uncontrollably, tearing out the pages of 'Little Red Riding Hood' and ripping them into pieces with her teeth.

Martha and I flew into action, trying to calm her. "Miss Alice, the chloroform's next door in the bathroom, over the sink!" She shouted. I ran next door to retrieve the bottle and some cloth.

When I came back Martha was wrestling with a wild mass of hair and flailing limbs. Grace was howling louder and louder; to a pitch that was almost unbearable.

"Quick, Miss, you know what to do!" Martha struggled to make herself heard over the din. I fumbled with the bottle and the cloth like an old woman, but didn't finish the task as I was knocked to the ground with a force I will never forget, the chloroform bottle sailed through the air and shattered somewhere out of reach. I felt my hair being pulled and my face being scratched by sharp little claws, all the while howling filled my ears so that nothing else could be heard. Was this a nightmare? It felt so unreal. I screamed and lifted my arms up to protect my face.

After what seemed an eternity the weight was lifted from my legs and the assault was over. I sat up, terrified and disorientated, looking for the door to escape. Instead my eyes fell on Martha, holding down a spasming figure. I stood up and saw immediately that Grace was having a convulsion. Her mouth was contorted into a macabre grimace, saliva frothed and dribbled down her chin. Her eyes were inhuman; I couldn't see her brown irises or dark pupils as they had rolled back so far. Her long, thin body shuddered and contracted as if an electric current passed through it.

I heard a new scream and turned to see Charlotte wide-eyed in the doorway. "Come on," I scrambled up and grabbed her arm, dragging her away. "We need to call the doctor at once."

Shortly after we called Doctor Scott, Grace's fit passed and Martha was able to put her to bed. She carried her into her own bed so the maids could clean up Grace's room. The doctor administered some medicine and tonic to calm her, but made it clear that she would need to be tested to discover what caused the seizure.

"Are you sure she hasn't suffered from fits before now?" He pushed his thin-rimmed spectacles onto the tip of his nose and looked at me over the top of the frames.

I shook my head, "Never. What do you think might have triggered it?"

"I couldn't possibly say for definite, but knowing Grace's need for stability and routine my guess would be that she is feeling an unprecedented amount of stress. Her life has been turned upside down with the upset of the war and then your parents passing away, people coming and going more frequently, it's bound to have had an impact on her more than anyone with a normal capacity to cope."

Doctor Scott had once described Grace as 'an enigma' - a confusing and unpredictable case. I knew he felt as powerless to help as the rest of us.

"I shouldn't have been so insistent on making her wear those wretched glasses. I should have known something like this would happen." I said miserably.

"Nobody is to blame for this, Miss Goldhurst. Not even doctors can predict these things, so don't blame yourself." He snapped shut the clasp on his leather bag. "Now, I can arrange the tests for you, if you'd like."

"Yes, that's kind of you. Is there anything we can do for her in the meantime? What can we do to reduce the chance of her having another fit?" I said.

"I would advise you to keep her as calm as possible, no excitement or loud noise, no sudden changes of any kind for the time being, and plenty of fresh air and exercise."

"That sounds easy enough. Thank you, doctor." Charlotte said, leading him out.

Nauseous, I retreated into the drawing room and collapsed onto the chaise longue. Closing my eyes I willed my parents to be there when I opened them again, my mother reassuring me that she would take care of everything. I wondered whether she had felt this guilty and helpless. Maybe she had suffered with these feelings for years, hiding them from all of us, not wanting to trouble us.

"Alice, are you all right?"

"Hmmm?" Charlotte loomed over me, a rare look of concern on her face.

"You should have asked Doctor Scott to look at those scratches. They look dreadfully sore!"

"They're fine; Mrs. Brickett bathed them for me. They look worse than they feel."

"I can't believe she attacked you like that! The howling was echoing around the entire house and when I came upstairs and saw you on the floor...I thought she'd killed you!"

"Don't exaggerate, Charlotte."

She ignored me, "And then when she was having the fit, heavens it was frightful! It looked as if she was possessed by a demon. You know, I think we should seriously consider a special hospital or asylum for her again. After what she did today, who knows what could happen? She could attack Sophie, or a guest; it's not safe."

I stood up so suddenly that blood rushed to my head and I felt faint. "No Charlotte! No, don't ever say that, do you hear me? She is not going into an asylum and that's not going to change. Ever. She's our sister and we need to look after her; she's our responsibility and we are not going to get rid of her because we cannot be bothered to look after her."

Charlotte's mouth hung limp in surprise at my outburst. "Don't get upset, Alice, I didn't mean to sound heartless, I...well...you have to admit we are somewhat out of our depth with her and I for one feel uneasy around her. She's become even more strange and violent since Mama and Papa died."

"Of course she has! Who could blame her? She's still a child and she's lost her parents. She doesn't understand why her life has completely changed, is it any wonder she's behaving the way she is?" I snapped.

"I see your point, but she has been like this on and off for years, it's just worsened over the past few months. Perhaps we could cope with her behaviour when our parents were here, but I honestly don't think we can cope now. Edward's away constantly, Sarah is no use to anyone; Lord knows when we will see Louisa and Miles again. And I don't plan on being here much longer myself, you know that." She glanced over at the drinks cabinet. "Do you want a drink? I'm going to have a sherry." I shook my head and sat down again. She strolled across the room and poured a large tot of brandy, which she gulped down, then a smaller glass of sherry. Although some of her words made sense I resented her attitude towards Grace. I turned away from her, feeling hopeless. Hot tears of defeat began to form.

"You know I'm only thinking of you, dear." She said, joining me on the sofa. I sniffed and she gave me her handkerchief.

"I feel such a fool, earlier today I was congratulating myself on how well I was coping without Mama and Papa, I felt so independent and strong; now I feel utterly incapable and I wish they were here. I wish Louisa and Edward were here so we could all be together again and the guilt I always seem to feel could be taken away."

Charlotte had her arms around my shoulders and pulled me close. "You have no need to feel guilty! Edward will be home tomorrow and we'll look into hiring an extra nurse for her; how about that?" She looked so pleased at her small suggestion that I found it difficult not to smile back.

"There, that's better! Now let's go and clean those battle scars properly, it could be worse, you could be on the frontline with my poor Henry."

Chapter Nine
5th March 1917, Stamford, Lincolnshire
Alice

The sewing machines whirred, theirs needles dancing, forcing the factory floorboards and windowpanes to rattle to the rhythm. I looked at the neat rows of women, all bent attentively over their machines and smiled to myself. I was proud of them, proud of their work and satisfied that I had proved Edward wrong.

We had received twelve large orders for army uniforms so far and business showed no sign of slowing. I had to employ eight more women to cope with the demand - fifty-five had applied for the positions.

There was a knock on the door of the small office. Without waiting, Edward entered, "Hello, Alice." He stopped to gaze at the machinists. "Looks productive, long may it continue."

"Take a seat, Edward; I've got the accounts ready for your inspection."

"When is this order due for dispatch?" He hung up his coat and hat and settled into the chair opposite.

"This Friday."

"And you're on schedule?"

"Ahead of schedule. It should be finished by five o'clock tonight."

"Hmmm, good." He nodded and pulled the account books towards him.

"Excuse me a moment, I'll tell Mrs. Birch and the girls to go for lunch." I said.

"How long do you give them?"

"Three quarters of an hour."

"Do they complain?"

"No, we negotiated a shorter lunch and two slightly longer tea breaks."

"Negotiated? No wonder half the women in Stamford want to work here!"

"They're human beings, Edward. If they're happy and feel respected they do their job better."

"An interesting philosophy." He smirked. I ignored him and went to stop the machinists.

"How much is their weekly wage?" He said as soon as I returned.

"One pound and six shillings."

He raised his eyebrows, "Is it wise to pay them that much?"

"They're working a fifty-two-hour week at least."

"They're earning more than some of the men in the area."

"And why not? The work is equally important and equally demanding. These women are skilled machinists so I'm paying for their expertise."

"All right, Alice, save your suffragette speech. Just don't put it up any more, will you?"

"Why not?" I asked, folding my arms and raising my eyebrows.

He stared at me for a few seconds then slowly lowered his eyes, "Because there'll be trouble with the men. The wage you're paying these women is on a par with, and in some cases higher than, the wages of some of my men. I don't need them finding out about it and protesting."

"Your factories are miles away. How could the men find out about it?"

"Easily, you can't be too careful about these things. You're doing a good job but there's still a lot you don't know about business. And don't forget I'm still your boss, you need to impress me and if I were you I wouldn't adopt such a sanctimonious tone."

I wasn't sure whether he was joking, but knowing Edward's caprice, I apologised. "If you've read those books properly you'll see that there's plenty I know about running a successful business, though."

He looked down and nodded, "Yes, I admit these figures are impressive." He sat back in the chair, "But this is a small business, it's quite different running a national or international business successfully." He smiled and winked pompously at me, inviting me to challenge him. I smiled back, holding my tongue. I still needed to keep him on my side; he could disband the business whenever he chose.

After a few minutes he closed the book. "A nice profit you're generating here, I'm impressed. You'll have more than enough to resume your dressmaking after the war."

"Thank you. I've decided to give the profits to a charity, though."

He looked up, startled.

"I know you won't like it, but I don't need the money and nor do you. I want to help the returning men and their families. It's the least we can do."

There was a long pause before Edward spoke, "A wonderful idea, Alice. I support you wholeheartedly!"

"You do?"

"I've been to France, remember, I fought, I know what it's like." He twitched his shoulder to remind me. "Furthermore, no one will be able to accuse Goldhurst and Son of profiteering. It will reflect very well on the family business."

I wrinkled my nose. I hated the idea of people assuming I was doing it to gain credit for Goldhurst and Son. "All right, well, I'm glad you approve."

"Alice, you're doing a solid job here, I can see this factory is in capable hands. I was dreading coming here this morning; I thought I would have to spend hours sorting out the books." He stood up and retrieved his hat and coat, "who would have thought you'd become such a good businesswoman! You were always such a dreamer when we were younger and terrible at arithmetic as I remember."

"I've improved since then." I was not about to tell him that Mrs. Birch had helped me.

"Oh, by the way, can you make sure you're back by six o'clock tonight?" He said.

"Why?"

"That chap, Doctor Clancey, is coming to see Grace."

I groaned, "Are you sure he's qualified? Have you checked his history?"

He waved a hand at me, "Yes, yes, of course. His qualifications are very impressive - educated at Oxford."

"I thought he was American?"

"He is, originally, but he's lived in England since he was sixteen. He's the best so far, I can tell."

The last thing I wanted was another pushy quack trying to make money from my sister. "I hope you told him he's not to use any electric shock treatment. I'm not letting him wire her up like Frankenstein's monster. It's inhumane."

"Don't worry; he doesn't do that sort of thing. He's a psychotherapist, deals with the mind, talks to his patients a lot. He worked with some of the Russian royal family." He looked over and read my face instantly. "Listen, I don't want you being rude to the fellow, it's taken a good deal of favours to get him here. That judgemental face will scare him off."

"It's difficult not to be sceptical. There have been so many of them and none have been any good for her. Is he really going to be the answer to all our prayers? I doubt it. What's the point?"

"All I ask of you is to keep your mind open and your mouth closed." He said, clearly losing patience.

"Edward!"

"Just be there to support your family, please?"

I sighed, "I'll be there, for Grace's sake."

"Good." He opened the door, a peal of soft, female laughter floated into the office. He closed it again. "I must talk to you about Charlotte later as well. I won't keep you now; your women will be back soon, their three quarters is nearly up." He tapped his watch.

Mrs. Birch returned just as he let himself out. Both acknowledged one another perfunctorily.

"So, did we pass, Miss Goldhurst?" She joked when he had gone.

"With flying colours, thanks to your help with the accounts."

She clapped her hands together, "And did you tell him about the charity idea?"

"I did and he was very keen, thankfully."

Mrs. Birch smiled, "We should have that order done by half past four at the latest." She hung up her coat.

"Excellent. Send the girls home as soon as it's finished. I have to be home by six o'clock tonight."

"Anything interesting happening?"

"Oh, not really. My sister is back from London and I like to get the news from her." I lied.

"That's something to look forward to then." She said leaving the room.

Doctor Clancey arrived at half past seven. He had caught the same train as Charlotte, who I assumed would find no pleasure in travelling with a dull, bookish doctor. This was not the case, it seemed, when they walked through the heavy oak doors into the hallway. Charlotte was laughing and throwing her head back in mirth; the doctor politely stepped back to allow her to enter first but she whirled around away from us suddenly, hissing in his ear, "For Heaven's sake don't tell them what I just told you, Doctor Clancey! It's a surprise!"

Judging by the way she was tottering towards me, I guessed she had had a few drinks on the train. She had never mastered the art of discretion when drunk.

After greeting us over-zealously, Charlotte retreated upstairs to change for dinner, "I have some *very* exciting news for you all!" She called over her shoulder as she wobbled towards the staircase. "Remember what I said, Doctor Clancey?" She winked so obviously at the beaming doctor that I winced with embarrassment, before click-clacking noisily up the stairs, weighed down with gold and pearls.

Edward threw me a look of panic. Although we hadn't managed to talk about Charlotte yet, I knew what was coming.

"Good evening, Mr. Goldhurst, it's a pleasure to meet you." Doctor Clancey held out his hand with confidence for my brother to shake. Faint as it was, there was an unmistakable hint of American in his Oxbridge English. It was a calm, self-assured voice, the voice of one who speaks for a living and has confidence in its own proficiency. I liked it. I was not expecting such a voice, nor was I expecting him to be so young. He couldn't have been much older than Edward. The first thing I noticed was his skin and his teeth. The teeth were like polished pearls; not a hint of disrepair could be seen in his mouth. His skin was golden and formed a perfect contrast to the whiteness of his teeth. No wonder he smiles so much, I thought to myself.

Edward was introducing me to him. I smiled self-consciously, without baring my teeth, which were only an average shade of white.

"Pleased to meet you, Doctor Clancey. I do hope you can help our little sister." I said, noticing his eyes for the first time. Both were a cloudy blue, but the right iris had a dark brown patch covering roughly a quarter of it. I tried not to stare, but found my eyes drawn back to the spot. I searched his face for other anomalies and found none. His rich brown hair sat obediently, thick and coiled at the front. The only hint of his age was the delicate imprint of furrows that I now traced across his forehead.

"It's a pleasure to meet you, Miss Goldhurst, I've heard a lot about you. And don't worry about your sister, I will look after her."

Despite my best efforts my eyes roved back to the dark brown spot. I was staring so much that I began to feel tears. I blinked and looked away quickly.

"I'm sure you will." I said. "Please excuse me; I must get ready for dinner."

"I thought you were ready?" Edward said.

I blushed and lied unconvincingly, "No, no, Edward, I haven't quite finished getting ready yet, won't be a moment."

I hurried away from the two men as the doctor called, "Perhaps we can talk more at dinner."

And dinner was uncomfortable. Sarah barely ate two mouthfuls or said three words together owing to a headache and sore throat, whereas Charlotte, still mildly drunk, was making her opinions known on all subjects from the progress of the war, to whether the French Riviera was a better holiday destination than the Italian Lakes. She had informed the entire table that Doctor Clancey could not serve on the frontline because he was partially sighted in his right eye and interrogated him on his family, his upbringing, his marital status and his leisure pursuits. Although I disapproved of Charlotte's impertinent prying, I was just as keen to find out more about the man. His remaining family lived in New Hampshire and in Surrey; he was born in New York and moved to England when he was sixteen years old; he was unmarried; he enjoyed fishing and playing the piano. I could tell my brother was irritated with Charlotte, but disliked the idea of berating her in front of a guest.

"So, tell me about your work, Doctor Clancey," I said, trying to add some decorum, "my brother speaks very highly of you, but I must confess, I don't know anything about your methods."

He set his magnificent eyes on me and grinned. I swallowed, desperate not to show too much interest. "Well, Miss Goldhurst, I suppose the word I would use to describe my methods is: humane."

I turned to Edward quickly and narrowed my eyes. His face remained blank and he shook his head. He had obviously tutored this man to say what I wanted to hear.

"You mean you don't use electricotherapy?" Charlotte interrupted.

"Electrotherapy." I corrected.

He laughed good-humouredly, "I do not. Nor do I restrain the patient or use any physical force. Mainly, I use a modified form of psychoanalysis."

"Like that fellow Freud? Was it Freud?" Edward said.

"Yes, I do apply some of Freud's theories to my practice, and Carl Jung's, although not all. It's important to tailor one's methods to the needs of the patient rather than blindly following a popular theory."

"And what is your success rate? Have you managed to cure many patients?" Edward pressed.

"You truly would be a miracle worker if you managed to cure Grace!" Charlotte guffawed taking another hearty gulp of wine.

Edward turned his attention to her, barely able to hide his disapproval. "Right, you've had your fill of wine, Charlotte."

"Oh, Edward, you're bringing out the champagne are you? How awfully generous!" She teased.

His face reddened, "You're embarrassing me and everyone else at this table." He turned to the footmen, "bring her a glass of water." The two men looked at each other nervously. One nodded his head and scurried out of the room.

"Why don't you come up with me now, Charlotte? I'm feeling a little under the weather so I'm going to retire for the evening." Sarah said, her voice quiet and thin. The gentlemen stood, but she waved her hand delicately to halt them. "I'm fine, Edward, I just need some rest. Are you coming, Charlotte?"

"No, you go ahead, Sarah, I'm waiting for dessert."

Edward placed his hand on the table heavily, "You can have dessert, but absolutely no more wine. It was reckless of you to drink so much on the train, especially when you knew we had a guest."

Doctor Clancey apologised for causing upset. My heart went out to him. He was so gallant and amiable; I hoped he would be good for Grace.

Charlotte snorted, "Please spare me the honourable, brotherly concern, Edward. You won't be able to boss me around like this when I'm married." The footman had returned and placed a large glass of water in front of Charlotte. She looked at it in disgust.

"When you do marry your husband can regulate your drinking, until then the happy task falls to me, so drink that water and calm yourself down, for God's sake."

"Ha, well it's going to be a lot sooner than you think!" She exclaimed.

"What?" He shot back.

"My marriage, Henry proposed to me yesterday and I accepted!" She grinned and raised her glass to the astonished table. Water slopped over her lilac satin gloves and I winced. "Here's to marriage and freedom!" She announced slopping more great drops onto the tablecloth as she drank.

An uncomfortable silence permeated the dining room as my brother's face grew redder. "Go to bed, Charlotte. We will discuss this in the morning." I looked down and noticed his fist clenching and unclenching. I looked at her, my eyes pleading her not to argue.

She rolled her eyes and exhaled dramatically. "Fine, I will go to bed but there's no point in discussing this in the morning, unless you want to wish me well and help me plan the ceremony. There's nothing any of you can do to change my mind. I love Henry more than I'll ever love anyone; he's the only man I want for a husband and he feels the same way about me. To keep us apart would be cruel and a waste of time as we'll always find each other. Our love has survived a war after all! I know you don't like him, Edward, but it doesn't bother me in the slightest. I know when you get to know him properly, and not through city gossips, you will grow fond of him too."

"Go to bed." He repeated, rubbing his temple.

"Good night, everyone." She tottered towards the door, making a point of glaring defiantly at Edward as she left with Sarah still hovering in the doorway.

The raspberry pavlova arrived in all its splendour but remained virtually untouched. Edward brooded and my heart was beating with humiliation.

"I'm terribly sorry about that, Doctor Clancey." Edward finally said when the footmen had finished clearing away the plates. "All these sisters to deal with," he shook his head. "Sometimes I wish I had another brother to help me with them all! Alice here is a very sensible young woman, though, thank God." He put a patronising hand on my arm.

"Maybe Miss Goldhurst can help me tomorrow when I speak to Grace?" the doctor said, turning to me.

"Oh...yes I will help, of course, if you really need me to help." My eyes were dancing in their sockets, avoiding his gaze.

"I usually ask a family member to be present at the first few interviews and observations, a family member who knows the patient well."

"Martha would probably be of more help than I will. She's Grace's carer; she's spent almost every day with her since she was a baby." I said, fiddling with my bracelet.

"I would like Martha to be present, but I will need a family member as well."

"Would you mind, Alice? Sarah and I may be busy with Charlotte in the morning. Besides, you know Grace better than I do; you have the best relationship with her out of all of us."

I could resist the gaze no longer. Doctor Clancey was smiling at me, his eyes full of hope, full of kindness and promise. I swallowed, "All right, what time would you like to start?"

"I want to stay here. I don't want to meet him." Grace sat on the floor of her bedroom, her back hunched, her gangly legs drawn into her chest and her face buried in her skirts, so that her words barely penetrated the fabric buffer.

"Now, that's very rude; he's travelled an awfully long way just to meet you. The least you can do is say how do you do? Where's the harm in that?" I failed to persuade her.

Martha sidled into the room giving me a sympathetic smile. "Did you get the..." I whispered into her ear. She patted her pocket to indicate the chloroform bottle.

"Come on, Grace. If you're a good girl and come to meet Doctor Clancey I promise we can visit the farm today."

The body wailed and sighed; Martha knew how best to bargain with her, "When?" She lifted a serious face and looked at her.

"After luncheon."

Grace turned her face away from us, considering this offer then jerked up suddenly, as if someone had pulled her strings.

"Or, the Mid-Lenten fair is in town, we could go there!" I exclaimed.

"No!" she cut me off, "the farm!"

"All right, bossy boots, the farm it is, but only if you're downstairs in two minutes."

Her tuneless humming echoed around the hallway. The house was empty; Charlotte was still in bed and my brother and Sarah had taken Sophie to see her grandparents.

"It's jolly nice of Edward to be so supportive." I muttered.

"Sorry, Miss?" Martha whispered.

"He invited this doctor here and asked only for my support, yet here I am dealing with him on my own." I glanced at Martha, "with your help, obviously. And he said he was going to talk to Charlotte about this silly engagement of hers and he's disappeared for the day."

"Hello, there!" Doctor Clancey's voice rang out hearty and warm in the draughty space. He had caught me off guard and I blushed.

"Hello, Grace, my name is Doctor Michael." He held out his hand ceremoniously. I stared at him, until I realised that he was using his Christian name. "There's no need to be nervous or afraid, I'm simply going to talk to you, your sister and Martha."

Grace looked through him as if he wasn't there, rocking lightly on her feet ignoring the proffered hand. Doctor Clancey slowly withdrew it and beamed.

"Shall we go into the sitting room?" I began to lead the way; Doctor Clancey followed and Grace allowed Martha to guide her towards the door after us without presenting any signs of struggle.

As I expected, Grace was reticent during the first meeting, which lasted half an hour. She answered Doctor Clancey's questions with as little detail as possible and only when prompted by Martha.

After Martha had whisked her away I found myself apologising to the doctor, "Please don't take it personally, she rarely talks to strangers and finds it difficult to make eye contact with anyone, even her own family."

He smiled once more and changed chairs so that he was closer to mine. He smelled of soap and musk, lighter than the one my brother wore. I glanced his way and instantly remembered his peculiar iris. Again, I tried to avoid staring.

"You need to stop apologising for your sister's behaviour; I see people with mental illnesses every day; it's my job and I know what to expect. I don't want to see Grace on her best behaviour, I need to see the real her otherwise it's pointless my being here." He spoke steadily and reassuringly. I enjoyed listening to his soft tones.

"You can't have gained much from her answers."

He smiled, "On the contrary, I wasn't really concentrating on her answers as much as her behaviour during the interview. I have noticed many significant things and your family's doctor is sending me a copy of her medical record, which I'm sure will prove useful. I would like to visit her once a week at the same time, if you and your brother will allow me to."

"Here, every week? Are you sure you have the time for that, Doctor Clancey? You must be very busy; are you not based in London?"

"I am, but the train journey is fairly swift. Besides, I came here with a view to helping your sister and I believe I can, but I can't begin to make progress until I build some sort of relationship with her; she has to trust me, she has to get used to me. Is Saturday afternoon convenient?"

"Saturday?" I looked at him, confused.

"To visit her?"

"Oh, yes, of course. Thank you. My brother will be fine with that arrangement."

"Good. Now, I wonder if I could trespass on your time a little longer, Miss Goldhurst? Could you tell me a bit more about your sister? How old is she, firstly?"

"Fifteen. Sixteen in July."

"And what about her habits, her interests and so forth?"

I dared myself to look at him. The features were just as handsome as they had been the night before: he exuded warmth and confidence. I couldn't decide whether I wanted to spend more time with him or to flee with embarrassment.

I swallowed before responding, "Well, she adores animals. In fact, she wouldn't have left her bedroom this morning if Martha hadn't charmed her with the promise of a visit to the farm this afternoon."

"Really? Where is this farm?"

"It's only a few miles away. The farmer knows Grace and Martha; he doesn't mind them visiting for a look at the animals now and again. Martha usually buys some produce to bring back for the cook as payment."

Doctor Clancey nodded, "Would Martha and Grace mind if we accompanied them this afternoon? It would be a wonderful chance for me to get to know her and observe her behaviour discreetly. We could have a talk about her at the same time."

"Oh, um, that sounds...possible, I suppose."

"I'm sorry, that was presumptuous of me, you must be busy."

"No, I'm not particularly busy today; I didn't want you to put yourself out. Like I said, you must be occupied with your other patients."

"It's no trouble. In truth, I take any opportunity to walk in the countryside. I grew up surrounded by farmland so I enjoy spending time outdoors."

"As long as you're sure, we'll leave straight after we've eaten."

"Tremendous!" He announced, beaming. "Excuse me, Miss Goldhurst, I have a few notes to write up, would you mind if I used the library?"

"Not at all, I'll see you at luncheon."

I stood awkwardly and retreated upstairs, my heart pounding. I had never been so anxious around someone. I felt a desire to impress him and was disappointed with myself for failing to appear interesting or intelligent or even pretty in front of him yet.

A half-completed dress lay across the table next to my sewing machine. I ran a hand along its length - burgundy cotton with a black satin trimming. I glanced at the clock on the wall - eleven o'clock. Luncheon would be served at half past twelve. I sat down at the machine to finish the dress.

Grace skipped towards the farm gate with the grace of a crane fly. Her bonnet was askew and her boots already bore a layer of dirt. The land was open and the wind was fresh and strong. With a hand, I shielded my eyes against the gusts and the low-lying sun. The farm buildings had been rebuilt recently and Grace seemed familiar with the place, running straight towards the sheep pen; she had forgotten about us already. The baas soon rose a note in protest at the intrusion. Martha strode ahead to supervise.

"She seems very content now," Doctor Clancey observed, "what a transformation!"

I followed his gaze to where Grace was standing waving at the sheep from a safe distance. "As I said, she adores animals, especially farm animals, for some reason. As long as she's pleasing herself she is perfectly lovely. When she's made to do something new, or something that she doesn't want to do she can be quite formidable."

We approached the sheep pen in silence. Martha was coaxing Grace towards the pig sty. Once they were out of earshot again, Doctor Clancey said, "Has your sister shown any violent tendencies in the past?"

My heart ground to a halt then leapt forward. Had Edward mentioned anything?

"If you don't mind my asking, that is."

"She can be violent, but only when she's frightened." I inclined my head towards the pig sty, "much like these animals, I suspect. She isn't malicious, she only lashes out when she feels threatened or suffers a convulsion, when she can't control herself."

The doctor nodded, "And what, may I ask, happens when she suffers a convulsion or lashes out? Is she restrained?"

"Martha normally pacifies her before it gets too dangerous. Doctor Scott has prescribed some medicine to help control her seizures, but if all that fails we usually have to resort to chloroform. I don't like the idea of it...sometimes it's the only way."

"Do you know what causes the seizures?"

I shook my head, "She's had tests but the doctors can't tell for certain. Stress, perhaps, that's all we know."

"Hmm, I will talk to Doctor Scott about her medication. There may be some alternatives we can try."

As we watched Grace gambol around the farm in bliss I answered Doctor Clancey's questions as faithfully as I could. By the end of the visit he knew all about her daily routine and habits; her diet; her favourite game, storybook, toy and place; her academic aptitude and difficulties; her response to my parents' deaths and her reliance on Martha.

When we returned to Goldhurst Estate he thanked me, with all politeness, for my help, but I had one last question for him.

"Have you come across any other patients like Grace? I mean, anyone with similar ...behaviours and habits?"

He met my eyes and smiled reassuringly, "Yes, many patients I have worked with have exhibited similar cognitive dysfunction. Don't get me wrong, no two patients are exactly the same in terms of their...." he trailed off, "behaviour, but yes, I have seen this type of psychosis before."

I nodded. "And these others, how did they cope moving into adulthood? Did any of them progress enough to live a normal life? Or are they all..." I waved my hand at the house in front of me, "trapped, living with their relatives or in mental hospitals forever?"

Sensing my anxiety, he placed a hand on my arm. It was warm, despite the wind, firm yet gentle enough not to cause alarm. "Don't worry. Your sister will still be able to live a happy, fulfilling life. It will be a different sort of life to yours and mine, but it will be satisfying to her." He withdrew his touch and led me into the house. His presence was so comforting; I felt I could trust him. "She's a very lucky young woman to have such a caring family; it pains me to admit it, but not all of my patients have such a good life."

"There you are!" Charlotte strode towards us, "don't tell me you dragged poor Doctor Clancey to the Lenten fair!"

"No, we went to a charming little farm, actually." He smiled.

Charlotte's jaw dropped then she laughed. "That awful farm?"

"I enjoyed it," he answered immediately, "I love the outdoors."

Defeated, Charlotte changed the subject, "Are you staying for dinner? You're more than welcome."

"Thank you, but I'm afraid I must get back to London. I planned to catch the half past four train from Peterborough."

"Our driver will take you as soon as you're ready." I said

"That's very kind, thank you, Miss Goldhurst. I will be back next Saturday at two o'clock to see your sister."

"She hasn't scared you off, then?" Charlotte giggled.

"Of course not." He replied, smiling. "Excuse me ladies, I must finish packing." He brushed past and up the stairs.

Charlotte waited until he had gone before hissing "Where the devil is Edward? How could he leave us to deal with all this? Honestly, the selfishness of that man!"

"Us?" I said incredulously.

"Mind you, a part of me is glad; he would only try to lecture me on how much he disapproves of my engagement. He can stay away for the whole weekend for all I care!"

"He should be back for dinner." I said, but she seemed not to hear.

"So, why is he coming back next weekend?"

"He wants to visit Grace once a week at the same time. He doesn't want to overwhelm her with treatment too soon."

"He's going to spend his weekends travelling up to Rutland? Edward must be paying him a grand sum!" She laughed, "Still, I'm not complaining, he's terribly good-looking. I'm sure that hasn't escaped your attention, Alice." She grinned mischievously at me; I blushed.

"Is that all you think about, Charlotte? I thought you were madly in love with Henry?"

"Oh, I am! But I can still think a man is attractive." She winked lasciviously, "American too. If I wasn't madly in love with Henry I would probably like to marry an American. They are so charming and handsome."

I shook my head and headed upstairs. "I'll see you at dinner, Charlotte."

"Aren't you going to wave bye-bye to the dashing doctor?"

"I'll leave him in your capable hands." I called without turning around.

"Oh no, no, I wouldn't dream of depriving you of that pleasure; especially as you went to the trouble of making a new dress just to wear to a dirty old farm!"

Doctor Clancey visited Grace every Saturday for four months. Although Martha acted as her chaperone during their treatment sessions, he would often ask me to join them or speak to me in private to discuss the progress they had made. I saw no tangible difference in Grace at first, but by the third month she was noticeably calmer and talking more coherently.

In myself, however, there was a significant change. Doctor Clancey dominated my thoughts; when I wasn't thinking about him I was worrying about how often I thought of him. Terrified as I was that Edward, or worse still, Clancey himself, would notice my infatuation, I tried to keep a respectable distance. However, at times, our being alone was unavoidable. During those moments I tried to detect a hint of meaning in every look, every wave, every word that passed between us, yet I could never tell with confidence that he felt anything for me other than polite interest. Whenever we seemed in danger of drifting towards affection he would find an excuse to change the subject or leave. Charlotte was the only person who seemed to comment on my preoccupation for the doctor, and she only ever mentioned it to tease me for her own amusement.

Following a session in July, Doctor Clancey informed me of his attempts to encourage Grace to make more eye contact. "It will be a challenge for her, but I am optimistic."

I was grateful for any chance of speaking with him alone, "It will be a challenge for both of you; Grace has never made eye contact with strangers and she rarely does so with her family. We've grown used to it, I suppose."

"Her ability to make eye contact is crucial if she is to cope with adult life."

I looked away, embarrassed with myself for being flippant about her defect, "Yes, indeed, forgive me, I didn't mean you shouldn't...I'm sorry."

"You must stop apologising, Alice." He laughed. "I'm going to charge you a shilling every time you try to apologise!" It took me a while to realise that he had addressed me as 'Alice'. My heart jolted. "Miss Goldhurst." He corrected, standing up awkwardly. He must have seen my red face and thought he had made a faux pas.

"I must head back to the station." I tried to hide my disappointment. We hadn't spent much time together on this visit.

"Won't you stay for tea?" I tried.

"I'm terribly sorry, but I must get back." He smiled an apology and headed for the door. "Your sister tells me that you're coming to London this week."

I brightened, "I am, our cousin is getting married and I'm making the dresses. It's the fitting on Friday."

"Your family's very lucky having such a talented dressmaker at their disposal."

I felt my cheeks burn afresh, "They certainly like the convenience of it; I enjoy designing and creating. It suits us all."

"What about your own wedding? Would you make your own dress?"

I looked into his face with its perpetual smile and mirrored it, "I suppose I would like to, yes. I can't say that I've thought about it before."

"Well, if you get tired of fitting dresses I would be honoured if you would join me for dinner on Friday."

I froze. My feelings wavered between elation and dread, "That's very generous of you, but I'm not sure what Charlotte has planned for us."

"Actually, I bumped into her at the theatre a few days ago and mentioned it. She said you didn't have any prior engagements. She is invited as well, of course." He added.

"Oh, in that case we would be happy to join you, thank you very much."

His lips expanded into a magnificent grin, "Wonderful! I will contact you with the arrangements next week." He tipped his hat and fairly bounced out of the library.

"Grace seems to like him, as far as I can tell. He's very patient and gentle with her." Before leaving for London I asked Martha to give me her honest opinion of Doctor Clancey. "He understands her more than the others and certainly captures her imagination..." She paused and narrowed her eyes as if searching for her next words.

"So, do you think she's making progress?" I prompted.

"Oh yes. She's having fewer fits and bouts of anger, certainly."

"That's good, isn't it?"

"Oh yes." She said again.

"What does he usually do with her on Saturdays?"

"Well, he does some breathing exercises, then they sing a song, he reads to her, occasionally he gets her to read to us, he asks her to draw, we sometimes walk to the lake. A few weeks ago we went into Kinwell and he tried to get Grace to buy some bread from the baker's. Mostly they just talk, though."

"What about?"

"Anything, really, erm, last time it was about God, they have spoken about the war, your parents and animals is usually a popular choice." I nodded. "I think he's very good for Grace. I wouldn't exactly say she looks forward to their meetings but she certainly doesn't resist him like she has done with all the others. She trusts him."

I smiled, "Thank you, Martha you've been very helpful."

She looked relieved that the interview was over and headed for the door.

"Oh, have you heard word about your brother?"

She spun around, "Ah, no Miss, not since his last letter home."

"I expect he's too busy to write, or the letters are taking longer to reach England." I smiled.

"Perhaps...yes you're right." She said clasping her hands together.

"Try not to worry, we only received one letter from Edward when he was in France, it's frightfully slow."

"I can imagine." She shifted uncomfortably before adding, "Enjoy your time in London, Miss."

Poor Martha. Her brother had not written for three months and she was obviously worrying herself sick - she always looked pale and serious these days. I would have to send her back to Derbyshire for a few days when I returned.

The train journey to London had never been enjoyable for me. It was a cumbersome necessity, a tedious trial before the rewards of the metropolis. On this occasion though, the train became a place to sit and dream. I pictured myself in the finest gown I had brought with me: mauve with an indigo satin trim and appliqué on the back . It was the first time I had worn it since the outbreak of the war and I had had to ask Miss McEvilly, my maid, to clean and iron it. Doctor Clancey would greet me - handsome - in an immaculate black dinner suit. He would listen and be fascinated by everything I had to say and he would speak with eloquence about everything from food to foreign travel. He would admire my dress and compliment me on my talents, encouraging me to pursue my dreams. He would fall in love with me tonight, and, for the first time, I would allow myself to show the depth of my feelings for him.

"A doctor's wife," I muttered to myself. It was strange and thrilling to think of it. My parents, God rest them, would have been appalled; Edward would be displeased. Charlotte would giggle and say 'I knew it'. Could I face them? True, I had never envisioned being a doctor's wife, would the life suit me? True, he wasn't like an ordinary doctor, not like Doctor Scott, but he didn't have the wealth or the family connections that my parents would have insisted on. But what did that matter now? All that elitism seemed so insignificant during the war.

By the time I reached King's Cross Station I had convinced myself that we were perfect for one another. Above all, I knew he wouldn't prevent me from pursuing my business ambitions after the war; he was a modern man, indeed. Furthermore, he knew Grace and wouldn't object to her living with us one day. If things went well this weekend, how long would it be before he proposed? My face glowed with the thought; exhilarating yet terrifying.

The only flaw in my fantasy stood on the platform crossing her arms impatiently - Charlotte. She would be there too, she had to be, but how I wished she wasn't.

She hurried towards me, an agitated peahen in her chocolate brown coat and hat.

"You're late."

I looked down at myself in mock surprise, "I'm sorry, I didn't realise I had miraculously turned into a train on the way here." I smiled to myself at the thought of getting married before her; she would be livid.

"Ha ha, you're quite the funny woman. Come on, I have a surprise for you!"

I groaned, "I don't like your surprises. No one likes your surprises except for you."

"Bosh! I'm the queen of surprises! Come on, the car's outside." She grabbed my wrist and dragged me towards the exit.

"Charlotte, wait! Miss McEvilly..."

"What?"

"My maid, she's getting the bags."

Charlotte emitted a sigh to rival the stationary train's, "For goodness sake! I'll be waiting in the car."

Once Miss McEvilly and the bags had been safely deposited, the driver whisked us through the streets of Central London. It was a relief to be back; I sat in silence, digesting the scenes appearing before me. London was so alive and on show. Every building couldn't simply be a building; it was a story, a painting, a song; justifying its right to be here. Likewise, each person moved and spoke with a different manner and air, people here were confident and ambitious. I felt a wave of jealousy towards them: they were part of it, I was not.

"I may have had a shop around here by now, had it not been for the war." I thought aloud.

"That's very selfish of you! My poor Henry is risking his life in the name of freedom and you're wittering on about a shop! Anyway, you've got a whole factory now; I'd say you've done pretty well out of this war; it's made you rich."

I winced, "Don't be ridiculous, I told you I'm giving all the profits to charity."

"How very noble of you," she sniggered, "if I were you, though, I would use the money to buy a shop here after the war, if it means that much to you. You'd be able to dine with Henry and me every week."

"Well luckily you're not me. The profits are going to charity and I will start from the beginning. I've done it once before and I didn't have any experience of managing a business then."

"How middle class of you!" She said, popping a cigarette between her lips.

I raised my eyebrows in derision, "Our ancestors were *working* class."

She curled her lip, "Only on Papa's side."

A few minutes later we arrived at a familiar street in Knightsbridge. "This is Louisa's house, why have you brought me here?"

Charlotte grinned like an excited child, "We're staying here! On our own!"

"What, are you sure? How on earth did you persuade Miles to agree to this?"

"I told them you needed your old sewing machine to make alterations to Cousin Miranda's dresses, and that you were bringing Grace and Martha with you." She grinned, pleased with her story.

"I don't like you using me in your lies." I said.

"Oh please, I can tell you are just as excited about it as I am. Now, come along, we need to get ready for dinner, I've invited some of Henry's family and friends, and the cousins, of course, you know they'd be griping tomorrow if I didn't invite them."

"They're all coming here for dinner? Are there going to be enough servants?"

"Alice, do you take me for a fool? I've arranged all that." She exhaled a plume of smoke and grinned. "Stop worrying and go and get ready. Enjoy yourself; you're not in your factory now!"

We both stepped out of the car, Charlotte leading me confidently into Louisa's house. "Oh, I invited your sweetheart, Doctor Clancey." My eyes widened like a startled deer's; Charlotte laughed. "Unfortunately he was out of town tonight, but he's very much looking forward to our dinner tomorrow evening." She gave me a crude wink and I blushed.

"Do shut up, Charlotte. Let's concentrate on tonight's dinner first, shall we?"

The following morning I left without Charlotte, who was still in a deep, wine-induced slumber. It was a relief to have some peace, her voice was still ringing in my ears from the night before; cackling at every question or comment that she didn't listen to properly and assumed to be a joke. Being around Charlotte was tiring, Cousin Miranda and I concluded at the dress fitting, "But not as tiring, perhaps as being Charlotte!" She giggled, "Oh, we shouldn't laugh at her, the poor thing has taken your parents' deaths extremely hard."

I looked up from my work, "You honestly think that's why she's such an exhibitionist? No, Charlotte's been like this for years. When we were children she would pretend to be ill to get more attention. Once she even lied that a boy from the village bit her arm so everyone would fuss round her; it later transpired that she bit herself! The poor boy got such a smacking for no reason!"

"Oh, poor Charlotte!"

I snorted and stood up to inspect the dress, "There, that should do it, just don't lose any more weight before the wedding."

"Ooooh, thank you so much, Alice, it's beautiful, I hate taking it off!" She gushed. "Enjoy your evening tonight with Doctor..."

"Clancey." I said.

"And please be nice to Charlotte." I rolled my eyes but promised her I would, "unless she pretends one of the waiters bit her!"

That evening Charlotte was running late for dinner. After twenty minutes of arguing I headed to the restaurant angry and alone with Charlotte's unreliable assurance that she would meet us there in half an hour.

Doctor Clancey greeted me with a smile full of warmth and a kiss on the hand that sent a shiver up my arm that I prayed had gone unnoticed. For once I was grateful for Charlotte's tardiness, perhaps she was trying to play cupid and had planned this after all.

We worked our way through apologies and pleasantries; he apologised for not making dinner the night before; I made my excuses for Charlotte's late arrival.

"I'm afraid I won't be able to visit Grace tomorrow. An old colleague of mine is visiting from New York and tomorrow is his last day in town. I'm dreadfully sorry."

"Please don't apologise, you've done so much for Grace, you're more than entitled to a reprieve." I said, smiling and taking a sip of wine.

"Thank you..." he leaned in closer, "am I allowed to call you 'Alice'?"

My cheeks burned and I looked away, "Yes, you can if you like." I muttered.

"Would you like me to? Only I don't want to make you feel uncomfortable."

"It's fine with me, I won't feel uncomfortable." His cloudy eyes were all I saw, the dark brown in his right iris seemed to pulse and shine with each beat I felt in my chest. For God's sake, Alice, compose yourself, I thought, taking a longer sip of wine for courage.

"Do you miss America?" I asked.

"The States? I suppose, in the same way I miss London, or Paris when I'm not there. It's been so long since I lived there I don't regard America as my home anymore. It's always nice to see old friends, though. Have you ever visited?"

"No, we had all planned to visit my sister in New York, but after what happened to my parents I wouldn't dream of it until peacetime."

He nodded, his eyes softening in sympathy, "It must be hard being separated from her all this time. Perhaps when they develop aviation you will be able to travel there on a passenger aeroplane."

"Oh no, I don't think I'd ever be brave enough to try that!"

"A friend of mine took me to watch the Wright brothers once. It was quite fascinating; I'd love to try it one day."

The waiter brought us a bottle of champagne and I tried to avoid the lure of his gaze again as we watched it tinkle and fizz delicately into the glasses.

"You shouldn't order things like this, it's not necessary."

"You're my boss, I want to impress you!" He joked. I blushed and looked around the room to check that Charlotte hadn't arrived. At least half of the men were wearing army uniforms and I suddenly felt guilty drinking the champagne.

"It seems so strange being here, enjoying myself, when thousands of men my age are sitting in dirty, water-logged trenches as we speak, facing death or injury. If it wasn't for these men in uniform, you wouldn't realise there was a war going on tonight." I shook my head, "I feel so ashamed sometimes."

"Why?" Doctor Clancey leaned in again, his eyebrows raised in concern.

"Because I can't do more to help, because I feel so helpless and pointless. I see all these posters ordering men to go and fight for their women, and I know it's just propaganda, but some men truly believe they have a duty to fight for us all. I hate to think of all those men going through hell for me and others like me."

"Alice, you shouldn't think like that. Men join up for many reasons, not just because they think it's what women expect of them. Anyway, you of all people have no need to feel ashamed. Look at what you've done for the war effort. You're donating an incredible sum to help these men." He glanced around the room. "How many others here can place their hand on their heart and say they've done their bit?"

"I know all that, but I also know that I will never truly understand what these men are going through, there's always going to be that divide. Edward never talks about the war because he knows we won't understand. It hurts me that there's nothing I can say to ease the pain of his memories."

He placed his hand on top of mine; it was warm and comforting; I looked up at him, "Every day I see men returning from France wounded, traumatised and angry. But I've yet to find one who blames a woman for what has happened. Most men want someone to listen to them and help them return to normality. Some of my patients tell me that it's love alone that helps them to keep going." His face was so close I could see a tiny image of myself reflected in his eyes. I recognised his cologne - light and musky. Perfect. "Believe me, no man is going to be disappointed with a woman who is sympathetic and caring." For an alarming moment I thought he was going to lean in and kiss me; my heart was beating its way out of my chest. Instead he cupped my hand in both of his.

"Alice, I was wondering, would you..."

His sentence was interrupted by a bejewelled Charlotte, who was bustling towards our table at a great speed. I looked down at our hands and yanked mine away from him before she could see.

"Doctor Clancey, I'm so sorry I'm late." She heaved herself into a chair next to him. "Champagne! How wonderful!" The waiter poured her a glass. "Let's toast!" She raised her glass in the air.

"What would you like to toast?" Doctor Clancey said, back to his easy smile.

"Us three, of course!"

"How about the men fighting on the Western Front?" I said.

"Oh, yes, my poor Henry. To Henry!"

"And all the other men out there." I added. Our glasses clinked and I noticed Charlotte's dress properly.

"You're wearing my dress!"

Charlotte started and began to giggle. I realised then that she had already been drinking. "Oh, I hoped you wouldn't notice! I had nothing suitable and I knew you wouldn't be wearing it tomorrow."

"It's exquisite." The doctor nodded in approval.

"Thank you." Charlotte simpered. "Have you ordered anything yet? I'm ravenous after the day I've had."

Two hours later Charlotte's laughter was once again ringing in my ears. I longed for another moment alone with Doctor Clancey, but Charlotte's barrage of questions, anecdotes and laughter had drained me of all hope.

"Alice," Charlotte addressed me suddenly as I stifled a yawn, "Cee Cee and Vera have invited us to meet them at a music hall on King's Road." She turned to our companion, "You should come with us, Doctor."

"That's very kind, but I have to be up early in the morning. You ladies enjoy yourselves, though." He said fixing his eyes on mine.

"No, Charlotte, I'm tired after last night and I need to catch the train tomorrow." I leaned closer to her and lowered my voice, "I don't think you should be drinking in some London music hall with people you barely know either, especially after last night."

She moved away from me and laughed, "I'm sorry, mother! Come on, sis, you need to let your hair down - no work tomorrow!"

"Charlotte, please..."

She set her wine glass down with a thud and huffed, "If you want to go home, suit yourself, but I'm going to meet my friends and have some fun." She stood up and headed for the door.

"She's driving me dotty at the moment. She just won't listen." I whispered. Doctor Clancey put a steady arm around my waist.

"I know you want to protect her, but I don't think you're going to win. Is a driver meeting you here?" I nodded. "I'll come with you and after he's taken you home I'll make sure she meets her friends inside and ask the driver to wait outside for her."

I dared myself to meet his gaze. I wanted to run a finger along his smooth cheek. "That's so kind of you."

"It's my pleasure." He smiled and led us both out into the rain soaked London night.

The shrill note of a woman's laugh drifted through the window, rousing me from a depthless sleep. I glanced at the ivory wall clock. Two o'clock in the morning. The woman's laughter continued, accompanied by the hint of a man's voice. Now conscious, I realised the voices were closer than I first imagined. I sat up and looked around the dark room. The bridesmaids' dresses were still hanging on the back of the wooden screen like elegant spectres; pearls, pins and spools of thread in varying shades of cream lay undisturbed on the dresser. I was so tired that I had fallen asleep on top of the quilt; perhaps I had drunk more wine than I thought. The woman's laughter sounded once more then came to an abrupt stop. Silence. Drowsy, yet in no mood for sleep, I moved across to the window. I had not drawn the curtains and only the nets protected the room from the jaundiced glow of the electric street lights. I eased the flimsy net aside; a couple of inches were enough. The first thing I noticed was a large black motor car sitting patiently by the curb, directly in front of the house next door. I frowned; I didn't recognise it.

I drew the net curtain aside a further inch and noticed a man and woman tied together in an embrace close to the car. I squinted; they were just beyond the glare of the streetlight, making it hard for me to identify them. The man wore a dark suit and hat, blocking his face completely; the woman had her back to me. Eventually they pulled away and the woman giggled again. The man grasped her hand and pulled her body towards his again, kissing her passionately before releasing her. I realised before I saw her face that it was Charlotte. Her tipsy giggle gave her away first, then, as she moved into the circle of streetlight, I caught sight of my purple brocade skirt. She turned around and blew a coquettish kiss at the man, who had not yet moved. He reciprocated by removing his hat and bowing slightly, he said something to her, but he spoke so softly I couldn't decipher any of it. Charlotte giggled irritatingly and called, "Goodnight, Doctor!" I breathed in. My heart pounded. I couldn't blink, my eyes shot towards the man again. It couldn't be him, it must be somebody else. Although I could see no more than his silhouette, I knew. His height, frame and clothing matched. I knew it was my Doctor Clancey.

I stood back, my legs suddenly felt too weak, too fragile to hold my body and I sat down heavily on the edge of the bed. I stared at the carpet and held both hands over my heart to try to prevent it from galloping faster and faster. I felt faint. I focused on the carpet; night had stolen its usual crimson hue, replacing it with black. Everything was coloured with shadows.

Downstairs the door opened and slammed; the car roared into life outside and drove away. I waited and listened in the darkness. The clock ticked faithfully; Charlotte tottered drunkenly beneath the floorboards where I sat; something somewhere hummed languidly and my heart slowly returned to a monotonous beat. I lay back on the bed and closed my eyes, waiting for the blackness to cover me.

"Trafford, could you call a cab to take Miss McEvilly and I to the train station in half an hour? McEvilly is just packing; I'm afraid I didn't give her much notice."

Mr. Trafford, the butler, frowned but complied, bowing courteously. I didn't know the man well enough to offer him any further explanation for our premature departure.

I had risen early, at five o'clock, and packed my cases right away. I needed to get away from the place, but the first train didn't leave until half past nine.

I was glad of my old sewing machine which offered some distraction while I was waiting for the cab. I began altering the maid of honour's dress, thinking of nothing except the hammer of the needle and the resistance of the wheel. I passed ten minutes in blissful monotony until a screech cut through the beautiful, steady noise of the machine, "Why the hell are you making so much noise at this time in the morning? What *is* wrong with you? Why can't you sleep like normal people?"

She was wearing a white cotton bed jacket, her hair hung wild about her shoulders. I hated her.

"For God's sake, Alice, the wedding's not for two weeks, have you got nothing better to do? Something that doesn't involve waking me up at this beastly hour."

"Quarter to nine, you mean? It's not my fault you dragged yourself back here at two o'clock in the morning, drunk and roaring like a common alley cat. You weren't so bothered about getting some sleep then, were you?" I spat the words at her, I couldn't help it.

She blinked, unprepared for my tone, "What? No one woke up last night...and it wasn't two o'clock..."

"Wrong on both counts. You woke me up and it was definitely two o'clock."

"Well I'm sorry I woke you, now can you please stop rattling on that machine for a couple of hours. If we're meeting Miranda for luncheon at one I *need* to sleep..."

"I'm not going anywhere with you, I'm catching the half past nine train to Peterborough."

She narrowed her eyes and scratched her head, "What? Why?"

I stood up, my eyes boring into hers, my fingers twitching with anger, I wanted to rush across the room and shake her, "Because I don't want anything to do with you!"

Charlotte bridled at my display of anger, but recovered herself and smirked. She was more adept at arguments than me. "For God's sake, Alice, what's the matter with you?"

Her nonchalance was infuriating, "You disgust me, the way you can just lie so easily and deceive me, Henry, yourself."

Charlotte narrowed her eyes and laughed mockingly, "I have no idea what you..."

"I saw you kissing Doctor Clancey on the street last night."

Time seemed to slow. Charlotte's smile drooped and she furrowed her brow, "I...I..."

"All that rubbish about how much you love Henry, how he's the only man for you..." Charlotte prepared a reply but I raised my voice, "lies! All of it. Does your fiancé know that he's marrying a *slut*?" Her mouth dropped open. "Of course he doesn't, he's conveniently out of the way fighting the Boche in France, which leaves you free to throw yourself at every man that buys you a drink. You're a drunken whore and I'm ashamed to call you my sister!"

My heart was thumping so fast my ears were ringing. I breathed heavily, unable to tear my eyes away from my sister who now stood cowed near the door.

"My cab will be here soon, please remove yourself from my sight until I've gone."

Charlotte's head had dropped to her chest and she covered her face with her hands, sobbing. I felt no pity, only revulsion. "I used to worry that *Henry* was the one not to be trusted, that he was going to be unfaithful to *you*." I hissed, "it's him I feel sorry for now; you don't deserve his love."

"Alice," she murmured, lifting her head.

"Shut up! Just go!" I shouted. In the hallway beyond the door I heard nervous whispers and pattering feet.

"Alice, please, listen to me!" She begged, moving closer. Her face was contorted and slick with tears. "It didn't mean anything, it was a mistake, I've never done anything like that before and I'm ashamed...I love Henry!"

I laughed with mirth, "No you don't! You don't know how to love anyone except yourself."

"I do, I do! I was stupid, I shouldn't have drunk so much, I didn't know what I was doing, he kept buying me..."

"Stop! You need to take responsibility for your own shameful behaviour. You're forgetting I was there last night, I saw you flirting with him, along with every other man who gave you a smile or a drink."

"All right, I was drunk; I probably flirted too much, I regret that; I won't do it again, but you can't tell me I don't love Henry; I do, more than anything!" She exploded with a fresh batch of tears and sobs. "I...I've been so lonely...I miss him....I suppose I was just flattered by the attention, it reminded me of being with Henry." She sniffed and dabbed her eyes with the sleeve of her bed jacket. "I don't expect you to understand."

I clicked my tongue impatiently, "I'm not interested in the slightest. Save the feeble excuses for your *fiancé*. I have to go."

I cut the thread and gathered up the dress. Charlotte blocked the door. "Please, Alice, I know you hate me, but please, please don't tell Henry!" Her eyes were wide and earnest.

"What?"

"I know I've behaved awfully and I promise I will not even look at another man again. Please, promise you won't tell him!"

"Your selfishness is astonishing! You really do only care about yourself. I would be doing that poor fool a huge courtesy if I told him what you're really like."

She folded her arms defiantly, "Why are you doing this? You're my sister! Did that doctor really mean so much to you that you're willing to destroy two people's happiness to get revenge?"

The venom inside me rose slowly and terribly, "How dare you! *You* are the one who has destroyed your relationship, not me!"

She saw my weakness and badgered on, "I knew you liked him, that's what this is all about, isn't it? You're jealous because he preferred *me* to *you*! Pathetic! He's only a doctor; you should really aim a little higher." She stood up taller, her hands on her hips, gaining confidence, "But who can blame him? How could any man possibly enjoy the company of a boring, plain, spinster seamstress?"

The venom inside me was burning the edge of my temper and ignited my arm into action. My hand propelled forward and delivered a hard slap across her right cheek. The force of it sent her falling to the floor, gasping. It shocked me almost as much as her, and I instinctively stooped to see if she was all right.

"You lunatic! I can't believe you hit me!"

"You deserved it!" I spat, standing up straight away. "Since we were children you've been selfish and vile, tormenting me, ridiculing me, putting yourself first, I'm sick of it! I thought after our parents died we could support each other and finally put our differences aside, but you're worse than ever! Drinking, flirting, and showing us all up in public..."

"That's rich! When did you ever make an effort with me when we were younger? You always acted so superior to me and locked yourself away with your damn sewing machine! I tried to include you, but you were so haughty and difficult all the time. Are you honestly surprised that I drink and go out so much? Nobody in this family even talks to me! Edward's never around, his wife's crippled with illness, Louisa's in America, Mother and Father are dead, Grace is...well, mad, and you disappear to your factory every time I come back. I'm lonely!" She wailed.

"Plenty of people are lonely but they don't behave the way you do." I said.

"I beg your pardon, m'lady," there came a timid knock at the door, "your cab's arrived."

I nudged Charlotte away from the door; she was still clutching the right side of her face. "Don't hurry back to Goldhurst, will you? You won't be welcomed." I rushed out of the room without waiting for a response.

The next day I approached Edward in his study to speak to him about the deceitful doctor.

"What about him?" He said, without looking up.

I swallowed and tried to regulate my voice. Separating the emotional from the rational had never been my forte. When I didn't reply immediately, Edward looked up, concern on his face, "What is it?"

"I-I don't think he should continue to visit Grace. She's making little to no progress and, to be frank, why waste time and expense on something that isn't working?" I blurted.

Edward frowned, "I thought he was doing a good job? I recall your last account of him was glowing, was it not?"

I blushed, "Yes, I was impressed with his impact on Grace at first; however, it has been weeks since I've seen any real improvement, or new methods. I think he showed us all he has to offer within the first few sessions." My heart was beating hard in my chest.

My brother lowered his head and squeezed his lower lip between his fingers, the way he did when he was deep in thought. He looked at me, "All right, if you think that, but this all seems quite sudden, Alice. Are you sure there isn't more to this? Something you're not telling me?"

I felt my face burn. Did he know? "I don't want to embarrass you. You can tell me, you can trust me, I'm your brother!" He smiled and patted my hand awkwardly. "Did he...you know...did he make a pass at you or something?"

I looked at him quickly, shocked by the suggestion; Edward reacted immediately, "I knew it! That swine! Sarah said weeks ago she thought he was enamoured with you and I dismissed it..."

"No, no, Edward, he didn't make a pass at me."

"Are you sure? Don't feel ashamed, my dear, you're not the one in the wrong." He looked back at me suddenly, "My God, he hasn't hurt Grace, has he?"

"No, no, nothing like that, but I must admit I don't feel comfortable around him and I don't want him around our sister, either."

"He must have done something, then, to make you feel like this. You were fond of him before."

"I was, he's a friendly, charming sort of man, but I don't trust him. I saw him in London this weekend and, well, I didn't approve of his behaviour."

"Why, what did he do?" Edward looked serious.

"He...drank rather a lot and was quite...flirty with myself and Charlotte. I thought it most unprofessional and I don't want to see him again." Much as I despised Charlotte for what she had done, I couldn't bring myself to tell Edward the truth. Or anyone, for that matter.

Edward snarled and turned away. "I knew it! How dare he! I shall contact Oxford and the hospital that he's working for and tell them about this. A man of his position ought to control himself." He paced over to the window and poured himself a large draught of port from the decanter. "Bloody Americans! Uncouth lot, I tell you. They need to learn how to conduct themselves amongst decent people. He's not in the Wild West now!" He drank quickly and poured another. "Does he think because you don't have parents that you're unprotected? I'll show him!"

It struck me how much he looked and sounded like our father. "Edward, please don't write to the hospital. By all means, get rid of him, but don't cause trouble for him elsewhere. He has always been very good to Grace and he deserves some recompense for that."

"You're too forgiving, Alice. His employers need warning. Who's to say he won't behave despicably elsewhere with another honest family? He may prey on another impressionable young woman...No, it's my duty..."

"Then at least let me write the letter? I know the details better than you and I don't want him to lose his job. He doesn't deserve that."

"Of course he does! He's abused his position and behaved inappropriately around two respectable young women. Of course he should lose his job."

"Please, don't, he is working with soldiers, remember. If they dismiss him will there be anyone to take his place? I know what he did was wrong, but no real harm has come of it. He made a mistake, which I'm sure he regrets; he doesn't need to lose two jobs."

Edward took another long gulp of port and placed the glass on the sill. He gripped his lower lip once more in thought.

"I'm sure you've made mistakes that..."

"Oh for God's sake, Alice, of course I've made mistakes, who hasn't? But I would never have behaved as brazenly as he has." I cowered slightly; an involuntary act when my father used to shout. "There are some things you don't understand. It's my responsibility to look after you all. Father would never let that Yankee cad get away with treating you like that, and neither will I."

I felt tenderness towards my brother for the first time in years. I smiled at his protective gallantry, despite his obstinacy.

"You don't have to worry about us all the time. You're our brother, not our father and, believe it or not, we can look after ourselves. I will write to him explaining that he should not come anywhere near Goldhurst Estate again."

Edward started to work himself up into another tirade so I hurried on. "I will also inform him that he should leave the country at the earliest opportunity after the war, otherwise we will expose him as the opportunist he is to his employers and to as many respectable families in England as we can."

Edward looked at me suddenly; a smile slowly diffused the animosity on his face and he began to laugh, "Brilliant! That will teach the scoundrel."

I smiled, "So you don't need to worry about Clancey, I will deal with him."

He sighed, "Yes, if you wish, but let me see that letter before you send it." I nodded and rose. I felt exhausted and longed to be alone.

"Will you tell Grace?" He said.

Grace. I hadn't thought about the impact it might have on her. I felt a stab of guilt, "Oh, yes I will."

"It's a shame, she's lost another doctor. Still it can't be helped." He turned back to the decanter. "I'll see you at dinner."

I turned to go, but remembered, "Edward, I would appreciate it if you didn't tell people about this. It's...a little embarrassing."

He waved a hand to silence me, "I won't mention it, of course."

"Thank you." I said and slipped upstairs.

I could smell the Mansion Polish as soon as I entered the room. My sewing machine and the gramophone had been dusted too, the latter shining with renewed vigour. Both seemed to glow with excitement at my return and beckoned to be used once more.

Their presence was comforting; occupation was the best way to forget the unpleasant business of the last few days. If I kept as busy as possible, the memory would fade before I had time to dwell on it.

Carefully, I unfolded the bridesmaid dresses and hung them from the back of the wardrobe doors. When I had finished them I planned to start on the bridal gown and finish the maid of honour's. There were at least twelve guests who had requested bespoke dresses, and the wedding was less than two weeks away.

The only music I had was my father's old copy of Mozart's Requiem, which now filled the room, transporting me to the simple world of childhood as my fingers eased the fabric through the needle and the presser. I imagined myself in my bedroom with my mother and father downstairs, as it used to be. Absorbed as I was in my own escape, I didn't notice Martha had entered the room until she was in front of me. I jumped, narrowly missing a pummelling stab from the thin needle. Her mimed apologies looked quite comical with the powerful orchestra providing the backdrop. I lifted the needle on the second machine and broke the spell.

"I'm sorry, I'm so sorry, Miss Alice! Are you hurt?"

"No, no, I'm fine, Martha. What did you want?" Her face was bloated and patchy with salty tears. "Lord, what's happened? Is it Grace? What's she done?"

She shook her head, "Grace hasn't done anything, it's...I received a letter from my mother." She sniffed.

"Oh no, is she unwell?"

"My brother, he's missing in action, he has been since May but the letter's been lost in the post." I stood dumb, turning the information over in my mind. I wasn't surprised, the women in the town had spoken about men they knew going missing in France and Belgium. It was an unbearable fact of war.

"You mustn't think the worst, my dear." I said.

"I may never see him again." Her mouth quivered. I thought of my parents; my father's gramophone winked from the bureau.

"You must go to your mother. I'll ask Griffin to drive you tomorrow morning. Take as long as you need, I'll see to Grace."

"Oh no, no, I couldn't ask that..."

"Nonsense, besides, you're not asking me, I'm telling you to go and be with your family. They need you. Now go and pack."

"I can take Grace with..."

"No you won't. I said I'd look after her, she'll be fine."

"Miss Alice, that's incredibly kind, thank you..."

"You don't need to thank me, please, go and pack, I'm giving you the night off."

Tears pooled in her lower lids, "I-I'll write you a few notes about Grace - her routines and what not before I go."

"Don't burden yourself..."

"I insist, Miss, you may need it."

"Thank you," I said. She smiled tremulously and sniffed, I followed her to the door.

"Your brother just told me Doctor Clancey won't be coming to see Grace anymore."

My face fell, I had just managed to blot him out, "That's right. He-he's terribly busy and I don't think..." I trailed off. For some reason I hated lying to Martha.

She nodded and smiled sympathetically, "It's probably for the best."

"Yes," I said, "I daresay it is."

Chapter Ten
30th October 1918, Goldhurst Estate, Rutland
Alice

Ghostly. The only way I could describe the factory was ghostly. Each machine was covered under its own black veil, creating a procession of miniature pall bearers; the floor and the sills were starting to gather a film of dust, slightly thicker each time I visited. The motes trickled down the faint insinuations of sunlight that escaped through gaps in the window blinds. The most ghostly aspect, however, was the quiet. Not long ago the place had droned and danced with activity - voices, hammering needles, feet on pedals and scissors on khaki - now all gone.

"Good morning, Miss Goldhurst, you're early." Mrs. Birch beamed at me with her comforting pink face as she walked through the factory door.

"I thought I'd take one last look at the place. The end of an era, one could say..."

"Aye," she shrugged off her black coat and unloaded her bag on an empty table top, "but just think what the future has in store for you. Have you thought any more about your dressmaking business?"

"I've thought of nothing else." I walked across to the window, pushed the flimsy blind aside and glanced down to the small delivery yard. It had never been a pleasant view. "Although I can't make any definite plans until the war comes to an end properly."

"That won't be long, thank the lord. But, if you need to be in London couldn't you stop with your sister and her new husband? They're setting up home there, aren't they?"

I grimaced, "Perhaps I'll visit them now and again but I can't imagine anything worse than living with Charlotte and her husband. And I'm sure the feeling's mutual!" I laughed.

Mrs. Birch looked at me, puzzled, "I find that hard to believe, you're one of the most pleasant young ladies I've met."

"You flatter me, Mrs. Birch! Charlotte and I have always had...a fraught relationship. My older sister and her family are set to return to London from New York after the armistice so hopefully I can stay with them whilst I'm establishing myself there."

"Sounds like you have it planned out. Your brother and his family will miss you, though, and little Grace."

"Yes, but I will be back some weekends, I daresay. The baby's due in December so I'll wait until he or she is a few months old before I commit to anything. That's if it's all over by then."

Mrs. Birch's eyes drifted wistfully around the room, "Ah, life goes on as it always has."

"Are you certain you want to sell up? It's not too late to pull out." I said.

She smiled and shook her head. "I'm too old to start all over again; I'll leave that to young'uns like you! Besides, my daughter and grandchildren need me."

"When do you leave Stamford?"

"This Monday." She said whilst reaching for her bag. I suspected that she didn't want to see the business she had nurtured for over ten years transformed into a car factory in a matter of weeks.

"Since this may be the last time we meet, I wanted to give you this as a thank you for everything you've done for me." From her bag she proffered a little box.

"What's this? You shouldn't have troubled yourself." I opened the little box to find a blue velvet pin cushion spiked with gold dressmaker's pins, some of which were topped with tiny pearls.

"I ordered it from a hoity toity tailor's in London back in 1906 – that was our best year so I thought I'd treat myself. I thought you could get some use out of it."

"Mrs. Birch, this is far too generous. You keep it, or give it to your daughter; it must be worth a lot."

She held her hands up and shook her head, "Please accept it, Miss Goldhurst. You saved me from ruin; I'd never be able to retire now if it weren't for your kindness. This is only a trifle compared to what you've given me."

I looked down at the pin cushion again and smiled, "I think we've helped one another. I will miss you, partner, but I hope you'll write to me often and who knows, our paths may cross again one day."

"I hope they will, Miss." She beamed and held out her hand, "The best of luck with your business."

"And to you." We shook hands and parted ways.

I couldn't bear to linger any longer amongst the abandoned Singers, but since only boredom awaited me at home I decided to walk back along the river. The day was unseasonably mild and the water looked beautiful bathed in the autumn sunlight. The leaves underfoot formed a dense, crackling carpet and those still crowning the trees were resplendent in all their October glory: flaming red, ruddy bronze, tawny yellow, dusky orange…I vowed to bring my watercolours to The Meadows before the November chill arrived.

The further I headed away from the town, the more peaceful it became. After walking for an hour or so I stopped on a quiet little bridge about an hour from the house and stared at the water below, listening to the soft susurration of a tiny waterfall underneath. A few ducks swam languidly upstream, propelled by a sudden gust of wind which almost blew my hat into the river. The letter I had received from Louisa yesterday was still inside my coat pocket so I took it out and perused it again, smiling at her funny stories involving the children and cherishing the gentleness of her prose. I had never heard Louisa utter an unkind word about anyone; she was the only person I told about Charlotte and Clancey and, in true Louisa fashion, she persuaded me to forgive Charlotte and not to cause trouble for her and Henry. It had been more than four years since I had seen Louisa, Miles and my nephews and niece. Moira would be fifteen by now, just two years younger than Grace, though their futures could not be more different.

I hurried on in the direction of Kinwell, daydreaming about my future. Edward had promised me that he would loan me as much capital as I needed to establish myself and would help me to rent a shop space and hire staff. He had even gone so far as to offer to be my business partner, he had that much faith in me, he said. Although I was grateful, I told him that I wanted to be as independent as possible. I smiled to myself. With his support I had much to look forward to.

Chaos greeted me when I arrived home. I had chosen the wrong day to walk the five miles back to the estate rather than taking the driver. Housemaids and footmen scurried in and out of doors with anxious expressions. Mrs. Brickett rushed my way and ushered me into the morning room.

"What on earth's going on?" I demanded. She wrung her hands and asked me to sit. "Oh God, it's Grace, isn't it?"

"No, Miss Alice...it's Mrs. Goldhurst, she's lost the baby."

I stared at her for a long time and she stared back at me. I sank onto the sofa. The silence was broken only by the noisy ticking of the clock. I hadn't noticed how loud it was before.

"I'm so sorry, Miss."

I tried to swallow but my mouth was dry, "Is Sarah all right?" I managed to croak. It was a stupid question but I couldn't think of anything else to say. I wanted to be alone to take it in.

"Doctor Scott's with her at the moment. We've called her family; her mother and sister are on their way."

I turned to her sharply, "What about my brother? Has anyone told him?"

"Of course, Mr. Brooks telephoned straight away. He's on his way back from London." She looked a little affronted by the sharpness of my tone, but I didn't care.

"Thank you, Mrs. Brickett. Please send Doctor Scott to me after he's finished. And can you ask the maids to make up the guest rooms?"

She nodded, "Of course, m'lady", and bustled out.

I watched the clock's minute hand creep its way around the face ever so slowly. The ticking seemed to grow louder and louder until I could bear it no longer. I rang the bell and asked Gordon, the second footman, to take it away and destroy it. He looked at me in shock but bowed and scurried from the room, the clock in his hands, when he realised I was serious.

Silence swept the room and I stared at the thick red Persian rug. The garish circular patterns blurred and moved in time with the ticking that still sounded in my ears. Another baby dead. A third tiny ghost to haunt

Goldhurst Estate. I didn't want to see Sarah – what could I possibly say to her? The intensity of her grief would consume me and reduce me to nothing.

A soft knock at the door interrupted my quiet despair. Mr. Brooks led Doctor Scott into the room, bowed and closed the door behind him.

"How is she? What happened? She seemed fine when I left this morning." I cried, remembering how I had risen early and breakfasted alone. Sarah had only just woken when I announced my departure. "Perhaps I shouldn't have left her."

"It was a miscarriage, m'lady, the baby's heart was weak; there was nothing anyone could have done. It's a terrible tragedy of nature, I'm afraid."

"She must be heartbroken."

"Indeed. She's weak and emotional. I've given her something to help her sleep and, I hope you won't object, I've called two nurses to stay with her – one has just arrived."

"That's good of you, thank you, Doctor Scott. Won't you stay for tea?" I wasn't sure whether this invitation sounded crude given the circumstances, but convention prevailed in me.

"I won't, thank you, I need to get back. I'll return in the morning to see how she is. You have my details if you need me. And I'd advise you to let her sleep undisturbed for the next few hours."

I nodded and walked with him to the front doors. A large black undertaker's cart stood in the driveway. I turned away from it, ran into the morning room and vomited into an empty vase.

The clop of footsteps on the polished wood floor echoed louder until I heard someone call my name. Martha had her arms around my waist and guided me onto the sofa, taking the stinking vase.

"I'll ask Gordon to run and fetch Doctor Scott, I think he's still on the drive."

"No, no, Martha, I'm fine, really. I just need to sit for a moment." Grace stood by the door, clutching a knitted duck, staring at the vase in Martha's left hand.

"I'll fetch you a glass of water at least. I think Cook has a ginger tea recipe for an upset stomach. Grace, stay and look after your sister, duck."

Grace shuffled further into the room and slid onto the sofa, drawing her knees up to her chin, balancing the duck on the end of her feet.

"That's a nice duck, is it Jemima Puddleduck?" I smiled weakly.

"No, it's Jimmy." She said with a serious expression. "Why were you sick?"

"I'm feeling a little under the weather – it will pass though."

"Why was Doctor Scott here?" She continued, her expression still grave.

I inhaled and exhaled quietly; the nausea was passing. "He was here to see Sarah – she's very poorly. In fact, she lost her baby."

She frowned, "She's in the big nursery, isn't she?"

"Not Sophie, she lost the baby she was carrying. The same way Mama lost Gregory."

"Oh." She slithered onto the floor and began playing with her toy, quacking and lifting its wings.

"Gregory was a silly name." She said after a while.

"Hmm?"

"Is the baby going to be buried next to Gregory and Robert?"

"I expect so." I hadn't considered the funeral.

"Was it a boy?" I hadn't thought to ask Doctor Scott the child's gender either.

"I don't know, my darling."

"Do you think Martha will take me to feed the ducks?" I stared at her. Had she even understood anything?

"Here you go, Miss." Martha swept into the room with a bowl and towel and a steaming mug. Behind marched Gordon with a carafe of water and a large glass.

"Can we go and feed the ducks?" Grace jumped up and flung her toy into the air. Gordon caught it and handed it back to her.

"Not now, Gracie." Martha placed the bowl and towel on a side table and insisted that I drink the strange, brown spiced concoction in the mug. Gordon poured a glass of water, bowed and went out.

"Don't worry about me, Martha, I'm already feeling better. Perhaps Grace should have some fresh air." Grace was lying on her back on the rug, throwing the duck upwards and attempting to catch it with little success.

"Are you sure you're feeling well? We can stay with you, it's no bother, is it Gracie?"

"I want to feed the ducks." She whined. I assured Martha that I was fine. Grace's restless presence, in fact, was making me feel queasier.

"I'll tell Mrs. Brickett to keep an eye on you." She said. I thanked her and she led the quacking girl away.

Knowing Grace as I did, I was still surprised by her arbitrary reaction to the death of her niece or nephew. Although I didn't expect her to mourn in the conventional way, her response to Mr. Healy's death, her howling tears, moody silences, tantrums and depression proved that she was capable of expressing grief and sadness. So why didn't she grieve in this way for her family? It unsettled me.

Mr. Brooks knocked and entered. "I'm sorry to disturb you, madam, Mrs. Goldhurst's family have arrived. Shall I show them into the drawing room?"

I stood slowly and took a draught of water; the sickness had passed but my stomach was hollow. "Please do, Brooks, and could tea be served there in fifteen minutes?"

"Very good, madam."

I heard the great doors open and high-pitched voices awaiting my arrival.

Sarah's family stayed for several days before returning to Lincolnshire with Sophie. The poor girl cried for hours at a time, sensing the fraught atmosphere. Meanwhile, upon my suggestion, Martha took Grace to stay with her mother in Derbyshire for a week. This would allow Martha to visit her brother, who had been released from a prisoner of war camp in Germany, but I was also keen for Grace to avoid Edward, who lost all patience during times of emotional stress. Edward sat with Sarah for days, but it wasn't enough. On November the sixth, Sarah died. She had a blood infection that had gradually spread through her body and poisoned her from the inside out so that I barely recognised her.

My brother regressed to his former state after he first came back from the Front. He sat in his library or in his bedroom, refusing to speak with anybody, staring, like the living dead. After the second day he disappeared, returning only for Sarah's and George's funerals (I later discovered that the baby had been a boy).

Five days after the tragedy, the Armistice was declared across Europe. We must have been the most solemn house in the country; not one of us was in the mood for a celebration.

Chapter Eleven
5th April 1919, Goldhurst Estate, Rutland
Alice

By the time Edward finally introduced his mistress, Annabelle Tressider, to us at Goldhurst Estate her name had already achieved a level of infamy within the household. She was the mysterious woman with whom my brother had struck up a three-year affair whilst his poor wife's health slowly deteriorated. Just as Sarah's health failed her, so too did her husband's faithfulness. His absences became longer and more spontaneous until it was obvious that his heart was planted elsewhere.

Of course I disapproved of my brother's behaviour and, for a while after Sarah's death, he was overcome with guilt. He lost weight, couldn't sleep and disappeared for days, or even weeks, at a time. I never asked him directly about his mistress but I sensed that he had decided to give her up after his wife's demise, out of respect. A few months later, however, here he was formally introducing her, offering up the guest room next to Sarah's old bedroom with no trace of his initial shame.

I decided to reserve judgement when I met her. The same could not be said of Charlotte, who informed me that Miss Tressider was practically 'a social pariah' in London, where she lived, on account of her adulterous relationship with Edward (of which, I was told, *she* ruthlessly pursued *him*) and furthermore due to her 'conceited self-belief and ungracious attitude to others'. This coming from Charlotte meant little; she was not known for her open mind and was most likely threatened by a woman who was probably too similar in character for them to ever get along. Still, I was determined to prioritise Edward's happiness. After all, the war years had been particularly cruel to him and I was pleased that he had met someone who made him happy again.

The object of my brother's affections was, as I was told, from a wealthy family on her father's side but her mother was from lower middle-class stock, and had achieved fame as an actress before she married. Her story sounded very glamorous but was not without its scandal. Her father was a dedicated drinker and an even more committed gambler, leaving the family almost destitute after his death.

"Annabelle Tressider is a fortune-hunter and a social climber just like her unscrupulous mother. She dug her claws into some American financier, Mr. Boule or was it Bowler? I forget, but I do know that she remarried just seven months after her husband's funeral! Apparently it was just in the nick of time; they would have been out on the streets on account of her late husband's debts."

"You can't really blame the woman then. She was clearly just trying to save herself and her daughter. She didn't have much choice." I offered.

Charlotte gave me a look of disdain, "She didn't have to steal someone else's husband though, did she? He was *married* when she pursued him, the same way Edward was married."

I wasn't sure how to respond. The Tressiders' reputation seemed to precede them. I attempted to change the subject. "Has she inherited her mother's passion for the stage?" Charlotte rolled her eyes and pointed her nose skywards.

"She sings very badly, in my opinion, and plays the violin tolerably well. As for acting, the closest she gets to the stage is sitting in the *stalls* at The Empire."

"What does she look like? Is she pretty? Of course she must be otherwise Edward wouldn't..."

"He wouldn't have treated his family so abominably!" Charlotte interrupted in a shrill tone. "She is moderately pretty I suppose, but one tends not to notice when she opens her mouth - ghastly laugh! She wears far too much make up as well. I really don't know what Edward sees in her. What is it? What spell has she cast over him? I know he's not the most desirable husband in England, but he can certainly attract someone better than *her*." She spat out the last word with renewed venom.

I smiled at Charlotte's performance; she spoke as if her record of past behaviour was stainless. "Maybe he's in love?" I said. Charlotte spluttered on a mouthful of tea and stared at me as if I had slapped her. "Well, she must have some redeeming features. Perhaps we just need to get to know her better. I will judge for myself when I meet her next week."

Charlotte grimaced, "I can't believe she's coming here. You can do what you like but I've had more than my fill; I'm staying away. Oh, and trust me, she has no redeeming features so if I were you I wouldn't waste my time trying to discover them."

I witnessed Annabelle's charms, or lack thereof, for myself a few days later. I first glimpsed her out of a window at the top of the grand staircase. She was a beautiful figure - tall and graceful - walking towards the front doors with swan-like serenity, dressed in what looked like Parisian couture. Perhaps Charlotte was wrong; this woman looked charming enough.

"Annabelle, my dearest, this is my sister, Alice, and this is Mr. Brooks, the butler and the house staff." My brother could barely control his grin as he made the introductions. I smiled warmly and shook her hand.

"Welcome to Goldhurst Estate, Miss Tressider. It's so nice to meet you at last." She was not looking at me as I uttered my salutation. Her eyes roved the inside of the house, from the staircase, the ornamental vases, the regiment of housemaids and footmen, before finally resting on me. She looked me up and down and I noticed how heavily powdered her face was.

"Alice the entrepreneur!" She giggled and smiled delightedly at me. I bridled at the familiarity of her greeting. "I would just love to see these darling dresses Edward has told me so much about. They sound exquisite! Perhaps we could discuss it over dinner? I would love you to make one for me." She leaned in and spoke with the confidence of someone completely at home, addressing me as if I was the visitor, despite this being her first visit to Goldhurst. I felt myself getting flustered, wanting to impress her and just as I opened my mouth to reply she was already sweeping past me, pulling my brother along with her like a pet. Her manner towards me seemed so earnest and involving for a moment that the alacrity with which she shifted her attention elsewhere seemed like a shove out of the warm circle that encompassed her. I began to realise why Edward was so besotted with this woman; she was certainly adept at drawing one's attention.

"Come on Edward, I'm dying to see the rest of this beautiful house." With these words the servants began to scurry out of sight and off the couple glided towards the drawing room. As my brother gushed with Annabelle he strode straight past the nanny holding Sophie's hand.

"Edward." I called and they spun around, visibly irritated that somebody had interrupted their intimacy. "Sophie wanted to say hello to you." I moved across and rested my hand on the little girl's blonde head. She was holding onto her nanny's hand sheepishly, probably wishing she was back in the nursery away from the attention. Edward stared at her for a moment then, recovering himself, he grinned and scooped her up, kissing both cheeks with affection. Sophie craned her neck and looked back at Bridget, her nanny, who smiled encouragingly. Edward, sensing the girl's nervousness, let her down and began to ask the usual questions about whether she had been good, what she had been learning and so forth. I watched Annabelle's reaction to this display with keen interest. For the first time since her arrival I saw discomposure in her mannequin face. The mask had slipped momentarily. She looked around her for any means in which to claim back her lover, noticed me looking at her and smiled, back to her previous self-assurance.

"My, what a charming dress you have on, Sophie." She exclaimed. Sophie looked at her in shock and nestled against Bridget's side. "Did your Aunt Alice make it for you?" Annabelle's smile stretched taut across the lower half of her powdered face, undeterred by the child's reservation. Sophie said nothing.

"I made it for her last birthday. It's one of your favourites, isn't it?" I brushed one of the ringlets away from her cheek and tucked it behind her ear. It was time for me to rescue them both. "Sophie, why don't we go upstairs and finish that painting from earlier? We should leave your papa to show Miss Tressider around the house."

Annabelle seemed relieved; Edward said his goodbyes and kissed his daughter's wispy curls before leading his lover away, leaving me to stare after them.

The couple didn't surface again until dinner was served that evening. Annabelle had applied a thicker layer of powder, a generous smudge of colour turned her eyelids midnight blue and a brighter hue of red stained her lips. The scent of eau de toilette clung to the air, leaving me light-headed. She had changed into an outrageously tight burgundy gown with elaborate ruffling and silver beading.

"Good evening, Alice. This house is quite impressive, isn't it?" She trilled, smiling at me.

"Good evening, Annabelle. Yes, Goldhurst is one of the most beautiful houses in Rutland; although I am biased." I smiled back.

"That's a lovely gown", she pointed, "did you make it yourself?"

"Not this one. It was a present from my sister Louisa; it's from a dressmaker in New York."

Annabelle lifted her nose upwards, "For me, nothing beats Paris for couture, wouldn't you agree, darling?" She covered Edward's hand with her own.

"I confess I don't know as much about these things as you two ladies, but I gather the general consensus is that Paris is the best." He said.

"Precisely!" Annabelle said, triumphant. "Perhaps it's because my mother always had such fine clothes from the House of Worth; I grew up around the finest, you see, now nothing else will do!"

"Ah, yes, being on the stage I expect your mother must have had some grand costumes. Where did she perform?"

Annabelle narrowed her eyes and cleared her throat. "My mother hasn't performed for a great many years, not since she married my father. Anyway, Alice, I'm simply dying to hear about your dressmaking enterprise. Edward tells me you're quite the businesswoman these days."

She certainly shared Charlotte's habit of unsubtly changing the subject. As she stared at me, smiling, I blushed despite myself. Her look and tone were friendly enough but a part of me felt that she was mocking me and I felt the need to defend myself. "I confess I'm no Worth, but I am building up a reasonable clientele of London families as well as those around the county, some of whom have spread the word to relatives from further afield." Annabelle's face was locked into a sweet smile. "I have more than enough requests to occupy my time. Edward has been very generous in letting me run the business from here, although I am hoping to open a shop in London eventually."

"Oh! I didn't realise you worked here." Annabelle turned to Edward.

"Alice has a few rooms on the second floor. I never thought she'd become such an apt businesswoman." He grinned.

"I see. How kind of you to support her, Edward." She placed a hand on his again, but kept her blue-lidded eyes on me until the first course arrived.

We ate watercress soup in silence, Annabelle barely touching the spoon. Eventually I dared to ask how long she was planning to stay. She set down her spoon as if it were made of gold, "A week, I believe. Although Edward and I were debating whether to head for the coast for the Easter weekend."

"Perhaps you could join us, Alice!" Edward exclaimed. Annabelle's eyes darted towards my brother. "It would give you ladies time to get to know one another better." He smiled, finishing off his soup. Annabelle welded on her smile again and nodded.

As dinner progressed, she praised every dish that was served, yet ate virtually nothing. Instead she seemed rather keen to find out as much as possible about my business. "I hear you did rather well out of the war, Alice, with the factory. Surely the profits from your little enterprise would be more than sufficient to buy or at least rent a shop on Bond Street."

I stole a glance at my brother who was gazing at Annabelle like a besotted school boy. He had clearly kept her abreast of family matters.

"I did make a healthy profit from the war contract but I don't have that money anymore."

"Of course, you must have re-invested the money into the family business." She said.

"No, I donated it all to the Red Cross." Her face fell.

"It was jolly generous of Alice, I think. I tried to persuade her to keep a sum of it, after all, she earned it, but she wouldn't listen." Edward had caught up with our conversation and was beaming with approval which induced in me a similar grin. Annabelle joined us by smiling broadly - a smile that didn't reach her eyes.

"How...saintly of you, Alice." She said, taking a sip of wine.

"We hardly saw Alice for five years before the war, she was always up in her room tinkering with her sewing machine or sketching designs; she was utterly obsessed! I didn't understand it at the time, but now I'm pleased she's doing something she enjoys and making a bit of money for herself at the same time. You must see the charming dresses she's made for Sophie." He added.

"So, Alice is a thoroughly modern woman! Are you also one who shuns marriage in favour of ambition and independence?" Her tone was teasing but her eyes seemed to blaze. I smiled and sipped some wine.

"Well, it is nineteen-nineteen, Miss Tressider, I would like to think a woman is allowed to have a little ambition and enterprise as well as marry when she chooses."

"So you do want to marry?" The question was thrown at me with disarming force.

"I, well, of course, but I'm in no hurry. I would prefer to concentrate on my business for now."

"Do you not feel left behind now that both of your sisters are married and settled?" I felt my cheeks starting to heat.

"Not at all. I miss them from time to time, but I have my own life. Besides," I continued, "Grace is still here."

"Grace?" She frowned.

"Our younger sister."

Annabelle put her knife and fork down quickly and turned to Edward. "You have another sister? Why didn't you tell me about her?"

Edward grimaced and looked reproachfully at me for getting him into trouble. "I was going to tell you about Grace tonight, dearest. It is a somewhat...delicate subject, you see."

She pursed her lips, "What on earth are you talking about? Why is the subject 'delicate'?"

"Yes, Edward, why is the subject 'delicate'?" I turned towards him, suddenly irritated by his evasiveness. Did he see her as an awful family secret? Something to be ashamed of?

"Grace is...different; she's not very well, unfortunately, Bella, and her illness prevents her from leading a normal life."

I raised my eyebrows at him; Annabelle gripped his hand.

"Oh how terrible! What is the matter with her? Is she in a private hospital somewhere?"

"No, she lives here, that's why I said 'Grace is still here' a moment ago." I said, abandoning all efforts of politeness.

"She lives upstairs and has a full time carer to look after her." Edward clarified.

"Is she bedridden?"

"No, not exactly."

"Not at all." I corrected, sitting back to allow Edward the full benefit of my glare.

He dropped his knife and fork and turned to me, "Well how would you describe her condition, Alice? Since you're getting all high and mighty about it, maybe you would care to explain it more accurately than I have."

"It would be my pleasure." I faced Annabelle, "Grace is a lovely young lady, if you take the time to get to know her. She is sometimes prone to fits if she becomes distressed, but is otherwise completely fit and healthy. What my brother is referring to, albeit not very eloquently, are her *mental* health problems. She does not have the same capacities as the rest of us."

"Mental health problems, yes, very eloquently put, Alice, thank God we have you here to clarify everything for us." Edward interrupted, stabbing at a slice of beef. Annabelle ignored him.

"What do you mean? In what capacity is she lacking?" She stared at me, panic tangible on her face.

"Well, for instance, she can't write very well and her reading isn't good either. She has an incredible memory, though, and she's very good with numbers."

"Oh, so she's a slow learner then." Annabelle said, looking relieved.

"I suppose that is one facet of it, but her difficulties are not as black and white as that. It's not simply her academic ability; her illness manifests itself in many other ways, but learning was certainly never easy for her."

"So your sister is a slow learner, has fits and needs full time care..."

"Annabelle, my darling, you don't need to worry yourself about Grace. She is well looked after and I doubt you will see much of her; she has a set of rooms belonging only to her and her carer on the second floor. She lives in her own little world...in more ways than one!" Edward soothed, stroking her hand like a small pet. She snatched it away, noticed me watching and switched on a powerful smile.

"I'm sure you do look after her. It's very generous of you to care for her here." She took a delicate sip of wine. "It seems that everybody occupies the second floor!" She laughed. Silence permeated the room for a minute before she spoke again, "I would love to meet your sister, Edward. You don't have to be ashamed of her. After all, every family has its secrets and its oddities!"

The sun's rays bore down on the back of my neck with unusual fervour for springtime. I sat back and closed my eyes, feeling the heat brushing my lids, my brows, my hands, making me drowsy.

"No, Grace, that's one of mine!" Martha's patient voice wafted on the clement air. I held a hand up to shield my eyes. Martha was trying to teach Grace the rules of chess for the fourth time this week. She still hadn't mastered the game.

"No, you have to keep with the colour you chose at the beginning - the white pieces are yours."

The next thing I saw was a chess board and various pieces scattering across the tartan picnic rug towards Martha, and a thin, gangly figure retreating down the slope towards the rose garden. At nearly eighteen, she had lost the young, childlike appearance, but had not gained any of the adult traits of her peers. She was in a sort of developmental limbo; inside a chrysalis that would never burst open.

"Grace! Come back and apologise this instant..." I stood up and yelled after the retreating mane of mousy hair.

"It's fine, Miss Alice," said Martha with a benign smile.

"She has to learn, she can't behave in that way, Martha, it's not fair on you."

"Don't fret, Miss. She knows when she's done wrong; she'll apologise later and she knows she won't have as many pages tonight."

I frowned. "Pages?"

"We always read before she goes to bed. If she's naughty I won't read as much. You know, she's actually getting very good at chess but she can't bear to lose. She starts cheating to save face." She chuckled.

Just as Grace had disappeared behind the rose bushes, Annabelle and Edward glided down the stone steps, my brother simpering with infatuation.

The object of his affection received the praise willingly, but behind the heavy makeup I still wasn't convinced of her devotion to him. Annabelle held a garish turquoise parasol with an oriental print. Her dress was of the same hue, with a wide belt and long collar - far too fussy and elaborate for a hot spring afternoon. Edward wore a beige flannel suit with a ridiculous purple silk neck chief. I suspected the whole ensemble had been put together by Annabelle; I hadn't seen my brother wear anything of the sort before.

"Teddy and I were just saying how heavenly the weather is for this time of year."

"Teddy?" I whispered to him. He looked down at his shoes and mumbled, "Yes it is uncommonly warm for April."

"It would be a shame not to make the most of it, so we thought we'd spend a few days in Bournemouth. What do you think?"

"That sounds very nice. Will you take Sophie?" I directed my question at Edward.

"Actually, Annabelle was hoping we could all go. She can get to know the family better; we could all do with a little holiday."

"That's very generous of you both but it's a bit far to travel. Would it not be easier to stay somewhere a little closer to Rutland?"

"Well, Bella's got her heart set on Bournemouth you see. She used to go there as a girl and longs to see if the place has changed."

Annabelle flashed a sweet smile from underneath her parasol. I suddenly realised Martha was still standing next to me, an uncomfortable intruder to our conversation.

"Forgive me, Annabelle, this is Martha Pick. She looks after our sister, Grace."

Martha bowed her head politely. "How do you do, ma'am?"

"Oh, where is your sister? Is she around? Can I meet her?" Martha and I exchanged nervous glances.

"I'll just go and fetch her, ma'am." Martha walked quietly towards the rose garden leaving an awkward silence to settle on the three of us.

"So, when were you thinking of going to Bournemouth? And where would we all stay?"

"A friend of mine has a couple of cottages near the seafront that he can rent to us for the weekend. We're leaving after breakfast on Thursday morning and staying the night in London before heading to the coast early on Friday." He sighed, "Do you remember when we went there as children, Alice?"

"Yes, of course. I remember you used to grumble so much about going there, Edward. You were always desperate to return to London or Oxford. How things have changed!"

He laughed, "Things have changed. I'm too old to be running about like I used to. I'd much rather spend some time in the country, or by the sea, when work permits it." He glanced sappily at Annabelle.

"I'm very glad to hear it, Teddy. You work too hard, you know. I want you all to myself until next week, at least."

I shuddered despite the closeness in the air. "Well, I would certainly enjoy a little break, thank you. Are you going to invite Charlotte and Henry?"

My brother appeared not to have heard me, but Annabelle certainly had. Her raw blue eyes fixed on mine, forcing me to break the gaze and look away first. "I don't think there will be room for any more people. Eight is the most we can take." I was surprised by the authority she had when speaking to me in my own home; she had only been at Goldhurst Estate for a day, after all.

"I see. Who *is* invited then?" I asked trying to lighten the starchy atmosphere between us.

"You and your sister, and her nurse, of course; Sophie and her nanny; Teddy and me and my mother and stepfather." Annabelle replied easily. I sensed this holiday was more Annabelle's doing than Edward's. I supposed that Edward had persuaded her to invite us because I certainly couldn't imagine it being her idea.

"Ah, well, maybe another time. Have you met my sister Charlotte, Miss Tressider?" I was aware that I was being provocative. I knew they had met and instantly disliked one another. Annabelle's lips pursed and her eyes challenged mine once more. This time I was ready for them; I stared back, refusing to be silently intimidated.

"I have met Charlotte, once," her mouth stretched into a smile which again escaped her eyes, "we didn't have much time to speak, unfortunately. There's plenty of time, though; Edward just has so many sisters!" She laughed and looped her arm through his with a touch of impatience. "Teddy, dearest, I would love a stroll around the lake before luncheon."

"Then stroll you shall, my dear!" He beamed, guiding her down the stone steps onto the lawn. "Would you like to join us, Alice?" He said, turning back. Annabelle's face fell as she waited for my answer.

"Thank you Edward, but I have some sketches to finish. I'll see you at luncheon."

He nodded and was towed away by his companion lest I should change my mind.

A gentle breeze stroked past my cheek and ruffled the leaves of the horse chestnuts. Saucepans clattered over the sound of urgent voices in the kitchen. I tried to focus on my sketches, but Annabelle refused to disappear from my thoughts. She had not been overtly unpleasant; still there was something strange about her. I couldn't be sure that everything she did wasn't an act: her histrionic affection towards Edward, her eager interest in Grace and I, her manners at dinner; I didn't trust her. The way she looked at me disturbed me most - those cool, emotionless blue eyes. They were eyes belonging to one who is capable of cruelty.

I looked up from the half-formed sketch to see Martha walking towards me.

"Have Mr. Goldhurst and the lady gone, Miss?" She was breathless.

"Yes, Miss Tressider wanted to see the lake again. It's probably for the best, given Grace's mood. Take a seat, Martha, you look worn out! Where did Grace disappear to?"

Gratefully, she sat down opposite me. "I tried to coax her out of the garden to meet the lady guest, but she's having none of it. She's in one of her stubborn tempers."

"Leave her, then. Annabelle has plenty of time to meet her."

"She hates losing."

I laughed, "I've never known such a bad loser! Poor thing!"

Martha sighed. "What is she like? Mr. Goldhurst's lady friend?"

I leaned closer to her, "I'm not entirely sure what to make of her yet. She seems perfectly nice on the surface."

"Maybe you just need time to get to know her, Miss." Martha said.

"Mmm. Perhaps you're right. We will have plenty of time this weekend; they've invited us to Bournemouth."

"You and Miss Charlotte? That will be lovely, especially with this weather."

"Not Charlotte. You, Grace and Sophie, along with her parents."

Martha looked perturbed, "All of us together? Where will we stay?"

"Edward's renting cottages."

"Bournemouth's quite a long way. I'm not sure how Grace will react to that. She's in a queer mood at the moment and all these new people may...set her off." She looked at me quickly then blushed, "Oh, Miss, I'm sorry, I must sound ungrateful. It's a kind invitation, but..."

A thin figure lumbered awkwardly across the grass towards us. Her rag-like hair had broken free from its ribbons and dangled over her shoulders. Her blue dress was daubed with mud stains.

"We can ask Grace her opinion now." I said nodding my head in her direction. Martha stood to greet her. At the same time two figures in gaudy colours made their way towards the table from the opposite direction. I could hear Edward gibbering, accompanied by Annabelle's falsetto giggle.

Grace reached us first and Martha hurriedly wiped her face with a clean handkerchief. She squirmed and moaned.

"Oh! Is this Grace?" Annabelle had appeared at the bottom of the steps and looked up delightedly at Grace, the same way one would view a quaint art exhibition.

"How do you do, Grace? My name is Annabelle Tressider. I'm a...good friend of your brother's." Annabelle shouted in Grace's direction, stretching her mouth around each word. Grace said nothing and looked at no one.

"Say how do you do to the lady, Grace." Martha coaxed. She ignored her and turned her body towards me, kneading the white handkerchief Martha had given her.

"Can we play a game?" She croaked.

"It's a bit late now, Grace, we need to have luncheon." I said.

"Can we play afterwards?"

"That sounds like fun!" Annabelle cooed loudly. "What game shall we play?"

Grace's eyes darkened. "I don't want them to play."

"That's not polite." Martha said, trying to keep her voice light.

"Yes, that's jolly rude, Grace. You do not speak to a guest in that manner." My brother chimed in heavily.

"It's fine, Edward, she doesn't understand, poor dear." Annabelle replied with a patronising look.

"What game do you want to play after luncheon?" I asked.

"Find my knight."

"What? I haven't heard of that game before! Tell me how you play it?" Annabelle exclaimed, stretching her mouth into an unnaturally wide grin.

Grace's head slowly retreated to her chest, "Not telling you."

Edward's face flushed, "Bella, darling, come on inside and get ready for luncheon. You're wasting your time with her when she's in a mood like this." Grace continued to stare sulkily at the ground. Her long, bony fingers twisted round and round the fabric of the hanky.

Annabelle obeyed, eyeing Grace amusedly as they passed. "Isn't she funny, Edward!" I heard her squawk as they entered the house.

Martha sighed and gingerly touched Grace on the shoulder. "Come on, duckie, let's get you some lunch."

"My knight's buried in the garden. You have to find it after lunch!" She blurted as she turned and ran towards the kitchen.

"What?" I stared after her in puzzlement.

Martha groaned, "Her chess piece, the white knight. She did this last week; it's her new favourite game. I think she prefers it to a normal game of chess."

I smiled, "I can't imagine Annabelle mucking in to look for it, can you?"

Martha sighed, "I wish she'd picked the black pieces, the white ones are going to be ruined!"

I gathered up my still unfinished sketches and followed her into the house.

"Oh look, Sophie, there's the sea!" The little girl scrambled onto my knee for a closer look, her eyes shining with excitement. The journey to Bournemouth had been a good deal more pleasant than the journey to London when Annabelle's pungent laughter had filled the train carriages and every other utterance was a cry of "Oh, Teddy, stop it!", "Teddy, darling, what do you think about...?" and, "Teddy, what would I do without you?".

Now I shared a car with Sophie, Grace, Martha and Bridget, Sophie's nanny, who had dropped off to sleep as soon as we left London and was now slumped quietly in the back seat. Grace too was fast asleep, her pale face resting on Martha's shoulder. They had taken a car to London since Grace was no longer able to travel by train without suffering a fit.

Edward and Annabelle had left earlier in the morning, collecting her mother and stepfather (who I later discovered were called Mr. and Mrs. *Buhler*) on the way. The only other detail I had was that Mr. Buhler was a wealthy American financier based in London and New York.

Our car rolled to a halt outside an elegant cottage overlooking Boscombe beach, a relatively peaceful and picturesque part of the coast. Being creatures of landlocked counties, we all stood transfixed by the wonderful spectacle of the sea, absorbing the sound of the distant waves and bemoaning our lot for being starved of such a majestic a sight.

After a while my mind wandered to my parents. Somewhere in the depths they struggled and perished - victims of the same vast sea. I shuddered and turned back to the cottage.

I had to applaud Edward; it was the finest cottage I had seen in a very long time. The walls were whitewashed to perfection and the front garden was bursting with spring flowers and twisting pine bushes that flanked the front door. The roof was thatched, much to my delight; I remembered walking in the countryside as a child, counting all the thatched roofs I saw, a game at which Grace was always much better.

Grace was still fast asleep on the rear seat of the car and Martha was negotiating the best way to rouse her. In the end I persuaded her to let her sleep a little longer.

"Unpack and enjoy the place while she's asleep," I said, "Thompson won't mind keeping an eye on her, will you Thompson?"

The young chauffeur looked alarmed but nodded dutifully, adopting a sentry-like stance six feet away from the car once he had taken in our luggage.

The cottage was as beautiful inside as it was outside. A huge hearth dominated the front room, adorned with fresh flowers; the walls were painted cream and oak beams supported the roof. A spiral staircase led us up to the five pretty bedrooms, where we found a startled housemaid, "I beg your pardon, ma'am, have you got the right cottage? Only Mr. Goldhurst and his guests have already given me instructions to prepare the rooms for them."

"Hello there!" An unfamiliar voice boomed up the stairs, making me jump. I leaned over the banister to see a middle-aged gentleman with a huge tawny face grinning at me.

"How do you do? You must be..."

"Theodore Buhler," he interrupted, grasping my hand and drawing it to his lips. His palms were sweaty and his lips were wetter still. "I'm afraid we've marked our territory here, well, the two lovebirds had their hearts set on this place!" He chuckled good-naturedly and the ample flesh around his stomach jiggled. Behind me Martha, Bridget and Sophie shrunk into one person, unsure of what to make of this loud stranger.

"I can see why." I said, extricating my hand from his grip.

"How do you do? You must be Edward's sister," another, less congenial voice wafted through the sitting room. "I'm Mrs. Buhler, Annabelle's mother." She proffered a dainty hand and flashed me the same sugary smile as her daughter.

"Alice Goldhurst, pleased to meet you. This is Sophie, my niece, Edward's daughter."

"Hello beautiful!" Mr. Buhler boomed, his brown eyes locked on the little girl who clung to Bridget, a look of terror in her eyes. "Aren't you a precious little thing?" He continued, advancing on her, lips puckered.

"This is Bridget, Sophie's nanny and Martha, who looks after our sister, Grace." I said, hoping to distract Mr. Buhler.

"Where is your sister? Edward was just telling us all about her." Mrs. Buhler said.

"She's still asleep in the car. Long journeys tire her out." I explained.

Mr. Buhler stood up and scratched the bald patch on the back of his head. "I think it's wonderful that you encourage her to lead a normal life. What a lucky girl she is to have a caring family!" Mrs. Buhler nodded in unconvincing agreement and stretched her mouth into the Tressider forced smile.

"Would you be so kind as to tell us where we are staying?" I asked.

"Allow me, ladies!" Mr. Buhler began to lead us outside when I heard a familiar vinegary laugh. Annabelle was leading my brother up the garden path.

"Oh hooray, you've arrived!" She simpered, "I see you've all met."

"Yes, I was just asking Mr. and Mrs. Buhler where we're staying, Edward."

Before he could respond a wolfish howl, pierced the air, followed by a shout for help. Martha and I ran down the path and were greeted with the sight of the lower half of Thompson's body bent over and twisting like a caught fish. His top half was inside the car.

"Grace, let go!" Martha bellowed. She had grabbed onto the poor man's hair and was screaming with abandon. She ignored Martha's order and pulled harder, wailing and howling louder still.

"My God!" I heard Mr. Buhler exclaim.

Annabelle and her mother gasped and wailed, "Do something, do something! Edward!"

I called to my brother to help us loosen her grip. Martha had taken hold of Grace's hands on the opposite side of the car seat; I went to help her while Edward reached around the struggling chauffeur, who was now crying hysterically. Together, and with much difficulty, we prised her fingers open and freed Thompson. Bridget immediately ran over to tend to him, leaving a traumatised Sophie wailing next to Annabelle.

"What on earth was that about?" Mr. Buhler said, goggle-eyed.

"She...she screamed and grabbed my hair! I was only asking her if she was all right!" Thompson sobbed on the ground. "She's crazy! She was like a wild animal!"

"Yes, yes, all right, Thompson. I'm very sorry for leaving you alone with her. Go inside and have a sit down." I indicated towards the cottage. Mrs. Buhler shot me a disgruntled look but remained silent.

"Take Sophie to the house." Edward spoke quietly and with anger in his voice. "It's at the bottom of the hill; the servants are already there." He walked over to Annabelle, who was sobbing and fanning herself, and pulled her into an embrace.

I picked up the little girl and glanced at Martha through the car's window. She was talking soothingly and gently rocking Grace into a state of calm; the howling gradually subsiding.

The next day it was generally agreed that we should spend the day at the beach. Martha suggested that she and Grace join us after luncheon, since the latter was still asleep. On hearing this, Annabelle and her guests did little to hide their relief.

"She's not fond of sand anyway, doesn't like it getting between her toes." Edward added, offering Annabelle an arm and a fawning grin as we made our way down the hill.

"Who does?" Mr. Buhler chuckled.

"It seems strange to bring her here if she dislikes the beach and the long journey." The mother said, ignoring her husband. Edward, ensconced as he was in his lover's consuming gaze, seemed not to hear.

Her comment bothered me, "Because she's family; that's why she's invited." She opened her mouth to respond but was interrupted by a collective cry of joy as Boscombe Bay came into view. Sophie, Bridget and Mr. Buhler ran ahead, followed by Edward and Annabelle who, in their excitement, dropped one another's hand and quickened their pace. Mrs. Buhler and I walked together in silence until we reached the beach when she commented on the novelty of being close to the sea. As I turned to go she added, as an aside, "You needn't take offence, Alice, I'm merely stating an opinion. An opinion which most people here share."

"I beg your pardon, Mrs. Buhler, but Grace is none of your business. She's mine and Edward's sister and you are not family, so I would appreciate it if you kept your opinions."

At that moment I hated her. Not so much for the comment itself but for the presumptuous complacency with which she expressed her views about our family after one brief meeting. I felt my face grow hot. I couldn't be around her. She seemed to sense my annoyance and smiled, apparently enjoying my discomfort.

"I think you'll find that I am, or I will be, very soon."

"Mama, there's a deck chair for you here, come on." Annabelle trilled. Mrs. Buhler winked at me boldly and I watched her saunter over to the chair next to her equally insufferable daughter.

I seethed in helpless anger; my good mood was ruined; I didn't want to be on this holiday and longed for the haven of Goldhurst Estate and my Singer. Until it dawned on me that it was not likely to be a haven for much longer.

"Edward, I'm going for a walk." I called to him as brightly as I could.

"We've just got here. Sit down for a while and enjoy the sun; Bella and I can come with you in an hour or so." He gestured to Mrs. Buhler, who was now lifting her skirts to expose slim ivory calves. "Look, there's a chair next to Marianne."

I shook my head, "I won't be long."

"I don't mind accompanying you, young lady. I am partial to a little dander along the seashore." Mr. Buhler stepped forward, a sweating, panting knight with a shining face that grinned and squinted at me.

"Thank you, Mr. Buhler." I grimaced, "But I'd like a little solitude, if you don't mind. I'll be back within the hour." I said to Edward.

"Well make sure you're back for the Punch and Judy show at eleven. And don't wander off too far, I know what you're like." He said. Annabelle giggled and he began coaxing her into the water. I walked away with her coquettish peals of laughter ringing in my ears.

Despite the odd bout of cloud the sun remained a constant beacon overhead, rising steadily as the day galloped on. The cool tide lapped rhythmically around my ankles and the watery sound of an organ playing drifted in and out of my consciousness. On any other occasion I would have drawn much pleasure from the surroundings. I adored seaside holidays as a child and I could spend hours staring at and listening to the waves without a thought for anything else. However, it was wasted on me today. I couldn't put Mrs. Buhler's words out of my mind. My brother couldn't marry Annabelle; it was out of the question. The woman and her family were vile, yet there was an air of officiousness about them; a deluded self-pride. They seemed convinced that they were equal to, if not better than us. The audacity! "She's not good enough for him." I muttered. I had never been a snob, not like Charlotte or my grandmother, but I knew that they were inferior in every way. What could be done? Annabelle and her mother had ensnared him. Would he even listen to me or Charlotte? For the second time in as many days I longed for my parents.

I stopped walking. The sun was almost directly overhead so I calculated it must be close to midday. A group of young boys played with a ball in the shallows, their calves were hard and thin like rounders' bats. I had walked a considerable distance so that I could no longer see the stretch of beach from which I had set off. Up ahead was a cluster of rocks and pools and, considering I had already missed the Punch and Judy show, I decided to rest there for a few minutes before heading back.

I had fond memories of rock pools. One particularly adventurous nanny had taken us exploring one summer in Wells. I remember being fascinated by the amount of life to be found in each small puddle.

I found a relatively dry, flat rock and perched, swinging my body round to face the sea and drew my legs up away from the water and the splashing boys. Edward had discovered the hard way not to place his feet in the pools in case a crab was lurking beneath a rock. I smiled at the memory of him yelping and crying and blaming the nanny when one pinched his toe. The pool before me was not exactly teeming with life but captivating nonetheless. Bedraggled manes of seaweed clung to the crusty surfaces of the rock; anemones sucked the sides and tiny black fish darted in and out of crevices. Sadly there were no crabs or starfish but there were some pretty shells - pearly and ornate - beneath the rippling water. I reached in to pick one; the fish shot to the other side of the pool. It was a perfect cockle shell: white, speckled with brown; its ridges were still smooth with saltwater. I decided to keep it for Grace and headed back the way I had come.

It took me longer than expected to reach the group; they were packing up when I arrived, minus Edward, Sophie and Bridget. Annabelle and her mother were deep in conversation and didn't notice me approaching.

"I suggested to Edward that we dine alone tonight."

"I don't blame you darling; you don't want the mob interrupting."

"I know, they're...Alice! Where have you been?" Annabelle's face flushed when she saw me and she grinned maniacally.

"Where are the others?"

Mrs. Buhler placed her hands on her slim hips, "Your brother went to look for you, he was worried sick! Why didn't you come back when you said you were going to? It was rather..."

"Thank you, but I don't want or need a lecture." I said turning away. I was hot and bothered and repulsed by them both.

"Oh, Alice! Mama didn't mean any offence; she's merely concerned about Teddy."

"And we're late for luncheon." Mrs. Buhler added. They stood side by side: two harpies working together to defeat their prey. A small boy belonging to a nearby family was staring at me, sifting handful after handful of sand through his fingers.

"Which way did he go?" I lowered my voice so the boy couldn't eavesdrop.

"There he is." Mr. Buhler appeared from behind the blue windbreaker, beaming contentedly.

"Teddy! Cooeee!" Annabelle and her mother bounced up and down waving their arms at my brother like schoolgirls at a cricket match.

He looked stern as he approached. "Where did you get to? I thought you were coming back for eleven? We were worried out of our senses!"

"I wanted some time alone." I turned my back on the two women, trying to add meaning to my words.

Edward just tutted and shook his head. "Well, you're back, that's the main thing. I was beginning to think the tide had got you. Let's head back and eat; I'm ravenous after that walk." Annabelle looped her arm around his and led him towards the steps.

"Teddy, after luncheon let's go into Bournemouth and take a stroll along the promenade. We can have our photograph taken!"

"Capital idea, Bella! Will you three join us?" He twisted his neck round and smiled. Mr. and Mrs. Buhler confirmed that they would like nothing more. I declined, blaming a headache.

"I'm not surprised, young lady, walking all that way in the midday sun!" Mr. Buhler chortled.

"You were gone for an awfully long time. How far did you go?" Annabelle said.

"I'm not sure. Quite a long way."

"Doesn't it get boring, walking all that time on your own?" She pressed.

"Not really."

Mrs. Buhler leaned closer to me and whispered, "Perhaps you ought to find a sweetheart to wander beside, like our darling Annabelle has."

I glanced at my brother, oblivious to the insidious plans unfurling in this woman's mind. I couldn't bear it; I had to talk to him alone; I had to try to warn him. The very least I could do was try.

I had never experienced such relief as that which greeted me on my return to the cottage. Sophie and Bridget were eating at the kitchen table and Grace and Martha were in the garden playing chess. Grace was glaring at the board with the intensity of a lioness stalking her prey.

"Come on Gracie, make your move, we'll be out here till midnight at this rate." Martha said.

"I'm not Gracie." Grace mumbled back, continuing to stare at the board, unblinking, unmoving.

Martha sighed and smiled at me, "Did you have a nice time at the beach, Miss?"

"Lovely, thank you," I nodded. "I went for a walk and found this, I thought you might like it, Grace." I offered her the cockle shell from the rock pool but her attention was monopolised for the next hour at least.

"Say thank you to your sister, it's a perfect shape, Miss, no dents or scratches. It reminds me of that song, 'Mary, Mary, quite contrary, how does your garden grow?'"

"I'm not Mary." Grace interrupted, moving her knight suddenly, "check mate."

"No duck, you say 'check' first, it's only 'check mate' if your opponent's king can't..."

"I think it is check mate, Martha - look." I said. We all stared at the board. Sure enough, Martha's king was surrounded by dangers that could not be avoided. She sat back and exhaled from the side of her mouth.

"Well I never, Gracie. I didn't see that coming. Perhaps you'd better play your sister from now on; you're clearly too good for me."

"I'm not Gracie," she grumbled and took the shell from my hand. "Thank you, Alice." She said and pottered inside.

"Remarkable. She was awful last week; you've obviously taught her well."

Martha raised her eyebrows, "Not me, Miss, she's been practising all hours every day, often on her own. I just showed her the basics. She's very clever in that way."

"If only she could earn a living being a chess genius." I said.

"Or counting flower petals." We both smiled. "Miss Alice, I think I'm going to take Grace back tomorrow."

"Back where?"

"To Rutland. The driver's taking us after breakfast."

I stared at her. She blushed and looked down. "What on earth for? Has she been unwell? Doesn't she like it here?" Martha squirmed. "Listen, you don't have to leave because of what happened yesterday. Edward's so smitten with Annabelle he'll have forgotten it. Do you think he'd let Sophie stay here if he thought Grace was a risk?"

"I-I don't think the ladies are comfortable with her. We're all used to Gracie's ways. I think it would be best if we left you all to it this time. There'll be other chances like this I'm sure..." She blushed again, her neck and cheeks aglow.

"Well, if Annabelle has designs on my brother she'll have to get used to his family." A thought suddenly came to me: had Annabelle said something? Or her ghastly mother? Was she behind her decision to leave? I asked Martha, who squirmed and coloured even more, suggesting that I was correct. "How dare they! The audacity! Neither of them have the right to tell you what to do, she and her family are nothing to Edward and they never will be if I have anything to do with it." I was shaking with fury; to think that someone could have the presumption to overrule Edward or myself on family matters was too much to bear. I left Martha stuttering in the garden and stormed into the house.

"Oh, Miss please, don't say anything, it's nothing, really, they probably just want some time to themselves." She said, following me inside.

"They shouldn't have invited us if they wanted to be alone. It's downright impudent and I won't stand for it anymore. I'm going to talk some sense into Edward."

My brother had gone out for his stroll by the time I reached their cottage so I left a message for him to meet me in private before dinner. He arrived in good spirits, oblivious to the urgency of my message. I had had three hours to calm down and was less sure of how to broach the subject of Annabelle. Edward, however, was less reticent, "I'm going to ask Annabelle to marry me."

In front of us the endless blue sea and the chalky cliffs and the cloud-spotted sky grew grey and insignificant. I folded my arms around my waist and shivered.

"I'm going to propose tonight. Do you think I should ask her during supper? Or at sunset on this hill? It's rather romantic here, but then again, she is a sophisticated woman and the table I've reserved at the restaurant is superb."

I groaned inwardly, willing the conversation to end. I couldn't let him propose. At this moment in time there was nothing I wanted less. But how could I tell him that? He was besotted with her and all he wanted was my approval. "Edward, I've barely known her a week, how would I know what she'd prefer?"

"You get on very well with her, though, don't you? She is wonderful, isn't she? So kind and tremendous fun."

I couldn't bear it. "Edward, listen, please. I know you're smitten with Annabelle and you seem happy now, but what about in five, ten, fifty years from now? Are you a suitable match? Will she be a good stepmother to Sophie?"

He frowned; this wasn't the response he had expected. "Of course I'll be happy; we'll be happy. I'll be with the woman I love."

"I'm worried about you, Edward. You're rushing into this. Remember we hardly know her, your daughter included. What's the hurry? It wouldn't hurt to postpone your proposal for a few months. Then she can get to know the family better and we can get to know her properly."

"Nonsense, Alice, you've spent plenty of time with her over the past few days and you can get to know her before the wedding. You've seen who she is." He turned his face away, his smile long faded. "I thought you were getting on famously."

"She *appears* nice; I just don't think we've got to know the real Annabelle yet, or her family. You included, perhaps." I didn't know whether to mention her meddling with Martha since she would most likely deny it and Edward was so enamoured he would certainly believe her.

"What do you mean 'The real Annabelle'? Are you expecting to uncover some sort of scandalous secret life? Well, I'm sorry to disappoint you, but there is nothing to uncover - she's perfect - and I'm proposing tonight." When he was angry, Edward always spoke like the intractable boy he used to be.

"Don't be cross; I'm trying to give you some perspective. I just think...you have a young daughter who lost her mother less than a year ago;

you need to put her first. Is she ready for a stepmother so soon? Will Annabelle love her as if she were her own? And then there's Grace to think of."

"Grace? What the devil's she got to do with it?" He interrupted.

"You know change upsets her; new people make her feel threatened. Annabelle only found out about her a few days ago. Does she realise that you have a responsibility to her as well? If she's marrying you, she has to be prepared to love and care for your family in the same way. She has to accept Grace, not try to shut her out."

Edward stood suddenly and paced towards the cliff edge, "Responsibility, responsibility. How I hate that word!"

I was annoyed by his single-mindedness, "Like it or not, it's not going to go away."

"I wish, just for once, that I could put myself first rather than the world and his wife." He shook his head and turned to look at me. "When I'm with Annabelle I feel happy and...free. She makes me feel like everything is possible; all my troubles disappear. I know it sounds clichéd but...I...I love her."

I stood up and took his hand, "I don't doubt that you love her. I can see how happy you are around her. You're my big brother; I just want to make sure that she deserves you and Sophie." A flock of seagulls flew overhead, calling noisily to one another. I squeezed his hand. "Whenever and however you decide to propose I wish you all the best. But please, Edward, promise me you'll wait a little longer. You should only do it when you know for certain that it's the right thing to do." At that moment I should have voiced my concerns about Annabelle and her mother. I should have been honest and tried harder to discourage him, but I didn't want to ruin our relationship. He had stood by me for years and was helping me realise my dreams; I owed him my support, even if I didn't approve of his decision.

He sighed and shook away my hand, looking back towards the cottage. "I promise." He said quietly. I smiled and went to hug him but he began to walk down the hill, "Thank you for your advice, Alice." He called over his shoulder. I sat on the bench and watched his retreating back until it disappeared from view.

Annabelle Tressider. I read her name, immaculately calligraphed, on the order of service. She had well and truly infected my brother with her charming manipulation. I had never considered Edward to be one of those weak men who found it impossible to resist women, but clearly all it took was one very sly and persistent one. The poor fool.

"I can't believe this is happening. Are you certain there's nothing we can do to stop it? Is he so besotted with her?" Charlotte hissed in my ear, reading my thoughts.

"No," I hissed back, "I tried, you tried, we even convinced Louisa to try. He's smitten."

"More likely bewitched." She hissed back. Henry coughed and gave her a nudge, which she ignored. "Oh Alice, she's so awful. Have you seen the decorations at Goldhurst? Vulgar barely begins to describe it. Pink everywhere! Can you imagine? It reminds me of a child's tea party."

"I could cope with a bit of vulgarity if I thought she was a nice person, if I thought she could make Edward happy."

Charlotte tutted, "You weren't saying that when she snubbed your dresses." I felt my face flush and glared at my sister; realising that she had taken it too far, she apologised. "You know *I* adore your dresses, that's the point I'm making, she doesn't fit in and she's made it quite clear that she doesn't intend to."

We lapsed into silence until the bride appeared at the back of the church, escorted by the beaming, shiny-faced Mr. Buhler.

Mrs. Buhler and Edward wore similar fawning smiles as they gazed at Annabelle from the head of the aisle. Charlotte's lips pursed as she looked the bride up and down. "That dress isn't a patch on one of yours."

"Charlotte, pipe down!" Henry hissed.

I had to be grateful to Annabelle for one thing - our mutual dislike for her had brought Charlotte and I closer than we had ever been.

"To Annabelle Goldhurst." I raised my glass limply and joined in with the chorus. From the top table, Annabelle smiled and laughed like a giddy schoolgirl, kissing Edward coyly. I turned away.

"Where's Grace?" I wondered aloud. Sophie, in her puffy coral bridesmaid gown, was being petted by Aunt Cynthia at the next table, but there was no trace of Grace and Martha.

"Hmm? I'm not sure?" Charlotte replied with disinterest, taking a gulp of champagne.

"I saw Martha earlier; she said she would keep Grace away from the reception as she was quite distressed this morning with all these people around." Louisa said.

"Are you sure she hasn't been banished on Annabelle's orders?" I said bitterly.

"Why do you think that? I think she wanted Grace here. She really isn't all that bad when you get to know her; you should give her a chance." Louisa said.

Charlotte rolled her eyes and took another glass of champagne from the footman. "Please tell me she hasn't cast a spell on you as well, Louisa, I thought you had more sense than that."

A fresh wave of sugary laughter sounded from the top table. "Excuse me." I slipped out of the marquee towards the lake.

It was cool and peaceful away from the lawn. The willows created an umbrella of refuge, the grass, which was long and wet on the descent, soaking my shoes and the hem of my frock, was shorter here and blanketed with cottony debris. The willows sighed as the breeze ruffled their tops and the distant sound of instruments competed with the frogs' noisy chorus. I waved to Martha and she came to greet me.

"Hello, Miss Alice. I didn't think I'd see you down here." Grace trotted after her and I noticed she had changed into a pretty violet frock embroidered with pansies.

"That's a gorgeous gown, Grace. You look ever so pretty."

"Of course it is, you made her this one, Miss! I did have to alter it, mind you, she's grown so much."

I laughed, "I've made you so many I'm having trouble remembering them all! You must stop growing!"

"I didn't like the other one." Grace sat down on the bank, cross-legged, decapitating a patch of daisies.

"The pink one?" I asked, knowing full well that Annabelle had given her a hideous, frilly coral gown that was too short for her long legs.

"Pink is horrid, bows are horrid and I wear purple on a Saturday."

"I'm not keen on pink either." I said.

"I can hear the frogs, can we find them? I want to count them." She rose suddenly and fidgeted as if a line of ants were trooping the length of her spine.

"We can as long as you keep your dress clean. That means staying well away from the water." Martha warned, but she was already lolloping around the edge of the lake, extending her right arm so that her fingers brushed the bulrushes. We trailed behind.

"Tell me the truth, Martha, did Annabelle or Edward tell you to keep Grace away from the wedding?" I whispered.

Her eyes widened. "No, Miss; they haven't said anything. In fact, Miss Tressider, sorry, Mrs. Goldhurst, was very understanding and encouraged me to bring her. But you know what Grace is like, she hates big crowds; she'd just cause a fuss."

I nodded feeling slightly ashamed. Perhaps I was being too harsh in my criticism of Annabelle. Louisa seemed to like her after all and I always trusted Louisa's judgement.

"How's the wedding going?"

"Fine - a little tedious," I paused to admire the stillness of the lake. Dragonflies swooped and lingered over the surface. The frogs' croaks echoed through the willows.

"Truthfully, what do you make of Miss Tressider, Martha?" She looked away and cleared her throat. "Don't worry, I haven't been sent to test you. I just don't know what to make of her and I suppose I need to hear someone else's opinion - someone outside the family."

She shot me a strange look, but continued in a steady tone, "I think she's a nice woman. I haven't spoken to her much but when I have she seems pleasant. And Mr. Goldhurst is happier than I've seen him since his first marriage."

I considered this. "I suppose it worries me that Edward is so enthralled. There's nothing he wouldn't do for her; she has such a hold over him."

Martha smiled, "They're in love. A man in love can be the soppiest creature alive, it's normal. My brother was the same when he married. I went to stay with the pair of them after the wedding and neither had eyes nor ears for anyone else; I thought them quite rude until I realised the reason. Once they've been married a while it will return to normal, believe me, Miss."

I nodded. Perhaps she was right. Poor Martha, did she long for someone to love? I gazed at her now - the calm expression, the dark hair streaked with grey, the lines across her forehead and around her eyes. Although she didn't look old I couldn't deny the fact that this job had aged her.

The music from the marquee was swelling, threatening to overcome the frogs' full-throated belches.

"I should get back. Would you bring Grace up after she's seen her frogs, if only for a short while?"

"I will." She said, continuing to follow the track leading to Grace.

"Bye, Grace." I called, but she was half hidden by a willow tree and engrossed in finding the lusty amphibians.

"Twenty-four so far!" I heard her call.

"Where have you been?" Charlotte, half-drunk, accosted me outside the marquee as I climbed up the slope. A cigarette dangled half-heartedly from her left hand whilst the other clutched her umpteenth glass of champagne.

"For a walk; I had a headache."

"I'd keep on walking if I were you; Cousin Lyle is looking for a dance!" She began to snigger then gasped abruptly. "Oh God, the wicked stepmother is heading our way. Henry! Henry darling, dance with me!" Charlotte was off before Annabelle appeared.

"Oh dear, your sister can barely compose herself to walk in a straight line," she smirked, "perhaps her husband had better take her to bed."

"She's just enjoying herself." I didn't like her talking about my sister in such a haughty manner, wedding day or not. I quickly changed the subject by offering my congratulations, which she lapped up with great gushing declarations of love.

"It's such a perfect day. Edward and I are so blissfully happy!" On the other side of the marquee Edward was looking equally blissful. She did seem to make him very happy.

"So, what do you think of my dress, Alice? Do you approve?"

I took in the billowing lace, the excessive pearl detail, the snowy whiteness of the silk, the never-ending train. "Lovely, really lovely."

"Not the sort of dress that you would wear for your wedding, though?" She teased. This was the woman I disliked: the over-familiarity, the playful hectoring, the deceptive sweetness.

"No, but every woman has her own taste and style."

"Said like a true professional! I'm sure it won't be long before you're designing your own wedding dress; it must be strange living with your brother at twenty-six."

"Twenty-five," I corrected, "I don't spend all my time in Rutland, and when I am here I have my rooms..."

"On the second floor." She said with a hint of irritation threatening the grin.

"Quite, so don't worry, I won't be in your way."

"Forgive me, I didn't mean to imply that we wanted to get rid of you! Quite the opposite, it will be wonderful to have a sister around. I was an only child and now I have three and a half!" She laughed.

"Well I hope you like your new home."

"I just love Goldhurst Estate. It's everything one could wish for in a home," she simpered, staring back at the house. "Of course there will be a few little changes and then I know I will be very happy here."

I looked at her suddenly. Her eyes roved the grounds before meeting mine. They twinkled with dull satisfaction.

"What sort of changes?" I said as lightly as possible.

"Nothing much, you know." She waved her hand flippantly; her eyes retained their intensity. "Every bride has to make a house her own, as you'll find out."

I wasn't sure how to respond.

"Please excuse me, Alice; I must speak to Lady Manners."

She floated away in a cloud of self-satisfied scheming. There was still so much I didn't know about her, and that worried me.

"By jingo, you're looking particularly enchanting today, Cousin Alice!"

I had been so immersed in the mystery of Annabelle that I hadn't noticed that I had become the unfortunate prey of Cousin Lyle.

Chapter Twelve
Goldhurst Estate, Rutland 10th May 1921
Alice

The familiar crunch of tyres on gravel roused me from a light sleep. I was home at last. The seven o'clock train from London had been delayed twice and it was a relief to end the long journey. The not so familiar sight of a red and yellow striped helter-skelter drew me to the lawn which had been almost completely hidden by a giant merry-go-round with wide-eyed, buck-toothed horses suspended on golden poles; row upon row of stalls advertising cakes, ices, sweets, knits, farm produce and even shoes; a coconut shy; a tombola and a large poster promoting a raffle, tug-of-war contest and a 'guess how many sweets are in the jar!' competition. My garden had been taken over by an army of men and women scurrying and shouting, getting everything prepared. I stared in amazement until a pair of grinning men tipped their hats causing me to turn away, embarrassed.

I didn't recognise the footman as he carried my luggage into the house; had I been away that long? It had been two months at least and I would soon be leaving again, possibly for longer.

Mr. Brooks, greeted me comfortably and someone was soon dispatched to bring some tea to the morning room. However, there was no sign of my family. Mr. Brooks brought the tea in himself and I thanked him.

"Mrs. Goldhurst sends her apologies, Miss Alice; she's busy with Mrs. Quince, putting the finishing touches to this afternoon's fête. They're in Stamford at present."

I frowned, "Who's Mrs. Quince?"

"The new housekeeper, Miss, I beg your pardon, I should have told you that."

"What happened to Mrs. Brickett?"

"She retired and moved down south to care for her sister."

"Oh, that's a shame. I didn't get the chance to say goodbye. Do you think you could write down her address for me? I should like to write to thank her."

"Very good, Miss." He turned to leave.

"Wait a moment, Brooks, is Mr. Goldhurst at home?"

"He's on his way back from Liverpool; he should be back for luncheon at one o'clock, before the fête."

I started and set my cup down, "I was led to believe that the fête was tomorrow. Why has the date changed?"

He looked at me with a blank expression, "I'm afraid I don't know, Miss Alice. I haven't had much to do with it. Mrs. Quince has dealt with it all." He looked down at his shoes, "I'll get you Mrs. Brickett's address."

"Thank you." I called as he bowed and exited.

I made myself comfortable in the morning room. It had retained the same comforting smell over the years; a mixture of roses (Mr. Healy's legacy) and Mansion Polish - a peculiar combination - but it was old and familiar, reminding me I was safe, at home.

Brooks returned with the address and a bundle of letters which had been delivered in my absence. I had nearly finished reading them when Edward walked in.

"Ah, Alice, I didn't think you were getting here until tomorrow morning."

I rose and kissed him on the cheek. "I did telephone several times yesterday to forewarn you."

"I had to go up to Liverpool on Thursday. Bella was here, though."

"Brooks said she's busy organising this fête. Why did she change the date? She wrote and told me it was Sunday."

"Hmm?" He raised his eyebrows as he lit a cigarette.

"Never mind. How's little Freddie? Has he stopped crying?"

"Frederick." He corrected me straight away. "Annabelle hates people calling him 'Freddie' or 'Fred'."

I rolled my eyes but Edward didn't see. "The little chap's still wailing, I'm afraid. He had colic, but I think that's cleared up." He trailed off, inhaling.

"Are you sure Annabelle's not taking on a bit too much? I mean, Fred…erick is only three months and if he's unwell..."

Edward exhaled smoke and sighed, "I've tried talking to her, but she won't listen to me." He sat down next to me, "Do you think you could talk to her, sis? She might listen to you."

I spluttered, "If she won't listen to her husband she's unlikely to listen to me!" His face fell. "Oh for goodness sake, all right, I'll talk to her. Where is she anyway?"

Edward's brow furrowed. "I thought she was here."

"Brooks said she's preparing for the fête this afternoon. I'm sure she'll appear. I must tell you about what's been going on in London." I said, pleased to have a moment alone with my brother.

"How is the business going?" Edward tipped some ash into a glass ash tray and snapped back to a more business-like tone.

"It's incredible, Edward. I've been inundated with requests during the two months I've been in London; I can scarcely keep up with the demand! It's jolly hard work but of course that's what I wanted."

He nodded seriously. "I'm pleased for you. We must hear all about it at luncheon. You must excuse me, Alice, I need to telephone the factory. It's super to see you, you look well."

He kissed my cheek and walked out of the room, leaving me alone and feeling somewhat out of place.

"Hello, Miss, welcome home." Martha's familiar voice sounded from the doorway a few minutes later.

"Thank you, Martha. How are you?" I replied, smiling.

"Sorry to disturb you, Miss. You haven't seen Grace, have you?" Martha hung by the doorway staring at me, breathing heavily.

"No, I only arrived about twenty minutes ago. Is she missing?"

"It's very quiet upstairs." She said, hurrying away towards the staircase.

A minute or so passed before I realised what she was suggesting - Frederick wasn't crying. Could Grace be responsible? I shook my head; trying to shake away the awful thought but headed towards the nursery anyway.

The first floor corridor was quiet and gloomy. The day was overcast and the sun had once again disappeared behind a blanket of grey, dimming the light that normally streamed in through the large windows. I quickened my pace, impatient to reach the nursery and quell the ill-feeling in my stomach. Where was Annabelle? I prayed that she was still out, or at least away from this part of the house, away from Frederick.

I heard the faint rumble of voices as I neared the room and stopped and strained to detect some words or at least a tone. Two female voices, shrill and quick. Arguing, perhaps? The door was closed so I couldn't be sure, but there was no sound of the baby. The knot in my stomach twisted. Annabelle couldn't be in the room; she would have been railing and screeching around the whole house if something had happened to her precious son. But did it matter? If the nanny had caught Grace it was only a matter of time before Annabelle and my brother heard of it. I had to go in and find out what was going on.

Gripping the door knob I was embarrassed to feel the film of sweat lubricating the metal. Taking a deep breath to steady my hand, I strode into the nursery, expecting to see Martha. Instead Annabelle and Miss Woodley, Frederick's nanny turned to face me, brows furrowed. Their torsos faced one another, like duellists, Annabelle's hands were placed on her hips, but relaxed into a more neutral position when she registered who she was now looking at. Miss Woodley looked on the verge of tears. Her gammon-pink face was rumpled, her fists were balled up and hung pathetically at her sides.

"I'm sorry, I heard voices and..." I tailed off, noticing straight away that the Frederick was absent from the scene. The knot untied slowly, allowing relief to wash through me. "Mr. Brooks told me you were in Stamford, Annabelle."

Her face gradually contorted into her usual broad smile, "I just arrived back. How are you Alice? I thought you were arriving tomorrow."

"I left a message yesterday." I felt like an intruder and wished I had stayed out of it.

"Well at least you'll be able to enjoy the fête. Please excuse me, I've got so much to do." She bustled past me, her smile still planted in her cheeks.

"We will discuss this tomorrow, Miss Woodley." She called back, leaving me alone with the harassed nanny. I asked her if she had seen Grace or Martha in an attempt to kill the silence.

"I haven't seen them since this morning m'lady." she squeaked.

"Sit down, Miss Woodley. You look upset." I gestured to the wooden rocking chair in the corner. "What was all that about?"

She arranged herself in the chair, her short legs barely reaching the rug underneath, all the while looking at the door, as if waiting for Annabelle to return.

"Don't worry about Mrs. Goldhurst. She's rather highly strung and this is her first child; she's probably worrying herself unnecessarily. She will have forgotten about it by tomorrow, what with this fête she's organising."

"I-I'm sure she will." Miss Woodley muttered, visibly shaken. Annabelle must have given her a roasting.

"What was she saying to you? Because if she's bullying you I am more than happy to speak to her."

"No, no, Miss, please don't, it's fine, honestly." She jumped up as quickly as one could from a rocking chair, her eyes suddenly wide and imploring. "I wanted to go to my sister's wedding next week, only Mrs. Goldhurst says I can't as I'm needed here."

"Is that it? Oh really! I'm sure allowances can be made for your sister's wedding. It's not like it happens every week and you've been doing a grand job looking after little Fred. I will speak to my brother about it and see if we can make alternative arrangements. How long will you need off?"

"Oh, no m'lady. Thank you but it doesn't matter. Please don't say anything to Mr. Goldhurst, will you?"

"Nonsense, Annabelle shouldn't be allowed to frighten you like this. You're entitled to some time off. Leave it with me." I smiled encouragingly and turned to leave.

"Oh, Miss, please!" I felt plump fingers clasp my arm and bridled. I wasn't expecting it. Miss Woodley realised her mistake and let go as if she had been burned.

"Oh, dear! Forgive me, m'lady, I didn't mean to do that. Please, I beg you; don't say anything to Mr. Goldhurst yet. Let me talk to Mrs. Goldhurst again first. Please." She looked on the verge of tears again. It was strange. Annabelle's spell was certainly strong in this part of the house.

"If you insist. I don't want to make life more difficult for you. But promise me you will tell me if my sister-in-law is being too heavy-handed with you."

"Thank you, Miss, I will, but she's not."

I nodded and turned to leave, realising that Frederick and Grace were still missing.

"Miss Woodley, I forgot to ask, where is my nephew?"

"He's with his father, m'lady."

"Oh, thank heavens! I thought we'd lost him!" I laughed. Miss Woodley laughed nervously back.

I made my way up to Grace's room on the next floor and heard Martha's warm, familiar voice.
"You found her then? We were worried about you, Grace." She didn't look up; but continued to arrange her stuffed animals on a large wicker chair my uncle had given us years ago. My mother detested it, so gave it to her.
"Yes, she was up here the whole time, Miss Alice. Sorry to alarm you."
"That's quite all right. Actually, I was wondering if you two would like to go for a little walk down to the lake before luncheon. I could do with stretching my legs."
"No." Grace shot back whilst still fussing with the toys.
"Don't be so rude, Grace, we could do with some fresh air and you haven't seen your sister for weeks." Martha said.
"I want to play chess."
Martha rolled her eyes, "We played chess all morning and you beat me every time! I'm sure we can have half an hour away from chess."
"I'm not going." The husky voice was decisive.
"That's a shame because I heard that there are some little ducklings nesting there with their mother, just born yesterday. I suppose I'll just have to go down and see them myself. It'll be a shame for you to miss out, though." I said.
She stopped and sat still for a moment, unsure whether to trust me. "Are they really there?"
"I hope so. I tell you what we can do - we'll take some food down for them and if they are there we can feed them; if they're not we can walk on to the river and feed the ducks. What do you think?"
She stood still, only her dark eyes sprung from her stuffed animals, to the chess board atop the bedside table, to the door, weighing up her options.
"It sounds like a wonderful idea to me." Martha added.
"Yes, I'll go for a walk to see the ducklings."
She stood up and shuffled out the door. Martha winked at me and followed close behind with her coat.

As I thought, there were ducks nestled amongst the reeds on the lake, but no ducklings. I convinced Grace that the ducks were due to lay their eggs any day now so we should leave them alone. She seemed satisfied with this and we carried on towards the village.
She gambolled ahead of us, a tall, ungainly young woman with a slightly unkempt appearance, despite Martha's best efforts to spruce her up. Poor Grace, I thought; almost twenty years old and trapped in the perpetual mind of a child. She would never be able to work, fall in love, get married or have children of her own; in fact, she would never be able to cope without

Martha or someone like Martha. That was another worry. It would be naïve of us all to think that Martha would be around forever. She had hinted to me once or twice that she was averse to marriage, and past the stage of thinking about children, so there was no immediate danger of her leaving. But the war had taught me well - situations can change in an instant and alter your life forever.

"I was so worried earlier when you couldn't find Grace. I thought...well, you know what I thought as you were thinking it yourself."

"Yes. I feel quite embarrassed for worrying you like that, Miss Alice. I know you have more important things on your mind and, well, I know Grace would never do anything like that again. She's changed so much since then and I would be shocked if she ever," She hesitated, "behaved in that way again."

"I agree that she has improved no end, thanks to you. I know we don't always say it, but you've been a godsend to our family, Martha; your manner with Grace and the things you've taught her have had an incredible impact." I paused. "Therefore I don't want you to be offended by what I'm about to say." She looked at me, expectantly. "The truth is I feel an incredible sense of unease with Grace being under the same roof as a baby. I just keep expecting to hear some awful news about her smothering or strangling Freddie because of his crying."

"I've been watching her like a hawk, Miss. And the nanny is in the nursery all the time so there's no way she could do anything." Martha said in hushed tones.

"I'm sure we both thought that eleven years ago."

Martha looked at me and away again hastily. Grace had stopped and was staring up at a canopy of trees, hooting like an owl. We halted a few yards behind.

"I didn't mean to be abrupt. You're the only person I can talk to about it. I often wonder whether I did the right thing."

"What do you mean? Telling me?" Martha said.

"No, I mean should I have told Mother and Father about it?" I trailed off.

"You did the right thing, of that I am certain." Martha said. "If you had told your parents, God rest their souls, you know how they would have reacted. Your mother would have been devastated and your sister would have been sent away."

I nodded, watching Grace lope along the path in front again.

"Do you remember that time we went to Scotland to see that macabre hospital? With Mr. Irvine?" I said as we continued walking.

"How could I forget? You wouldn't have wanted Grace sent away to a place like that, would you?"

"No of course not, but, I feel like I ought to say something now; I don't want to put innocent people at risk."

"Miss Alice, do you seriously think your sister is a risk to your family?"

"I don't know, Martha; outwardly, no, but I thought that when…"

"Please trust me. She made a mistake then, a terrible mistake I grant you, but I know that she will never do anything like that again. She learned her lesson. As I keep saying, Grace is not as stupid as people assume."

I relaxed, "She hasn't tried anything? Or exhibited any strange behaviour around the baby?"

"Nothing to cause alarm. She hates the noise he makes, but she deals with it in her own way and I help her through it. Remember I spend every hour of every day with her, Miss, I would know if there was something wrong."

"If you do think something changes in her behaviour you must tell me straight away, Martha. Do you promise?"

"I promise. Stop worrying so much, Miss. All is under control." She smiled at me and I smiled back, the foreboding in my stomach slowly subsiding.

"Isn't this simply wonderful?" Annabelle exclaimed as another bus trundled up the gravel drive, belching out people of all ages, their reactions all the same – a gasp, a cry of delight and a run or a quick walk down the slope into the throng. There were easily over two hundred people in our garden and the noise was incredible: laughter and cheers from the coconut shy; screams and wails from the helter-skelter; the sound of an organ and an accordion playing somewhere amidst the crowd; the buzz and whirr of the merry-go-round and general chatter and bartering at the food stalls. I didn't recognise my own garden.

"I have a feeling that this is the beginning of a long and happy tradition - 'The Annual May Fair at Goldhurst Estate'."

I smiled, feeling queasy from the wafting scent of pies and beer from a nearby stand.

"When I heard the Kinwell fête had been cancelled again I just had to intervene – the poor wretches need something to look forward to." She sighed and fanned herself, despite the coolness of the early evening air. I smiled and waved at Edward and Sophie as they clung on to a deranged-looking horse's mane on the merry-go-round.

"Edward told me that your mother used to hold an annual fête like this until Grace was born; I was quite delighted by the idea of resurrecting the family tradition. It's such a shame she can't enjoy these sorts of things."

"I remember one or two fêtes being held here, vaguely." I said. "They were never as – colourful – as this one, though. My mother organised it for the servants and the villagers, she wouldn't have thought of sending buses to collect people from Stamford."

Annabelle laughed, "See, Alice, you're not the only one in the family who does her bit for charity!"

"Are you donating the funds to a charitable organisation?" I said.

"What? Oh, I should think so, but we might not turn a profit."

A stout woman with a square jar and swarthy face chugged up the slope towards us, clutching in her huge hands a jar crammed full of sherbet lemon sweets.

"I beg your pardon, Mrs. Goldhurst, but – Miss Goldhurst, you've won the sweets!"

She held out the jar towards me, her eyes gleaming with excitement.

I frowned and stared at the jar, "I'm sorry, I think you've made a mistake, I didn't enter the contest."

Her hands slowly withdrew and she frowned back at me. "It definitely said 'Miss Goldhurst' on the paper – you were one sweet off – there's three hundred and fifty two and you guessed three hundred and fifty one."

I realised straight away what had happened, "My sister Grace must have guessed – she's very good with numbers."

"Oh, I'm very sorry, m'lady. Where is your sister?"

"I'll take it to her. She gets rather tired; she's inside resting. Thank you so much, Mrs…"

"Boyle, Miss." She beamed, handing me the jar. Annabelle winked at me with all the subtlety of a mating frog. "It's incredible, we've never had a guess that close before!"

"I will be sure to tell her." I smiled. "Excuse me, Annabelle."

"How nice for Grace! Congratulate her for me, will you?" She simpered and flounced towards the merry-go-round calling my brother's name.

"Grace, look what you've won!" I opened the door to her bedroom only to find it empty.

"Martha?" I called.

"We're in here, Miss Alice."

I followed the voice into the adjoining bathroom where Grace was hunched in the corner, wedged between the bathtub and the wall, covering her ears with her palms, rocking and moaning softly.

"What's wrong?" I mouthed to Martha. She shook her head and pointed to the floor.

"It's the crying again and the noise outside." I had noticed Frederick's crying when I first climbed the stairs, but up here it was all the more audible for his nursery was directly beneath Grace's room. Furthermore, the cacophony of the fête, however, boomed and burst its way in through the closed window.

"It's not so bad, Grace. Do you want me to fetch my gramophone for you?"

She didn't respond but rocked harder.

"Look – you won the 'guess how many sweets in the jar' competition." I laid the jar on the floor so it was eye level with her. "Mrs. Boyle said your guess was the closest they'd ever had – only one sweet off!"

"Well done, duckie!" Martha exclaimed. She ignored us and continued her ritual moaning.

"Will she be all right?" I said to Martha quietly.

She nodded, "I'll keep a close eye on her."

"I'm sure the crying will stop soon, Grace. You used to cry like that, you know! I remember it."

"I hate it!" She shouted, kicking over the jar of sweets which smashed and disgorged three hundred and fifty two sherbet lemons across the bathroom floor.

Chapter Thirteen
15th May 1910, Goldhurst Estate, Rutland
Grace

My little brother is called Robert. He is twenty-six days old and he makes a lot of noise. I don't like him because he makes the house so noisy that I can't hear anything but his cries. We try to read books like 'Little Red Riding Hood' but I can't listen to the words because I can hear him crying all the time. Martha told me I used to cry like that but I don't believe it. She said that I cried just as much as Robert. I always get told off for making a noise in church but no one ever says anything about Robert. Alice said everyone likes him because he is a boy. Mother and Father said it's very good to have another boy. When I was born I had a twin brother called Gregory which I think was a silly name. He died as soon as he was born so he's not my brother anymore.

Sometimes I go and see Robert, but not very often because I don't like him. He is red and wrinkly like a bird when it's first born and he doesn't really do much but cry and wriggle in his bed. When Martha tried to hold his hand he just squeezed his hand shut which means he didn't want to be friends with her. I don't want to be his friend either.

Alice and Charlotte sometimes hold him but he just screams even louder and wriggles like the worms I have seen Mr. Healy dig up in the garden. He said he sometimes accidentally cuts the worms in half with his shovel and they carry on wriggling even though they have been cut into two pieces. I don't believe him.

Mother and Father don't like the crying and the screaming either. Father shouts a lot and stays in his study and Mother is always too ill to look after him. She has been ill since he was born and stays in her bedroom. I think she might be hiding from the noise too. Maybe she is in there trying to read her books as well; I don't know how she concentrates.

Instead there are two nannies that look after Robert. One is young and has orange hair and the other one is old and has grey hair. I can't remember their names but they are not doing very well with their jobs because they never get Robert to shut up.

Yesterday was rainy all day which was horrid because I was going to go to Stamford with Martha, Alice and Charlotte, to go to the toy shop and get a new toy to play with. Then after lunch I was going to help Mr. Healy tend the roses. He says I'm very helpful.

We still went to Stamford (but Charlotte didn't want to come because she didn't want to get wet and we had to take the old car because Father didn't want the new one to get dirty).

I didn't like the umbrella Martha gave me. She only had a black one and it looked like a bat (I hate bats). If I had gone to the toy shop on a day that wasn't rainy I would probably get a book or a teddy bear but today I could only see one good toy: twenty eight dominoes.

Alice didn't come to the toy shop with us, she likes going to the dressmaker's shop, that is her favourite. I hate it. It's boring because there are no books or toys. Stamford has lots of people in it and they all like wearing dark clothes. Today there weren't as many people. Martha said it was because it was raining.

When we got back I wanted to play with my dominoes straight away but Martha said I had to eat my lunch first (a jam sandwich with white bread, two biscuits and an apple). I ate it quickly but Martha told me off because she said I would probably choke with too much food in my mouth. I didn't choke today, though.

A normal twenty-eight domino set has one hundred and sixty-eight dots and when you add it to my old set (that Edward gave to me at Christmas) there should be three hundred and thirty-six, but two tiles are missing so there are three hundred and twenty-five. I like playing dominoes, so Martha and I played three games (I won every game). But I prefer standing them up in a snaky line and pushing them over. I did this for four hours and twenty minutes (two hundred and sixty minutes), which I think is the longest time I have spent playing dominoes.

Martha told me she was going to fetch my supper but I didn't realise she was gone until five minutes past six. It was still raining outside but not as much as before and it was grey outside. I couldn't hear anything except Robert crying. I can't remember if he had been crying the whole time I was playing dominoes, but he was really noisy at five minutes past six. I put my hands over my ears but I could still hear the noise so I decided to go and find Martha.

In the hallway he was even louder, but not as loud as when his bedroom was on the same corridor as mine. Mother moved his room to another part of the house but still on the same floor, which I hate. I had not looked at Robert for a long time but his noise hadn't changed; it was the same annoying noise with no words. I wanted to tell his nanny to get him to be quiet.

Robert's bedroom is like mine but with too much blue and white. Martha told me that because he is a boy everything has to be blue and everything else is white because he is a baby and all baby things are white. His crib is brown and wooden with bars like he's in prison.

The nannies were not in his room at seven minutes past six and Robert was howling so loud that I had to put my hands over my ears.

I went over to his bed and he screamed in my face, waving his fists around like he was a boxer. He was just the same: red, wrinkly and wriggling. I was about to get out of the noisy room but then I had a good idea.

I didn't really want to touch Robert's mouth because there was dribble all over it and he might bite me, but I didn't want to listen to his horrible noise anymore so I tried it with one of his blue blankets. It worked quite well, he was still making a noise but it was quieter. I kept the blanket over his mouth for about ten minutes and he stopped crying completely! He was asleep and it had worked! I had stopped my brother's horrible crying and it was so easy. Mother and Father might even let me have another toy this month as I had been so helpful.

Then Alice came running over to me; I hadn't even seen her come into the room. She looked at Robert and back at me, she looked funny, like she couldn't believe he was so quiet.

I said, "Look Alice, I stopped him from crying!" I was so excited to tell her but she wasn't smiling. She reached in to the crib and touched Robert's mouth and front. Then she put her hands over her face and fell to the floor making a funny noise. She was happy that the noise had finally stopped as well. I copied her and kneeled down next to her.

I said, "It's nice and quiet. We should tell the nannies how to do it so they can get him to sleep every day."

Alice turned and looked at me, her face was all red and her eyes were watery. She looked funny. She suddenly got up and grabbed my arm. I was about to say something but she hissed in my ear like a snake, "Grace, come with me now, we need to get back to your room." She pulled me along and I screamed because I don't like people touching me like that.

In my room Alice shut the door and most of the dominoes fell over. I knelt down to start picking them up but she told me to sit down on the bed. I didn't want to do it so she kneeled in front of me; her face was still red.

She said, "Grace, listen to me now. Do not tell anybody that you were in Robert's room just now and don't tell anyone what you did. Do you understand me?"

I thought this was another game that I didn't understand. She grabbed both of my hands and her eyes were watering even more. I told her to let go and she did.

"This isn't a game, Grace. You have done a very, very bad thing." She stopped and looked out of the window. I looked out as well as I thought there was something outside, but there wasn't. I could just see the grey sky and the treetops, the same as always. Then she said, "Robert is dead. When you put that blanket over his face he wasn't able to breathe and he died." She was making a sniffing sound.

"You must promise not to tell anyone that you did it because you will be in so much trouble...you will get sent away and Mother and Father will be incredibly upset. You must promise not to tell Martha, even."

This seemed like a hard thing to do because Martha was my favourite friend and we talk all the time.

"Do you understand what I'm saying, Grace?"

"I don't want to be sent away." I said and I carried on picking up my dominoes.

Then she said, "This isn't a game, Grace, this has really happened. You have killed our brother and you will be in a lot of trouble if anyone finds out, so please, please don't talk about it at all, to anyone. Promise me? Just imagine this never happened and you were in your room playing dominoes the whole time, like a good girl."

I said to her, "Am I bad, Alice? Am I like the wolf?"

She said, "No, you're not like the wolf because you didn't mean to kill Robert, did you? But you still need to promise me not to tell anyone else about what you did because you will be in lots of trouble and it will make everyone very upset."

I wanted to know where Martha was with my supper as it was nearly half past six. I asked Alice.

"Stay here, I'll go and find her. Remember, no talking about this to anyone, all right? If you do then...then...people will think you're bad like the wolf and they'll send you away."

I hate the wolf. He's dangerous, so I told her I wouldn't tell Martha.

"Good girl." She said and she kissed me on the head which I wiped off because I don't like it. She left my room and I carried on picking up my domino tiles. It was nice and quiet when Robert was dead.

Chapter Fourteen
20th October 1922, Goldhurst Estate, Rutland
Martha

"Good Afternoon, Goldhurst Couture of Bond Street, Clara Harwood speaking."

The mouth piece was slick with sweat and was in danger of slipping out of my shaking hand. I could see the outline of Mrs. Quince behind the net curtain of her sitting room, listening in, no doubt. I lowered my voice as much as possible.

"Can I speak with Miss Alice Goldhurst, please?"

"I'm sorry, Miss Goldhurst is busy. The line is poor - I can hardly hear you." The girl said.

"I do need to speak to her urgently." I said a little louder, the trembling was travelling down to my knees forcing me to sit in Mrs. Quince's leather chair.

"Like I said, she's busy with a client so you'll have to make an appointment."

"It's a family matter," I interrupted. "It's about her sister, Grace; I'm her carer. Please can you ask her to speak to me for a moment?"

There was a brief silence then the haughty voice said, "Hold on please."

I heard a rustle then an abrupt silence, punctuated with crackling on the line. I closed my eyes and told myself aloud that it would be all right. Miss Alice would know what to do. Miss Alice would help us.

"Martha?" The voice made me start.

"Miss Alice, is that you?"

"What's the matter? Has something happened to Grace?"

I swallowed and lowered my voice so as not to include Mrs. Quince in our conversation. "Oh, Miss, you must come back as soon as you can. Grace...she..." I heard voices in the corridor outside - some of the housemaids. I heard Ms. Quince shush them and shoo them on.

"What's happened? Tell me what's wrong!" she cried.

"She's done it again, you know?"

"What?"

I swallowed again and whispered, "Like what she did to Robert."

I heard her gasp, "Not Frederick?"

"He's fine, but Mrs. Goldhurst and the nanny found her in the nursery. Mr. Goldhurst is in such a temper...I've never seen him so angry and Mrs. Goldhurst wants to call the police."

"Oh God! Please tell me she hasn't."

"No, no, Mr. Goldhurst wouldn't let her. But he's locked Grace in her room and won't let me near her. He insists he's going to send her away and they want me to go." The lump in my throat erupted into a sob and my voice wobbled. "I tried to talk to them; I really have tried..."

"I know, I know. Don't worry, I'll be back tonight, I'm leaving now, tell Edward." She said.

"Miss Alice, there's something else." I didn't want to tell her, but what choice was there now?

"What is it?" I could tell her heart was pounding as much as mine.

"Your brother knows about Robert." I could almost feel the colour drain from my face; a cold sweat broke over my brow. The secret we had kept for so long was loose and about to destroy us all.

"What? How? Who told him?" She spluttered.

I rubbed tears of shame out of my eyes and sniffed. "Miss Woodley, the nanny, overheard me talking to Grace about Robert. She told Mrs. Goldhurst and she wouldn't leave us alone until I told her the truth." She cursed and exhaled. "I...I didn't have a choice. She said she'd sack me and I'd never see Grace again if I didn't tell her."

"The blackmailing bitch!" She shouted suddenly. "What exactly did you tell her?"

"I didn't mention your part in the concealment, Miss. I kept telling her it was an accident, I tried to explain." A sob escaped my mouth, "I'm so sorry, I've ruined everything."

She cut me off, "How did Grace get into the nursery?"

"We were outside looking for her book one minute then – I heard screaming – she must have sneaked up there. I was distracted by Mrs. Quince talking to me – I thought she was with Mr. Gribble in the garden."

There was a long silence, then she said, "I must leave now. I'll catch the first train I can to Peterborough and hire a cab to Goldhurst. Martha?"

"Yes Miss?"

"Please try to stop Edward from doing anything rash before I get there. Do everything you can."

I assured her I would and she hung up, leaving me to stare at the black contraption that was now covered with clammy fingerprints.

"Ahem, have you finished?" Mrs. Quince had entered the sitting room without knocking and glared at me, eyebrows raised and arms folded. She reminded me of my old schoolteacher with her greying hair pulled back and her drab black dress. She had been a miserable, heartless woman too. Even though we had never been friends I had to admit that I missed Mrs. Brickett. At least she had a heart underneath the cold hard outer crust of reserve.

"Yes, thank you." I pushed past her and out into the service yard. I needed fresh air. I needed space to think. One of the footmen was leaning against the wall smoking. I asked him for a cigarette. He looked surprised but handed me one and his box of matches. I lit it, inhaled the smoke and held it in my lungs for a second before collapsing into pealing coughs. I had never been a smoker, and it did little to calm my nerves. The footman smirked and went back inside.

I just needed to think. Why was Grace in the nursery? I didn't understand. We were looking for her missing book in the garden, so how did she end up in the nursery? She always stayed as far away from the first floor as possible. Normally I couldn't drag her there – it didn't make sense. If only I could get to her to hear her explanation. I couldn't believe she meant to harm the baby. She was so much better at controlling herself these days, she knew better than to do something like that. This had to be a misunderstanding.

A tiny drop of rain spotted my hand. My eyes roved skywards - grey cloud upon grey cloud. I clenched my teeth and raised my chin. I had to find Edward Goldhurst and convince him to let me see Grace somehow. Surely he wouldn't send her away? He was angry but after he calmed down and Miss Alice had spoken to him he would change his mind. I could take her to Bradcote for a few weeks to let the dust settle, perhaps, and if the worst happened and she was sent away, I would follow her – to Miss Louisa's home in London or wherever she was sent.

"Martha, are you there?" a voice called. I pushed open the door to see Jill, one of the housemaids. "Martha, Mrs. Quince wants to speak to you at once."

"What does she want?" I asked, annoyed that I couldn't go directly to Mr. Goldhurst.

"I have a message for you from Mr. and Mrs. Goldhurst." Mrs. Quince's long angular face glared at me from the kitchen doorway like a demon's. "Come into my sitting room."

Chapter Fifteen
20th October 1922, Goldhurst Estate, Rutland
Alice

"Excuse me, can you drive a little faster?" I called to the cab driver as we whittled our way through Stamford.

"I'm going as fast as I can, madam. There've been a lot of accidents on these roads due to maniacs thinking they're in some kind of motor race. The law's the law, you know."

I gritted my teeth and tapped my foot on the floor of the car. I had to get to Grace and Martha first somehow, to get the full perspective. When I had all the facts I could appeal to Edward's better nature. I wasn't sure how he would react when I told him that I knew about Robert. I wasn't even sure if I should I tell him at all.

"Madam!" The driver was glaring at me from the mirror. "Can you stop making that noise? It's distracting me!"

We had barely crunched to a stop at the end of the gravel driveway when I smacked down money on the passenger seat and threw open the car's door.

"Hey! Don't yer want yer change, madam?"

"Keep it!" I yelled back and ran around the side of the house to enter through the morning room's doors, which were always unlocked during the day.

As I jogged into the hallway, Mr. Brooks saw me, his face changing from stern to surprised to humble in a matter of seconds. "Miss Goldhurst, we weren't expecting you!"

"Brooks, where is Martha?"

"Martha has gone." A vinegary voice interrupted. Mrs. Quince stood behind Brooks, her hands folded in front of her, her long face giving nothing away.

"Gone where?"

"Mr. Goldhurst dismissed her from his service earlier this afternoon, with immediate effect. A car took her to the station about an hour ago."

My mouth opened and closed pathetically. I looked at Brooks, who looked away, confirming that it was true.

"I need to see my brother right away, where is he?" I moved towards the library but Mrs. Quince stood in my way.

"I'm afraid Mr. and Mrs. Goldhurst are busy; they don't want to be disturbed by anyone."

"Mrs. Quince!" Brooks began to protest on my behalf.

"It's all right, Brooks, this woman is still new to Goldhurst; therefore we must forgive her if she hasn't quite grasped how to speak to people in their own home." Her eyes locked onto mine: grey and unblinking. Clearly

Annabelle had trained this Mrs. Quince herself. "Now tell me where Mr. Goldhurst is or Brooks, the footmen and I will have to scour the house ourselves."

She pursed her lips, "I'm only following instructions from Mr. and Mrs. Goldhurst, I meant no offence, Miss." She carried on staring at me; I said nothing. "He's upstairs in his rooms."

"Thank you," I ran past her up to Edward's rooms and knocked on every door until I got a response.

Edward, grim-faced, opened the door and ushered me inside. I hadn't seen him looking so sombre since Sarah died. He was pale and rubbed at his bleary eyes and temple. I looked past him and, to my dismay, Annabelle was sitting on the sofa, her face heavily powdered and rouged, wearing a black chiffon velvet gown that made her look even more like a witch as she glared at me.

"I heard what happened, how is Frederick?" I asked Edward.

"Absolutely terrified, no thanks to that murderous mad woman! He's been crying all day, my poor innocent little boy." She let out a little sob and covered her mouth with her handkerchief.

"Where's Grace? I need to talk to her, Edward. You don't honestly think she meant to hurt him?"

Annabelle gasped so loud that Edward and I started, "I saw her! I saw her trying to strangle my son! Her lunatic hands around his little throat…God forbid if I hadn't have been there, she would have killed him without a care, just like she killed your poor little brother. Well, she's not going to escape justice this time…"

"Shut up will you! What right have you got to speak about Robert? You know nothing about it, it was an accident…"

"How do you know about it?" Edward said, narrowing his eyes at me.

Annabelle gasped again, "I knew it! They're all in cahoots! Her and the nanny worked together to cover it up!"

"I need to talk to you alone, Edward. I can't talk to you with all this noise in the background." I said without looking at her.

Edward turned his gaze to the window, slowly. "Annabelle, dearest, go and check on Frederick, please."

"Oh no, Edward, I'm not leaving her to manipulate you…"

"Just go, please, I won't be long." It was the first time I had heard him raise his voice to her and the shock was visible on her face. She huffed and walked towards the door, offering me a bitter glare as she passed.

"She's going to get what she deserves this time. Nobody attacks *my* son and evades punishment!" She slammed the door as she left and we listened to her footsteps retreat down the corridor.

"It's true, then, you knew about Robert?" Edward said finally.

I swallowed and leaned against the window sill. I expected to see rain pelting onto the gardens; the sky was such a murky shade of grey.

"How long have you known?" he pressed.

The temptation to lie was great. Martha had gone, Grace was ruined, what good would it do to tell him? Edward was staring at me, his eyes hard and incendiary. This must be how one felt being cross-examined in a courtroom. I couldn't lie.

"I-I was there. I came into the room shortly after she…" I was unable to look at him. "I know it must sound awful but it was an accident, Edward, she didn't realise what she was doing and I was young and afraid. I panicked, I didn't want her to be sent to prison."

Edward's eyes were filling with tears; the sight made my throat constrict until I thought I would faint through lack of breath. "Our own brother, Alice! You let her get away with murder!"

"It wasn't like that. I love Grace, I didn't want her to be sent away. Don't suggest that I didn't feel desperately upset afterwards. I cried myself to sleep for over a year after that day."

"Annabelle was right, she's not going to get away with it this time." He wiped his eyes and snarled.

"You don't mean that. She doesn't understand…"

"You know the only reason Father didn't send her away was because Mother begged him not to. He knew that we were out of our depth with her and foresaw the trouble she would cause later in life. The day before I was married Sarah he said to me, 'after we've gone, if she's no better, I won't blame you if you decide to put her in a home'. But he loved our mother and knew that sending that child away would break her heart."

I stared at him, desperately trying to think of the right words that would save us, but my thoughts were interrupted with the re-entrance of Annabelle, who was followed by the small, plump figure of Miss Woodley.

"Tell her what you saw, nanny," Annabelle barked at the woman, "and show her what she did last week."

I stared at Miss Woodley, trembling and watery eyed. She opened her mouth and emitted a strange whimpering sound before closing it again.

"You're not in trouble, Nanny Woodley. Be honest, tell Miss Goldhurst." Edward said quietly, turning to the window and rubbing his temples again.

"Well, I…I saw the younger Miss Goldhurst, well, actually I heard her first, she was in Master Frederick's bedroom. I asked the servant to fetch Mrs. Goldhurst quickly and I went in and…and she was trying to strangle Master Frederick, Lord have mercy!" She sniffed, covering her face with her hands.

"There! Do you understand now? Tell her the rest, nanny, what did she do to you last week?"

Miss Woodley dropped her hands and gave Annabelle a pleading look as if she were unable to continue, but she merely arched her eyebrows and nodded her head indicating for her to continue.

Miss Woodley took a long breath and said, "She attacked me last week."

"What?" I gasped.

"Yes, look." Annabelle pointed at Miss Woodley's arm and she slowly eased her sleeve up to reveal a pattern of angry scarlet cross-hatching on her forearm. "And this isn't the worst of it, look at this-"

"No, Mrs. Goldhurst!" Miss Woodley shot a frightened look in Edward's direction.

"Never mind Mr. Goldhurst, he needs to see this too." Annabelle proceeded to button the nanny's dress while she looked miserably at the floor. Edward turned to face the room once more and glared at me before fixing his eyes on the strange scene in front of us.

"Here, here and here, can you see the bite marks as well as the scratches? She did this last Saturday when Nanny found her in Frederick's bedroom and confronted her. She flew into a wild rage and attacked her, the beast! We moved Frederick to another room in the house, as far away from her as possible and she still came looking for him today. Thank God we were here to stop her!"

"But...what about Martha? She'd never let Grace roam the house alone, she'd never let her..."

"Oh, oh, I haven't even started on Martha yet! She's as much to blame as the girl, if not more."

"I don't understand. Martha never leaves Grace's side unless she has to." I protested.

"Ha! That's what you think is it? Martha has been letting her have the run of the house; she's been negligent for months now, that's how she managed to get her vile hands on my poor boy! And if that wasn't bad enough, she's been bribing Nanny Woodley to keep it quiet."

"What!" Edward and I cried in unison.

Annabelle sighed, "It's true, Edward, I wanted to tell you alone but *she* needs to hear it too. She needs to realise what her partner in crime is really like - a devious, lying..."

"Stop! You're the liar! Martha would never do that."

"Nanny Woodley, what did Martha say to you?" Edward interjected. The nanny shuddered, her face reddening. "You're not in trouble," he said, more gently, "I just want to establish the truth."

Annabelle nodded manically again, folding her arms and pursing her red lips.

"Martha said she would give me half her pay if I kept quiet." She squeaked.

"Kept quiet about what, exactly?" Edward pressed.

"About Grace being in Master Frederick's room and about her attacking me. She didn't want you or Mrs. Goldhurst knowing, Sir." She hastily added, "I didn't take the money, Sir."

"No one's accusing you, Nanny Woodley and thank you, you may go now." Edward said. The small woman hurried to the door gratefully, stroking her forearm.

"Well? What have you to say about your dear, darling sister and her dutiful minder now? What further evidence do we need?" Annabelle's eyes burned into mine and I looked at Edward, willing him to look at me and reassure me the way he had when we were younger.

"You ought to be ashamed of yourself, putting us all in danger when the whole time you knew what she was like! How could you live with yourself if Frederick had been murdered by her? If it were up to me I'd have all three of you arrested."

"That's enough, Annabelle." Edward said. I looked at him, thankful, hoping to catch his eye but he turned away and muttered, "Go to your rooms and take what you can now. I'll have Mrs. Quince send the rest to Louisa and Miles in London. Thompson can take you to the station in quarter of an hour."

He went on staring out of the window, his shoulders rising and falling. I felt dizzy, Edward's back blurred into two, then three, dancing in front of me in some awful vision.

"Edward, please, listen…"

"Get out!" He spun around and thundered across the room, towards me, his face terrifying, like a warrior's. "I want nothing more to do with you or her, do you hear me? I don't want to see you or hear you; I want nothing to do with your business; I want you to leave my house for good. Now get out!"

The tears that had been pooling in my lower lids poured forth in torrents. I ran past Annabelle, not daring to look at the triumphant look that I knew she would be displaying. I ran from the room, tears gushing down my cheeks without shame, no longer caring who saw me.

I opened the door to my bedroom and threw myself onto the bed, unable to control the spasms and the tears. Guilt and despair washed through my insides and raced back up from my stomach out of my mouth and I retched into an old basin under the bed. I had been a fool. A reckless, reckless fool. Grace could have killed my nephew, Edward's child and I had all but allowed it to happen. Although I had my fears about Grace, Martha had always been so adamant that she was better, that she would never be a danger to anyone again. Hadn't I seen her improve with my own eyes? Was I so deluded that I had convinced myself that she was fine? Or was it all a lie? It couldn't be, where else would Miss Woodley's sustain such injuries? It must be the truth, Grace really was out of control and I had stood back and said nothing. She would have to be sent away now, it wouldn't be safe to have her live with Louisa and Miles, or any family for that matter. Perhaps this was the answer all along. I had been naïve in thinking she could live at home forever. This was the end.

I had only one suitcase as I had left the rest of my luggage in London. There wasn't much that I could take; the best of my clothes were already at Louisa's house, so I packed a few undergarments, perfume and paint brushes. I wanted to take my old Singer with me, but of course it was too heavy to carry on the train. I stroked it several times, not wanting to leave it and felt a surge of painful nostalgia. I sat down on the stool and mimed threading the needle. Edward was the eldest and a man. This was his house now. "His and Annabelle's." I muttered. That was one of the hardest truths to bear - Annabelle had been right and she had made me look like I didn't know my own family.

I stood and took my suitcase, looking around me once more. Edward was angry, it was to be expected, but after his anger was spent he would forgive me, and maybe Grace too, with time. I knew my brother, he had a temper, but his moods never lasted that long. He would apologise and invite me back when he was ready. Then Louisa and I could visit Grace, wherever she would be, once she had settled in.

I wiped my eyes with my handkerchief and left the room. I didn't stop on the staircase to admire the portraits or the antique vases. I didn't pay attention to the sounds of the house, the doors opening and closing or the voices of servants hidden below stairs. I didn't breathe in the scent of the old house – roses mingled with polish. I was used to it all and I knew I would be back before long. Even as I walked out of the front doors, greeted by Thompson and the Rolls Royce, I didn't think to go back and say goodbye to Brooks and the other servants, some of whom had been at Goldhurst longer than I had. Instead I left upset but hopeful. My brother loved me. I knew it.

The car crawled out of the Estate and cruised through Kinwell towards Stamford. I said a prayer for my parents as we passed the church. What would they think of it all? Would this have happened if they were still here? I couldn't fathom Martha's role in the incident. To leave Grace unattended and resort to bribery seemed absurd, but why would Nanny Woodley lie?

I leaned my head back to rest on the seat and watched the fields and hedgerows whiz by. The thick grey clouds that had threatened rain grew darker still and soon spots appeared on the windows. On leaving Stamford I leaned forward for a glimpse of Burghley House before rehearsing what I was going to tell Louisa and Miles.

She was sitting in the drawing room, waiting for me when I arrived. I could tell from the look on her face that she knew. She had been crying; her face was blotched and lined. Edward or Annabelle must have telephoned her and told her everything, including my involvement.

"I'm sorry." I said as soon as the footman closed the door behind him. She gestured for me to join her on the sofa then drew a handkerchief to her nose and sniffed. "I didn't want to upset you like this, Louisa."

"Why didn't you tell me about Robert's..." She closed her eyes and grimaced.

"I-I didn't tell anyone because, well, because I didn't want her to be sent away, or imprisoned, or hanged."

"You knew she wouldn't have been hanged or sent to prison; she was a child."

"Exactly, a child who didn't understand what she was doing and...if I told everyone they wouldn't understand, they'd just think how awful it was that a baby was killed and not take into account her condition."

"So you'd rather let her get away with it!" I had never heard Louisa raise her voice before and it stunned me into silence.

"Look, what's done is done, as terrible and cruel as it is, it cannot be undone, so there's no point in arguing about it. But you must understand, Alice, that Grace can never live with any of us again; she's dangerous; she needs psychiatric care."

I had thought of nothing else during the journey back to London. Horrified as I was by Miss Woodley's claims, part of me could not bring myself to believe them. The only conclusion I could draw was that Annabelle was behind it all, but could even she be that evil? I put this to Louisa who listened patiently before speaking again.

"Alice, I know you and Charlotte have taken a disliking to Annabelle and, as far as I can see, this disliking is merely borne from some sort of juvenile jealousy and not founded on anything." I began to protest but she silenced me immediately, "You do realise that this secret kept by yourself and Martha Pick could ruin you? You could even be investigated by the police. You were an accomplice to murder, after all."

I stared at her, unblinking. Louisa had always been so sweet, so gentle and understanding, to hear her speaking like this frightened me. "Of course none of us want to see you ruined; we're your family and we love you very much, but Miles and I will no longer protect you if you fail to realise the severity of Grace's illness and continue to cause trouble between Edward and Annabelle. Now, we have decided to bring forward our move to Paris. I want you to come with us. Miles will help you get started with your couture business there and I want no more talk of Grace."

She rose and smoothed the front of her dress. "Perhaps I'm partly to blame, I left you all when you were very young and I've hardly been around since then. I've been too indulgent and diplomatic on this subject and it's time for me to put my foot down. You must leave Edward to decide what to do with Grace, he is her legal guardian after all, not you, and you mustn't interfere. As for your friendship with Martha, that has to be severed, for both your sakes, so no running away to find her, do you hear me?"

I looked down at my feet and nodded, feeling like a child again.

"Good, well," her voice had changed from acerbic to her usual calm, soft tone, "I don't think we need to speak of it again for the time being. It's late, you must be exhausted. Would you like me to call Trafford to fetch you something to eat?"

"No thank you, I haven't much of an appetite." I mumbled.

"Very well, I'll say good night then. We'll discuss the arrangements for Paris tomorrow." She touched me lightly on the arm and went out, leaving me lost and alone.

Chapter Sixteen
20th October 1922, Goldhurst Estate, Rutland
Grace

I hate being locked in my room. Mother and Father used to do it, but they died. I screamed so much when they locked me in my bedroom. I wanted Martha but Edward told her to go so I screamed and kicked the door.

After I had breakfast this morning (two slices of brown toast and one egg) I went to get a book to read from my shelf. 'Little Red Riding Hood' wasn't there and it's always there – it's my favourite. Martha and I looked for it everywhere. It wasn't in my room, it wasn't in the morning room, it wasn't in the upstairs nursery or the big nursery, it wasn't in the drawing room, it wasn't in the kitchen, it wasn't in the library, it wasn't in Alice's room, we couldn't find it anywhere in the house. It made me cry because 'Little Red Riding Hood' is my favourite book of all and Martha has read it to me since I was a baby, which I can't remember but I remember her reading it to me when I was three (although this book is my third copy).

I wanted to look outside in the garden because we read it out there yesterday. Martha said no because it was going to rain but I really wanted to find 'Little Red Riding Hood' so I went out to look in the rose garden.

Mr. Gribble wasn't in the rose garden so I had to look on my own (I don't like Mr. Gribble much. I really liked Mr. Healy but he's dead). I looked under all the bushes but it wasn't there. I wanted to go to the lake to look as well but Annabelle (the lady who is married to my brother) came and told me that she had seen it in Frederick's room. Frederick is my nephew which means he is my brother's son. I don't like him because he screams and cries really loud like all babies do. I don't like babies. I don't like Annabelle either because she shouts at me or laughs at me sometimes.

Even though I don't like going in Fredrick's room I had to find my book, so I covered my ears so his crying wouldn't hurt them. I was pleased because he wasn't crying but he was making a squeaky sound and scrunched up his face which meant he was about to cry.

I looked for my book quickly so I could leave, but it wasn't on the bookshelf. I had to look everywhere: under the crib, inside the toy box and in all the drawers but I couldn't see it.

Annabelle came in again and told me the book was on the shelf (even though I had looked there twice). She told me to look again, which I did, but it wasn't there.

Then Frederick screamed louder than I have ever heard a baby scream. I screamed as well. Annabelle was pinching him! I told her "stop!" and she did but then she covered his face with his blanket. I told her "stop!" twelve times. I hated the noise. She finally let go and then started screaming at me.

It made me cry because my ears were hurting from all the screaming. I wanted Martha. I sat in the corner, closed my eyes and covered my ears.

I don't know how long I was on the floor - I couldn't time it because I couldn't see my watch because it was on my wrist and my hands were over my ears.

When I opened my eyes lots of people were in the room and Annabelle was still screaming and saying things but I still couldn't hear very well. I wanted 'Little Red Riding Hood'. It was still missing and I wanted to find it and get back to Martha.

Finally I saw Martha but she looked funny. Her face was all wrinkled up and she was crying too. Edward was yelling at her then she took me to my bedroom but she was pulling me by the arm, which she has only done once before when I smashed Mother's old vase when I was thirteen.

I was still crying when we got back to my bedroom and I tried to tell Martha that I was just looking for 'Little Red Riding Hood' and then Annabelle came in and started screaming at me for ten minutes and thirty-one seconds. She said I was a lunatic, but she is wrong because I am a human being, or a girl. I don't know what a lunatic is.

Then Edward came back and shouted at her to get out of my bedroom then he locked the door and I was left alone.

I screamed and cried for a long time. I only stopped when my throat hurt. Then the rain started making a loud noise. There were too many different loud noises and it made me feel sick. So I had to close my eyes and hum for a long time.

I never found 'Little Red Riding Hood'. This was the worst day of my life.

Chapter Seventeen
19th April 1932, St. John's Wood, London
Alice

"Hello, darling." My husband, James, held my shoulders and kissed me on the cheek when I announced my arrival. "How was Lady Caroline?"

"Oh, you know, charming yet very particular. I shan't bore you with it all."

He laughed, "I never tire of hearing about your customers."

"I know, you're very patient."

"Charlotte's in the sitting room, I asked her to stay for supper, is that all right?"

"She's back from Paris?" I said, removing my coat and hat.

"I'll let you two exchange gossip. See you at supper." He kissed me again and went upstairs.

Charlotte was lying on the chaise longue poring over a copy of *The Lady* with all the earnestness of a scholar when I entered. She soon abandoned her reading when she saw me and greeted me with a hug and a smile.

"I take it you both enjoyed your time at Deauville?" I said as I replenished her wine and poured myself a glass.

"Penny adored every minute. She's so interested in fashion already – she even started taking notes of the outfits she saw! I'm still dreaming about the shows, you know." She clapped her hands together in delight. "Your collection was the best by far, of course."

"Thank you. That's very sweet of you but I don't think it's my magnum opus; it's not as good as last year's. I'll have to raise my game next year, especially as there are so many excellent couturiers around now."

Charlotte scoffed and shook her head, "I disagree, I thought it was your best collection yet, those little suits were exquisite, much more feminine than some of the others I've seen. Oh, it's such a shame you couldn't have stayed a little longer. Louisa and I missed you!"

After initially whisking me away to Paris and helping me to start a new life, Louisa and I had drifted apart over the years. After I married James I moved back to London to work and I saw her perfunctorily, every few months or so, and only for a day or two at a time. Our relationship was never the same after the night Grace was sent away. I knew Louisa blamed me for what had nearly happened to Frederick and I resented the heavy-handed approach she took with me at first. Our opinions of one another had changed irrevocably so it was easier to avoid one another rather than confront our feelings.

"I'm sorry for that, but I'm so busy at the moment; everybody's getting ready for the season. I had Lady Caroline Paget today and the Duchess of Brabant is coming later in the week."

"There! You see? Your collection must have impressed."

Francis, the footman, entered carrying a plate of biscuits. "Supper will be ready in half an hour, ma'am."

I thanked him, he bowed and left. We both took a biscuit. I was pleased to see Charlotte back to normal after her separation from Henry the year before. He had run away to California with an American actress without leaving as much as a note by way of explanation for his wife and two children. It had been common knowledge for many years that Henry was a bounder and a womaniser. Charlotte, however, refused to believe these reports until it was too late.

"Where is Penny this evening?" I said.

"The poor thing was exhausted so I thought I'd leave her to sleep."

"And Harry's gone back to Harrow?"

"Yes, can you believe he's almost finished his first year?"

"How is he getting on?"

She pursed her lips and set her glass down. "He adores the sport; he's the most talented athlete and rugger player in his year, but he said he finds the academic side difficult. Like his father, I suppose."

"Better than his father." I corrected.

"Oh yes, he's very polite and respectful; he won't turn out like him, I'll make sure of that."

I smiled. "Oliver went back to Warwick the day before yesterday."

"Oh, I'm sure it broke your heart - he still seems so young!"

"I did have a little tear when we left him at the station, but he loves it there. He got the highest grade in his year in his arithmetic test; he's very good with numbers – he must get that from James because I've never been a natural."

"No, you were always the artist! Do you think you'll send him to Harrow with Harry?"

"Harrow or Eton, we haven't decided yet; he's still got four years to go."

"Freddie's going to Eton." She said.

We lapsed into silence. I hadn't seen Edward or Frederick for nearly a decade and I always felt like an interloper when Charlotte or Louisa spoke about either of them.

"Have you seen Edward lately?" I said finally.

"Not since Christmas." She reached for another biscuit. "I don't go there often anymore, and he never visits me in Knightsbridge."

"I thought you went to Goldhurst every two months or so." I was surprised; Charlotte had always looked forward to taking the children to her old home.

She took a sip of wine and leaned in closer, "I used to, especially when Henry was away. Edward was an absolute darling when he and I separated. He had the children a couple of times and he listened. He never once said 'I told you', he just listened and let me cry." She paused and shook her head. "But I just couldn't stand being in *her* company." She grimaced and took a hasty gulp from her glass, as if mentioning Annabelle left a bitter taste.

"She grows haughtier with age and she has no reason to be! What has she done? She's not successful like you and she hasn't aged well at all." She huffed, "She's still incapable of making civilised conversation; she's only happy talking about herself or bragging about Frederick. She made it very clear that she didn't like Penny and Harry coming around and 'leading Frederick astray'. Not Sophie, just Freddie. I overheard her whinging to Edward. It's become so unpleasant that we only go there once every six months or so to be polite. It's such a shame, but it serves Edward right for staying with such a ghastly woman."

"What can he do? She'd never agree to a divorce, she'd make his life hellish." I said. Charlotte nodded in agreement. "It is sad, isn't it? Goldhurst was our home for years. We were born and brought up there and now it plays no part in my life and virtually no part in yours." I said.

"Dreadfully sad. Anyway, let's talk of more interesting things. What sort of gown did Lady Caroline Paget request?"

After all these years, I was still amazed by Charlotte's ability to glide from a serious subject to a trivial one so easily. "Charlotte, you would have been fantastic on the stage."

She frowned, "What an odd thing to say!"

When I arrived at the Bond Street shop the next morning, another letter was waiting for me underneath the pin box housing Mrs. Birch's gold pins, which had been allocated the role of paper weight over the years. The same small white envelope with the clunky black handwriting sent from Derbyshire. This was the third. He was persistent, but then, he loved his sister. I felt the envelope - it wasn't as thick as the last one – perhaps he would tire of writing soon enough. But what if he arrived at the shop one day, or at the house? I winced and tore open the envelope.

"Let's hear what he's got to say this time." I sighed and read.

Dear Mrs. Hartwright,
As this is my third letter and having checked your address several times I can assume that you are away from London on business. Or perhaps you do not wish to respond. If it is the latter, I must plead again on my sister's behalf.

I did not want to tell you about Martha's illness in a letter, but if you are reluctant to write back perhaps it will convince you to change your mind.

Two months ago, Martha was told that she had cancer and that it is so advanced there is little the doctor can do for her. He was reluctant to give us an exact time but we know we will be lucky if Martha lives to see her forty-ninth birthday in June. As I am sure you can imagine our family is devastated. Martha has been coping with it remarkably well, at least on the surface.

Martha has never spoken much about her time working for your family until recently. She has always been very private about that part of her life. However, she had a visitor several months ago, a former servant, who has lately been dismissed from Goldhurst Estate. Martha will not tell anyone the nature of the visit, or the news given to her, but she is adamant that she must speak to you as soon as possible as the information regards your family.

I understand that you are very busy but it would mean a lot to my sister if you could find the time to visit her before she passes. She has been quite restless since this woman's visit. I know there is something troubling her that she refuses to talk about to me.

I hope you do not find me impertinent for sending you another letter; Martha has spoken very highly of you and I want to help her as much as I can in what little time we have left together.

Our address is on the top of the first page. I only hope this reaches you before it's too late. I sincerely hope to hear from you soon.

Yours sincerely
Mr. William Pick

I wasn't surprised to read of Martha's illness. Her brother had hinted at it twice in his previous correspondence, but the visitor from Goldhurst Estate - this was new. Who had she seen? If indeed she had seen anyone at all. It could be a ruse to get me there. But something inside me knew it was about Grace. How could it not be? Upon Louisa's instruction I had forced myself to forget her and start again after that day. Now I couldn't bear to see her name or visualise her face, let alone think about the past. I didn't want to go. Poor Martha. I still felt guilty when I thought about the way she was treated. It was far easier to forget.

"Anything interesting?"

I jumped. "James, you frightened me! What are you doing here at this time?"

"I thought I might take my beautiful wife out to luncheon."

Of course I hadn't told him anything about William Pick's letters. He didn't know the full extent of the family secret and I was keen for it to stay that way for as long as possible. When I was pregnant with Oliver I had expressed a desire to try and find Grace again, but Louisa had threatened to tell James about everything and I was afraid that it would change his opinion of me, so I abandoned the idea indefinitely.

"What a lovely thought but I'm afraid I'm too busy. I have a fitting in twenty minutes."

"There I was, trying to be romantic." He took my hand gently and kissed it. "Telephone when you're ready to leave later and I'll collect you myself since I'm a man of leisure this week. Are you sure you're all right, Alice? You look a little pale."

"Yes, fine, just a little tired. I didn't sleep too well last night."

"Well don't overdo it."

"I won't." I waved him goodbye and as soon as he left I started writing my reply.

Chapter Eighteen
24th April 1932, Bradcote, Derbyshire
Alice

Bradcote looked like a village well-loved by its inhabitants. No part of it had fallen into disrepair and no garden was slapdash. Every patch of grass was cut to a modest height, every stone had its proper place in the walls, every cottage was proudly cared-for. I usually found villages like these to be so uniform that they lost all their character, yet each cottage was sufficiently different to its neighbour to be considered unique. Some had thatched roofs, some were slate-grey; some were white-washed, others were painted beige or sand or pink; some had large front gardens bursting with flowers and shrubs, some preferred a simple garden path and a few plant pots. The village itself was small and functional. From what I saw it contained a pretty local church with adjoining village green; a small main shopping street with a public house at one end and a post office at the other. No doubt all businesses were run by local families - I remember Martha telling me that her brother had owned the butcher's shop. A couple of motor cars trundled up the streets, but mostly people got around on foot or on bicycle. A view of rolling green farmland and peaks appeared beyond the village. It was a peaceful and welcoming place. It reminded me a little of Kinwell, which drew me into a reflective mood. I imagined Martha walking up the main street, frequenting the local shops, walking in the countryside, trying to forget the past.

"This is it, Clematis Cottage." The cab driver chirped.

It was one of the thatched and whitewashed variety, although the walls were dabbled with ivy, unlike the others. The garden was neat and sufficiently pretty without being ostentatious.

"Thank you," He opened the passenger's door for me and I stepped out, hoping that nobody came out to greet me on the street. "Please could you pick me up from here in two hours? I will need to go back to the station."

"Of course, madam." He tipped his hat and retreated to the driver's side. "Enjoy your visit," He called, leaving me to stare at Clematis Cottage.

The gate groaned as I passed through and approached the front door. Despite its charm I had an overwhelming urge to turn my back on the cottage and run after the driver. Why had I agreed to come here? I hadn't seen Martha for ten years; I had no allegiance to her anymore, and she had none to me. Why was I being summoned like this? Why couldn't she just leave the past alone? I had tried to reconcile with Edward, but it was never going to happen. Of course, the answers were obvious. I knew what the theme of our conversation was likely to be.

I knocked on the door three times. Immediately I heard shuffling within. Oh God, what should I say? I was useless around sick people; I'd had almost no experience, thank heavens.

The door opened and a tweed-clad man stood in front of me, beaming like a friendly garden gnome. Instantly I felt guilty for contemplating escape moments earlier.

"How do you do, Mrs. Hartwright? William Pick. Thank you so much for taking the trouble to visit us." He held out his hand for me to shake.

"How do you do, Mr. Pick?" I replied.

"Please, call me Bill. Do come in, I bet you're famished after your journey." He stood aside to let me by. The house was just as immaculate inside. The furniture looked new and every surface had been polished to Goldhurst standards. I blushed at the knowledge that it was probably for my benefit. Bill Pick took my coat and enquired about the length and quality of my journey, to which I answered positively. A small grey-haired woman, who I assumed was either Martha's mother or Bill's wife, I was never very good at guessing ages, bustled into the room, smiling broadly. She carried a tea tray which she set down on a small dining table. It was laden with food and plates, again, clearly for my benefit.

"Mrs. Hartwright, this is Ivy Dodman, Martha's neighbour. She's been helping me look after her. I don't know how I'd cope without her."

I went to shake her hand but the woman suddenly curtseyed so low I was afraid she might fall flat on her face.

"It's such an honour to be in the same house as a lady of your esteem," she said, fixing her eyes on my face with a smile so wide her face was contorted. "I know this is inferior to what you are used to, m'lady," she continued gesturing sadly at the table. I noticed her hand - two fingers were missing and part of her face had been badly burned. It must have been an old injury; the scars had settled into place, snaking across the right side of her face, cheek, jaw, eye socket. The papery creases had forced her right eye into submission; it was smaller than the other and lacking lashes and brow. Her blue iris was several shades lighter than her left and the pupil was dilated.

"No, no of course not," I assured her. "It looks delightful; I can't wait to try some of it."

The woman's face brightened, she wasn't as old as I had previously thought. "Oh thank you, m'lady. Such a compliment! I was a cook before the war, you know. I re-trained as a nurse and was sent to the Front, hence." She held up her scarred hand apologetically. I opened my mouth and closed it again, trying to think of a suitably sympathetic reply before Bill cut in.

"Martha was going to join us, but unfortunately she's feeling unwell."

"Oh. Could I perhaps take some food up to her?" I said.

"I took some up to her just before you arrived. She hasn't got much of an appetite at the moment. She said she'd like a rest." He looked at the floor. "How about we have some tea down here and afterwards you can go and see her?"

"Of course," I smiled, "do you know what Martha wants to talk to me about? You mentioned my family in your letter."

He glanced at Ivy, who scurried back into the kitchen. "She's told me very little. I think she wants to tell you herself."

The last time I saw Martha, and the final image I had of her, was in 1922, a few months before the three of us had been banished from the house. She would have been thirty eight; a year older than Edward. I remembered her appearance: dark brown hair, hazel eyes, pale skin, a smattering of freckles and a few lines around her eyes and across her forehead. I also remember her demeanour: calm, quiet, patient, kind, devoted to Grace, nervous yet confident at the same time. The woman I saw when I climbed the creaky stairs and entered the main bedroom of Clematis Cottage looked like an elderly relative of hers. It was as if a creature had visited her while she slept, sucking the life from her body, ageing her by about forty years in ten. She was propped up by three pillows and swaddled in cream blankets. Still she shivered.

"Hello Miss Alice," a voice within the figure croaked.

"Hello Martha. Please just call me Alice," I replied, trying not to wince. "Dear me, it's been so long since we last saw each other."

"Nearly ten years." She swallowed loudly and grimaced.

"Would you like some water?" I said, reaching for the glass. She waved her hand feebly.

"No thank you, Miss. Bill didn't tell me you were coming until this morning. I would have made more of an effort; forgive me."

"Don't be silly, Martha. You know I wouldn't expect it." She closed her eyes, her brow furrowed. The lines I remembered were as deep as trenches now. "I'm sorry. I shouldn't be here, you need to rest."

"No, no. The reason you're here is to talk. I can spend the remainder of my life resting. Please sit down."

I was about to object to her addressing me as 'Miss' once more, but thought better of it.

"What is it, your condition?"

"Breast cancer. And I recently had the 'flu which turned out to be pneumonia. Poor Bill's taken it harder than I have. We only lost my mother two years ago." She stared out of the cross-hatched window. "And his wife left him three years back. Apart from his children, whom he hardly sees, I'm the only family he has left."

"But is there nothing the doctors can do? I know lots of very good doctors in London who specialise in cancer. Please let me help, let me make you an appointment," I pleaded. Martha shook her head.

"I am grateful for the offer but it would make no difference. It's too late for me. Look at me!" She chuckled throatily, "the doctor says I'll be lucky to see Easter."

I looked away, unused to this kind of talk. The old Martha was long gone, but I still felt a tie to the stranger lying enervated before me. I felt ridiculous for not replying to her brother's letters sooner. The very least I owed her was a visit.

I caught sight of a painting hanging on the far wall in a gilt frame. "Is that Edinburgh?"

Her eyes bobbed towards the painting like the hand on a compass. "Do you remember giving it to me, Miss? You'd spent so long on it and then you said you didn't like it."

The old, dusty memory came flooding back; it had been the day before we visited St. Giles' Hospital. My mother must have been pregnant with Robert at the time. I walked over to inspect it.

"Arthur's Seat, I remember." I recognised the clouds and the pile of stones constructed by Grace. Then, in the foreground, were two figures, one dressed in dark brown, sitting patiently on a rug, gazing at a small girl with wispy hair and a blue dress. "It's not bad, actually. I don't know why I didn't like it at the time."

A cough brought me back into the present and I hurried back to the chair by her bed. "I'm so sorry for not getting in touch with you before now."

"Don't apologise." She said sincerely.

"So, what did you do after...after that day we all left Goldhurst?" I asked. Her eyes closed and she started coughing again. I passed her the glass of water and noticed the bones shallow beneath her shrunken fingers.

"Why...don't you...tell me what...you've been doing since 1922?" She uttered the words breathlessly, her eyes watering.

"Are you sure you're up to this, Martha?" She nodded her assent so I began.

"Immediately afterwards I went to live with Louisa and Miles in London. Then they left to live in Paris so I went with them and set up a new shop there. I spent most of my time at the shop, which turned out to be a very good thing as the business flourished. I have more shops in London, one in Edinburgh and Manchester as well as the one in Paris. Many customers want a shop in New York so I'm planning that next. I've been most fortunate..." Guilt crept over me again; I must have sounded spoilt and self-serving to her. But she looked so happy, which made me feel even worse.

"And you're married now?"

"Yes. I met my husband in Paris. He was working with Miles and we married on New Year's Eve in 1923. James is a wonderful man and always very supportive of my business."

"Do you have any children?"

"One, a boy called Oliver. He's seven and doing extremely well at school."

Martha smiled. "You have the perfect life, Miss Alice." I shifted uncomfortably on the hard chair.

"Anyway, enough about my life, what about you?" I was keen to shift the focus away from me. Her eyes clouded over as she took a deep breath.

"I came back here, to stay with my mother after..." She trailed off and was silent for a moment before starting again, "I didn't have anywhere else to go. After a few weeks of dwelling and fretting about what had happened, Mother encouraged me to apply for other positions with wealthy families around Derby. She arranged several interviews for me; all of them involved looking after children. But I just couldn't go through with it. It seemed wrong. I couldn't bear the thought of looking after children again. Besides, I could hardly ask for a reference. So my brother took pity on me and gave me a job working in his butcher's shop and here I've stayed quietly ever since." She closed her eyes for some seconds. "Of course I had to leave the butcher's three years ago when my mother became ill. I had to care for her; she had done so much for me I wanted to be there for her too. Since then I've nursed quite a few people around the village, including Ivy, whom I'm sure you've met." I nodded. "She lived in the next village; there was a fire in her house. She was lucky to escape alive."

I frowned, "I thought she got her injuries during the war?"

"She injured her hand in the Great War, her face was burned in the fire. She's had an awful time, yet still she's smiling."

"It sounds like you've been busy, Martha."

She sighed; a heavy, weary sigh. "I tried to start again after I left Goldhurst Estate. I tried to forget everything. I won't ever forget her." She leaned closer to me. "I was quite relieved when I found out I was dying. I have nothing else to live for." I was shocked by the statement and looked away. "I don't blame you for moving on with your life, Miss. You were young and you deserve all your success. I'm very happy for you."

I gazed at the picture of Edinburgh. "I admit, I have pushed her out of my mind, I have created a life that doesn't involve her. It wasn't easy though. I thought about her all the time to begin with. I couldn't sleep with worry, I lost weight and everyone thought I was going mad. That's why I spent so much time working; it was the only thing that took my mind off her. It saved me really."

Martha's eyes were closed and she was so still I thought she may have drifted off, until she finally spoke.

"Frederick's old nanny came to see me a few months ago - Miss Woodley - do you remember her?"

I nodded. How could I forget the red marks across her back that Annabelle revealed to Edward and I so unceremoniously?

"It was all very strange. No one from Goldhurst contacted me after what happened, but I wasn't surprised as I didn't have many friends there. She told me Mrs. Goldhurst had dismissed her after ten years of service."

I still hated Annabelle being referred to as 'Mrs. Goldhurst'. "Did she say why?"

"Mrs. Goldhurst claimed that she spoke in an impudent and patronising manner to Frederick."

I laughed mirthlessly, "That sounds like Annabelle. So why did she seek you out?"

There was a long pause. "She told me something which has troubled me ever since."

"About Grace?"

"Hmmm. That day when she and Mrs. Goldhurst found her with Frederick, when she tried to harm him." Martha's small body heaved up and down. I stood up, about to call for help until I saw tears and realised she was sobbing. I sat again, taking her bony hand.

"She didn't do it, Miss Alice. She didn't touch him or her. I knew it all along, I tried to tell everyone but no one was listening!"

I heard the words as if in a dream. "What?"

"After Mrs. Goldhurst found out about Robert, she set it up. Miss Woodley never saw Grace near the cradle, but Mrs. Goldhurst made her lie to Mr. Goldhurst and say that she had seen her try to strangle him. She said she'd dismiss her with no reference if she didn't help her."

I stood up too quickly and placed a hand on the back of the armchair to steady myself.

"What about the marks? I was there, she showed us the red marks on her arms and back where Grace had attacked her, how did she explain that?"

Martha was quiet for what seemed like half an hour before she said, "I didn't know about any marks. Miss Woodley did tell me something about a dog attack that she suspected had been set up by Mrs. Goldhurst, but I confess I didn't have a clue what she was talking about and I was already so shocked I didn't question her further on that."

I focused my eyes on the window. I felt sick. "How can we be sure the nanny is telling the truth? She probably wants revenge on Annabelle for how she's been treated."

"True, she probably does hold a grudge. But I've been thinking back to that afternoon. Grace kept saying that Annabelle did something to the baby to make him cry and she covered his head with a blanket. Grace was never a liar, Miss, she may have been reticent, but she couldn't lie. And I still maintain what I said back then - she was much better and I never let her out of my sight for longer than a minute. Besides, Miss Woodley said she wanted to tell someone sooner but she was afraid of losing her job and damaging her chances of getting another one."

I walked over to the window sill to try and hide my nausea that must have been evident. Inside I knew that Grace had been innocent all along, now we had proof and I felt so bitterly ashamed.

"I don't think she did it, Miss. I think there's been a huge mistake. You're the only one who can do anything about it now."

I turned around slowly, tears in my eyes, guilt and anger swelling inside my stomach. I didn't think it was possible to hate anyone as much as I hated Annabelle Tressider.

"Edward will never believe me. That bitch has complete control over him; he won't even agree to see me."

"You must try, though. We owe her that. We must try to clear her name and get her back."

I realised the magnitude of the task and felt faint.

"I can't rest for thinking about her. She's been in my thoughts every day for the past ten years. Now she's there constantly. I can't die not knowing..." Thin rivulets trickled weakly from one eye over the ashen surface of her face. I handed her the tissue box on the night stand, her shaking hand struggled to grip and pull at one.

"I know I had no right to but I loved that girl as if she were my own child. I still love her, wherever she is. I was the first person in the world to hold her. I was there every day for twenty-one years and I tried so hard to protect her. I pray constantly for her protection, but it's not the same." Suddenly she took my hand. I blinked back shameful tears. I had spent the last decade forgetting my sister and building a new life; Martha had spent the time remembering her, unable to move on because of the loyalty and love she felt for a girl who wasn't even her blood relative. Everything I had told myself - Grace was better off, there's nothing I could have done, I need to move on with my life; was washed away in less than fifteen minutes.

"Please try to find her, Alice. I need to know she's safe and she has something to look forward to - a life of some form. Promise me you'll try." Pain was woven into every crevice of her face. She had a look of desperate hope in each iris and pupil. I knew what I had to do.

"No. I can't promise you that." I heard the paltry gasp as I uttered the words. "I promise you I *will* bring her back. Merely trying won't do. I've ignored this for far too long; Annabelle's lie needs to be exposed and Grace needs to come home. If anyone should bring her back it should be me." I was facing her now, fists clenched, tears in both of our eyes. It was about time.

Chapter Nineteen
25th April 1932, Goldhurst Estate, Rutland
Alice

Trundling along the long gravel driveway towards my old home stirred up the very memories that I had spent the last decade repressing. Emotions, too, that I thought were long dead suddenly rushed through me like the torrent of water that used to cascade from the fountain in front of the house. I absorbed my surroundings during the approach and tried to summon former, happy feelings of the place in which I was born and raised. Alas, I could feel nothing but sadness and regret. It was almost absurd to think that I once lived in this estranged house, for it no longer represented a home to me. It was merely a building - bricks and mortar - nothing more remained.

My last few moments here were by far the worst of my life. However, it wasn't simply the past colouring my feelings; there was something more, something had changed at Goldhurst Estate. The old house wasn't the same. I saw it as we approached; I could feel it too. I was under no illusion that the nostalgia of youth distorts one's memory of the childhood home. I loved Goldhurst Estate growing up and, although these feelings of adoration had long since vanished, I could not deny that this house was barely a shadow of its former self. The building itself appeared run down and in need of painting and I noticed a good deal of drawn curtains at the windows, making the house appear to be slumbering, or that its inhabitants were under some kind of witch's spell. It was April but the primroses and irises no longer lined the driveway like they used to and the fir trees were unkempt, lacking that sharp, needle-like shape of which Mr. Healy had always been so proud. The once-majestic fountain that my mother had adored was littered with leaves and other debris and the stone figures were coated with a slimy green film. I only had a partial view of the gardens that we all loved as children, but what I could see was much the same as the house - dishevelment and neglect. The lawns and hedges were not nearly as carefully clipped and I could no longer see the lake; it was blocked by a curtain of foliage, separating the woodland from the gardens which were almost equally overgrown. Worse still was the palpable absence of the rose garden. Grace's rose garden. Goldhurst was famed for growing the best roses in the county - surely they hadn't been forgotten too?

Tearing myself away from the bleak picture I glanced at James, remembering that this was the first time he had seen the estate. I wondered what he saw.

"So, what do you think of the house?" I said.

"It's..." he eyed the house and half smiled. "It's a bit much for one small family. I'm sure it was quite impressive once, but like so many of these great houses, its glory days are long gone, I fear. More's the pity." He smiled apologetically.

I turned my attention back to the house as the car came to a halt. "Yes. I think you're right."

As I rang the front doorbell of the house I realised that, in the twenty-eight years of calling it my home, I had never once used it. I relayed this to James who laughed good-humouredly and took my hand as the great oak door opened.

An unfamiliar young man with fine sandy hair and ruddy cheeks greeted us politely but with reserve, opening the door just enough so as not to seem rude.

"Good afternoon." I said. "I need to speak with Mr. Goldhurst as a matter of urgency. It won't take long, but I do need to see him immediately." The young man glanced uncomfortably over his shoulder.

"Uh, can I ask what the matter is concerning if you don't have an appointment, madam?"

"Kindly tell him that his sister, Mrs. Alice Hartwright, needs to speak to him about an important family matter."

The footman's face reddened, colouring his cheeks a darker hue of rouge. He yanked the door open wide and fairly sprang out of our path.

"Oh! I beg your pardon, ma'am. I didn't know any of the master's family were visiting. Please come in and wait in the sitting room."

I thanked him but stated that I would prefer to wait in the hallway while he delivered the message to my brother. He seemed uncomfortable with this, but bowed nonetheless, assuring us that he would go directly to announce our arrival.

Standing in the hallway allowed James and I the opportunity to study the interior of the house. As with the external prospect it had not altered a great deal in its general appearance: the same solid oak staircases, polished wood floors, carpets and rugs of thick pile; galleries of portraits and vistas adorning the walls and stairwells; antique vases and the odd new figurine posing atop dressers or little decorative tables once picked out by my mother. My grandmother's old Persian rug also remained intact at the far end of the hall. However, the same air of partial abandonment and bereft shabbiness hung about the house like a spectre. The distinct smell of roses and polish had been replaced with a stuffy, slightly stale perfume. Perhaps time had worn the estate and its contents down into poor shape; or perhaps a depleted supply of money was a bigger problem than I first thought. I had heard that the family business had been affected by the 1929 crash, which could explain the lapse in attentiveness on Edward's part. I was, however, surprised at Annabelle since aesthetics were sacrosanct to her.

James was quietly inspecting some vases, of which I was about to make some trivial comment to break the silence when an unmistakable, abrasive tone struck us from the first floor landing, "What in God's name are *you* doing here? You're not welcome in this house!" She began to clatter down the stairs towards us. Like the house, her style was the same, but she was badly desiccated. She still wore an excessive amount of make-up – her powder no longer smoothed her face into a mask; instead it formed a cakey film on her skin, emphasising the papery creases that had formed around her eyes and mouth. Her lips were a violent shade of red, and her hair, a good two shades darker than I remember, was piled high in a fussy, ornate style, an oriental comb tucked into one side. Her attire was predictably expensive-looking and brash, although more forgiving as she had clearly put on some weight since we last spoke. She faced us, her hands on her hips in confrontation.

Some of the servants were appearing in the doorways, unsure of whether to intervene, disappear or simply loiter out of curiosity. I squared my shoulders and raised my eyebrows at her, for I had never been intimidated by her haughtiness and the years certainly hadn't changed that. Furthermore I knew her secret now; I could expose what she really was.

"I'm here to talk to my brother. It's a family matter and it won't take long." She opened the thin reds lips of her mouth to respond, but I was quicker. "I won't be leaving until I have spoken to him. I wouldn't be here if it were not very important."

Her eyes darkened with menace and her voice rose shriller still. "How dare you come into my house making demands? My husband doesn't want to see you now or ever again so leave now before I call the police!"

I snorted. "Still as histrionic and as interfering as ever, I see. This is Edward's house and I've come to speak to him, not you." I heard a titter coming from the direction of a door where the servants congregated. They were in no rush to come to their mistress' defence and I couldn't blame them.

Annabelle began to upbraid me for my audacity and ordered me to leave once more; I paid no notice, instead scanning the rooms upstairs to see if I could glimpse the footman. Edward must have heard the ruckus if he was at home. James was using his most diplomatic tone to pacify the shrieking harpy, "Please, Annabelle, Alice just wants to have a few minutes with her brother, surely you can indulge her after all these years? I'd also like to get to know you and Edward, you are family, after all."

I was about to tell him to give up when I caught sight of a middle-aged man with dark, oily hair and a pencil moustache knocking and entering one of the rooms on the first floor, just within eyesight from where I was standing. The sandy-haired footman emerged almost immediately after and made his way downstairs with the middle-aged man.

Disappointed by my lack of reaction, Annabelle had fixed her attention on my husband, bleating over his every word with a torrent of insults.

I waited until the footman and the other man, who I assumed to be the butler, had descended and were almost at Annabelle's side and shot past them, up the stairs and into the room on the first floor.

The room used to be my father's bedroom, but had been used as a guest room after his death. Since I had left it had been redecorated and had changed considerably, but I still remembered it being one of the largest and best rooms in the house in terms of its view of the grounds, with windows all along the far wall. My brother stood in profile to me, staring out the window closest to the door, seemingly oblivious to the commotion downstairs. Despite our ten year separation he glanced at me and back again as if my being there was commonplace.

Knowing we were soon to be interrupted I spoke with haste, "Edward, believe me I wouldn't have disturbed you if this wasn't important, please listen..." the door flew open and Annabelle rushed forward, panting like an excited dog.

"Get out, get out now! The very impudence of it, trying to push me around in my own house! Edward doesn't want to see you, he's..."

"Annabelle, Annabelle." Edward held his right hand up towards her and rested the fingers on his closed lids, massaging them. He was unwell; I noticed it straight away. His weight must have halved since I last saw him; he stooped slightly and his breathing was laboured. His eyes, although I had only seen them for a moment, were tired and glassy. Altogether his appearance was that of an old man - thinning grey hair and a frame that barely filled his clothes.

"My dear, it's fine. I think reconciliation is long overdue."

Of course, Annabelle objected, complained and argued, directing as many slurs at me as she could, but her husband paid her no attention. He shook James' hand and made a cursory introduction before interrupting his wife.

"This is Mr. Hartwright's first visit to Goldhurst, Matthews. Please give him a tour of the estate and then make him some tea and something to eat." He spoke to the man with the pencil moustache, who bowed in assent. Then he spoke louder, without looking at Annabelle. "Mrs. Goldhurst may or may not choose to accompany him, but in any case I do not wish to be disturbed whilst I am talking to my sister." Annabelle was powerless to continue her tirade but shot me a look full of contempt, eyes narrowed and lips pursed tight.

They all followed her out of the room, leaving Edward and I alone. My brother suddenly shrank back into a chair and subsided into the frail man I saw when I first entered.

"Edward, you're ill. What is the matter?"

He smiled grimly, "I had pneumonia last November and I never quite recovered. I'm wasting away slowly." On cue he coughed and his whole body seemed to rattle. It reminded me of Martha. "I haven't the strength I used to, I'm afraid." I poured him some tea that another servant had brought up and pressed him further on the subject of his health, to no avail. My brother had always been reticent on the subject.

"You're not the only one in a bad way, which is part of the reason I'm here."

Edward raised his eyebrows. "It's not Charlotte is it? Or Louisa?"

"No, They're fine. I've been to see Martha Pick. I haven't spoken to her since I left the house. You do remember her?"

"Of course I remember her, I'm not senile."

"She's dying and her brother wrote begging for me to see her before she went."

He listened in silence, sipping his tea. I noticed his hands quivering.

"A few months ago she received a visit from Miss Woodley, Frederick's old nanny. She told Martha something quite shocking. A secret she has kept since that day."

He put the tea cup down with a clatter. "For goodness' sake, Alice. I thought you came here to apologise, to build some long overdue bridges. Have you honestly come here to gossip about a servant and drag up the past?"

"Listen, Edward, Annabelle lied to us. Grace didn't touch Freddie that day. Annabelle tricked her and made Freddie cry so it looked like Grace was trying to harm him. Then she blackmailed the nanny into supporting the story. She framed Grace because she wanted you to get rid of her."

He looked perturbed but made no attempt to speak, so I went on, "Believe me, Edward, I understand what Grace did to Robert was abominable and, with hindsight, I know I should have told our parents. I completely understand why you were appalled, but at the time I thought I was doing the right thing. I was trying to protect her because I knew she'd be sent away and treated like a criminal if people knew the truth. She was an innocent killer, I suppose, she didn't realise what she was doing." I looked up to gauge his reaction but he continued to stare at nothing. "She actually thought she was helping Mama by keeping him quiet. She never had the capacity to understand her actions, don't you see?"

He leaned forward and covered his face with his hands, still saying nothing. "Grace may have been dangerous once, but Martha changed her. She taught her what was right and what was wrong and she came to understand. I believe the nanny; I don't think she laid a finger on Freddie." I leaned back and exhaled. "I want to bring her back to London with me. Please Edward, she's still our sister and she's been punished enough. We still have a responsibility to look after her. I promise I won't ever bring her near Goldhurst Estate, or your family. I'll keep her with me and look after her. James and I can employ the best nurses to care for her in our home. But I can't go on pretending she doesn't exist; especially now I know for sure that she's innocent."

I sat back to wait for Edward's response. To my surprise he started laughing softly.

"You're insane, Alice, if you think I'm going to listen to anything that you, Martha Pick or the nanny say over the word of my wife. How dare you come here and accuse her of lying! That lunatic nearly murdered my son, my only son! How would you feel if it was Oliver?"

I looked away, surprised by his reference to Oliver, the nephew he had never met.

"I don't regret sending her away. I don't care if she's family or not, she's dangerous; she needs proper professional care."

He breathed out heavily and went on, "I'm never, ever going to consent to her release from the hospital; you're wasting your time here. Go back to London and concentrate on your dresses."

He paced over to the desk in the corner, opened a drawer and ripped a page out of an old journal buried under a pile of papers.

"Here," he thrust the scrap of paper into my hand. "This is the name and address of the place." I glanced at the paper. My eyes widened when I saw 'Switzerland'.

"You may write to her or visit if you wish. But I don't want to speak about this again."

I gripped the paper, tears in my eyes. How could I make him believe me? Were Annabelle's claws implanted so deep that nothing could be done to remove them?

"Edward, Can't you see what she's like? Can't you see what she's done to our family? You're not happy, she wanted us all out of the way and she's succeeded because you are so blind to her wickedness. I know Grace better than you, Martha even more so. Why would Miss Woodley take the trouble to find Martha and tell her this after ten years? Don't you think it's strange that none of us saw anything except her and Annabelle? Grace was telling the truth. She's been punished enough; she's had to endure ten years without any familiar faces, without any love." My voice rose into a desperate plea. "Please, let me take responsibility for her, you won't have to do a thing, just let me have your consent to release her. I know our parents would have wanted it."

Edward bridled a little at my final comment and he faced me, anger woven into his face. "Do you think they'd want it if they knew the truth? If they knew she had smothered their son? You seem to forget that she actually killed a human being – a baby – and she could do it again. Have you forgotten how ill Mother was after Robert? How much she grieved?"

He turned away and paced back to his original spot, staring out the window, his back rising and sinking rapidly.

"Annabelle's a liar, Edward."

"Well if she is, then you're no better! You kept quiet about Grace's action for years, you saw her kill your own brother and you said nothing. You make me sick." He spat, his face wore so much contempt I had to look away.

"Get out, Alice, I've nothing else to say to you."

My heart heaved and pulsed so quickly that I gasped for breath. I wanted to leave that room and the house as quickly as I could before I collapsed. I hadn't felt like this since the last time I was here, arguing with my brother. Why had I come?

As I neared the door I shoved the hospital's address into my bag and felt the edge of a business card belonging to Mr. Hemingford, our solicitor. Composing myself, I walked back to Edward's desk, slotting the card into a wooden letter rack.

"Thank you for the address. We will make plans to go and see her as soon as possible. Just so you know I won't be swayed off course so easily. I won't rest until I get her out of there and back home with me, with or without your help. Obviously I would much prefer your approval so I'm leaving my solicitor's card, should you change your mind at any point." Edward remained quite still. "I am aware of Grace's crimes, her faults and the risks involved with looking after her. But a sister is a sister, irrespective of her flaws. I withdrew my love ten years ago when she most needed it and now it's time to make amends."

I didn't wait for a response. Slipping from the room I began the slow descent back to the front door. This time I wasn't so naïve. I knew there was no chance of my return.

Chapter Twenty
27th April 1932, Charbonnier, Switzerland
Alice

Twenty miles inland from Lausanne, La Clinique de Charbonnier protruded between the mountains like a large abandoned nest. Starkly out of place amongst the alpine beauty of the surrounding countryside, it appeared a functional, melancholy building - grey, square and featureless.

Entering the heavy iron gates for the first time I felt unease, followed by dread, quickly succeeded with hopelessness and I found myself checking for the nearest means of escape. A place like this demanded absolute submission or retreat. Everything about it whispered 'leave now and we'll say no more about it'.

James and I were led through the grounds by an equally morose young nurse in a drab grey uniform that couldn't have been more than two shades lighter than the building's exterior. I watched her move briskly and noiselessly a few steps ahead, forcing us to match her stride. The bun on her head was so tightly welded that it could have been made of the same iron as the gates.

I was aware of the patients either side of us, exercising in the gardens. I tried to avoid staring at them, but felt an irresistible urge. The people I saw were placid and sedate, some barely capable of shuffling along without assistance. There was a mixture of men and women, small and large, dark and light-haired, but all seemed old and appeared to be wearing a uniform of beige flannel pyjamas. Most of the patients had orderlies escorting them around the gardens like doting nannies, except their expressions were grim and stern, and they held onto their charges with tight fists, almost anticipating a violent break for freedom. I thought of the way Martha used to accompany Grace around the grounds of Goldhurst so lovingly, without complaint or resentment. She always showed her such patience and kindness, virtues that were sadly lacking in this place.

As we neared the entrance I caught sight of a man of about James' age, sitting cross-legged on the ground near a small rose bush. He was one of the few who were unsupervised and, to my surprise, he seemed to be counting the petals on each bloom. I smiled for the first time as I recalled Grace's penchant for counting rose petals and, for a brief moment, I wondered whether I had been too quick to judge the clinic. Perhaps Grace was happy here, maybe it was an ideal home for her; a place full of people that understood and helped her in a way that we never could.

Guided through the front doors into the large, cold mouth of the building I stole one last glance at the man by the rose bush. I stopped to make sure I had seen it correctly. He was plucking the velvety petals from the flower and popping them into his mouth one by one.

I had spoken to Doctor Bracken on the telephone the day before, and now he sat on the other side of a bulky but immaculate desk, interlacing his fingers as he regarded us in a way doctors often do. He reminded me of a croquet mallet - thin and straight with an abnormally wide head. His face was clean-shaven and mauve; a pinched nose gave way to long, thin lips, curving downwards giving him the look of a melancholic. Were all the staff created from the same substance as the building? His hair was black, streaked with silvery-white and lay flat and slick on his head, parted to the side giving it the appearance of an oily beret.

His office was similar to many doctors' I had seen before with its dark wood furnishings; over-filled bookcases on two walls; a writing desk lined with paper and envelopes and various medical objects, including a child-sized skull at which I couldn't stop staring. It seemed to be an odd thing to have in one's office, even for a doctor.

"Now I must inform you, visitors are expected to make an appointment before I allow them to enter the clinic, let alone see anyone. You're fortunate that I have a light day today, ordinarily I would have had to turn you away." He smiled at me and I disliked him instantly.

"We understand that; we're sorry for the inconvenience. You see, my wife and I haven't visited before and thus are not familiar with your protocol. Mrs. Hartwright and I would be extremely grateful if you could make allowances on this occasion. In future we will make an appointment." James smiled congenially at the doctor, which irritated me.

"I don't understand why there should be a problem. She is my sister after all and I wish to see her. I gather my brother is paying you plenty of money to care for her, therefore I don't see why you should have any complaint when her family decide to visit, especially as no one has visited her since she arrived."

He turned from James to me and smiled, "Mrs. Hartwright, this is not a typical hospital where you can come and go at your whim; it is a secure clinic; the patients are vulnerable and, in some instances, dangerous. Therefore I have to be especially careful about whom I allow on to the premises, as much for your sake as for my patients'." His face barely moved as he spoke, but his tendency to interlace his fingers and rub his palms together reminded me of Mr. Irvine.

"Mrs. Hartwright and I appreciate that, don't we, dear?" James dealt me a pleading look.

"Yes." I said.

"We've travelled all the way from London to see my sister-in-law; my wife has not seen her for years and is desperate to be reunited with her. I know we haven't gone about this the right way and I know that you are a busy man, but please can we see Miss Goldhurst for half an hour today? It would mean so much to both of us."

"Please," I added desperately, "please, I won't be able to rest until I see her."

Doctor Bracken sat back, his face seemed to soften slightly although his eyes remained hard and fixed. "I suppose I can make an exception this once."

The corridor leading to Grace's room was on the second floor, as it had been at Goldhurst. That, however, was where the similarity ended. It was long and straight, colourless and clinical, so dark that one could not see the end. The other main difference was the smell. No polish and roses here; this corridor smelled of disinfectant and despair.

The sound of the doctor's quick, clipping footsteps melted into the walls as we passed each nondescript door and I noticed how well they had blocked out the brilliant Swiss daylight.

We finally stopped at a door on the left-hand side of the corridor: number sixteen, according to the enamel sign. Doctor Bracken stopped abruptly and faced us.

"I must warn you, she may be...changed since you last saw her." He leaned closer and muttered, "She has received the very best treatment from medical experts across Europe here but, sadly, she has not yet responded all that well...I mean, she largely refuses to cooperate and has become more and more introverted. She barely leaves this room," he paused, then added quickly, "though she has plenty of opportunity to do so."

James took my hand and squeezed it gently. The doctor produced a key, turned it in the lock and pushed open the door.

The light dazzled me after the gloom of the corridor and it took me a while to realise where she was. From behind the figure in the room looked like the stumpy carcass of a large bird, fallen from its nest. She didn't look up or change position as we entered the room. All three of us circled her vulture-like, not sure what to do next. My initial thought was that Doctor Bracken had shown us into the wrong room, for this couldn't be my sister. This woman was old, with greying, mousy hair that hung in wispy tendrils around her shoulders. Her clothes were wrinkled and worn, and predominantly brown. This woman was plump and thick around the middle from inactivity. But when I looked into her face I knew. Behind the years of loneliness and rejection and neglect was Grace. The eyes were the same, except they had glazed over and lost that enquiring look. She wore the same serious expression, albeit with more sadness than before. The years had been cruel to her and I could barely breathe for the guilt that was churning inside me. I looked away but knew I was the only person who could break the silence. It was the least I could do. I fixed my eyes on her again and spoke.

"Grace?" I was annoyed by how watery my voice sounded and tried to steady it before opening my mouth again. "Grace, do you remember me? Do you know who I am?" Would she remember my voice? Had it changed? I hunched towards her; she didn't react to my closeness. I might as well have been a ghost to her. I glanced at James, who smiled encouragement.

"Be careful, Mrs. Hartwright, Grace is not used to seeing strangers." Bracken said.

I glared at him, although I knew he was right, I was a stranger to her. "Grace, it's me, your sister, Alice. I know we haven't seen each other for years, gosh, it must be at least ten years now." Still no reaction. I went on. "This is my husband, James." James waved and smiled despite Grace's lack of interest. "We've been married for eight years and we have a son called Oliver - your nephew! You have so many nieces and nephews who want to see you. And of course, Martha is longing to see you again." I thought I saw a flicker in Grace's eyes when I mentioned her name. Not much, but enough to give me hope. "Yes, Martha really wanted to come with us to bring you home but she couldn't because - " I thought of what to tell her, "because she wanted everything to be just right for you when you returned."

Her face remained immobile, staring out of the window towards the mountains. I stood up and looked around the room for the first time. It was neither large nor small but the huge windows made it appear bigger. It was a fairly comfortable room but, like a hotel room, it had little personality. The window ledge was large enough for two people to sit on and was painted white. A single bed was positioned opposite the window, with a green plaid duvet that matched the curtains. A bookcase and small chest of drawers stood along another wall and a white bowl and jug sat atop the small sink with a yellowing bar of soap. Finally, a white wooden dressing table was placed between the bed and the window with a hairbrush (which looked like it hadn't been used), a toothbrush and some perfume. The only remotely familiar sight in the room was the rows of books lined up perfectly straight on the shelves of the bookcase, their spines facing out. I walked over to them and gently ran my finger along the spines. Some I recognised: The Wizard of Oz, Sleeping Beauty, Cinderella, various Beatrix Potters, Treasure Island, Hansel and Gretel, The Elephant's Child along with some new ones that looked untouched. Grace flinched slightly as I did this, as if their spines had some kind of invisible connection to her own.

I remembered Doctor Bracken standing near the door, awkwardly observing this scene. "Doctor Bracken, would you be so kind as to leave us alone for a while? Half an hour or so?" He looked from me to Grace and back again.

"Ahhh, well you see, Mrs. Hartwright, I'm afraid I can't. As I explained in my office we have a duty of care for the patients here as well as any visitors and I wouldn't feel entirely...comfortable leaving you alone in here without supervision." His eyes darted back and forth between Grace and I. Squaring my shoulders I began to close the gap between us. His eyes darted towards the door and back towards me, standing his ground.

James, registering my annoyance, interrupted, "Doctor Bracken, my wife has just been reunited with her sister for the first time in *ten years*. A sister who is very dear to her and, through no fault of her own, removed from her home and hidden from the rest of her family. You seem like a reasonable man, a family man, am I right?"

Doctor Bracken shifted, visibly irritated at the knowledge that here were two people who were not to be reasoned with. James went on.

"I'm sure you understand how my wife must feel and you can comprehend how important this first meeting is. I am asking you kindly; please allow her some time with her poor sister. I will ensure that no harm comes to either party."

A sigh of resignation escaped his creviced mouth. "All right, but I will be back in twenty minutes. I'm very busy," he whined.

"Thank you." James said. Defeated, the doctor left the room muttering to himself and as the sound of his footsteps was sucked into the corridor's thick walls I turned urgently to James. "We have to get her out of here, now." the quietness of the room amplified my words, yet still Grace remained lifeless, a worn mannequin, staring out of the window.

"We need to tread carefully here, Alice," he led me to the other side of the room so our backs faced her, "this Doctor Bracken already resents us for causing him aggravation. We don't want to upset him further." I tutted derisively; partly due to my dislike for Doctor Bracken's interference and partly because I disliked James' insufferable pandering.

"Can you not see what these so-called doctors have done to her?" I looked over at the still image of my sister. "They've sucked the life out of her; she has no friends or family here - They don't see her as a human being; all they want is Edward's money and a subject for their experiments."

"We don't know that."

Every time I looked at Grace I became more resolute. "I am not leaving this place without her, James. That Doctor can just go and..."

"Alice!" James had been saying my name for some time before I heard him. "Darling, I agree with you, I'm on your side. But you heard what Hemingford said to us before we left; Edward is her legal guardian and he has consigned her to the care of this hospital. He's also set up a trust to pay the fees for her to stay here indefinitely. Don't you see? They're not going to just give her up. We need to find a solution by thinking logically, not by making an enemy one of the hospital's most senior physicians."

Grace sat motionless as we discussed her fate. "So what do you suggest we do?" I said, stepping over to the bookcase.

"I suggest we talk to this doctor properly when he comes back."

"And find out how much it will take to get her out of here?" I pulled 'Cinderella' from the immaculate line and brushed the thin film of dust from its edges. I thought I saw Grace move a fraction, or was I imagining it?

"It's not going to be as simple as all that. I don't think this is the sort of place that will accept an envelope under the table, a hand shake and a farewell, do you?" He raised his straight eyebrows into arches.

"Why not? After all, institutions like these are businesses; their main aim is to make money so as long as we offer more than Edward is giving I don't see why there would be any problems getting her out of here."

"Let's talk about it later." He whispered.

I started to protest but he motioned to Grace, "Spend some time with her, he'll be back in a few minutes." He sat on the edge of the bed and gazed out to the distant summits of the Alps.

Gingerly, I sat down on the window seat, eager not to startle her. "Hello, Grace, dear. Would you like me to read 'Cinderella' to you? Like I used to?" I settled down and began to read, lifting each word off the page and offering it to my sister as a token of forgiveness; or maybe a promise for a better future. She remained frozen.

Half way through the story I stopped reading, at the point when the fairy godmother had arrived and transformed her into a young lady worthy of catching the attention of a handsome prince. The irony was not lost on me, but I had no illusions; I knew that I in no way deserved to be regarded as a kind of fairy godmother.

I sighed, "I'm afraid I have to stop there for today, darling. The doctor will be returning soon. I'll be back tomorrow to finish the story, though. Would you like that?" I began to get up and replace the book, trying one last time to extract some words from her.

"Do you still have a copy of 'Little Red Riding Hood'? I can't see it on the shelf and I know it was your favourite." No reaction. I continued, "I remember you used to drive Martha potty with the amount of times you asked her to read it. Hopefully it won't be long before she can read to you again."

The wooden door groaned open and Doctor Bracken's ovoid head peeked around, his mauve lips spread into a convex smile. "We'll be back tomorrow Grace, I promise." I thought about kissing her on the cheek, the way she sometimes let me in the old days, but it seemed an inappropriate gesture now we were strangers. I touched her lightly on the shoulder and rose from the seat. James was by the door speaking in a low voice to Doctor Bracken. If the room hadn't been so quiet and had I not been so close I may not have heard it - Grace's voice. It was quiet and fragile like a new born chick's - shaky and timorous through lack of use. I rushed to sit back down and held my face close to hers.

"Mmmm...mmmm." A simple sound, but a glorious one. I was elated but kept my voice to a low decibel to parallel hers.

"What are you trying to say, dear? Come on, you can do it."

She continued to stare straight ahead, uttering the, "Mmmm" sound once more. Then it stopped as suddenly as it had started. I stayed close by her, waiting for something to happen, some acknowledgement or recognition, but she just stared out at the mountains as if I wasn't there. I followed her gaze and imagined her doing this every day for ten years: staring at the Alps, waiting for someone to rescue her. No wonder she couldn't acknowledge me – to her no one was there.

Doctor Bracken claimed he was too busy to talk to us after leaving Grace but arranged a meeting for one o'clock the next day.

Reluctantly we allowed ourselves to be steered from the building and its grounds by the same po-faced nurse with only a brief and unfriendly goodbye to cheer us.

The next day, James and I sat in Doctor Bracken's office, behind the same imposing desk, monitored by the same grey walls, looking at this man - an unwanted obstacle that refused to be moved. I tried to remain composed but frustration coloured my every action and word.

"I'm very sorry Mrs. Hartwright; it's simply out of the question. Your brother is the legal guardian and he has signed..."

"Yes, I know, we've established that, but I am Grace's sister and I'm not leaving this place until you allow me to take her with me. She doesn't belong in here; she should be with her family, with people who love her."

James placed a placatory hand on my arm, "Doctor Bracken, you cannot fail to see my wife's point. As a physician you must admit the advantages of Grace being looked after by her own family. I can assure you we have plenty of room at our house and intend to employ the best doctors and nurses to care for her."

Doctor Bracken pursed his mauve lips, "What makes you think Miss Goldhurst is not adequately cared for here?"

"We're not suggesting that, merely that this is a large hospital and, well, who can care for one better than one's own relatives? Switzerland is so far from us that we can't hope to visit her more than twice a year; it doesn't seem fair."

I said, "You admitted yesterday that she hasn't reacted to any of your treatments. Have you thought, perhaps, that being locked away in here has done her more harm than good?" Doctor Bracken's eyes grinded into mine, a mixture of green and grey, pebble-cold and defiant, daring me to match his stare. I held his gaze with stoicism; returning the challenge.

Seconds passed and his face remained stagnant before he averted his eyes and spoke, "Again, I am very sorry but I cannot help you. Unless Mr. Goldhurst formally consents to her release, Miss Goldhurst must remain at the clinic. My hands are tied." He held his hands behind his back by way of demonstration. Each word he uttered brought a wave of despair that washed through my stomach and up into my throat. I wasn't sure if I was going to cry or be sick. Doctor Bracken's face suddenly brightened. "However, I must reiterate that Grace is receiving some of the best care in Europe, if not the world, at this clinic. You will not find an institution to match ours in Britain or France, I assure you. She is in the very best place possible to treat and moderate her condition."

"I want to see her," I interrupted.

Doctor Bracken narrowed his cool eyes and raised his voice. "I'm afraid that won't be possible today, Mrs. Hartwright. Grace is receiving psychotherapy this afternoon and I am not sure how long she will be with the doctor."

James responded before I could, "We would like to see her tomorrow then, Doctor."

"Our policy is that patients should not receive visitors more than once every four weeks. It can impair their progress and disrupt their routine. We have been working extremely hard to regulate Grace's behaviour and her convulsions. Seeing you again yesterday left her quite confused and distressed. It would be unfair to excite her again so soon."

"It's unfair that my sister hasn't had a single visitor in all these years because my heartless brother refused to tell any of the family where she had been sent. Now you have the audacity to tell me I'm visiting her too much? How can you be so cruel? How can you be so lacking in scruples?" My pulse was pounding in each ear; I felt my face grow hot with fury.

"I need to consider her welfare and the welfare of other patients," was the cold reply.

James intervened, "Please, can we see her one last time tomorrow? I promise we will not visit again for four weeks. Consider, Doctor Bracken, the poor old girl has gone so long without a visit, surely you can grant us a reprieve?" James shot me a pleading look. I kept quiet and waited for the reply.

"Well...I suppose I can make another exception given the circumstances, *if* you promise to behave with decorum and composure." He huffed, directing his mirthless pebbles at me.

"How could you say we won't come back for four weeks?" I had held the words in my mouth since leaving Doctor Bracken's office and spat them out as soon as we closed the car's doors.

"Because, my dear, you were perilously close to angering him and then he would certainly not let us see her at all."

"Who on earth does he think he is? Dictating when I can and can't see my own sister! I can't abide him." I glared out the window at the lush greens of the mountains behind. I was in no mood for their beauty. "Doctor Crippen - that's who he reminds me of. Do you think they're related?"

James smirked, "Now, now, Alice, that's slander! He's only doing his job, after all. It's your brother that really stands in our way."

"Yes, I know, and that meddling slut Annabelle." I closed my eyes and let my head roll back to rest on the seat, silently begging for a solution. "Don't you find him strange?"

"Edward?"

"No, Doctor Bracken. There's something creepy about him. I don't trust him." I said.

"He's a medical man, there're all rather eccentric. I don't think there's anything sinister about him, though."

"I do, he seems intent on keeping us away from Grace and hasn't once offered to explain what treatment she's receiving, if any. Her appearance the other day was not that of one who has been looked after with attentiveness." James was quiet. "Grace was never the neatest of children but she was certainly never that dishevelled when Martha cared for her."

"I remember you saying yesterday. Well she's your sister, you know her better than I do. If you're worried about the care she's receiving you had better raise the subject with the doctor tomorrow." James said. "And try to do it diplomatically, for God's sake!"

"I was going to mention it today but you cut the meeting short."

"Alice, I've already explained why I did that and it's a jolly good job I did. What's wrong with you? I haven't seen you this belligerent since your little disagreement with the French chap a couple of years ago, the one who tried to pilfer your designs before the Paris show."

I winced, "François Leclerc."

"That's the one," he smiled, "and we both know how that ended."

"Why are we talking about that vile little swine? He was a dishonest fool, yes, but he's not in the same league as this Bracken fellow. You know, I think Grace may have turned mute again."

James frowned, "I think she was just confused and a bit scared the other day. She will start speaking when she gets to know you again. You haven't seen her for an awfully long time, Alice, don't forget that."

I stared out across the happy green tapestry towards the heavy, snow-topped Alps. They seemed to be staring back with the same intensity as Doctor Bracken, carrying the weight of my mistakes. My head was heavy and swollen with guilt.

"Believe me, I have never forgotten that fact."

Chapter Twenty One
30th April, Charbonnier, Switzerland 1932
Alice

On our return to the hotel after being denied a visit by the odious Doctor Bracken, a telegram was waiting from Mr. Hemingford, informing us that he was on his way to Charbonnier as he had some urgent news.

"We should expect him by Thursday evening." James looked at me and smiled. "That's today, then, the telegram was sent not long after we left."

"I do hope it's good news. Maybe Edward has changed his mind. Oh, please let him bring some hope with him! I can't bear to leave her in that frightful prison another night. He wouldn't trouble himself to come all this way if it were not something positive, would he?"

James put his arm around me, "I'm sure he wouldn't, darling. But please don't get your hopes up too high." He paused, kissing my head, gently. "I'm rather worried that you're getting yourself worked up with this business."

"Nonsense!" I shot back. "If anything I think I've been too passive."

James opened his mouth to say something then closed it again, shaking his head.

"I'm sorry, I shouldn't take it out on you, you've been so wonderful throughout all this." I said.

He smiled and held my hand. "Why don't we go for a walk after breakfast? We've hardly spent any time out of doors and look," he gestured to the window, "it's so beautiful, it seems a terrible waste not to make the most of it."

"What time is Hemingford arriving?"

"Not until seven o'clock at the earliest." He said. I could eat little at breakfast and I was in desperate need of a distraction so I proposed that we set off in half an hour.

We ventured out into the hills shortly after breakfast and reached a small plateau atop one of the many surrounding peaks. "This is a fine spot, well, as fine as any around here, you'd be hard pressed to find a bad one!" I was grateful for James' enthusiasm. Without him I would certainly have crumbled. He dropped our bag to the ground and began erecting the easel I had brought with the somewhat naïve hope that I could spend some time painting with Grace before heading home. I followed suit and began arranging my watercolours, gazing across the vista.

"Quite something, isn't it?" James said

"Yes, certainly is." I replied, taking in the view in all its glory: a flawless green baize covered the hills and lower ground as far as the eye could see, broken only by clusters of bottle-green pine trees, blessing the air with a gloriously fresh scent. Omnipotent behind, in stark contrast to the verdant rises, were the craggy slopes of the Alps, quietly observing the profound beauty lying at their feet like a sacrificial offering.

However striking the scenery, the depth of silence was more prominent. We had seen no more than ten buildings during our two-hour walk and from our current vantage point one could see even less. The houses that could be seen appeared miniature and insignificant, tucked away neatly into nooks in the landscape, tiny wooden huts, mere children's playthings compared to the mighty peaks that ruled above them. The silence and isolation was so intense that one could almost see it, enveloping us into its peaceful folds. If it were not for the breeze and James' breathing I could almost believe I had lost my ability to hear altogether.

On any other occasion the fresh Swiss breeze would have swept away all my cares and the views could rejuvenate even the most wizened of souls. But try as I might I simply couldn't forget our last meeting with Grace. The canvas in front of me, which usually brought relief, irritated me today. Each stroke appeared on the white background mechanically, as if another hand were painting, and doing a poor job at that. After a while I put the brush down and leaned back, staring at the swirling mass of diluted colours dancing and merging into an oblivion of white in the far corner. What a mess, I thought.

James' voice broke into my thoughts, "So, my dear, *if* we manage to take Grace away with us, what are your plans for her?"

I set my brush down. "Isn't it obvious? We take her back to London and she lives with us. And of course I must take her to Derbyshire as soon as possible to see poor Martha. If you're worried about carers for her, don't. I've already asked Mrs. Lawrence to look into employing several. I want her to be involved in our lives more than she was at Goldhurst."

James nodded and looked away. He had never been able to hide his feelings from me. "You're worried about her living with us, aren't you? It will be fine, leave it all to me. I'll spend some time away from the business." He still looked troubled. "You will grow to love her, I promise." He looked at me then away towards the mountains again, shaking his head. I sighed and walked towards him. "What is it?"

He sighed and patted the space on the rug next to him. He had the same deep furrows lining his forehead that he got when completing a difficult crossword puzzle on Sundays.

"Louisa told me about what happened with your brother Robert - and Frederick and the nanny..." He tailed off. "You mustn't blame her, I overheard her talking about it to Miles and I wouldn't relent until she told me the truth. She made me promise not to tell you I knew."

I stared at the easel and at the superficial blotches of colour on my canvas. They danced and blurred together as I heard myself speak, "And did she tell you that she used you to emotionally blackmail me?"

"What?" I could feel his gaze on me.

"She told me that if I ever tried to find Grace or help her in any way she would tell you that I was an accomplice to murder and you would be sure to leave me. Those were more or less her exact words."

"I'm sure she didn't mean that, she was probably just distressed and taking it out on you. You were only young when it happened, who could blame you for being afraid?"

"How long have you known this?"

"About two and a half years."

I put my face in my hands, "If I'd known perhaps I would have sought her out sooner."

"Well, we're here now, thanks to Martha."

I sat up straight again. "I haven't told you everything that Martha told me when I visited her."

He raised his eyebrows, "Another secret?"

"The last secret, I promise." I relayed everything Martha had told me and James listened quietly, the furrows returning once more.

"Hmmm. Is there any way this Miss Woodley can be traced? We ought to get a statement from her. I'll speak to Hemingford about it when he arrives."

"I think Charlotte was looking into it, but she's hardly the most likely detective."

"So you believe this incident with Frederick was a fabrication?"

"Yes, of course. I think I've known all along really. She had not been violent for years, excepting the odd outburst; Martha was very good with her."

James interrupted, "But we must acknowledge that she has serious mental health problems."

"Well, yes, but, what I mean is she's not a dangerous beast."

"But you have to realise, Alice, that it is our responsibility to guarantee everyone's safety if we bring her home."

"Are you suggesting she might try to harm Oliver?"

"I'm suggesting nothing, I just want to make sure we're completely prepared. This is going to completely change our lives, you know?"

"I don't care, I welcome the change. The alternative is leaving her here, which will drive me insane."

He stood up and placed a palm on his forehead, breathing deeply.

"Listen, I intend to take on at least three nurses for her to start with, so someone will be with her at all times. One of the problems at Goldhurst was that Martha was her only carer. Therefore, when Martha was asleep or preparing breakfast and whatnot, Grace was unsupervised. Then, once we've observed her behaviour, we can decide the best course of action for her."

He paced across the plateau, into the wind. "I worry that it's all going to be too much for us all. I think you're taking too much upon yourself. You seem to have this ludicrous idea that you alone are responsible for every unfortunate thing that's happened to her and this is your penance. It's not your fault that she was born..." He waved his hand and grimaced as if trying to prevent the words from escaping.

"Born what? A lunatic? A madwoman? An imbecile? Say it! If you think that's what she is. You certainly not the first person to think it and you won't be the last, for that matter."

"You're putting words in my mouth, Alice! You know I want to help her, why else would I have come all this way with you? But you're not rescuing Rapunzel from her tower; you can't pretend that we'll all live happily ever after when we bring her back. Her condition may worsen, she may detest us, she may grow more aggressive and I for one don't feel prepared for it. We've got to take her back on the train, what if something happens then?"

I stood and followed his steps, "We will get through it together, as a family. I'd much rather try than accept defeat because I'm scared that it's not going to work." I grasped his arm to steady him. "Please, just think about that woman we saw yesterday, miserable and alone. You must pity her - her face, her clothes, and her hair - everything about her looks defeated. She has accepted abandonment. Imagine if she was your sister."

I felt my lips fluttering up and down and gave way to the sobs bursting for release. James didn't rush to comfort me this time; he just looked perturbed.

"Just because I don't fully understand her condition doesn't mean I can't understand her and love her." I said through each sob. "I have to do the right thing; I have to help my sister."

Whether he had been affected by my tears or by my words I couldn't tell, but I was relieved when he beckoned me to him and held me close.

"I don't think we've quarrelled this much in all our years of marriage!" He chuckled bitterly. "You win me round every time though."

I looked up into his kind brown eyes and smiled. We didn't need words now; I knew we shared the same purpose.

To my dismay, Mr. Hemingford arrived much later than expected, at half past eight in the evening. A whole afternoon of anxious waiting had induced a nervous headache and a maddening, overactive beating of my heart so that I could barely breathe without discomfort.

"Thank you so much for travelling all this way, Hemingford, it's jolly decent of you." James greeted the solicitor warmly, guiding him to the dining table. I sat next to him, but the sight of food made my stomach shrink.

"Well, I knew how much this meant to Mrs. Hartwright," he smiled at me. "I'll get to the point; I'm sure you're desperate to hear what I've got to say."

"Oh, yes." I breathed with eagerness.

Hemingford settled himself; tucking his middle-aged spread under the table and placing his palms flat either side of his plate. "I'm very pleased to tell you that your brother has changed his mind about authorising Grace's discharge from the clinic. I have here," he placed a slim white envelope, addressed to a name I didn't recognise at 'La Clinique de Charbonnier', on the table, "his written consent, witnessed by myself, which means you will be able to take Grace back with you immediately."

His words fell on me with the revitalising quality of rain on parched earth.

"That's wonderful news, Alice, isn't it? Bloody fantastic!" James grinned and kissed me with glee.

"I don't understand...what did you say to change his mind?"

Hemingford held his hands up "I must confess I had very little to do with it, your sisters were most instrumental in persuading Mr. Goldhurst."

"Charlotte and Louisa?"

"Indeed. In fact I have a letter for you from Mrs. Avery; I believe she explains it all here."

He passed to me an ivory envelope with what I recognised as Louisa's name and address on the back.

I held it for a few minutes then placed it in my lap and said, "So we can fetch her now?"

James and Hemingford exchanged glances. "It's too late tonight, dear, the clinic won't admit us now. First thing in the morning we'll go."

"It's not that late. Why should she spend any longer than necessary in that place now we have Edward's consent?"

Hemingford looked at me suddenly, "Now, I'm afraid I have some more news concerning your brother that is considerably less cheerful, Mrs. Hartwright."

"Go on." I said.

"I'm dreadfully sorry to tell you that Mr. Goldhurst is very ill. His doctors are incredibly worried. He took a turn for the worse last Friday, so he's been getting his affairs in order since then."

I gasped, "No! Oh heavens! I knew he had been unwell recently but I had no idea how serious it was."

"Your sisters are staying with him in Rutland, I believe."

"I'm shocked that Annabelle has allowed them to stay. Still, it would be jolly insensitive of her to send them away, even for a she-devil like her," I said, looking at James.

"I'm so sorry, my darling." He said, reaching out to take my hand.

"Is there nothing the doctors can do?" I continued.

Hemingford sighed, "In truth I don't know, ma'am. Let's hope and pray." I nodded and glanced out at the darkening sky. "I'm not completely sure what your sisters said to him, but he told me he hadn't been able to think about anything else but Grace since their visit. They did mention that they had been to see a Miss Woodley, but Mrs. Avery assured me everything is outlined in her letter. It's none of my business; I have the consent, that's all I need." He smiled and took a long draught of wine.

"Well, I'm pleased, for Grace's sake. It's all so sad though. It's so much to take in."

Two servants arrived to serve dinner, but eating was still intolerable to me after the news. I went to bed with my mind full of mixed emotions: elation at finally being able to free Grace from her miserable incarceration; sadness knowing that I may never be able to reconcile with Edward properly. I resolved to visit him as soon as we got home, if it wasn't too late.

I had been dozing in and out of a shallow sleep when I heard James enter our room. I sat up.

"Sorry, dear. I didn't mean to wake you."

"I wasn't really sleeping." I said. "What were you and Hemingford talking about?"

"Practicalities. The man's thought of everything for us," he chuckled, "travel arrangements, Grace's passport, nurses to assist us with her..."

"Nurses?"

"Two nurses from France are going to accompany us as far as Paris, just as a precaution. It's hardly likely that she's been near transportation for a long while and certainly won't have travelled by train in an age - it could upset her."

"Yes, you're right, good thinking; she never liked trains as I recall."

"Oh, you left Louisa's letter in the dining room." He handed me the ivory envelope which I ripped open straight away.

"What can she have to say for herself, I wonder." I said bitterly.

"Now, dear, it seems she and Charlotte have been doing a lot to help."

"Shall I read it aloud?"

He nodded. I unfolded the pages and began:

"Dearest Alice, I hope this letter finds you and James well and that Mr. Hemingford has informed you of Edward's change of heart regarding Grace. It wasn't easy to convince him at first, but Charlotte was quite the sleuth and managed to track down the nanny. Perhaps I should start at the beginning.

The day before you left for Switzerland, Charlotte and I visited Martha Pick and she told us about her visit from Miss Woodley. All this you know, so I shan't waste time repeating it. Charlotte questioned the housekeeper at Goldhurst Estate and managed to extract an address and we both called on her yesterday. She confirmed everything Martha said and more - she revealed that Annabelle has been having an affair with a man named Walter Murphy for at least two years and insinuated that this was certainly not the only dalliance during her marriage. Somehow, Charlotte persuaded Miss Woodley to come with us to Goldhurst (Charlotte has been simply marvellous

throughout this) and together we revealed it all to Edward. Oh, Alice, it was dreadful. Our poor brother is very unwell and I feared that this would kill him. Annabelle eventually confessed to everything; Edward threatened to keep Frederick from her if she did not tell the truth and it seemed to work. Oh, Alice, words cannot express how sorry I am; I should have believed in you; it seems you were right about Annabelle all along and Grace really was set up. I hope I can make amends for my lack of faith in you and for my cruel dismissal of Grace. Miles and I will be back in Paris soon after you receive this letter and would like you to stay with us for a couple of days before you continue your journey. Send word any way you can so Miles can send a driver to meet you at the train station. I do hope that Grace has been well cared for at the hospital; when I think about her I feel desperately ashamed and saddened by my behaviour. I hope in time you can both forgive me.
Your loving, contrite sister, Louisa."

I folded the pages and placed them back in the envelope.
"A nice letter. It seems she wants to make amends." James said. I didn't reply but rose and put the letter away in my travelling trunk. I could not forgive Louisa so readily.
"We should take her up on her offer; perhaps I should go downstairs and telephone them now."
"What time are we going to the clinic tomorrow?" I interrupted.
James shifted on the bed. "Hemingford and I were just discussing that." He began removing his cufflinks and loosening his tie. "I think it would be best if he and I collect her tomorrow and you stay here, getting everything ready for our journey."
I stared at him and opened my mouth to protest, but he continued hurriedly, "Now, please think about it rationally, Alice; you and Doctor Bracken didn't part on the best of terms and he may be less cooperative if you turn up so soon after your disagreement."
"Who cares about him? This is none of his business, this is about Grace, not him. Edward's agreed to her release so he has no say in the matter. If he refuses he's breaking the law!"
James hissed, "For God's sake, lower your voice; you'll wake everyone in the building."
"I'm her flesh and blood; surely I should be the one to collect her. She doesn't know you or Hemingford; she'll be afraid."
He fell silent and lay down on the bed. "Fine. Come with us and wait in the car to greet her when we bring her out. She won't be afraid then."
"But, James..."
"This is the best way, Alice. You won't have to endure Bracken again and you'll be in a far more pleasant mood to greet her."
I propped up my pillow and lay back, sighing, "I suppose what you say makes sense. Please, whatever you do, do not leave that place without her,

promise me? Don't let that old fiend fob you off with stories of how she cannot be released."

"Of course I wouldn't leave without her." He reached across and placed his hand on mine. "Besides, Hemingford just told me he sent a letter to the clinic on Monday explaining the situation. They must have received it by now, he sent it express."

I settled down again, mollified somewhat. "I do hope it goes smoothly; I just want all this to be over and to have her back."

James leaned across and kissed me. "I guarantee tomorrow night this worry will be forgotten and you will go to sleep with a smile on your face."

"I hope you're right." I said, closing my eyes.

"Now, I'll just be a moment."

"Where are you going?"

"To ask the hotel to telephone Miles and Louisa in Paris. I expect we'll arrive around supper time tomorrow."

"I don't know if it's wise, staying with Louisa. I'd rather arrange a hotel then continue the journey early the next day." With everything that had happened over the past few days the last person I wanted to see was Louisa. A part of me wanted to punish her, the way she had punished me all those years ago, as petty as it seemed to me as I thought it.

"Come on, Alice, we're far better off staying with family and you know it. You have to face her sometime."

"Grace?"

"No, Louisa." He said with a look that made me fear he could read my thoughts. "Don't blame her; she's your sister and she was only doing what she thought was best for you."

I sighed, "I do blame her; I blame all of us; we've all behaved appallingly, but, well, I suppose it's pointless getting into this now. Telephone them then; we'll stay for one night."

James smiled and touched my cheek, "If we've any chance of moving on we can't dwell on the past." He left the room closing the door softly behind him.

"Perhaps you're right." I muttered as I listened to his retreating footsteps.

We left the hotel as early as possible the following morning and headed once more along the steep road towards La Clinique de Charbonnier. One of the nurses had travelled from Lausanne early to accompany us to the hospital; the other was to meet us at the train station.

Anxiety wracked my insides as we climbed slowly towards the grey building. Grace had barely spoken to or even acknowledged me in our meetings, what if she didn't want to come away with us? What if she never spoke to me again? Was she even capable of making the long journey home?

Whatever the answer, it was too late now. We pulled up to the black iron gates and the car grumbled to a halt as James turned off its engine.

"A heavy car like this doesn't fare too well on these mountain roads," he smiled, "at least it's a relatively short journey."

We all exited the car without speaking, all with our own questions and fears. Hemingford tipped his hat to me and Anne-Marie, the nurse, "We won't be long, Mrs. Hartwright."

I gulped back the knot that had formed in my throat, "Good luck."

James kissed me and squeezed both of my hands in his, "The law's on our side, my dear, you have nothing to worry about." I nodded and he joined Hemingford at the gates before being swallowed into the miserable austerity of the grounds.

Minutes passed before I could look at anything other than the iron gates. Anne-Marie was a blessing in distracting me from the wait, allowing me to practise my French in telling her more about Grace. After about an hour there was some sound and movement at the iron mouth. I lurched forward, impatient for a glimpse of her in a state of freedom. The gates opened with a loud gasp and belched out James, Hemingford and a stooped figure in a brown overcoat, helped along by a grey nurse. I rushed to greet them, Anne-Marie following closely behind to speak to the nurse.

"Grace, my darling! I've got you back!" The well of tears poured forth a fresh supply down my cheeks. "You're safe, I'm going to take care of you from now on." The nurse mumbled a goodbye in French and retreated into the gloom, shutting the clinic off from the outside world once more.

Grace didn't respond to my welcome but shuffled heavily towards the car, head drooped, eyes fixed on the gravel road, clutching an ancient, saggy knitted duck. As Anne-Marie and James helped her into the car, I beckoned to Hemingford.

"What did Bracken say? Was he angry? Did he try to stop you?"

"At first, yes, he asked us to wait for a week to allow her time to adjust to the idea, but he very quickly realised that he had no bargaining position with Mr. Goldhurst's written consent." He frowned, "he's a queer chap, isn't he? Very nervous and twitchy, did you notice? He was practically sweating as we left."

"I didn't like him from the beginning and I made no secret of it." I said.

"Mr. Hartwright did mention it. Well, that's the hard part done, shall we?" He followed me to the car and within seconds we headed back into the Charbonnier valley.

Grace slept for the majority of the journey to Lausanne. During moments of consciousness I chattered away to her about everything: stories from childhood, Charlotte and Louisa, dresses, London, Oliver and Martha. She remained mute throughout, staring out the window clutching the bedraggled duck that smelled of mildew and disinfectant - the smells of the hospital. I vowed to get her a new one as soon as we got home.

Once on the train platform, Grace's expression changed. Her eyes widened and she trembled like a cornered hare. She covered her head with her hands and slunk to the ground, wailing quietly, rocking back and forth. I had been expecting it and had warned Anne-Marie and the second nurse, Lucille, that she hated trains. Both women hunkered down beside her, cooing and rubbing her back, which only distressed her further. James and Hemingford, who had gone to deal with the car and the luggage, were greeted on the platform with three women fussing round a crumpled heap of moans and I saw their exchange of uneasy glances. I stood up and realised that Grace was beginning to attract an audience. A young woman was openly staring and muttering to her companion. I glared at her and she looked away.

"I know you don't like trains, my darling, but this is the fastest way to get back to Martha." I said, crouching down to her level again. "If you go to sleep we will have arrived by the time you wake up. And you can see Louisa as well!" The nurses nodded encouragingly. "Martha can't wait to see you, if we miss this train who knows when another one will come along? Poor Martha will be so upset."

Grace eventually stood up again and allowed the nurses to guide her towards the carriage, wailing as she went. I was surprised by the effort it took her to walk. She had always been clumsy, but never lacking in energy. Now it seemed even short distances were arduous for her. She could barely stand up without assistance.

"Well done, dear." James put his arm around me as we walked behind the nurses. I shivered.

"I just want to get out of this place; I won't be able to relax until we've crossed the border."

"Switzerland has failed to make an impression on you, Mrs. Hartwright?" Hemingford said.

I shook my head, "It's a shame, such a beautiful country, but it will be a long time before I return after this visit."

Once inside the carriage Grace's wailing and rocking grew worse. When the train started to move she sank to the floor hissing, howling and rocking to such an extent that we feared she would bring on a convulsion. Anne-Marie, the more experienced nurse, administered an injection of morphine to quieten her. I watched the thin needle enter her skin and winced. James and Lucille were holding her as I tried to soothe her. The drug took effect quickly and she slumped onto the floor, allowing the nurses to lift her exhausted body onto the seat and encourage her to sleep. A lump was convulsing in my throat and I turned to the window to choke it back discreetly.

"My wife and I are just going to have some tea," James said to the nurses, "we won't be long." He steered me into the compartment next door and once alone I collapsed with sobs, unable to control them for ten minutes.

"Oh, James, we're no better than those monsters at the clinic. She's been in our care a matter of hours and we've injected her with morphine...it's not the way!" I wailed.

James sat with patience and listened to me before replying, "You haven't done anything wrong, Alice, the nurse gave her morphine because she was at risk of hurting herself, we had no choice. You must stop punishing yourself, it's not going to help your sister, or Ollie and I either, for that matter." He handed me a handkerchief. "She's asleep now, which is what she needs. She'd thank you if she could." He kissed the top of my head. "Now she's settled I suggest you take a leaf out of her book. You barely slept last night."

"Where's Hemingford?" I said.

"At the restaurant, but don't worry, he booked three compartments so he and I can sleep next door, you won't be disturbed."

"Do you think the nurses will be all right on their own with her?"

"Of course, they're the experts!" He kissed me again, "I'll be next door if you need me and stop worrying, please." He smiled and closed the compartment door as he left.

I don't know how long I listened to the pant and rattle of the train but I woke to find that we were making rapid progress through the darkening French countryside. James was dozing opposite me and roused when he saw I had woken.

"You slept well, I'm glad." He stretched his arms and legs out and checked his wristwatch. "We should be in Paris within the hour."

"So soon? How long was I asleep?" I teased the remaining pins out of my hair and shook my head.

"It was a fair old stint." He stood and brushed himself down. "Hemingford's snoring next door - he's a little squiffy - the old boy can't resist a drop of bordeaux!"

"How's Grace?"

"Still out cold, last time I checked. I'll head next door and see."

"I'll just freshen myself up and join you. Is Hemingford staying in Paris too?"

"No, he's travelling on to Calais tonight. He's catching the first boat in the morning."

Grace began to stir and grizzle as we neared our destination. The thick rural darkness gave way to the glow of city street lamps and the station platform appeared outside. Soon she began to wail, but this time it was an agonised cry rather than the dull groan of earlier. She cried relentlessly, as if in terrible pain. Together we managed to bundle her off the train and onto the platform, where she collapsed in a heap once more. Each cry became louder and sharper, creating a haunting echo under the station's rafters. A flock of pigeons, startled by the noise, took flight in a great grey swarm. James and I stood rooted like river islands, forcing the crowds from the train to weave around us. Most bustled past oblivious, but some stopped to stare at a safe distance. I knew something was wrong when I saw her clutching her middle and rolling back and forth on the dirty floor, tears streaming down her face.

"What's wrong with her? Is it the morphine?" I shouted.

"Appelez une ambulance!" Anne-Marie hissed to Lucille, who scurried away wringing her hands.

"It must be a seizure." James said, pale-faced as the crowds swarmed past him.

"No, no, it's not. What is it, nurse?" Then I saw it, the growing circle of crimson beneath her. Her clothes were soaked with it. I screamed, which only served to intensify the cries coming from my poor sister, her face was contorted to the point that I feared it may fold in on itself. Anne-Marie was shouting something in French and James was imploring me to stop screaming. Lucille came dashing back, gesticulating to Anne-Marie.

"We must get her to hospital as soon as possible, she is haemorrhaging." She said.

"Yes I can see that!" I barked back, "Why? What's wrong with her?"

Before she could answer a figure ran towards us, forcing the crowds to part like the Red Sea. He was shouting our names.

"It's Miles, Alice. Thank God, he can help."

"How can he help? He's not a doctor." I was nearing hysteria again. Grace's wails had dwindled into groans and the two nurses were desperately trying to staunch the bleeding underneath her.

"Jesus Christ!" Miles exclaimed as her reached us.

"An ambulance is on its way, Miles. We don't know what happened; she was fine on the train..." James said.

"Forget the ambulance, help me carry her to my car, we'll take her straight to the hospital, it'll be quicker." He spoke in French to the nurses and indicated for James to take her legs. Anne-Marie was protesting angrily but Miles swatted away the words with his hand. Just as Miles stooped to lift Grace, who was now whimpering, a thin porter with a grey moustache appeared with a wheeled chair.

"Merci beaucoup," I said as James and Miles lifted her into the chair, exposing the dark red stain on the ground where she had been lying. I gasped and turned away, but there was no time to feel squeamish, Miles was already propelling the chair towards the exit and his waiting car.

Miles' chauffeur took us to an American Hospital in Neuilly-Sur-Seine. The source of Grace's bleeding was obvious, but the nurses seemed reluctant to speak about it in detail in the presence of the men. As soon as we arrived, Grace was whisked into a large room with a battalion of doctors and nurses. Miles went directly to telephone Louisa and the nurses disappeared to change their blood-stained clothes, leaving James and I alone. I sat in a leather armchair and slumped forward. I didn't know what to think.

James remained silent and paced the empty waiting room. I glanced at him and was shocked at how pale he was; he clearly hadn't slept much on the train.

"You should go back to the house with Miles and get some rest, I can wait here."

He furrowed his brow, "Don't be absurd, I'm not leaving you. I was going to suggest that you go back and rest."

"I slept on the train, dear, you must be exhausted. Besides, this is my mess; it's not fair to expect you to wait here all night."

He stopped pacing and looked at me, "What do you mean 'your mess'? How many times do I need to tell you? None of this is your fault. You're not on your own."

I sighed and looked out the window at the twilight sky, the leaves of the resident trees offering a darker outline against the darkening sky.

"There are so many things that I should have done, James. I can't get that out of mind. I should have concentrated on looking after Grace instead of selfishly pursuing my dressmaking business; perhaps then Annabelle wouldn't have had the opportunity to frame her. In fact, I should have stopped Edward from marrying Annabelle Tressider in the first place. I saw her malice even before he had proposed, but I wasn't forceful enough with him. I could have convinced him; I should have exposed her." James was sitting in an armchair looking out at the same sky. "I was too deferential with my parents too. I didn't want them to sail to New York during the war yet, again, I was too diffident to say anything. Most of all, though, I should have done more to stop Edward banishing Grace to that place. I shouldn't have given into Louisa's threats; I shouldn't have given up on her so easily. I sloped away to lick my wounds like a coward instead of fighting for her. I wish I had plagued and harried my brother until he told me where he had sent her. But I did nothing except writing a couple of paltry letters. I carried on with my own life, pursued my own ambitions, lived out my own dreams without so much as a second thought for Grace." I turned to look at James, "If she should die now, how can I make things right? I'll never be able to give her the loving home she's always needed. She'll never see Martha again; I promised both of them...I've let so many people down, James. Too many people."

He continued to stare out the window for so long I was beginning to think he had fallen asleep with his eyes open. To my surprise, however, he smiled.

"How many people can honestly say all their decisions have been the right ones? You have a sister with a mental health disorder; you did the best you could, like anyone else would in your position. Maybe one day we'll live in a society that knows exactly how to deal with people like Grace, but believe me, you've done your best and *we* will continue to do our best to care for her." He crossed the room and perched on the chair's arm next to me. "I think your parents would be proud of you."

Having never met my parents James was clearly just saying this to be kind. Would they be proud? I doubted it, but could they have done any better?

It was another eight hours before the doctors gave us any definitive answers on Grace's condition. James had finally surrendered to my pleas and returned to Miles' and Louisa's house to sleep. Louisa arrived just as I was summoned by an American doctor called Dreyfus.

"Why don't you wait here?" I said, unable to bear the thought of her believing she was exonerated.

"Oh no, I want to come with you." She gripped my hand intently and I felt myself being led towards a corridor with a bottle-green door at the far end.

The office wasn't too dissimilar to Doctor Bracken's, except this was smaller and brighter, and thankfully devoid of a skull on the desk.

"Please tell us Doctor, is she alive?" Louisa said, dabbing at tears I silently scorned.

"Your sister is still in a critical state, she lost a lot of blood, but she's over the worst. She will need to stay here with us for the next few days at least, so we can keep a close eye on her."

"Oh, thank heavens." Louisa threw her arms round me; I sat rigid and eyed Doctor Dreyfus, who waited for her to compose herself before he spoke again.

"We managed to save the child; however, I cannot tell whether any permanent damage has been done. You'll have to wait for the birth, I'm afraid."

Louisa and I stared at him, dumb. "What child?" I said.

He raised his eyebrows, "The child your sister is carrying."

My body suddenly felt very hollow and weak. I reached forward to grip the edge of the desk to stop me from falling. Grace was pregnant.

"Did you know?" Louisa gasped. She could tell from my face that I didn't. "How? Who?"

Who indeed. Doctor Bracken's pebble-hard eyes immediately came into my mind. Was he capable of such a sin? It would certainly explain his strange behaviour, or was he concealing someone else's crime? "They raped her," I blurted, "the people at the clinic, it was them and they've tried to cover it up." I stood up quickly and steadied myself against the chair, "And an awful job of it they've done as well."

"No," Louisa stared at Doctor Dreyfus, willing him to agree with her, "Surely no one can be so evil. There must be a mistake, Doctor?"

"Oh, people have the ability to be very evil, Louisa." I turned to Doctor Dreyfus, an awful thought entering my mind. "Why was she bleeding?"

He looked uncomfortable and cleared his throat, then said, "An...instrument appears to have been used in a crude attempt to abort the child. We also suspect she was given a dose of a substance containing Pennyroyal."

"Louisa's hands flew up to her mouth."

"What's that?" I said.

"An abortificant," he said. "Luckily the dose wasn't very strong and hasn't had much of an effect." He looked embarrassed and added, "I'm deeply sorry, I thought you knew about the pregnancy."

I sat down once more and mopped at the constant supply of fresh tears, "Thank you for everything you've done and thank you for being candid with us."

He stood, smoothing his white coat. "I'll leave you alone for a few minutes; this has been a huge shock, of course. Can I telephone anyone for you?"

"No, thank you." I replied.

"If you believe your sister has been abused you ought to let the police know. At which clinic was she residing?"

"La Clinique de Charbonnier in Switzerland. And don't worry; I have every intention of speaking to the police." I said bitterly.

Doctor Dreyfus looked thoughtful, "Hmm, I don't know much about that institution, but I will help in any way I can." He clasped his hands together and nodded. "Well, Miss Goldhurst is in safe hands now." He smiled apologetically as he left the room.

"Oh Alice, how awful! I simply can't understand how anyone can be so barbaric. A hospital - of all places - it's beyond an abuse of trust..."

Louisa spoke on and on but I ceased to hear her. We had returned to the same waiting room and I steadied myself on the window ledge, staring at the street outside, but in daylight now.

"Alice..." her hand gripped my arm and I pulled away instantly.

"What? What Louisa?" I shouted. She stepped back as if I had struck her. "What do you expect will happen when a vulnerable girl's family abandon her to the mercy of monsters masquerading as medics? We did this to her, all of us. Annabelle may have been the root cause but Edward was naïve enough to listen to her lies; you supported him and blackmailed me into abandoning her too; I was too weak and idiotic to stand up to you and Charlotte, well, where was Charlotte? Too busy worrying about herself as always."

Realising I was panting, I stopped to catch my breath. "I read your letter. You seem to think that we can all forget the part we played in her ruin, but I can't. It's going to take a lot more than a paltry guilt-letter to right this wrong."

Unable to take her eyes away from the floor I saw tears drip from her nose and onto the carpet. Her words came out in a stutter, "I'm...sorry...I know I...I behaved badly...I should have believed you. I...I want to help now."

I sank down into the same armchair I had occupied for nearly ten hours. "I looked up to you so much when I was growing up. I wanted to be like you one day; you were always so kind and you understood things far better than Mama and Papa. You had this glamorous life in New York, a husband who adored you and four beautiful children. But more than that I loved the way you were so gentle and tolerant with Grace; you taught me that she was someone to be treasured, not ashamed of. I remember when you asked me to take care of her and protect her; I took those words so seriously; I tried my best but I suppose I failed.

I just couldn't fathom your behaviour towards me when I left Goldhurst; I thought you were on our side, but you weren't. You were no longer the person I admired and I hated you for it."

We both sat in silence for who knows how many minutes. I listened to the motor cars driving along the street below and the distant chatter of the nurses somewhere nearby, not caring about any of it.

"Alice," eventually Louisa sat up straight and faced me; her face was badly blotched. "I need to explain why I behaved the way I did." I looked at her as she inhaled and exhaled quietly. "Annabelle wrote to me several times before the...incident expressing her concern for you."

"What do you mean? What concern?" I snapped.

"She seemed to think you were working too hard and close to a nervous breakdown. She said you'd been behaving erratically and had become anti-social. She said you only ever spent time with Grace and Martha and that it wasn't good for you."

"What? I was staying with you and Miles for most of the time she was there, so I could get away from her, in fact."

"Well, in hindsight she was most probably lying or constructing evidence to aid her bigger lie later on, anyway, I really took it to heart. I spoke to Edward about it shortly before it, you know, happened, and it occurred to me that you were only twenty-one and Charlotte twenty-three when Mama and Papa passed away. You had no one to guide you through those difficult few years. I was in America, Edward was not quite himself for much of that time and still a young man himself, so I felt I had failed you. I thought I had brought this on myself and I was worried you were going to make the same mistakes as Charlotte - drinking too much and marrying the wrong person - I didn't want that for you."

She stared back at the carpet again before continuing quietly, "To make matters worse, Annabelle was threatening to report you to the police behind

Edward's back after you left. I was terrified you were going to be ruined, or worse, so I had to be firm with you; I was trying to do what I thought Mama and Papa would do; I wanted to protect you and that was the only way I could think to do it. I'm so sorry, Alice, maybe I was wrong, but I was honestly doing what I thought was best."

Again we sat quietly together in the stuffy little waiting room, Louisa silently crying and me trying to decide what to do next. I hadn't thought of it from her perspective before.

Finally I stood and held my hand out to her. "Let's ask the doctor if we can see her." Louisa gazed at my hand as if in a daze then her tear-swollen face lighted with a grateful smile as she took my hand and stood up.

She was still asleep when Louisa and I were finally allowed to see her. They had moved her from the operating theatre into a private room, which, excepting the medical paraphernalia, looked more like a hotel room. Her mousy-grey hair was spread across the white cotton pillow and a heather-coloured blanket tucked her up neatly to the collar bone. Her eyes were closed and her mouth was open; she was breathing deeply and her eyelids flickered restlessly. I sat on one of the brown leather armchairs at her bedside and stroked her hair.

"Goodness, Alice, she looks so old, the poor thing." Louisa said.

I nodded, "I thought the same when I first saw her at that place. She's been through too much."

We watched her in silence, her body rising and falling with each breath. I tried to imagine the child growing inside her at this very moment - Grace's child. I couldn't. Grace would always be a child to me. "A child should never have a child." I murmured under my breath.

After a few more minutes of silence Louisa nodded towards the mottled glass vase which stood atop a small mahogany table. "We shall have to get her some roses to go in that vase."

"That's a strange thing to think about at a time like this." I said.

"Roses were her favourites, don't you remember? She used to follow the gardener around for hours counting the things!"

"Mr. Healy, yes, I remember. A lot has happened since then..."

Louisa sighed, "We can't mope and cry forever, Alice. How will that help her?"

"And how exactly are flowers going to help her?" I snapped.

"Small things," she said gently, "small things can help..."

"Don't say they can help take your mind off things. It's precisely that which has brought us here." I looked at Grace's unconscious form. What sort of future lay ahead for her? For all of us?

"She's so miserable and scared."

She stood behind and put a hand on my shoulder. "Don't give up hope. I can help, Alice, we'll all help her."

"I want things to be different this time. I want to give her a good life."

Louisa crossed to the other side of the bed and sat down. "What about the baby? What if her child is...you know?" She avoided my gaze and smoothed the blanket around Grace's shoulders.

"It makes no difference to me; she or he will not be sent away to an institution to be...mistreated in the most inhuman way imaginable."

A knock at the door interrupted us.

"Come in." Louisa called. I turned around expecting to see James or Miles but it was neither.

"Charlotte! What on earth are you doing here?" I embraced her, I had never been so happy to see her and it felt wonderful.

"I came as soon as Louisa telephoned. How is she?"

"She's over the worst, thank heavens." I said.

"Oh, let me see her." Charlotte stared at the prostrate figure and gasped. "This can't be her! She's so..."

"Old," I finished. "Yes, ten years of imprisonment and abuse will add years to anyone."

"Alice, you ought to go home and rest." Louisa said, "You've been here all night."

"So have you. I'm fine, I'm staying with her. You should go home and see the children, you look tired."

"I'm all right but I should really go back to inform the men of all the details."

I nodded, "Yes, you go, Charlotte will keep me company for a while longer."

Louisa kissed us both and left, making us promise to return to the house for luncheon.

Charlotte questioned me for a while about Grace and the clinic and her current state. All the while she perched on the tip of the chair opposite me, eyes wide, mouth hanging open as I told her the entire story. By the time I had finished she was in tears. I was too exhausted to share her outpouring of grief, but proffered a handkerchief which she gratefully took and blew her nose.

"Oh, that's monstrous! Just beastly! Poor, poor little Grace. We must find whoever did this and...and..."

"We will, but Grace is our priority at the moment. Grace and the baby."

"The baby! Heavens! Grace can't cope with a baby, she can't even cope with herself. What are we going to do?"

"I will look into adopting the child, or at least legal guardianship. I'm sure Hemingford can advise us."

"Poor little thing, what a start in life." Charlotte shook her head and sniffed. "This is all so awful, I keep expecting to wake up and discover it's all been a terrible nightmare. I mean, how on earth is she going to give birth? I could barely face it so how can we expect her to do it in this state?"

"We'll look into all that once we get her back to London."

"She's staying with you and James?"

"Of course."

She looked thoughtful, "Alice, I know we haven't always been the best of friends but I feel we've grown closer these past few years, especially after Henry left." She let out a pitiful sob and dabbed her eyes again before continuing, "I want to help you and James, I want to be involved and help you look after Grace and the baby. Heaven knows I'm not proud of the way I treated her when we were growing up, I was so impatient and dismissive." Gingerly, she placed a hand on Grace's shoulder and stroked. "If I could have that time back I would behave so differently."

"Hindsight." I muttered wearily, "an enemy and a friend."

Charlotte stared at me with puzzlement on her face then shook her head. "When can we take her home?"

"I don't know. We'll have to wait for the doctor to pronounce her fit to travel."

"Well, Grace," She said, addressing the sleeping figure, "until then we'll be here for you. Your sisters are here for you."

The door opened suddenly and a young nurse I hadn't seen before strode in.

"Escusez-moi, mesdames. Ça appartient à Mademoiselle Goldhurst." She held up the bedraggled knitted duck Grace had had with her when we left the clinic. I had completely forgotten about it.

"What on earth?" Charlotte said frowning.

"Merci beaucoup." I took the toy and looked at it properly. There was white stuffing poking out of several holes in the duck's backside and front, and both eyes were long gone. The beak, which I suspected had once been orange, was a rusty colour, sewn on with red thread. No doubt it had required fixing at least once.

"It looks filthy. Throw it away! I'll get her a new one." Charlotte said, turning her nose up.

"No," I placed it under the blanket, in the crook of Grace's arm. "I have a feeling it's special to her."

"Mesdames, il y a un médecin qui voudrait vous parler." The nurse said as she moved towards the door.

"What did she say?" Charlotte hissed.

"The doctor wants to speak to us." I whispered back.

The nurse disappeared and seconds later a middle-aged man entered wearing a grey suit, a white, soft-collared shirt and a navy cravat tied loosely at his throat. He looked as if he had finished work and was about to go home. He was new - why did he want to speak to us?

As he approached the brighter sphere of light near the bed, his features became more distinguished. His thinning brown hair was peppered with grey, especially around his face, which was the honey hue of one who has spent two weeks on the French Riviera. His face was deeply lined around the eyes but his pearly teeth and smile were that of a young man - warm, confident and charming. It wasn't until I saw his eyes that I recognised the stranger. The cloudy blue iris of his right eye was blotted with a dark patch of brown that drew me in like a vacuum.

"What are you doing here?" I cried.

His confident smile wilted and he looked down. He had clearly expected a warmer welcome. I glared at him, but Charlotte still hadn't recognised him.

"Don't be rude, Alice! I'm sorry, Doctor, my sister has had a hellish few days. What did you want to talk to us about?"

I turned to Charlotte and raised my eyebrows, "Don't you recognise him?"

She turned from me to him and back again, shaking her head. She studied his face more carefully, then, her hands flew up to her mouth. "Oh my God! Doctor…"

"Clancey, yes. It's good to see you again, Alice, Charlotte."

"What are you doing here?" I repeated, refusing to be drawn into pleasantries.

He cleared his throat, "I work at this hospital. I saw your sister's name on the admissions list and, well, Doctor Dreyfus told me what had happened and…I…"

"I see, you thought you'd come and get all the details – satisfy your morbid curiosity – go home and tell whoever you could about how despicable we are."

"No, no, of course not. I want to help you." His eyes widened as he looked between me and Charlotte. "I know the clinic Grace was in. I visited it a few years back and I wasn't impressed with what I saw. And this Doctor Bracken fellow - he worked with me in London for a while during the war - I didn't take to him one bit; I always knew there was something strange about him. I can help you bring these animals to justice and get that place closed down so it can't happen to anyone else."

"Oh, thank you, yes, we want that more than anything, don't we, Alice?" Charlotte nodded with enthusiasm.

"We do, but we are going to deal with it ourselves, within the family. We don't need your help. Is that all?" I said, folding my hands in front of me with finality.

"Doctor Clancey, do you mind waiting outside while I talk to my sister in private?" Charlotte said.

"Not at all," he smiled with less self-assured charm than before and stepped out into the corridor, closing the door behind him.

Charlotte rounded on me, "Why are you being so petty? He's offering to help us and with his knowledge we could ensure these scoundrels are punished for what they've done."

I sighed and slunk into the armchair. "To be honest, all I can think about is getting through the next few weeks with Grace. Besides, I don't trust him."

Charlotte clicked her tongue loudly, "What happened between me and him was a stupid mistake. It happened years ago! I thought you'd forgotten it?"

"I have." I said.

"Well if you've forgiven me why can't you forgive him?"

"It's different – you're my sister. I don't have to forgive him."

Charlotte smirked, "If anything I did you a favour. Imagine if you'd married him? You wouldn't be half as rich. James is a much better catch!" A smile broke across my face and we giggled.

"I suppose you're right. But I wouldn't have ended up marrying him anyway."

"Let him help us, Alice. Louisa and I can deal with him; you won't even have to see him if you don't want to."

I thought for a moment. He had always been kind to Grace; I had no complaints there. "All right. But keep a close eye on him, don't let him seduce you like last time." She rolled her eyes and stepped outside to tell him the news.

I reached across the bed and held Grace's hand. Exhaustion had caught up with me at last. I laid my head on the mattress next to her shoulder and closed my eyes, listening to her steady breathing.

Chapter Twenty Two
21st July 1932, St. John's Wood, London
Alice

It was another two weeks before Grace was well enough to travel. True to her word, Charlotte accompanied us back to London and helped me to decorate and furnish Grace's new room. I employed three of the best nurses in London and James hired a doctor to visit her every two days. Between James, Charlotte, Louisa and myself we spent as much time as possible with our sister and sought to include her in our lives whenever possible. However, despite the attention she received, Grace did not speak or even make eye contact with anyone. She seemed unmoved by her new home and struggled to leave her bedroom. She cried and howled every morning on waking and had fits of temper when we tried to make her wash or dress or even eat. She dirtied herself at least twice a day and disliked being outside. To make matters worse, she suffered constantly during her pregnancy with sickness, pain and exhaustion, which made it impossible to even contemplate visiting Martha. I wrote to her every few weeks to remind her that I had not forgotten and prayed that she would live long enough for them to be reunited.

The summer weather disagreed with Grace. The stifling air and light mornings made her howl and grizzle more than usual, yet she would not move to a cooler part of the house. She had suffered a convulsion two nights before and was taken to hospital to be monitored. I had spent the majority of the two days with her, reading 'Little Red Riding Hood' and 'Cinderella' in an attempt to raise her spirits. As Charlotte was dealing with Doctor Clancey in Paris, James offered to take over so I could spend some time with Oliver.

When I returned home to St. John's Wood I noticed an unfamiliar car parked outside - a Rolls Royce. It looked far too expensive to belong to the doctor we had employed, so I assumed one of the neighbours had a visitor.

A refreshing draught surged through the front of the house when the door opened and I realised how tired I was. Although I had returned to spend time with Oliver, I longed for a nap. Mrs. Lawrence, the housekeeper, came to greet me and I asked her where Oliver was.

"He's out in the garden, playing with Master Harry and Miss Penelope." I frowned. James had not told me they were here. "Mrs. De Lisle is in the drawing room with a guest."

"Charlotte's back? She could have given us some warning. Who has she brought?"

"It's a gentleman." Mrs. Lawrence said.

I groaned. It was obviously Clancey. This was just like Charlotte; she knew I didn't want to see him, let alone welcome him into my home.

"Could you bring us some tea and sandwiches? I'm famished."

"Of course, Mrs. Hartwright." She hurried off to the kitchen.

I dragged myself to the sitting room repressing a series of yawns. I was not in the mood for this. I heard Charlotte's voice and Clancey's murmur. At least she wasn't giggling and flirting as I feared she might. I knocked and walked in without waiting for a response, fixing a polite smile. They both stood when I appeared. Charlotte smiled sheepishly when she said hello.

"Hello, Alice." The man said. I knew from the voice that it wasn't Doctor Clancey. I looked at him and froze as he said, "How are you?"

It was Edward. An older, more stooped version, but he was here, in my house. Charlotte had told me that his health had improved, so I hadn't been back to visit him like I promised myself. Even in the few months since we had been briefly reunited his hair had thinned considerably and the remaining tufts were grey. He held a polished walking cane and wore a heavy dark suit despite the warm weather outside, but some colour had returned to his cheeks.

I swallowed, "Hello Edward. I'm fine thank you, a little tired; I've just come from the hospital."

He nodded and cleared his throat. "How is she?"

"Not very well, I'm afraid. She's in a lot of discomfort, this weather doesn't help. She had a fit the other night."

"Mmm, Charlotte told me."

Mrs. Lawrence swept into the room and laid out the tea. We all sat down. I was happy to hear that my brother had recovered from his illness and grateful to him for changing his mind about releasing Grace, but still I resented him. If he hadn't been beguiled by Annabelle Grace may not have been sent away and she would not be suffering now.

"Has Charlotte told you everything?"

"I wrote to Edward a few weeks ago and told him what had happened," she replied.

"I'm going to sue that clinic. My solicitors are putting a case together..."

"Charlotte and Louisa are dealing with it," I interrupted. "And to be honest, Grace is my priority at the moment, and the baby."

He paused and softened his voice, "I understand that. I thought I could help by taking it off your hands. Honestly, they seemed to be a reputable institution, so many people recommended it."

"Well, they were wrong, weren't they? You should have visited it before signing her away to those barbarians." He looked at me. His eyes still had that glassy, cloudy appearance but none of Edward's old incipient anger behind them. All I saw now was anguish.

"Alice, please, this isn't helping." Charlotte said.

He rubbed his eyes, "I'm sorry. I'm deeply sorry. I would never have done it if I'd known the truth. I thought she was dangerous and I thought it was the best place for her at the time." He closed his eyes.

"He's got rid of Annabelle." Charlotte nodded approvingly, offering the information as consolation. I looked at him, surprised.

"After we confronted her, she flew into a rage and left. She returned the next day and admitted that she had been unfaithful, for quite a few years, in fact. I admit, I suspected it for some time, but that's not to say it was any less hurtful." He shook his head and massaged his right temple. "Anyway, I used it to my advantage - I threatened to prevent her seeing Freddie if she didn't tell the truth - and thank God she saw sense."

Charlotte placed a hand on his arm, "You're well rid of her. Vile strumpet! That man is welcome to her."

"At least we can all call him 'Freddie' again now, Frederick was always a bit of a mouthful." I smiled. Edward chuckled and then looked at me seriously.

"Alice, I've come here to apologise, sincerely. I was wrong and I behaved badly." His eyes began to water. "I want to put things right, I want to help you all. I don't expect us to go back to how we were, but please let me try and make up for my mistakes."

His eyes had a hopeful, imploring look, made all the more pitiful by his wan, tired face. I finally realised that it wasn't just me who had been tormented with guilt and regret. All three of us faced one another, needing the same thing - absolution.

"I've missed you, Edward," I said quietly. "I would like to get to know you again, but it will take time."

He tried to look serious but I could see the smile fighting to erupt. I grinned, giving consent for him to do the same. We both stood, beaming and embracing. Charlotte clapped her hands together in delight and embraced us both afterwards.

A knock at the door suspended our reunion. It was Mrs. Lawrence again.

"I'm terribly sorry for interrupting, ma'am. Mr. Hartwright just telephoned from the hospital...Miss Goldhurst has gone into labour."

My heart stalled then galloped into action, "What? She's not due until September! Are you sure?"

"He...he didn't say much, just asked if you could get there as soon as possible."

"Get the driver now!" I shouted. She raced from the room calling the driver's name. "Oh Lord, I should have stayed with her." I hurried out, snatching my handbag and hat.

"I'll come with you. Edward, could you stay and tell the children where we've gone?" Charlotte said.

"Would you like me to come with you?"

"No, stay here, we'll telephone you when there's news." Charlotte said and we left him lingering awkwardly by the sofa.

Grace was in an operating theatre when we arrived. James informed me that she had started bleeding heavily soon after I left and he hadn't seen her; a nurse came to tell him that she was in labour.

I could scarcely remember the happiness I had felt in the sitting room only a few minutes earlier. It seemed like a dream. All I could think about was her. What if she died, the baby too? I couldn't bear thinking about it. I glanced at Charlotte and knew that she was thinking the same. I prayed silently for over an hour, begging for their lives to be spared.

I had been in so many hospital waiting rooms recently that the clinical smell was more familiar to me than the freshness of my own lawn or the polish that the maids used to clean the floors. The garish pattern of the wallpaper had left a permanent imprint on my memory so I saw it when I closed my eyes to sleep. I had become part of the room.

"Mr. and Mrs. Hartwright?"

I jumped, having not heard the doctor enter. "How is she? What's happening?" I blurted.

I had seen this doctor once or twice before but never spoken to him. He was about fifty years old with white hair and a grey clipped moustache.

"Due to the premature labour Miss Goldhurst was in danger of miscarrying the child. We had to operate there and then. I've delivered the child by caesarean section."

I stared at him, my mouth dry and my voice hoarse, "Are...are they both all right?"

"Is it a boy or a girl?" Charlotte chimed in.

"It's a girl." He replied. Charlotte gasped and clapped her hands together.

"Doctor, are they both all right?" I said, studying his face for clues.

He remained calm and grave, his moustache barely moving when he spoke, "The baby is very small and weak. We're doing everything we possibly can for her. Trust me, she's in good hands."

"And Grace?" James said.

He cleared his throat, "Your sister was bleeding heavily and convulsing. The only way we could save her and her child was to induce a coma."

"She's in a coma?" James repeated. The doctor nodded. "How long before she wakes up?"

"I can't say at the moment. Hopefully it won't be too long. You can see her soon; hearing the voices of loved ones can encourage the patient to wake up."

The florid pattern of the wallpaper wrapped around me - a stifling melange of colour, feathers and leaves. The temperature in the room soared and I felt heating rising up my body and to my face. I felt faint and helpless. I went to sit down again, missed and landed on the floor. All three rushed to help me and I sat on the carpet leaning my back against the chair until the room stopped spinning.

"I'm sorry, I felt dizzy suddenly."

"Alice, dear, go home and rest, Charlotte and I will stay here."

"I can't leave her, she needs me." I moaned.

"You're not much use to her like this. Just go home and sleep and come back when you're feeling better. She won't be alone, I promise."

"Let me see the baby first, I need to see her."

The doctor led us down a series of corridors to an obscure section of the building. James held onto me like an elderly woman all the way, with Charlotte walking nervously behind. We went through several doors before stopping at one bearing the words 'Premature Baby Ward'.

"I'm afraid we can't let you hold or touch her just yet. Her heart is weak and she's more susceptible to infections. We're keeping her in a special incubator while she gains in strength and size."

Charlotte let out a sob that made me start and the doctor continued reassuringly, "She's not as small as we anticipated. Judging by her size and the development of her organs she's only about two months premature, she just looks tiny. I am optimistic that she will grow into a healthy child." Charlotte nodded and sniffed. "She's lucky, we may not have been able to do much for her as recently as two years ago, we've recently received all the latest equipment from America," he said.

James thanked the doctor and he left us with a friendly, red-cheeked nurse, who led us into the room. It was stark and clean, far too big for one infant for she lay alone inside her huge glass coffin in the centre of the room, barely moving. The doctor had been right; she was a puny little chick, all wrinkly pink skin and bone. I was quite relieved that the doctor had told us not to touch her; I would probably harm her just by breathing too heavily.

"She a brave little mite, this one." The red-cheeked nurse beamed, gazing at the tiny sleeping face. "She's a fighter, I can tell."

"She's so small! I've never seen a baby so small." Charlotte exclaimed, wide-eyed.

"We had a little girl go home yesterday who was even smaller when she was first born, if you can imagine it! She'll soon grow, don't you worry madam." We all gaped in silence, gasping with every slight movement she made, quietly astonished by this little miracle.

"Do you have a name for her yet?" The nurse broke in. James and Charlotte glanced at me expectantly.

"No, not yet. We'll wait until her mother wakes up."

Chapter Twenty Three
12th August 1932, St. John's Wood, London
Alice

"Are you bringing the baby home today?" Oliver hovered on the threshold of our bedroom, hands behind his back, rocking back and forth gently on his heels. The poor boy hadn't had much of a summer holiday; at Christmas we had planned to take him to France this summer with some of his friends. When he returned from boarding school in June he soon realised it was not to be and stopped mentioning it some weeks ago.

"Hopefully, darling, we shall have to see what the doctors say."

"I hope I can see her before I go back to school."

"You will, my boy, you will." James said, stroking a hand through his sandy hair and pulling him into a hug. "What about a bit of cricket practice in the garden whilst Mama finishes her hair?"

"My hair's done, can't you tell?" I said pretending to take offence.

"Oh, yes, of course, dear. Better concentrate on your make up then!" He and Oliver burst into giggles and ran off down the corridor.

"How dare you!" I shouted after them.

I went into the nursery, which had been newly painted yellow and cream, and began to gather some items for the baby. I had started this routine a few days ago, after the doctor uttered the promised words 'it won't be long now'. If today was the day we were allowed to bring her home I wanted to be prepared.

Engrossed as I was in my own thoughts I failed to notice that guests had arrived downstairs. James appeared at the door looking serious.

"What is it? Is it the baby? Or Grace?"

He shook his head and entered the room, closing the door behind him. "You have a visitor."

"Whoever it is will have to come back later." I said picking up the nursery bag I had prepared.

"It's Martha." I looked up at him quickly and lowered the bag to the floor. "Martha Pick," he clarified.

"It can't be Martha Pick, when I last saw her she was so ill she could barely open her eyes. She wouldn't be able to make it all the way to London."

"Well she's waiting downstairs in the sitting room. Admittedly she looks very unwell so I suggest you don't keep her waiting too long."

Slowly, I moved out of the nursery and down the stairs. I had been so preoccupied with Grace and the baby that I hadn't given Martha much thought of late. I calculated that it had been nearly three weeks since I had written to her, or rather, James had written to her, informing her of the little girl born prematurely and Grace's coma. I hadn't received a reply and since not much had changed I hadn't written to update her.

Taking a deep breath I pushed open the drawing room door and was greeted by a familiar looking man with a beard and bushy eyebrows wearing a brown suit.

"How do you do, Mrs. Hartwright? I'm Bill Pick, Martha's brother, we met a few months back."

"Yes, I remember. How do you do?" He smiled warmly and shook my hand and as he moved I saw the frail, shrunken figure in a wheeled chair behind him. My heart pounded when I thought of her last words to me: 'I need to know she's safe and she has something to look forward to - a life of some form.' With Grace lying comatose in the hospital I didn't know if any of these things were to be realised. I had to face facts: we were too late to rescue her.

"Martha, you look so tired, you shouldn't have travelled all this way. I'll ask Mrs. Lawrence to make up a bed for you so you can rest."

"I'm fine, Miss Alice, I look worse than I feel." She croaked. Bill was holding a half-full teacup while Martha's remained untouched.

"You're here to enquire about Grace and the baby, I assume," I said sitting next to her. "God willing we can bring her home today, I was just on my way to the hospital, actually. I'm afraid Grace is still the same. We do visit them every day and have been talking to Grace, but nothing has changed."

Martha listened quietly before replying, "Can I see her? Can I come with you to the hospital to see her?"

"To see Grace?" I wasn't sure whether Martha had heard me correctly, or understood what a coma was, but I didn't want to offend her by repeating myself.

"Of course I would love to see the baby as well, what's her name?"

"We haven't named her yet. We were hoping that Grace would wake up soon and name her. As it is we may have to pick a name on her behalf, we can't call her 'the baby' forever!"

Martha nodded, every action seemed to take twice as long and cause her pain. She exhaled throatily, "No one can believe that I've lasted this long, least of all me. I should have kicked the bucket months ago." I cast Bill an uneasy glance, which he returned with an apologetic smile. "I've never been a particularly religious person, but being this close to the end gives you a more spiritual perspective I suppose. I can't go until I've seen her. I mean, I need to see her one last time before I die. That's what God wants, I believe."

She fixed her eyes on mine, the saddest pair of brown eyes I had seen, worn out from years of worry and loss. "I know you tried, Miss Alice," she whispered so quietly I had to strain to hear. "You're a good person."

A lump grew thick and painful in my throat. I whispered back, "It wasn't enough to save her, though. I was too late."

"No," she said placing a withered hand on mine, exposing an emaciated, papery arm, "this disease hasn't given me much to be thankful for, but it has taught me a few things. Look at me, surely my being here is evidence enough that it's never too late. You tried. Maybe you didn't try very hard for years, but you did the right thing in the end. You didn't give up on her. She knows that, she's not stupid. Far from it, in fact."

I covered my face with my hands and sighed, letting the tears come. Martha patted my arm. "You are a good sister to her. Now, shall we go and see her?"

Those at the hospital were surprised to see such a big party arrive through their doors. Although we were only five (Charlotte had decided to join us) Martha's hulking wheeled chair, along with our bags and gifts, made us look like a welcoming committee. James and Bill offered to remain in the waiting room to be called upon if needed. Meanwhile, Charlotte went to speak to the doctor about the probability of our taking the baby home, leaving Martha and I to visit Grace.

A cheerful nurse informed us that during the night several of the nurses had seen some small movement in her face and hands; apparently a promising sign. Martha's chair was too wide to fit through the door of Grace's room so I suggested that I ask James to lift and carry her to the bedside. However, she gripped my arm to stop me, "Don't trouble him, I can make the few feet to her bedside, if you could give me your arm?"

I leaned across to help her stand and noticed that she had shrunk considerably since I last saw her active. I realised soon that she was stooping due to the stiffness in her legs. Together, we shuffled forward, my right arm around her tiny waist while her cadaverous fingers clung onto the left.

All at once she stopped. "Are you all right, Martha?"

"I'm going to keep my eyes closed until I sit down next to her." My heart sank. What would she say when she saw her so altered?

Slowly I delivered her into the chair closest to the sleeping figure and she exhaled, opening her eyes. I held my breath as I watched her face soften into a smile. She took the hand closest to her and kissed it gently.

"Grace, my darling girl, it's me, it's Martha. Look how you've grown!" I passed around the bottom of the bed to sit on the other side of her and noticed that one of the many pictures, drawn by Penny or Oliver and pinned to the wall, had fallen down. I crouched to pick it up. "My poor little duckie. Oh, my duckie! Can you hear me?" Duckie? I frowned, confused as to what Martha was talking about. She was stroking the side of Grace's face so delicately and with such a look of serenity that she appeared to have forgotten my presence. I carried on pinning the picture back up and caught sight of the tatty old knitted duck on the dresser, hidden amongst all the photographs and vases of flowers. Duck. Duckie.

"You gave her this," I exclaimed, holding up the toy. "I completely forgot you used to call her 'duckie'! Why didn't I realise? I remember her having this."

Martha stared at the duck with moist eyes, "My mother knitted that and sent it for her at the start of the war. She used to love the ducks. You remember Jimmy?"

"Jimmy the duck! Yes, of course." I paused, "I remember now."

"She's had it all this time." She clutched Grace's hand in hers. "Darling Gracie, it's Martha, it's Martha. I'm here, I'm not going to leave you again, I'm here for you."

I handed her a book from the small pile on the dresser. The pages were slightly more well-thumbed than the others. "I'm sure she'd love to hear you read." She took the book in shaking hands, bowed her head and sighed. "Are you sure you're well enough for this, Martha? Please tell me if you're feeling tired and we can come back tomorrow. You can stay with James and me for as long as you like."

She lifted her head and stroked the top of Grace's. "I know she's a woman now with her own child, but all I can see is the little girl I used to care for. My little Grace."

I asked her if she would like some time alone with Grace to which she quietly agreed, never taking her eyes off her for a moment. I told her I would find out how the baby was and bring her to see them both. She did not reply, so I left them.

"We can bring her home, Alice!" Charlotte bellowed as I entered the baby's room, causing her to grizzle and cry.

"Did Auntie Charlotte startle you, darling?" I cooed, taking the little bundle from her, "don't worry, you'll get used to her rowdy voice!"

"Rowdy indeed!" She scoffed.

"What did the doctor say?"

"She's been steadily improving over the past few days and is gaining in weight. We need to bring her in for regular checks, at least once a week, on top of twice-weekly visits from the nurse."

I nodded in approval, "You not only listened but remembered all that information? I'm so impressed, sister dearest!"

"I'm not as stupid as you would have people believe."

"I've never thought that." We smiled at one another with mutual affection and respect. "Now, how about we visit your mother and Martha before we take you home to meet your cousins?" Charlotte gasped suddenly and gripped my shoulder. "What is it?"

"Her name, it's so obvious!" I gawped at her. She rolled her eyes, "We have to call her Martha! It's the only name we know Grace would want."

I looked at the little girl's soft brown eyes, her downy hair and pink budding lips. Martha. I had been considering the name myself for some time but I wanted Charlotte to have this.

"What do you think? Are you a Martha?" She squirmed and stared at me in wonder.

"I think she agrees." Charlotte said, smiling and offering her finger, which the little girl gripped with all her might.

"That's settled, then. Come on, Martha."

As we walked down the corridor together, Charlotte leaned towards me, lowering her voice, "By the way, Doctor Bracken's been found – in Austria. He's being questioned by the police. We've built a strong case against him and the clinic, so he's got no chance of escaping."

"Good." I said, watching Martha's filmy eyelids quiver up and down.

"They've relocated nearly all of the patients now, so the place has been closed up. Michael has been an absolute gem throughout this."

"Michael?" I glanced at her sideways, raising my eyebrows.

"Doctor Clancey, then. It's just more natural to call him Michael, so I don't feel like I'm attending a consultation every time we meet!"

"Hmm, right well, I'm grateful to him for his help and yours too, of course. I suppose he's redeemed himself. The monsters at that clinic ought to rot for what they've done."

She nodded fiercely and then her face softened into a smile. "But this little one is the only blessed miracle to come out of it all." She stroked the top of her head until her eyes closed.

On returning to Grace's room we heard raised voices inside. I could hear Martha weeping and repeating Grace's name.

"Oh Lord, what do you suppose has happened?" Charlotte said. I handed her the baby and burst in, bracing myself for the worst. Martha was bent over the bed, crying and laughing in equal measure. The cheerful nurse from earlier, unsure of what to say to the hysterical stranger, seemed to appreciate our appearance.

"Your sister's awake, Mrs. Hartwright! I'll go and fetch the doctor."

Charlotte emitted a cry of joy and rushed to see. "Her eyes are open, Alice! Look!"

A mixture of relief and joy overpowered me so that, for a moment, time seemed to slow into a dreamlike waltz. No, time seemed to be reversing. I felt that we were back at Goldhurst Estate. We were all home and we were happy. Grace was soaking wet, having been hauled out of the lake by the under gardener and we were all laughing so much we were weeping. I stood at the foot of the bed, ready to introduce little Martha to her when I heard it - Grace was speaking. A fragile, barely audible whisper from fluttering mauve lips: "Martha...Martha… Martha."

Epilogue
1st May 1938, Goldhurst Estate, Rutland
Alice

"In loving memory of Grace Goldhurst, 20th July 1901-14th October 1932, forever in our thoughts, always in our hearts." The little girl followed the words with her thin finger and furrowed her brow.
"Do you know who is buried here, Martha?" I said.
"My mother?" She said, looking up at me for approval.
"That's right. Do you want to place these flowers for her?"
"Roses." She smiled.
"Her favourites."
"They're my favourites too." She took the roses from me and carefully placed them next to the headstone, rearranging them several times before she was satisfied.
"There's something else written here...Grace was in all her steps, heaven in her eye, in every ges..."
"In every gesture dignity and love." I finished.
"What does that mean?" She said.
"It's from a famous poem, it means your mother was a very loving and sweet person. Not everyone could see it, but she was."
"Was she pretty?" She said, looking up inquisitively.
"Beautiful."
She fell quiet for a few minutes and counted on her fingers. "She was thirty-one when she died."
I nodded, "Too young."
"Why did she die? You're forty-four and you're not dead."
"People can die at any age, sadly. Your mother was very unwell after she had you." She was silent again. "We can visit her here any time you would like."
"Is Uncle James my father?" She said suddenly.
"Oh, no, he's your uncle. But he's like your father, just like I'm like your mother."
"Where is my father?"
I bit my lip and inhaled deeply. "I'm afraid I don't know, sweetheart."
A gust of wind knocked the roses over and Martha stooped to replace them. "Who is Martha Pick?" She had noticed the plaque next to Grace's grave.
"Ah, now, I was just about to tell you about Martha Pick. You were named after her." I smiled.
"Why?"
"Because she was a very special person and a close friend of your mother's. She was your mother's best friend, in fact."

"Is that why she called me Martha?"

"Yes. You're very lucky to be named after such a wonderful person." I looked at the two names side by side.

"I'm going to call my daughter Helen because my best friend is called Helen."

I pretended to look affronted, "I hoped you were going to call your daughter after me!"

She looked thoughtful, "Maybe I'll call my other daughter Alice."

"You're having more than one daughter then?"

"I'm going to have three daughters but no boys!" She wrinkled nose and I laughed.

"Why hasn't Martha Pick got a big stone like my mother?"

"Martha was cremated, so only her ashes are buried here."

"What is cremated?"

"Her family chose to burn her body instead of burying it."

"I wouldn't like to be burned. I want to be buried."

"Hopefully it's a very, very long way off."

We stood quietly a little longer; I said a silent prayer for Grace and Martha and looked across the gardens towards the house. The midday light kissed everything on which it landed with gold.

"We had better go inside, Uncle Edward has planned quite a feast for us and Aunt Louisa wants to tell us about her holiday."

"When are Aunt Charlotte and Uncle Michael going to get here?" She said.

"I expect they're already inside. Let's go and see." I began to walk across the lawn but she lingered.

"Can we read on the bench first?" She said.

"Read? We haven't got a book."

"I know it off by heart."

I looked at her sweet, open face, the ringlets unravelling into wispy tendrils and her eyes: dark and curious, like a hare's.

"All right." She smiled and, taking my hand, skipped to the bench.

"Once upon a time there was a dear little girl who was loved by everyone who looked at her, but most of all by her grandmother..."

I listened to her recite the story with confidence and gazed at the two graves - together and undisturbed at last. They were separated in life and it destroyed them both; there was no question of them not being together in death.

"That was absolutely word-perfect! You tell that story very well." I gushed when Martha finished. She beamed and slunk off the bench. "Little Red Riding Hood was your mother's favourite story as well."

"I love it!" She jumped up in excitement and I laughed.

"Right, it's time to go inside. Make sure you wash your hands before you sit down."

"Yes Mama." She ran towards the house. I stood and watched the streamlined little figure darting across the garden and disappearing up the stone steps.

Kneeling closer to the headstone I dislodged half of the roses from Grace's bunch and placed them next to Martha's plaque. "Thank you for looking after my sister." I stroked the cool bronze and stood up to look at Grace's. "We all miss you, darling. You would be so proud of your daughter." I stooped and kissed the top of the stone. "Rest peacefully."

A grey cloud had sailed in front of the sun, changing the house from gold to brown. Two rays escaped through the grey and shone defiantly on the garden. I sighed and headed for the steps. I had tried. Perhaps not my hardest and not all the time, but I had tried.

Lightning Source UK Ltd.
Milton Keynes UK
UKOW04f0357010714

234333UK00001BA/15/P